SAVE ME, JULIE KOGON

A Novel

ALLEN RUFF

TRAFFORD

Note for Librarians: a cataloguing record for this book that includes Dewey Decimal Classification and US Library of Congress numbers is available from the Library and Archives of Canada. The complete cataloguing record can be obtained from their online database at: www.collectionscanada.ca/amicus/index-e.html
ISBN 1-4251-0320-0

TRAFFORD

Offices in Canada, USA, Ireland and UK
This book was published *on-demand* in cooperation with Trafford Publishing. On-demand publishing is a unique process and service of making a book available for retail sale to the public taking advantage of on-demand manufacturing and Internet marketing. On-demand publishing includes promotions, retail sales, manufacturing, order fulfilment, accounting and collecting royalties on behalf of the author.

Book sales for North America and international:
Trafford Publishing, 6E–2333 Government St.,
Victoria, BC v8t 4p4 CANADA
phone 250 383 6864 (toll-free 1 888 232 4444)
fax 250 383 6804; email to orders@trafford.com
Book sales in Europe:
Trafford Publishing (uk) Ltd., Enterprise House, Wistaston Road Business Centre,
Wistaston Road, Crewe, Cheshire cw2 7rp UNITED KINGDOM
phone 01270 251 396 (local rate 0845 230 9601)
facsimile 01270 254 983; orders.uk@trafford.com
Order online at:
trafford.com/06-2077

10 9 8 7 6 5 4 3 2

For Elsie and Teddy, *alevasholom,* and Ronald and Michael.

The tradition of all dead generations weighs like a nightmare on the brain of the living.
- Marx, *The Eighteenth Brumaire of Louis Bonaparte* (1852)

The past is never dead. It's not even past.
- Faulkner, *Requiem for a Nun* (1951)

Acknowledgements:

WORDS CANNOT ADEQUATELY EXPRESS my gratitude to all those who leant an ear and a critical eye to this work as it came to life over several years. Sitting around on successive Thanksgivings, my extended family of in-laws listened and offered needed encouragement as I read from various chapters. The late Peg Brei, Chuck and Linda and Tommy Brei, Ann, Jack, Peter and Michael Burton, Kate Grinde and Bill Bode all helped to move me forward. Critical reads by Kathy Rasmussen, Steve Kantrowitz, Tim Tyson, Marsha Rummel, and Sandra Austin-Phillips were invaluable, as was the friendship of Marc Rosenthal, Bill and Barbara Schwoerer, Pat Arnold, Ahmad Sultan, Paul Black, and those now gone and sorely missed -- Davíd Velazqúez, Joseph Cammarano, and Burt Somers. I remain indebted to Dwight Armstrong for his cover art artistry, photographic skills and continuing ability to laugh.

Ultimately, this project would not have come to life if not for the support of Pat DiBiase. Her companionship and unstinting generosity of spirit continually sustained my endeavors. Most importantly, her immense forbearance and patience once again afforded me the time and space I needed. For her, too, this book is especially dedicated.

Table of Contents

CHAPTER 1

New Haven

1989... LOUIE VELNER JUST SAT and stared at the body of his life-long friend, barely recognizable without any clothes, lying there on the mortician's table. The aged undertaker figured it must have been well over an hour since they had wheeled Harry in from the van, removed him from the zippered body bag, and slid him onto the slab. That made it more than two since they had gotten the call from Yale New Haven to come get his old crony. But Louie, dressed in a body length surgeon's gown, a surgical mask tucked under his chin, hadn't done a thing since he removed the hospital tubes from the corpse's nose and mouth and peeled the tape from its arms.

He just sat there and stared at the body as he sipped deeply from the glass of Johnny Walker, his long-time anesthetic of choice, and took a moment to pour another belt from the half-empty bottle resting nearby on the cart that he had wheeled within reach before sitting down. He realized that he was beginning to get as stiff as his old friend, knew he must get to work, but found it impossible to move. He felt as if he had suddenly lost all the skills and know-how that came with more than fifty years in the business. He reflected on how it had rarely troubled him before, after all he had seen, the thousands he had prepared. How it had suddenly become so very difficult, now that it had come time to bury so many of his old friends. And Harry was the most difficult to date. *"Time to get the hell out,"* he thought.

He found himself gazing at what somehow had become an old man, all skin and bones and belly, motionless as if asleep, lying there on his back, arms close at his sides, his knobby-kneed legs out straight.

"So, Harehleh," he said aloud, "you finally made it in. Yuh thought you'd be the last of the Mohicans. Yuh probably don't remember how yuh used to laugh when I told yuh, but here I am, you skinny son of a bitch. I outlasted yuh, just like I said!"

He paused and took another deep sip from the scotch as his eyes once again began their course of travel down the length of the body. He gazed at Harry's hair, thick and wavy, silver gray at the temples, but still dark unlike his own which had passed from gray to white years ago, a casualty of too much booze, the constant waft of formaldehyde in his nostrils, and too many decades of grief and sorrow, the *tsooris* that came and went, day in, day out, in an unending stream through the chapel and sitting rooms of his funeral home.

He focused in on Harry's left eye, closed as if his friend was taking a little snooze, and suddenly, the eye, caught in profile, opened. It blinked and peered up at the ceiling and Harry turned his head and looked at his pal.

Louie, unmoved, his glass in a calm, unnerved hand, responded. "Hey! Who yuh tryin' to kid? Yuh think yuh can con me, like all the rest over the years? You're dead, Harehleh. Deader 'n dick. You know it, and I know it!"

The corpse continued to stare and the lips began to quiver slightly, as if to speak. The light in the room turned as bright as a summer afternoon sun and Louie suddenly found himself looking at a youthful Harry, maybe sixteen or seventeen. There they were, lying side by side in their bathing trunks, sunning themselves on a blanket on the rough, stony beach at Woodmont, that Jewish enclave of simple gray summer cottages tucked against the Milford shore.

"Yuh know what, Louie?"

"What's t' know?"

"I can't wait to get the fuck o'tta here."

"Are you totally *mishoog*? It's only one o'clock! We just got here. Tons of *maidels* all over the place and already you wanna go back to N'Haven!?"

"No, yuh putz! I ain't talkin' about goin' home."

"Then what're yuh sayin'?"

"I'm talkin' about gettin' the fuck away from here. Away from N'Haven. Away from Oak Street. From my ol' man and his stinkin' chickens. From my goddamn brother and sisters and that crowded hole we live in! As soon as I finish school, I'm otta here. I'm gettin' the fuck out!"

"And where yuh gonna go, Mr. Big Shot, world traveler?"

"I don' know. Maybe New York. Florida maybe. Who knows? My father, he got these cousins in New York. His first cousin, Seymour, he once tol' me I could come stay by him in the garment district. He's got serious connections. My ol' man says he even knows Arnold Rothstein. He'd give me a job. I know it. I figure I can work a couple years shleppin' racks of ladies' dresses and then work my way into show bizz, or one of the rackets."

"Now I know you're totally *mishoogeh*."

"I'll tell yuh one thing... and this ain't no bullshit... I'm gonna get otta here."

Harry's eyes closed and he turned his head ceilingward as the light in the room dimmed.

"*Yeah, you really got out alright. You finally got out,*" Louie thought as another voice intruded.

"Dad... Dad! What are you doin'?"

Louie focused on the body, once again that of some skinny old man, quite dead, and then looked up in the direction of his son Steven's voice.

"What the hell? You've been sitting here like this for well over an hour. You're drinking too much and we got tons of work to do."

"I'm alright."

"No, you're not! We still have to..."

"Don't start tellin' me what I have to do. I'm tellin' yuh I'm alright."

"I know he's your old friend, your best friend, but at least let me help yuh with..."

"With what? Like I never done a stiff before? This one I have to do myself. It has to be done right!"

"Please, Dad, let me help. Everything'll..."

"You can help by leaving me and Harry the fuck alone!"

Realizing the futility of the situation, the son began to withdraw. He paused, thought about it an instant, and began to reach for the bottle of Johnny Walker.

"And leave *that* the fuck alone, too!"

Shaking his head, Steven turned and walked out of the room, without another word. His father resumed staring at Harry's corpse as his mind continued to wander.

The call had come early the previous evening, his oldest brother's voice on the line simply saying that the old man was gone and to come home. And there Davey found himself, crammed in next to the window as he and his wife flew east to bury Harry.

Not knowing exactly what to expect, but knowing fully well that it would certainly be a trip, he already realized that he had to make some attempt to prepare Annie. But he wasn't quite sure about how he should go about it. So he just stared out the window for some time, silently gazing down at the tumbly cloud cover several thousand feet below as images of the old man raced through his head.

He finally turned and glanced at his wife, her head back on the head rest, her eyes closed in that sort of in-flight stasis that she reverted to whenever they flew anywhere. He pondered a while longer on how to phrase it exactly, so as to put her at ease and at the same time bolster her for what was to come, and finally decided to go for it.

"You all right?" he asked, knowing she was awake.

"Yeah, I'm fine. And you?"

"Me? I'm okay. But would you do me a favor?"

Her eyes now opened, she turned her head and faced him with that skeptical look of humored suspicion, the one she gave him whenever he started out with that question. That "what now?" kind of look.

"No, seriously. I want yuh to do somethin' for me."

"Yeah, I know. Go on."

"Just do me one thing. That's all. From the time we land in New Haven until we fly home, do me and yourself a favor and just pretend you're watchin' a movie."

"A movie?"

"Yeah. I don't know what it'll be like. But from what I do know, the assorted cast of characters that'll definitely show, I imagine it could get pretty damn weird. I just don't wan'chuh to get overwhelmed by it all. It's my family, not yours, and you shouldn't have to be subjected to all the *mishigas*. Just play the detached observer."

"Like I'm watching a movie?"

"Yeah. Just pretend it's a film and you're just sittin' there front row lookin' up at the silver screen. Make like it's somebody else's story, that it really ain't happenin' and everything'll be fine."

She reached over and placed her hand atop his, partly to console and in part to connect with him.

"Okay," she replied.

Assured upon feeling her touch, he smiled and turned back toward the window and resumed his cloud gazing. In an attempt to prepare himself for whatever might come after they arrived in New Haven, he tried to relax. But as soon as he closed his eyes, he began seeing the faces of the various players, dead and alive. Peering out again, his focus shifted ever so slightly and he suddenly found himself looking at his reflection, somehow faint yet distinct, on the inner sheet of Plexiglas.

"Forty years old tomorrow, I got gray in my beard already, and I gotta bury the old man. Happy goddamn birthday!" he thought.

His gaze returned to the clouds and he found himself trying to remember when he had last been East. While he could fully remember being in New Haven with Annie, what came to mind was another time, an earlier moment, before they were together. It couldn't have been very long after he and Mona had split up, after she had dumped him, because he could vaguely recollect the post-bottom funk that he had been in at the time. That would make it '82, he figured.

He could clearly recall the sun being out and the broad green leaves, full and lush on the maples. His father had asked him to drive and they were going along somewhere in East Haven, with Harry sitting there next to him in that used, blue, mid-range Chevy, a borrowed clunker with faded paint, worn seats and threadbare tires that the old man would never have been caught dead in but a few years before. It must have been late spring or maybe very early fall before the leaves changed, maybe September, because he could recall the crisp morning chill in the air. Harry had just finished relighting his cigar and Davey asked him to crack the passenger window to let the smoke out.

They had only gone a few blocks when the old man, sensing something, sucked on the stogie, exhaled, coughed slightly to clear the phlegm from his throat, and asked his son, his favorite, what was wrong.

"So what's goin' on with you, lover boy?"

"With me? Nuthin'. Why?" David started. But taken aback, indeed surprised by the sudden display of fatherly concern, he proceeded to explain how he'd been down for months and months since Mona had gone. How her leaving had really taken its toll.

By that point Harry had taken to tapping. You know. That unconscious habit old people take on when they think no one is listening, when they want to make sure they're being heard. Nudging his youngest on the upper arm with the back of his left hand, in part to emphasize the obvious, in part to assure himself that his son was still in the car, the old man uttered some cliché about the passage of time and healing.

What Davey remembered then, as he sat on that plane heading to his father's funeral, was how annoyed he had gotten that day as they rode through that Connecticut shore town going who knows where. It was nothing the man said. He bitched and bellyached as usual about Mickey and how no good he was, and carried on about Howard and how selfish he was, prefaced with the proverbial "and that other brother of yours...." And it didn't matter what the old man said since Davey had heard it all a million times. The father griping about his other sons to the one seldom seen. Part of the New Haven homecoming ritual.

What pissed him off was the tapping. That staccato-like emphatic of a bony-assed hand, the index and middle finger extended, jabbing and poking across the seat with ever more frequency and force as Harry became more agitated with the thought of his other two boys. The old man had unconsciously switched the remainder of the cigar to his left after he inhaled and an occasional ash fluttered to the seat between them or onto Davey's arm as the tapping continued. Finally Davey couldn't take it any more.

"Would yuh stop, already!"

"Stop what? What the hell did I *do*?!"

"Stop with the hitting!"

"Hitting? Who's hitting? Me? Was I hitting?"

"Stop with the hand already. The poking with the finger, your ca-knocking me with the hand while you talk. Ashes are getting all over hell! You're drivin' me nuts!"

"Boy, she musta really done a job on you, sonny boy!"

"It's you doin' the job. With that fuckin' bony backhand of yours. You don't have to poke me with every sentence!"

"Is that some way to talk to your father? Excuse me for livin'!"

"You're excused."

And there they were, David and his wife Annie, flying to bury the old man.

"You're excused," Davey thought. *"You're excused."*

Mickey put the key in and opened the door to the apartment. Turning to Gina, he motioned for her to step in as he quickly glanced up and down the hallway.

"Now hurry the hell up. Remember, like I tol' yuh. I wanna be the fuck otta here before those other two assholes show up."

"Look, your brother, what's his name, he..."

"Davey?"

"Yeah, Davey. We figured before that his flight ain't due in 'til later."

"Yeah, I know. But that other asshole, Howard, he could show up here any time, lookin' t' score first. He thinks he's so fuckin' smart, that greedy fuck."

Gina looked around the small cramped apartment.

"Jesus, Mickey, your old man sure had a lotta stuff."

"Yeah, yeah. Just remember what I tol' yuh and don't waste no time botherin' with any bullshit. Go in the bedroom and take a pillowcase, like we talked about. Make sure to check through the top drawers and the jewelry boxes on the dresser and only grab what's worth anything. Don't bother with no clothes and shit. But make sure you check underneath everythin'. I gotta look for the cash. Don't forget the watch... And don't look to snatch nuthin'. I know exactly what the ol' man had."

Gina disappeared into the bedroom as Mickey began rifling through the accordian-doored closet along the narrow passage running between the back and the living room. *"There's got to be a stash here somewhere,"* he thought. *"Yuh always kept some around."*

Reaching up, he felt around on the top shelf beneath the piles of folded sweaters and starched, pressed shirts, neatly stacked in their cardboard and plastic bags, fresh from the cleaners. His hand bumped something under the blue cardigan tennis sweater, the one Harry occasionally wore when he was looking to make a sale to one of the new money *yiddels* from the country club in Woodbridge. He knew immediately from the touch what it was and took the snub nose down. Removing it from its shoulder holster, he looked to see if it was loaded and checked the safety before dropping it into the knock-off flight bag lying there on the floor.

"Hey, Gina!" he yelled. "You won't believe this! The ol' man had a piece tucked away up here!"

He shook his head as he laughed to himself and continued the search for the money and whatever else he could forage. Looking down at the rows of shiny shoes, easily thirty pair, neatly arranged along the back wall of the closet, he again chuckled to himself and quickly began to check each shoe. Pulling out the shoe trees, he pushed his large fingers into the toes of a pair of patent leather dress loafers, lightly covered with a thin film of Vaseline. He paused for a second as he remembered them, the ones with the black velvet bows the old man wore when they had gone to New York that time, to cousin Barry's kid's Bar Mitzvah. It was shortly after he had gotten out of the joint the second time, he could recall, and the old man was in his glory then, having his oldest back with him, back on the street.

Harry had small feet and Mickey's hands were too big for the shoes. But stretching his index and middle finger up toward the toe of a casual loafer, fourth in line, he finally felt something and retrieved the first tightly folded hundred.

"Who says I don't know the ol' man?" he thought.

Now on the scent and tossing them aside as he went, he moved quickly through the row of wing-tips, broughams and cordovans, the Scotch grain tie shoes and tasseled loafers, the assorted deck and tennis shoes, the array of knockabout discount specials, probably scored from some low-rent booster. He counted the old man's stash from the overturned pile and laughed to himself as he folded it away.

"Twenty-five hundred in your fuckin' shoes. Not bad, ol' man, not bad."

Gina reappeared from the bedroom carrying a pillowcase weighted down in the bottom and gazed at the mound of discarded footwear.

"Holy fuck! What the hell's your ol' man got so many shoes for? You'd think we was in one of them discount joints."

"Yep. Harry definitely liked his shoes. Always talked about havin' to wear his brothers'. After they were through with 'em. When they were kids. How he used t'have t' put cardboard inside to plug up the holes when it was wet out. T'keep his feet dry."

"And look at the clothes! You couldn't fit another goddamn thing in this closet!"

"There ain't one goddamn thing that'll fit me, neither. He took care of himself pretty good. Always looked out for number one, that's for sure.... Gimme the watch."

"I didn't find it."

"I ain't got time t' fuck around! I said gimme the watch."

"It wasn't there."

"Wudduhya mean it wasn't there? Did yuh check everywhere I tol' yuh?"

Wheeling around in the narrow hallway and half pushing her aside, he stepped by and went into the bedroom. She followed on his heels. He checked the three open jewelry boxes on the dresser, now just partially filled with various cheap cufflinks and stays and Elks Club mementos, the stuff Gina had left. He ripped through the drawers of socks and underwear and a small top drawer containing nothing but handkerchiefs. Turning, he grabbed her by the wrist and forced her against the wall. She winced at the grasp of his big hand.

"Leh' go! You're hurtin' me. I'm tellin' yuh I didn't find no watch!"

Still holding her, he quickly frisked her down, even taking a moment to make sure she wasn't concealing anything between her breasts, one of her favorite hiding places.

"Where the fuck can it be?" he said aloud. "I know it was here last week. It was sittin' on the jewelry box where he always left it. Right here on the dresser."

"Maybe he was wearin' it," Gina said as Mickey let go of her.

"Naw, he never wore it out, 'cept to somethin' special. Afraid some crumb would snatch it off his wrist some night when he was out partyin'. Or that some douche bag might swipe it. Ain't this a bitch! Where could it be?"

They spent several more minutes checking the rest of the apartment. They even went through all the kitchen cupboards and when Gina opened the cabinet under the sink to toss her gum in the basket, Mickey took a frantic second to check in the trash. They grabbed a few more things. Gina, insisting the faker Yves St. Laurent flight bags in the hallway closet were the real thing, gathered those up as Mickey snatched the box of cigars from its spot on the glass-topped coffee table. He then went over to the white enameled tea cart where Harry displayed his liquor and snatched up an unopened half gallon of Dewar's and a couple of fifths of Johnnie Walker Red, still in their red-ribboned Christmas boxes.

"Here, put these in one of those tote bags," he said as he handed them off to the girlfriend.

Knowing full well Mickey rarely if ever drank, she wondered why he would want the booze but didn't ask. His taking the cigars was a mystery as well, but she decided she'd better keep her mouth shut.

He paused to gaze at the framed photographs, dusty but neatly arranged on top of the TV. Pictures of Harry's parents, brothers and sisters, mostly all gone now. Old pictures. One of Howard and a couple of Davey, one of them taken in the early 70s, he figured. In his hippie days, with wire-rimmed glasses, a beard and his hair way long, tied back in a ponytail, wearing worn blue jeans frayed at the knees, an old khaki Eisenhower jacket and a checkered flannel shirt. He was holding a spinning rod and kneeling over a neatly arranged row of rainbow trout in a setting that was definitely out west somewhere, grinning one of those prideful "Hey! Look-what-I-caught" kind of grins, just like the guys in those fishing magazines they both used to look at.

"The one that got away," Mickey thought as his gaze then turned to the pictures of the grandsons, his own kids, taken when they were all still small and not yet into dope and trouble. His eyes then moved to the picture of Esther, a shot taken when she was younger, happier. Alive then.

He began to feel a remote tinge of sadness and guilt, but moved before it could take hold. Grabbing the pictures of himself with the old man and the one of his mother, he placed them in the pillowcase with the stash from the bedroom, and made for the door. Clutching the knock-off bags and the pillowcase, Gina moved out into the bright light of the hall in front of him and he closed the door.

"So what do yuh think happened to the watch?" she asked as they quickly moved down the hallway to the elevator.

"Who the fuck knows? I'll tell you one thing, though! Yuh can bet your sweet ass, I'll find out!"

Howard swiveled in his chair and peered at the digital desk clock. One o'clock already. He still had to see Rabbi Feldstein and he had promised to be at Velners' at two to finalize the arrangements.

He had already been there in the morning to take Stevie Velner some clothes for Harry and to pick out the casket. Knowing full well that Davey had little to spare and that he'd be lucky to see a penny from Mickey, he had selected something in the middle price range, with a veneer that looked like solid mahogany from a distance. He had come to realize long ago that there was no sense in burying too serious a piece of change and figured people wouldn't get so close as to notice anyway since the coffin would be closed.

He wondered how much he might get back from the old man's Social Security and if it would cover the costs. He tried to imagine what the bill from Yale New

Haven would end up costing, despite the fact that Harry was pretty much dead by the time the ambulance got him there. He figured that the funeral itself wouldn't run too high since Louie Velner had been friends with the old man since they were kids together on Legion Avenue and Velner the younger had told him not to worry, that they already had three come in and it was only Tuesday morning. That they would make it up in volume.

He picked up the phone, pressed the intercom and connected with the receptionist. "Yeah, Jeanette, do me a favor and call United Airlines. Please. Find out what time their afternoon flight from Chicago comes in."

"Yes, Mr. Rabin."

"Then, if yuh would, please call Fox's Deli on Whalley Avenue. Ask to speak to Hy. Tell him who you are, that you work for me, and make sure that everything'll be ready to go, as I asked. For after the funeral, tomorrow. And make sure they're going to deliver. I won't have time to run around in the morning. And hold any calls, unless there's one from my brother, Davey. I need some time to myself."

"Yes, Mr. Rabin."

"Thank you, Jeanette."

"Uh, Mr. Rabin?"

"Yes, what is it?"

"Sorry to hear about your father."

"Thank you, Jeanette."

Howard set the phone back on the cradle. He wondered for a moment what the hell he had come to work for, while knowing full well that the office had become his safe place, his refuge. Sliding his chair back and opening the desk drawer, he pulled out the watch and gazed at it. Turning it over and over in his fingers, he examined the workmanship in the gold linked band and the fine crafting of its crystal face and clasp, its rectangular Art Deco style. He read the inscription on the back. *"For Harry, Love Esther. 1937."*

He wondered about where the watch had been and thought about how he had retrieved it from Esther's belongings the day they buried her. *"What was it, now? Almost fifteen years already."* He thought about how long she must have worked to buy it with money she somehow managed to tuck away. Not having experienced any love himself and certainly no affection from the old man, he briefly pondered what might have possessed her to give it to him, even on their first anniversary. He thought about how much it must have originally gone for and speculated as to what it would be worth in current dollars, the value of the gold alone and the antique value. He wondered how much it would cost to have it appraised.

He found himself thinking about how Esther had kept it through those years after she and the old man had split up. How Harry had pleaded and played continuous head games and gambits to get it back when he found out who had it after she died. How he refused to return it to his father for years, in part because his mother didn't want the old man to have it, and partly out of spite for all the bad years, all the abuse.

His eyes now a little misty, he remembered how his father had embraced him the day he gave it back. How strange that felt. After all, Harry had never hugged him before, that he could recall. That had been the year before, after Davey had convinced him to make peace. Back after they had all gone out to Wisconsin for his baby brother's wedding.

He thought about how Harry had stopped by the office just a few days earlier, that Friday. He said he had just happened to be in the neighborhood, that he had just stopped in for a minute and had to be somewhere. Howard just sat there thinking how odd it was for the old man to show up at work, when Harry reached into his overcoat and came out with the watch.

"Here. I want yuh should do me a favor and hold onto this. I'm afraid one of those goniff maintenance men at the apartment might glom onto it. They got keys to all the apartments. In case of an emergency, they say. Emergency, my ass."

He had left as suddenly as he appeared, and Howard, now looking back in hindsight, found himself pondering what possessed his father to give the watch back. He wondered if the old man somehow knew that he was on his way out; that his time was up. He then smiled slightly when he thought how pissed Mickey would be when he discovered it was gone and that Harry had given it to him.

"He's probably looking for it right now," he thought to himself. "My brother, the putz! Wait 'til he finds out the ol' man gave it to me.... That I got it!"

The phone rang and Jeanette informed him that United flight #237 was scheduled to land at 2:15. He glanced at the watch in his hands, which he had taken to winding every day, religiously, after the jeweler in Westville had fixed and cleaned it. Quarter to one. He had plenty of time to stop by the funeral home and get to the airport to meet Davey.

He picked up the phone and pressed the intercom. "Jeanette, I'm going out. I'll be gone the rest of the day. If the people with Connecticut Savings call, inform them of my situation, and tell them I'll get back to them with more word on their mainframe early next week. I won't be in tomorrow, with the funeral and all. But I'll probably be here on Friday. Oh, yes, by the way..."

"Yes, Mr. Rabin, I talked to Fox's as you requested and everything is set. Just as you ordered."

 "Thanks for your help. For everything."

"You're welcome, Mr. Rabin."

Placing the phone in its cradle, Howard got up and turned to the wall. He touched the simulated walnut panel at the right spot and the door slid open. He pulled the topcoat on over his suit, the subdued charcoal pinstripe that Richie had picked out at J. Press. He wondered for a second about what he should wear to the funeral and if any of his associates from the district or his boss from the Manhattan office would show up. He took a moment to look at himself in the wall mirror mounted at the back of the closet. Brushing some lint from a shoulder and his lapel, he made a gesture at straightening the knot of his tie and buttoned the topcoat. Pulling a Kleenex from his right-hand pocket, he wiped his eyes, slightly red and irritated, and thought how he should stop and get some Visine on the way to Velners'. He unconsciously picked his nose, checked the tissue, and put it back in his coat pocket. *"Harry's finally gone,"* he thought. *"And I got the watch."*

CHAPTER 2

Izzie

1923... IZZIE RABINOVICH HATED THE rain. He hated being out in it. He hated it as a small boy when it drizzled down cold, numbing him to the bone in the *shtetl* outside Vilna and he hated it now as it banged on the roof of his rickety flatbed making its way along the county road, well north and east of New Haven.

He had been driving since before dawn and it had to be getting toward two and the rain just kept coming down. He got drenched loading the first batch of chickens and took another soaking with each successive stop as he pulled the tarpaulin off, loaded the crates, and covered his drenched birds. Now thoroughly chilled and not quite sure if he had missed the turn to New Haven, he pulled a large handkerchief from his work-a-day vest and wiped the windshield in order to see the road sign, a white blur barely visible across the intersection. He down shifted, slowed the truck to a crawl, looked both ways, and eased into the crossing. Squinting at the sign through the downpour, he made out the words "Entering the Town of Northford. Wallingford 5, New Haven 25," with an arrow pointing to the left. "Such names," he thought as he turned the truck. "Northford, Wallingford, Guilford, Branford, Milford. Everything they name for this man who makes the cars, and of course he's an *antisemit*. Such a place we came to!"

He glanced briefly at Heschie, asleep against the door on the other side of the small cab, curled up in his oversized hand-me-down jacket like some young shabby alley cat that had somehow smuggled itself aboard to get in out of the rain. Knowing full well the kid couldn't be much help, he had been reluctant to take him along. But the boy, off from school, had begged, "Please, Poppa, please!" with those pleading eyes of his as he promised to be good. Besides, Rivkah had given him that "So what's the big deal, you should just once take the boy along?" kind of look. And now he found himself enjoying the company, a rare occasion alone with his little one, riding along in the rain. "At least he's outta trouble for a change," he mused.

The boy stirred, and they spoke in Yiddish.

"Poppa?"

"Vas, Hescheleh, vas?"

"Where are we?"

"On our way home."

"Did we get all the chickens?"

"Most. More than half a load, almost three-quarters. It seems my good friend Teitelbaum, he musta been up this way again."

"Mr. Teitelbaum, the other chicken man? From home?"

"And what other Teitelbaums do we know?"

"Poppa?"

"What now, Heschie?"

"I'm hungry."

"You'll have somethin' for *essen* when we get home," Izzie responded. But as he said the words, he realized neither of them had had a bite since they had finished the bread and salami Rivkah had sent along, wrapped in the newspaper. That must have been before eight o'clock, certainly before their second stop, he figured. He wiped the windshield again and shuddering from the aching chill now overtaking him thought that stopping to get something somewhere, maybe some tea to warm up, wouldn't be such a bad idea. He once more silently cursed the rain as his son drifted off again.

Finally giving in to the chill, he pulled into the first place they came to, a small country store. Heschie stirred and raised his head as the truck creaked to a halt.

"Where are we?"

Izzie glanced past the boy to the front door of the store, beyond the gas pumps, a good thirty yards away. The rain, while not coming down as hard as before, was still tapping steadily on the roof of the cab and he immediately had second thoughts about getting out. Such places still made him feel self-conscious, forever the foreigner, anyway. He paused a second, still glancing at the storefront, then pulled out the small change purse from his vest and undoing its snap, dumped the contents into his left hand.

"Maybe we should get something to eat, Hescheleh," he said as he handed the boy two coins. "Here's twenty cents. I want you should go in. Get four slices of cheese and two rolls. Dat's all. Not'ing else. *Versteshteh*? This place isn't kosher." Knowing full well such a store would only have that horrible weak coffee he could never get accustomed to, he called to his son as the boy jumped down from the cab.

"And Heschie! Ask the man if he has hot water. If he does, get some. We'll have a *glas te*! And remember! Nut'ing else! It won' be kosher! An' don' forget *mein* change!"

The boy darted across the puddled yard, up the steps and into the store. The screen rattled and banged and the bell above the inner door rang as he stepped in and took his cap off. Shaking it quickly, he placed it front of him, ready to play the waif, and slowly moved forward, examining the interior.

It was one of those places, still common in those days, packed with a little bit of everything. Assorted dry goods and hardware of every kind, household items and bolts of cloth, farm tools, burlap sacks of flour and oatmeal. An old potbellied stove off to one side warmed the large single room. His eye immediately caught the penny candies in their large glass containers next to the pouch tobacco and chewing gum on the counter, and the big brass-fitted cash register. He peered at the large Coca Cola sign with its red cheeked gentile face offering up a bottle, painted icy cold. He gazed into the refrigerated display case to the right and his mouth immediately began to water at the sight of the various sausages, salamis and assorted cheeses.

A large woman in a light blue work dress and full store apron, big boned with high, full breasts and a thick head of straw colored hair tied back in a bun, in her early thirties, stepped out from a curtain concealing a back room.

"Now this is what the guys must mean by *zafdig*," the boy thought as soon as his eyes moved from the meats in the case to look up at her.

Sensing his gaze on her chest, she flushed a little. "Oh no," she thought, "Another one of these little Jews from New Haven!"

"Can I help you, young man?"

"Yes... uh... please. I'd like two rolls..."

"Rolls? Oh, you mean the buns! Yes. And what else?"

"Four slices of cheese, please. For sandwiches."

"And what kind?"

"The cheapest, please."

"The American?"

"Um...uh, yes. Please."

The woman slid the display case open and pulled out a rectangular orange slab and turned and placed it on the cutting board. With her back to him, Heschie found himself staring at her almost blond hair, something seldom seen on Legion Avenue. His eyes, propelled by the curiosity of such a different looking female, moved down the breadth of her broad back and halted at her wide, well-shaped back side.

"And this must be 'a *real tuchas*,'" he mused.

Finished slicing, she turned back toward the counter with the yellow cheese on a sheet of waxed paper in her upturned hand and noticed his gaze fixed upon her body. Agitated and slightly humored at the same time, she quickly turned again, grabbed the bulk cheese off the board, pivoted, and slid it back into the case.

"Anything else?"

"Uh... yes, please. Do you have hot water?"

"You mean from a sink? All we have is cold..."

"Umm... uhh... no. Like hot water to make tea. My Poppa thought maybe..."

The woman turned her gaze across the store and through the front door to the battered truck with its tarp-covered freight sitting on the other side of the pumps, as she wondered who would send a child out in such a rain. She looked back at the little ragamuffin of a boy standing in front of her.

"Yes. You see the kettle there, on the stove?"

"Do you have something to put it in?" she asked as she stepped out from behind the counter.

"Umm, uh... no."

"That's okay. I have a jar. We can put it in a jar."

Moving across the store, she bent and picked up the chipped canning jar, used by one of the regulars for summertime lemonade and long abandoned, still sitting there by the foot of the potbellied stove.

"I don't need this," she said as she wiped the inside with a corner of her apron and filled it from the piping kettle.

It was then, as she was filling the jar, that Heschie caught sight of the large hunk of boiled ham in the cooler. He hadn't had anything but that little bit of tea before leaving the house, back when it was still dark, and that bread and a small nub of salami after their first stop. He knew the cheese and bread wouldn't be enough, and the sight of the pink meat sitting there in its congealed juices, when combined with the smell of all the other delectables wafting through the store, made it all impossibly intoxicating. Glancing again at the woman's chest, suddenly there just above him, he succumbed.

"I'll... I'd like some of that," he said, pointing through the display glass at the ham. "Just a slice. And please don't put it in the bag with the rolls and cheese."

In one quick practiced motion, the woman yanked the meat from the cooler, moved it to the cutting board, and made a quick slice. Returning the ham to the refrigeration, she then placed a small brown bag with the bread and cheese and a pink piece of meat on its own sheet of paper on the counter, alongside the steaming jar of hot water. She fashioned an impromptu lid for the jar from a square of newspaper pulled from down below and fastened it in place with a used rubber band.

"That'll be twenty-cents."

Heschie gave her the dimes his father had sent him in with and placing his cap back on his head, rapidly undid the top buttons of his jacket as well as three buttons of his shirt as if he were going to undress. Taking the slice of ham, he folded it in half in its paper, and slid it gently inside, tucked almost under his armpit. Buttoning the shirt and jacket, he reached up into the right sleeve with his left hand, and rolled down the cuff of his oversized shirt till it covered his right hand to the fingertips. Drawing the hand in slightly to use the cuff like a pot holder, he cautiously grasped the jar by its rim so as not to scald himself. He picked up the bag with the cheese and rolls with his left and made for the door with the woman on his heels. Shaking her head and laughing lightly to herself in an embarrassed and contemptible kind of way, she held the doors open as the boy made his way back out into what had once again become a downpour.

Izzie, by this time wondering what could be taking so long, watched his son emerge from the store. The brim of his cap down over his eyes, the boy made his way as fast as he could without spilling the water and his father leaned over and opened the door for him just at the last second so as not to let in any more of the damp and chill than necessary. The boy handed up the bag and jar and climbed in.

Shaking off his cap, Heschie turned to his father. "I got just like you asked. Bread and cheese. And here's some hot water for tea."

"*Gut, gut,* Hescheleh, that's *gut.* And where's *mein* change?"

"There was none, Poppa."

"What? So much it cost? In what kind of place did we stop?"

"Well, uh, Poppa... uh...the *shikseh,* she charged me for the jar... for the tea!"

"For a chipped jar, she charged? Such a country!" Izzie exclaimed as he reached down under his seat.

He pulled out a small wooden box, some five inches high and four inches across, maybe ten inches long, his all-purpose odds-and-ends road kit that always stayed in the truck. Raising the hinged lid, he pulled out a cube shaped tin and pried it open with his nails. Again grasping the hot water jar with his sleeve, Heschie moved it toward his father and the man sprinkled a generous amount of black tea into the water.

"Set it down on the floor, it should steep a little," he directed his son. "Once they get good and soaked, the leaves on top'll sink."

With that he produced two battered tin cups from the box. Wiping the insides with the handkerchief, he handed one to his son. He then reached back in the box and came out with a small pocket knife as well as another smaller tin, this one with eight or ten cubes of hardened sugar.

"Your mother, God bless her, she thinks of everything!"

He unfolded the knife, cut the two rolls and handed them to the boy.

"Here, Hescheleh. Put two slices in each."

The boy unwrapped the cheese and did as his father said. He placed the sandwiches back on the paper, now spread between them on the seat, and his father told him to check the tea. He carefully lifted the quart jar from its resting place on the floor, between his feet.

"Here, let me take that before you spill," Izzie said as he reached over and grasped the jar in his big calloused hand, impervious to the heat of the glass.

Most of the tea had already settled and the water had turned a faint rust color, with a deeper reddish amber at the bottom. Wiping the knife, he gave a quick stir and the hot liquid took on a unified color as the black leaves swirled in their vortex at the center of the jar.

"Come, Hescheleh, *ess mein kindt,*" Izzie beckoned and the boy eagerly reached for a sandwich.

"But not before the *brocha,*" the father cautioned as he set the jar down and bowed his head to make the blessing.

Finishing the prayer, Izzie reached for the jar in an effort to capture some warmth in his hands before it all dissipated throughout the cab. He filled the cup in his left hand and reached over and filled his son's, sitting between them on the seat. Retrieving a sugar cube from its hiding place, he placed it between his front teeth as was the custom, and inhaled deeply through his nose, savoring the hot aromatic. Then drawing the cup to his lips, he took a full sip, pulling the tea through the sugar.

He had caught the first faint whiff, distantly familiar yet foreign, not long after the boy climbed back into the truck. He just couldn't place it and tried to pay it no mind. Suddenly, then, as that first full sweetened sip entered the back of his throat, the realization came. First he gasped deeply, then nearly gagged and coughed uncontrollably and the mouthful of tea and what remained of the sugar cube, half dissolved, splattered onto the windshield. In the same instant, his huge right hand fired across the cab, catching his son with a cracking backhand full across one whole side of his face.

"Where is it?! *Gibt me hier!* Give it here before I...!"

"What, Poppa, what...?!" the boy queried, stunned and terrified against the far door.

"You ask me *vas*? You *bummerkeh,* you! You no-good little bum! Such a nerve! You bring *traif, chazzerai* into my truck and ask me *vas*?! You thought this nose of mine, it wouldn't smell?!"

"But Poppa...!"

"Don't 'but Poppa' me! *Gibt me hier* before I give you such a *zetz* you'll never forget!"

Heschie undid his shirt buttons and reached in and pulled out the slice of ham, now warm to the touch, from its hiding place. He started to hand it over, but Izzie, not wanting to handle it himself, yelled, "Now open the window and throw it out! Out! Away from my truck!"

The boy rolled down his window and flung the piece of forbidden meat.

"And here for a moment, I t'ought to *mein selve* what in the hell is that *shtink.* No, it can' be! And then it *dawnt* on me. You sonovabitch! Get out from my truck!"

"But... but Poppa...."

"Don' 'but Poppa' *me*, you bum! Go on! Do like I say, *und geh,* get out! Go ride on the back with the chickens, in the *drek* where you belong 'cause you ain't ridin' with me no more. That's for sure!"

In shock, his face still stinging and beginning to swell, Heschie opened the door and started to climb down into the rain, his hand still clutching the cheese sandwich.

"What?! You t'ink yuhr gonna eat, yet? Throw that *sanvich* back up here," Izzie yelled as the boy's feet slipped to the ground. "Such *chutzpah*! The nerve! I don' believe!"

Izzie continued to bellow as Heschie tossed the roll up on the seat, closed the door and made his way through the slop to the back of the truck. Fighting back the tears, he hoisted himself over the tailgate boards. He pulled back the canvas and peered in among the chickens, asleep or cowering from the rain in their crated captivity, and as he did so, the smell of damp birds and chicken shit wafting up from under the covering nearly made him gag.

"So now," he muttered, as he hiked up his jacket collar and pulled down his cap, "I can either smother under the tarp or stay outside and drown like a rat."

Sitting down in the damp between the last row of crates and the tailgate, with his face toward the rear, he pulled the canvas partially up over his head. He sat touching his bruised face with his fingers and began to cry softly, quiet so his father wouldn't hear.

Izzie watched through the rear window of the cab as the boy climbed aboard and covered himself. Certain that his son was settled, he turned and started the engine. Wiping the windshield once again, he stuck the handkerchief in his jacket pocket and eased the truck into gear. He slowly let up on the clutch and the truck crawled onto the graveled shoulder of the road.

"Bringing *traif* into my truck. Imagine!" He peered through the windshield at the road and back to the wipers as they streaked across the glass. "I hate the *gotdamnt* rain," he grumbled. Feeling more sorry for himself than for the boy, he turned the truck toward New Haven.

CHAPTER 3:

Preparation

1989.... LOUIE HAD BEEN SITTING there for how long, he wasn't quite sure. At least another hour he figured, but he wasn't certain. Finally deciding it was time to get to work, he poured another long belt into the water glass sitting on the nearby cart, replaced the cap, and tucked the now dwindling fifth away on the bottom shelf. He slowly eased himself up and cautiously stepped over to Harry, pulling on a pair of rubber gloves as he approached. Taking the spray nozzle of the hose that extended from the ceiling at the end of the table, he wet down his old friend's graying head, poured a small puddle of the strong disinfectant soap into his hands, rubbed them together, and began to gently wash the scalp. Rinsing the hair, he then sprayed the face and upper torso. This time pouring some of the soap into a large sponge, he washed the man's forehead and temples, the brow and closed eyelids, the curve of nose. Following the contours of the face, the high cheekbones and line of the jaw and neck, his hands moved in a meditatively slow, almost hypnotic motion as if he were giving a facial massage, a soothing act of friendship. A lump slowly built in his throat.

As he worked his way down across the deflated chest and pallor of breast and rib cage, he thought about how it really would have been something if the bathing committee, the *chevrah kadishim* from the orthodox *shul,* maybe even some of the *hasidim* from upper George Street, had come to give Harry the ritual preparation, the whole *megilah* with the *brochas,* the immersion, the white shroud. He began to think about an appropriate send-off, something he could do special, when Harry's head raised up off the table and the face, full of lather, looked at him.

"What *special*? Who needs from *special*? Louie, how long we been friends? More than seventy goddamn years, *no*?!"

Hardly startled and determined to ride this one out, the undertaker just stood there, washcloth in hand.

"Again, you're talkin' to me? You gotta be kiddin'. You're dead!"

"Now yuhr catchin' on! That's my point! Just throw me in a goddamn pine box or maybe one of those jumbo-size zip-lock bags, the black ones yuh always got layin' around here. Save the frills for the suckers and just do me the favor, like I always asked yuh how many goddamn times, and bury me facedown so the whole world can kiss my skinny Sheeney ass!"

"Harehleh! Harehleh! You know as well as I do that funerals ain't for the deceased."

"*No*?! Then who they for? You want we should trade places so's I can go to *yours*? Look! If yuh can, I just want you should put me in a hole somewhere close by Esther, over in the Vilner Lodge section off by Fitch Street, maybe not far from Momma and Poppa and my brothers, *alevasholom*, if yuh can swing it. And if not...."

"Oh, so *now*, all of a sudden, you wanna get close back by Esther?"

"What? You gonna look to start with me *no*w?!"

"Hey, you're the one brought it up."

"Look, all I'm askin' is what we talked about years ago. I always told yuh that when the time came, if I went before you, that I didn't want yuh should make a big *tsimmes*, no big to do. That they should hold my funeral in a phone booth so's to cut down on the overhead. Just do me what I asked yuh!"

The eyes closed and the head eased back down. Louie turned and hurriedly went back to the cart. He drained the finger and a half of whiskey still sitting in the glass and reaching underneath, grabbed the bottle and poured another.

At that moment his son Steven reappeared. Looking first at his father's state, then to the glass in the old man's hand and the bottle on the cart, and then at Harry lying there with his face and half his body covered with soap, the young Velner just shook his head in disbelief.

Cued by his son's expression, Louie responded. "What?! Don't give me that look! You know damn well everything will come off just fine."

"*Fine*? Just *fine*!? Look at yourself! Someone might think you had been conversing with the dead, you look so bad."

"It just so happens that..."

"Stop already, would you please! Harry's son Howard is here. He and I made most of the arrangements earlier this morning when he brought me Harry's clothes and picked out a box."

"Yeah? What'd he choose?"

"The Forevermore. You know, the mahogany veneer with the fake silk."

"Harry always said he held a nickel so tight, he'd make the buffalo piss!"

"That's okay. We'll make it up elsewhere. I told him you were indisposed, but he really wants to see yuh."

"I guess I should go see."

"Yes, go and talk to him, give him a few minutes, and I'll finish cleaning the body."

"The body? Yuh mean Harry? Yeah, that sounds like a good idea, I guess. I'll go see Howard and you can finish with the washing. Give him a shave if yuh want, but don't do any cutting or connect the pumps. I'll do that myself. Everything's gotta be right!"

With that, Louie peeled off the rubber gloves, reached up behind his neck and undid the tie to the surgical smock and pulled his arms out. Rolling down his sleeves and buttoning the cuffs without looking and haphazardly straightening his tie, he grabbed his suit coat from the back of the chair where he had left it and cautiously and unevenly made his way toward the front door.

"And remember.... Don't start with the embalming or nuthin'. I'll do it. And don't talk with Harry while I'm gone. I don't want you should end up looking like me, God forbid!"

Howard was sitting there on one of the stiff upholstered chairs in the front parlor. He got up when Louie entered and the two shook hands.

"Howard! Howard! My god, it's been such a long time! I'm so sorry about your father. Me and him, I'm sure you know, we go back... oh, Jeez, more than seventy years, easy. We were kids together on Oak Street. Went to the same goddamn grade school together and then to Troupe, for god sakes."

"Yes, I know and..."

"Here, come Howard... Let's go into my office where we can talk."

Taking hold with that soft practiced touch to the outward bend of the elbow that came from decades of maneuvering the bereaved, he guided Howard down a hallway and through a door with the word "Private" engraved in cursive on its polished brass plate. They entered the tastefully outfitted office and Louie motioned for Howard to sit on one of the two matching leather uprights in front of the mahogany desk. Moving behind, he took his seat, opened one of the lower drawers and pulled out a cut glass decanter and two matching shot glasses set on a doilied sterling plate.

"You care for a drink?"

"No, I really don't."

Without missing a beat, Louie poured himself one and knocked it down as Howard's eye caught the glint of the man's diamond pinkie ring.

"L'chaim! For Harry!"

"L'chaim," Howard responded.

Placing the glass back alongside its twin, Louie returned the plate and bottle to its drawer, looked across the desk at Harry's son, sitting there with his topcoat unbuttoned, waiting, his legs crossed at the knee.

"You'll of course extend my condolences to your dear wife... I'm sorry, it's been so long, you'll have to excuse me, but I can't recall her name."

"Richie."

"Yes, of course. And the children? Did Harry mention that you had two?

Again, I'm gettin' so damn old, my memory isn't what it used to be."

Howard flashed on his and Richie's two Shelty collies, the ones they had raised from pups.

"Seamus and Lucy."

"A boy and a girl… and such nice names. *Mahzel tov!* And how old?"

"Ten and eleven."

"How wonderful! Bar and bat mitzvahs coming up, *no*? It's a shame Harry, *alevasholom,* he couldn't live to see."

"Yes, it would have been something."

"Anyway, Howard, I just wanted to let you know that if you have any concerns or questions about anything at all…."

The buzzer on the desk phone sounded and Louie picked up.

"What is it? …Who? …No, no, don't do that! …For cryin' out loud! …Okay, I'll come out!"

He hung up and came around the desk.

"I'm terribly sorry, but could you please excuse me for just a few minutes? Somethin's come up. I'll be right back as soon as I can. In just a couple of minutes. I do want to continue our conversation!"

Howard just sat there and watched as the man exited. His nose had picked up on the alcohol as soon as Louie had come close, but not one to say anything, at least under such circumstances, he now felt a little relieved to be alone.

"Seamus and Lucy having Bar Mitzvahs! What a *shmuck!*" he thought. "Wait 'til I tell Richie this one!"

Checking his watch, he thought about what a day it had been already. He thought about how he had hardly slept all night after finally getting home from the hospital, despite the two Valium. How he had lain there in the dark, with Richie snoring lightly and Seamus and Lucy twitching and whimpering from dog dreams on the end of the bed. How he just lay there thinking about Harry and how things had been improving between them, and how it was all cut short. The images of the horrible scene with Mickey at the hospital kept intruding. He had trouble keeping his eyes closed.

It was still pitch dark out when he finally gave up on getting any sleep and got out of bed. He threw on some around-the-house clothes and took the dogs out, came in and showered and shaved, put on his terry robe and killed some time putzing in the kitchen and den. He thought about vacuuming the living room but figured the noise would wake Richie, called Fox's Deli instead, knowing they opened at six, and finally changed into a suit and left the house before seven, with the dogs and Richie still asleep. He drove the fifteen miles through the early morning traffic to Harry's place and found the apologetic super who let him in. He retrieved some socks and underwear from one of the bedroom dressers, picked out one of the better suits, a dress shirt and tie, and grabbed a pair of dress shoes from the hallway closet.

He then drove back the ten miles to the shul in Westville to listen to Rabbi Feldstein insist that the old man had to be buried, according to custom, by sundown, and he had to explain that it wasn't possible. That David and the sister-in-law had to arrive from Wisconsin, and that there certainly would be *mishpocheh* coming from Florida and New York. Finally set on that end, but already talking to himself as he left the synagogue, he drove downtown to Velners' where he dropped off Harry's clothes, picked out the casket, and made most of the arrangements with Steven, after being told that Louie was somehow indisposed.

Remembering that he hadn't eaten anything and that he would pay for it later if he didn't, he had stopped off at the Greek joint, the American Diner, where he had his usual, a bowl of bran flakes with banana and skim milk and the daily glass of cranberry juice for his kidney stones. He killed another hour at the office calling friends and family and then stopped off at Whalley Pharmacy. Figuring there'd be lots of people at the house over the next few days, he picked up a couple of extra boxes of tissues. Remembering how David would probably be complaining about one of those airplane headaches of his when he arrived, he also had the pharmacist fill the scrip for the Percocets that he had tucked away in his billfold, the one that his shrink had given him "just in case". Trying to think of something they might need that he didn't already have in the house, he snatched up a couple of boxes of peppermint patties from the display near the check out.

And there he was, sitting in Louie's office, alone again, wanting to be done already, so he could make it to the airport to meet David and Annie. He thought about how he really didn't need the peppermint patties after all, that he really should return them since there certainly would be plenty to *nosh* on at the house. He began to wonder what he had done with the receipt.

Velner stepped into the hallway and again approached the front parlor. Mickey was standing there, looming big in the entryway. His eyes filled up with tears as soon as he saw his father's friend, someone he could remember from when he was a little kid, and he rushed forward and engulfed the old-timer in his arms, almost lifting him off the floor. They patted each other consolingly and broke their embrace, still holding on by the crook of one another's arms like two mismatched, out of shape street-clothed wrestlers.

"Mickey! Mickey! It's been so long! Look at yuh! My god!"

Mickey, all choked-up, lifted his yellow-lensed designer frames and wiped the tears from under both eyelids with the swipe of a puffy middle finger. He cleared his throat.

"Hey, Louie, what can I tell yuh?" He paused to catch a breath and a thought, coughed his quick smoker's cough, then started again. "I just come by t' bring yuh somethin'."

He turned to the walnut side table where he had placed the bottles. Picking up the larger one, he pivoted back and placed it in the undertaker's arms.

"What's this?"

"I sorta thought, maybe if yuh could... I stopped off an' got a bottle for the ol' man, a half gallon of Dewars. What he always drank. You know, so he shouldn't have t' go thirsty where he's headed."

"Yeah, it could get kinda hot," Louie quipped and they both guardedly chuckled as if there was someone else within earshot.

Going into his jacket like he was reaching for a piece, Mickey then pulled out a handful of cigars. "And here's some of his favorites, the Connecticut Valleys he liked to suck on."

Reaching over, he pulled the silk scarf out of Louie's breast pocket and slid the cigars in in its place. Placing the scarf in the suddenly silent undertaker's hand, he retrieved the second bottle from the table. He cradled it, red bow and all, in the man's other arm as if he was presenting a bouquet of cut flowers to some high school babe he once went with, back when he looked like something.

"I remember from when I was a kid how you always used t' drink Johnny Walker. With the red label."

Looking down at the bottle, Louie smiled and shook his head. "Your father always said you were somethin' else, a *real* piece of work. I'm tellin' yuh, boy...!"

Complimented, Mickey stood there, raised his glasses and wiped his eyes again and grinned as Louie, looking around first, removed the cigars from his pocket and placed them, along with the whiskey, behind the stand used for the condolence book.

Mickey started in. "Yuh know how the old man was. He always used to say he wanted to be buried facedown so everybody could kiss his ass."

"That's somethin', Mick. Those very words just came to me a little while ago."

"I thought you and I could make the arrangements."

"What? You don't know? Your brother Howard was here first thing this morning already. He worked everything out with Steven. I figured the two of you had been in touch, that you were too shook up to come down."

"Sonofabitch! I don't believe this! I'm the oldest, I should uh..."

"Look, Mickey, I hear yuh, believe me, but there's a time element involved here. After all, there's things that I have to take care of that gotta be done promptly. I couldn't sit around all mornin'. And neither could the old man. Howard did the right thing by your father, believe me, so let that one rest. Do it for me, and for the ol' man, would yuh?"

"Yeah, you're right. I hear yuh."

"Yuh know, Mickey, I probably shouldn't tell you this, but Howard's here right now. He's sittin' in my office. If you can act like a gentleman, then we can go in and the three of us can talk over what needs to be talked over. That make sense to you?"

"Hey, you don't have worry about me. I'm cool. I ain't got no beef."

"You sure?"

"Yuh got my word. There ain't gonna be no problem."

Guiding Mickey with that same back of the elbow touch, Louie led him into the office. Howard, still pondering the whereabouts of the receipt for the peppermint patties, jumped a little when the door opened. Surprised to see his brother there, he stood up and the two just looked at each other for what must have seemed like an eternity, in actuality a second or two. Their eyes simultaneously filled with tears and they came together and hugged quickly, without affection, and then parted, standing there face-to-face.

"Look, I just want yuh to know I ain't got no beef with anybody," Mickey slubbered. "I want everything to be done right. For the ol' man."

"I do too," sputtered Howard, already wiping his eyes with one of his tissues.

"I just want yuh t' know that you don't have t' worry 'bout nuthin'. I know David, he ain't got the bread so you and me, we'll whack everythin' in half, right down the middle, all the expenses."

"But that's what you said last time, when Mommy..."

"You believe *this,* Louie? You ask me to be cool, and he brings up some old shit from fuckin' twelve, fifteen years ago!"

"And how many times did you burn me before and since?!"

Having seen it all before, in a thousand different ways, Louie interceded.

"Gentlemen, gentlemen, please. Remember where we are. Your father, *alevashalom,* he's here in preparation for his final rest and I certainly didn't expect this from the two grown sons of my best friend."

Howard turned. "You're right, Louie. Have Steven give me a total and I'll write a check. You'll have it first thing Monday." He turned to Mickey. "And you'll give me half?"

"You hard uh hearin' or what?! Wha'd I jus' tell yuh? I ain't lookin' to put a hurt on yuh. No bullshit. Everythin' whacked right in half. T'marruh!"

"Okay, then. That's settled." Howard began to thank Louie, paused in mid-sentence as if he had forgotten what he was going to say, and looked at his watch.

"I have to get to the airport to pick up David."

"But I was gonna get him."

"You don't even know what time he's comin' in!"

"Oh! So yuh think you're so fuckin' smart! As a matter of fact, I had Gina call the airport this mornin' already. It don't take no fuckin' brains to find out when the only flight they got from Chicago might be landin'!"

Getting tired of the noise and wanting to get back to Harry, Louie again waded in.

"Excuse me, fellas, but look! I think the both of yuhs should go to the airport. Perhaps if yuh get into it over there, maybe you'll find a real Solomon, a man of wisdom that'll be happy to cut David in half so neither of you should feel cheated. Me? I got work to do yet and yuh interrupted a very important conversation I was having, long distance, when yuh showed up."

Howard, getting the message, thanked the undertaker and left. Mickey started after him but Louie grabbed him by the arm and the older brother turned.

"Let him go. You got plenty of time."

"He's somethin' else, that fuckin' brother of mine, ain't he?"

"You're both somethin', believe you me! Certainly Harry's kids!"

Mickey gave Louie another hug, raised his glasses and wiped his eyes one more time, began to make for the door, but paused and turned.

"Oh yeah, I just remembered somethin' I wanted to ask yuh. Sorta why I came."

"What's that?"

"You know anybody named Julie? Some ol' friend of the ol' man's maybe?"

"Julie? Julie who?"

"I don't know. That's why I'm askin'."

"Julie... I can't think of anyone off hand, no."

"That's weird 'cause I figured you might know. The last thing the ol' man says to me was somethin' about somebody named Julie. He said it when he collapsed in the yard at my place and says it again at the hospital. He said it several times."

"Said what? Wha' did he say, exactly?"

"Like he was callin' to some friend of his, someone he knew. At one point, when we was in the hospital, he motioned for me to come close, but when I bent down, he talked in a whisper like I wasn't even there."

"What did he say?"

"'*Save me, Julie!*' He said it twice, clear like I'm talkin' to yuh now. '*Save me, Julie.*'"

Velner paused as if checking his memory bank and looked back at Mickey.

"I don't know who it could be. I have no idea."

Mickey again moved toward the door and Louie's voice stopped him halfway.

"Do me a favor, would yuh please?"

"What's that?"

"Just slow down a little!"

CHAPTER 4:

Craps

1923. ... SEVERAL DAYS HAD PASSED since the chicken truck returned to its usual parking spot on Asylum Street and Heschie climbed down off the back from under the tarp, soaked and thoroughly chilled, his clothes spattered chalky grey with chicken shit, the side of his face swollen with a reddish purple welt visible for everyone to see. The sun had already begun to touch the roof tops way to the west when Rivkah once again stuck her large upper torso out the kitchen window of their fourth floor walk-up.

Gazing down at the group of boys playing in the narrow alley, she could see her little one, recognizable by the oversized tweed cap that he hardly ever removed, the brown one Dov, her eldest, had given him. Yelling in the *mama loschen,* her Yiddish mother tongue, she called.

"Heschie! Heschel Rabinovich! Do you hear me? Supper's ready! I'm not calling you again! Your father will be here soon! So you'd better come up here right now or you won't get nothing!"

One of the kids, the eight year-old they called Jakey, still ribbing his older friend about how he had looked when he had come home from his ride in the country, chuckled and teased.

"Hey, Chicken Drek, hurry up. Your mutha's callin' yuh again."

A third member of the scraggly crew, the one named Louie, stuck his head out from the clump of street kids huddled close to the ground by the brick wall and squinted up at the woman.

"Jeez, Chicken Drek, your mother's really getting mad! You better go,

Hesch!"

"I know! I know! I'll go in a minute. After my turn. One more roll! And stop with the Chicken Drek already! How many times do I have to tell yuh, the name is Harry!"

"Harry, Schmarry! Whatever your name is, you're gonna catch hell if you ain't upstairs when your father gets home. You won't eat again tonight!"

Ignoring his friend, Harry picked up the worn dice.

"A couple more rolls and that's it! Besides, if I don't eat home, I can get something later. At the *shvitz*."

Imitating the older guys that he watched play at the bathhouse, he blew into the fist cradling the dice and let them fly. Skipping across the concrete and caroming against the wall, they came to rest and a sigh went up from most of the others, crouching in to see the throw.

"There! Seven! I win!" Harry said as he grabbed up the pennies and nickels. "There, again! Who wants to play? Who's in!?" he shouted, gathering up the dice.

But before he could roll again, a blow struck him behind his right ear and a pain that made him see nothing but white light shot through his head. At the same instant, he felt himself being lifted off the ground in a rush, as if catapulted into space. He immediately recognized the hands, from their familiar force if nothing else, even before a second slap caught him on the other ear.

"So, you little *mamser*, my street *bummerkeh*! Again I catch you! And right here where everyone can see! Get your *tuchas* upstairs!"

Almost turning his son upside down while pinning him with one of his big arms, Izzie rifled the boy's pockets, shaking a small shower of change loose from the boy's hand-me-down jacket and oversized patch-worn knickers. In their silent glee, Velner and Jakey and the other boys scampered for the loose nickels and dimes as Harry returned to an upright position on the ground, only to be met by another cuff to the head, this time coming from his older brother Charlie, six years his senior, standing alongside his father with a chest puffed out like a young bull.

"Don't hit your brother, Casreel! If anyone's gonna hit around here, I'll do it! Now, both of yuhz get upstairs and wash good! Your mother should have supper ready!"

Harry, with Charlie dogging him on his heels, made his way through the back door of the tenement. Their father, in the meantime, turned to the other street kids, some as young as six or seven, still hunting for missed coins among the cracked concrete and half-paved cobble stones. "Go home already, you little bums! Go home before I *giff* you all a swift kick in the *tusch*! I'm surprised at you, Jakey Hirsch! And you, Louis Velner! You especially, yuh little *vantz,* yuh! Get your skinny *tuchas* home before I take you *dere meinself*, that yuhr father, he should know what you've been up to!"

The boys moved off, without a word, not wanting to provoke old man Rabin any further. Oblivious to the neighbors looking down on the commotion from the adjoining flats, he made a quick glance upward to see if Rivkah was in the window. Then shaking his head in disbelief, he half smiled at the thought of his youngest boy's relentless *chutzpah*, as he slowly made his way through the narrow doorway.

By the time he reached the top of the stairs and entered the small flat, most of his seven children were crowded around the kitchen table awaiting his arrival. Charlie and Harry, coming from the cramped hallway, still wiping their hands on the opposite ends of an old towel as they went, squeezed by their father and took their seats as he moved around them and into the closet of a bathroom to wash. Rivkah placed a large bowl of cabbage soup, hot and steamy, the small pieces of grayed *flanken* just barely visible in it, in the middle of the table alongside the plate of hand-sliced rye bread. She turned to Harry.

"See! See! You don't listen when I call and now you're in trouble again. When will you learn?"

"You think he can learn, Mama?" said Charlie.

"Yeah, and who are you to be hittin' me?" Harry shot back.

"Yeah! From up here I saw you take that poke at your brother after Poppa put him down. Who are you, anyway?!" asked an unintimidated Neshka, the third oldest girl, the one closest to Harry, older by just over a year.

Batyah, the oldest, almost eighteen and still not married off, chimed in. "You'd better all be quiet before Poppa hears, and then you'll all be sorry."

"Thank you, Batyah," intoned Rivkah, hovering over the table. "All of you take some soup before it gets cold. And pass the bread. Neshkeh, Batyah, help the little ones. And remember, not a bite until your father says the *brocha*."

Izzie reentered the kitchen and eased himself into his place at the head of the table with Charlie to his right and Harry to his left, just as the last steaming bowl made its way to Fageleh, the littlest one, just two and a half, sitting next to her mother now wedged in by the sink at the opposite end of the table. As Rivkah tore off pieces of the dark bread and placed them in the child's bowl, Izzie cleared his throat, a signal for the blessing, and began.

"*Baruch atah adonai, elohaynu melech haolom. Hamotzih lechem min ha'eretz.*"

"*Awmain,*" came the response from the table as the clattering sounds of dinner commenced.

No sooner did Harry begin to raise the first spoonful to his lips than Izzie's left hand shot out, halting it halfway between the boy's bowl and his mouth.

"So you think you can just come in here and sit down and eat from my table like a little prince?"

Even the little ones paused, already accustomed to such scenes.

"But Poppa... I... I..."

"Enough! Get up and get out! I work hard all day as does your brother and your older sisters. And your mother, she slaves here to make for a clean home and a good meal. And what do *you* do? Ten years old and he gambles in the street and God knows what else. Like the *goyim* or some *schwartzeh*. And you expect to come sit at my table? No, no! Go on! Get up and get out!"

Already having enough sense to know another word would only prove futile and merely serve to escalate the situation, Harry slowly got up from the table. As he did so, Izzie reached across and picked up the abandoned bowl of soup. Removing the spoon, he dumped the contents into his own dish. The boy, fighting back tears of embarrassment and anger, made his way down the hall to the tight little bedroom he shared with Casreel. Sitting on the worn springy bed that took up most of the room, the one where all three of them slept before Dov left, he listened to the sounds of the meal coming from the kitchen.

"Damn!" he thought to himself. "I almost got a taste!"

He turned and looked out the window, beyond the iron slats of the fire escape. It was already getting dark and pretty soon he'd have to get to work at the bathhouse.

"I'll get something to eat at the *shvitz*," the boy realized, as he sniffled and wiped the tears away with his sleeve.

Izzie remained at the kitchen table after the girls had cleared everything and wiped it clean. His spectacles perched on his nose, he gazed into the Yiddish paper raised in front of him. He paused for a moment, and fumbled in his vest pocket for a wooden match. Striking it underneath the table, he relit the pipe that hung from his lips. The little ones had gone out down the front stairway, accompanied by the older girls, to catch a few last moments of twilight. Casreel had also departed, saying he'd be home "not too late". Rivkah stood at the small sink finishing up what Batyah had left behind when she had gone down to keep an eye on the little ones, at her mother's request. Deciding to let it all sit rather than wipe everything dry as usual, she placed the last couple of utensils and a small pan atop the mound of dishes draining on the dish rack. She then cautiously tipped the dishpan, so as not to splash over onto the floor, and eased the gray soapy water into the sink. She waited, staring down at the small whirlpool as it formed in the basin, and then scraped the flecks of cabbage and specks of *flanken* from the top of the drain with her fingernails. Drying her hands with the old cloth that she used as an all-purpose kitchen towel, she draped it over the faucet to dry, and wiped the tiny beads of sweat from her brow with the back of her right hand.

Turning toward her husband, she exhaled through puffed cheeks and pursed lips as if to whistle, the sign that she was tired but not quite through with another long day. Pulling out a chair, she sat down across from Izzie with her large full forearms on the table, the tips of her middle fingers touching.

"You're being too hard on the boy," she said, talking to the newspaper raised across the table in front of her like the fortressed walls at Jericho. Izzie remained silent, in an attempt to avoid the conversation.

"Don't try and hide behind that paper, Izadore Rabinovich. I said you're being too hard on the boy!"

Izzie resignedly folded the newspaper in half, placed it on the table, and took his unlit pipe from his lips and balanced it in the small ashtray in front of him. Removing his reading glasses, he rubbed the bridge of his nose as his gaze moved across the table.

"What too hard? He's got to learn."

"Learn what?! His face is still swollen from when you hit him in the truck and now you humiliate him in front of the other boys in the alley and his brother and sisters, as well! You don't let him eat! And you take his supper! This is how a father should act?!"

"You know as well as me, he'll get something at the *shvitz*."

"That's not the point."

"Point!? What point?! All of a sudden, my wife has become a talmudic scholar, a lawyer? She talks in points! Rivkah, you don't..."

"*You* don't, Izzie! Don't tell me *Ich vershtehe nict*. I understand good. I know that you'll drive him out just like you did Dov. I can't have it. I can't have you doing this to *meine kinder*."

"And so now they're *your* kinder!"

"Yes, they're as much mine as yours! More, as much as you're around them!"

"Such talk from a wife! Whoever heard such..."

"Such talk? You Izzie, you! And you'll hear plenty more! I want you should hear that you have to stop before you lose another one of your sons to the streets! Please, Izzie..."

"But the boy has to learn!"

"Learn *vas*?! That the father must be cruel and hard, heartless? That a father should hit a small boy in the face, full with his hand!?"

"My father would have..."

"Your father is dead, *alevesholom*, and he lays in the ground far, far from here. We're not part of that world anymore. You're not part of that world. We've been here almost twenty years but still you live there!"

"Such talk I don't believe."

"Believe what you will. All I ask is that you think. That you don't be so quick *mit der handt*."

"I must have their respect!"

"Respect! Fine. Good. There's nothing wrong with respect. But sometimes you mistake fear for respect. Just think what you are doing!"

Cornered at that point, and knowing he was no match for his wife when she worked herself up like this, Izzie copped to his usual out.

"All right, enough already!"

At that moment, Harry appeared from the hallway. Rivkah and Izzie went silent as if they had forgotten and suddenly remembered that he was still in the small flat; that he must have heard every word.

"Mama," he said, "I have to go to work now."

"Yes, Heschie, I know."

The boy started for the front room, but turned and looked at his father, sitting there in silence, looking away.

"Poppa..."

"What, Heschie, what?"

"I'm sorry, Poppa. I'm sorry about bringing *chazzerai* in the truck and..."

"*Geh*, Heschie, *geh*. It's all right. Go to work already. Everything's all right."

The boy paused for a moment and let himself out, closing the door behind him.

Wanting it to be so, he wondered for a second when everything would really be all right. Moving more quickly then with each step, he headed down the hallway and the front stairway to the street, to the outside and away. Pausing for an instant to say good night to his sisters playing on the front stoop, he moved down Scranton Street, past the rows of aging three and four deckers crammed into the old narrow block, just as the streetlights came on. He turned into the alley that dog-legged through to Asylum and quickly made an arc, darting by the fence protecting Portovsky's Tin Works, still afraid that the wolf of a black mongrel watchdog barking, snapping and lunging at him from behind the boards and wire mesh, would someday, somehow get loose and tear into him. Holding his breath near the end of the alleyway as he moved by the row of trash cans leaning heavy with several days' garbage, he finally came out on Asylum Street. Making the quick jog to the left on the corner, he turned onto Oak Street, the heart of the neighborhood, still busy but beginning to close down as the evening sky darkened.

CHAPTER 5:

Homecoming

1989... DAVID CAREFULLY SQUEEZED HIMSELF past Annie so as not to wake her and made his way back to the plane's restroom. Grateful to find it unoccupied, he stepped in, latched the door and with an arm braced against the wall, steadied himself in the cramped space. He listened for an instant to the constant jet hum, the metallic vibration loud in his ears as he gazed into the mirror. It was then, as he stared at his reflection, that he suddenly recalled how the religious Jews covered their mirrors when somebody in the family died. He remembered being told that the custom had something to do with vanity, but he now realized that it also had to do with pain. For some, he imagined, the difficulty of facing, or not facing oneself.

He looked down at the stainless steel bowl, raised the seat, unzipped, and began to pee. As he did, that picture of Harry immediately leapt into view. There it was, that same image imprinted there in his memory, from when he was a little kid. The morning ritual that occurred every day for as long as he had lived under the same roof, his father standing there, as clear as if the two of them had somehow crammed into the jet's restroom.

There the old man stood, hardly awake, straddling over the toilet with nothing on but a tee-shirt, all bony legs and knobby knees, protruding belly and droopy balls, his black wavy hair tousled. Reaching over, he retrieved the partially smoked cigar from its resting place in the ashtray atop the tank. Grabbing the matchbook alongside, he let out a deep belch, "a good *krepz*" he used to call it, and placed the cigar in his mouth and *oyed* and groaned softly until the stream began to sound in the bowl. He then struck a match and placed it just in front of the stogie. The flame jumped and danced as he drew in and the bathroom filled with smoke as he rotated the cigar to assure an even light. He dropped the still lit match as he finished and David listened for the hiss as it hit the water. The beginning of Harry's forever daily routine and his son, standing there now, could even hear the cough, that same raspy, phlegmy cough, as the old man cleared his throat, spit into the bowl, and flushed.

He smiled at himself in the mirror as he recalled how he and Howard, and even Mickey, back before he moved out, used to kid about how the old man would some morning absentmindedly drop a match in too close, or that a hot ash would someday fall and catch him right on the tip of his *putz*. And that it really couldn't happen since his belly would get in the way. He heard Esther, like it was this morning, calling from the bedroom, reminding Harry to watch and not wet the floor, or to hurry up because she also had to *pish*.

He then recalled those horrible mornings after, whenever the old man had stayed out late, carousing. How he would wake everyone up with that horrific repeated retching and gagging and the sound of puke splashing in the bowl as his body recoiled and rejected the poison. And how they all knew everything was okay, that the storm had cleared, when the toilet flushed and the smell of the morning cigar filtered from the bathroom and Esther called for Harry to open the window and let some air in. He remembered the morning that Howard, annoyed that his dream sleep had been shattered, coined the nickname that stuck for years. "Old Gaggy Guts," he would mutter from under the blankets whenever the old man had one of those morning bouts in payment for the night before.

He looked up into the mirror and remembered where he was. Wondering how long he had been standing there, he arranged himself and zipped up. Then taking a quick look to make sure he hadn't dribbled on the front of his good corduroys, he eased around and opened the door to come face-to-face with some older guy, a casually dressed, thin gray Midwesterner in his mid to late fifties, standing there with a mildly pained impatient look, waiting to use the john.

David excused himself and slid by and as he made his way back to his seat, he mused about how mysterious the workings of the mind could be. He felt the subtle downward shift of the plane's nose that signaled the beginning of the descent toward New Haven and he found Annie awake, already going through her bag, upright and alert, released from her self-induced state of in-flight suspended animation. She too had sensed the descending tilt and extended her hand as he squeezed by her.

"Here, you want some gum?" she said, offering him a stick, still in its green wrapper. "It'll help with the pressure as we go down."

"You better give me another," he said as he unwrapped the first, put it in his mouth, and settled into his seat.

Now gazing out again, he found himself pondering his hometown, the place he never referred to as home anymore.

"New Haven. Goddamned New Haven! What a place!" he thought.

He had gotten out as soon as he could, eighteen and off to college. While the guidance counselors at Hillhouse and the parents of some of his friends had encouraged him to at least apply to Yale, he knew he had to get away. And that had been his sole reason for selecting the middle echelon DC college, the school farthest away from New Haven to which he was accepted.

Harry had always called him his *bocher* boy, his book child, and bragged about him to anyone who would listen, as if he had been somehow responsible. But it had been Esther who had given the boy a love for books and reading. Never having been much of a reader herself, but wanting things to be different for her third, the one that came three years after the doctors told her she would never have another, she read to him every morning from the time he was an infant until he began picking up books himself.

Her little one was smart to begin with. Everyone commented on it almost as soon as he began to talk. And since things were just a little better for that short time in the early fifties, and Harry needed her at the luncheonette anyway, she convinced him that "the baby" had to go to the nursery school, the one at the Jewish Home out on Sherman Avenue. That gave him a foot up, the head start his brothers never had.

He had learned how to read while in kindergarten, at least the basics. The teacher at Welch School had called Esther in and told her that Howard, already in second grade, was falling behind and that she should pay less attention to starching and ironing his shirts and spend more time helping him with his reading. So she sat on the bed with her middle one in the evenings after dinner in an attempt to help him with his Dick and Jane. David sat alongside, taking it all in, watching and listening as his mother struggled to help her middle one and the youngest surprised his first grade teachers with what he could read.

Besides books, he had TV. The family got their first in '51, not long after his second birthday, and it soon became his soothing black and white companion, his mentor and eye on the world, his time machine and getaway car. He watched it constantly when not preoccupied with his Golden Books, his few toys or the teasing games and challenges invented by his older brothers. The tube opened up worlds of wonderment and stimulated his fertile imagination, and he watched it all. It didn't matter what. Howdy Doody and Ding Dong School, Crusader Rabbit and Jerrold McBoing Boing, Mr. Wizard and Disney, Berle and Ceaser and Kovacs, J. Fred Mugs and Garroway, Captain Midnight, Morrow and Kronkite, Steve Allen and Sullivan. He watched wrestling alongside his Bubbie, Esther's mother, as she cursed at the bad guys in Hungarian, and the Friday night fights alongside Harry as he, too, yelled at the tube. And then there was "Shock Theatre" on Saturday night, after Esther and Harry went out. Bela Lugosi and Karloff, the Mummy, Frankenstein and King Kong, with him sitting on the sofa next to Howard, the both of them scared to death and loving every minute of it. And the Cold War paranoia sci fi, aliens from outer space taking over people's minds. Gigantic creatures, ants the size of utility vans and house-crushing tarantulas lurching up out of the ruins of some atomic desert test site. Nuclear madmen messing with nature and paying the price. He became so mad when something called the McCarthy Hearings preempted his morning kid shows that he lined up all his toy soldiers in front of the screen and ordered them to fire at the serious, puffy-faced men with their oily hair and baggy suits who his daddy said hated the Jews.

And Esther would talk years later of how she and Harry used to come home after a Saturday night out at one or two in the morning, and how she would find "the little one" sitting there alone by himself, in front of the tube. The entire house would be dark and both Howard and Mickey would be sound asleep and she and Harry would find Davey sitting there all alone on the floor close up by the screen, illuminated by its white glow, watching the only thing on, the test pattern.

He always did well in school without ever having to work hard at it, despite all the distractions of home and street. An honor student and a good test taker pretty much all the way through. He imagined going into government service someday or maybe to law school when he first went off to Washington, excited then about being in the nation's capital. He had always had a fascination and knack for history and it was there in DC that it caught up with him and smacked him upside the head, arriving when he did in the fall of 1967.

Yes, DC had been the place to be in those years. He realized it immediately, the very first day, when Harry and Esther drove him down to college and he spied the Georgetown hippie street scene along Wisconsin Avenue from the backseat of the Lincoln that Harry borrowed off the lot. Early on, in the first two years or so, before he began to acquire the beginnings of some fuller understanding, and long before he began to become political in any meaningful sense, he ingested it all, the whole scene, as if he were devouring a delicious hot fudge sundae or a slice of *abeetz* fresh from New Haven's brick oven pizzerias. The styles of the transient counterculture scene, the music sound and street heat tempo, the hipster affectations and experimentation into self, the discoveries of reefer and sex and left politics, the "be here now" and "do it" libratory excitement of the moment, it all grabbed him and set him free.

Pulled along by some of the guys from the dorm who seemed to know more than he did, he went to the demonstration against the war at the Pentagon a month after he began his freshman year. October of '67. He realized which side he was on then, at least in regard to what was still Johnson's war, and he never looked back. Turned off by all the pacifist talk of the well-heeled middle class peacenik liberals and religious types, he became curious about SDS, primarily because they seemed cool and bad. He watched the smoke billowing up over the city after King went down the following April. Riding downtown with a guy from the dorms with a car, he took a crash course that day on state power and popular rage as he watched the fires burning out of control along Fourteenth Street and the 101st Airborne placing barbed wire and machine guns in front of the White House. He joined the campus student power demonstrations the following year. He read and listened and read and listened and argued and laughed, and ran in the street, chased by tear gas and the cops. He got high and let his hair grow, lost weight and his virginity while gaining an awareness of who he was and what the country was about. He felt free, released, unencumbered, at least as long as he stayed away from New Haven and he never really returned, even when he had to.

Sitting there, still gazing out of the plane, he silently laughed to himself as his memory and imagination again began to wander. For some unknown reason he thought of the city's founders, those Plymouth Bay schismatics, purest of the Puritans, and how they broke away from the colony to the north, that city on a hill gone astray, in a futile effort to renew their utopian dreams. Looking downward in hopes of seeing the ground, he studied the cloud shapes just below the fuselage and suddenly, an image of the Pequots came to mind. He imagined how they must have dropped in droves when those very same New Haven colonists, in one of their more enlightened efforts at civilizing mission, gave them blankets contaminated with small pox. He thought of all that self-sanctified Puritan violence and how the Indians' blood, tainted and toxified by contact with whiskey and Calvinism, must have seeped into the soil, affecting the ground water. He imagined how it colored the land and how it trickled down through the aquifers of time like some deep-soiled curse, an infectious payback that lingered in the iron red earth only to surface on occasion across countless generations. He wondered about the Quinnipiac, the local tribe, now but the name of a river and a nearby local college.

His memory shifted to that one-time local boy and legendary hero of betrayal and deceit, Benedict Arnold, and then to the famed Eli Whitney, that New Haven tinkerer-entrepreneur. He thought of how Whitney, a founding father of American inventiveness and padded government contracts, developed that system of interchangeable parts while making guns for the military. And how his renowned gin, a simple device used to segregate black seed from white floss, revived the fortunes of King Cotton and pushed demands for slaves and land and expansionist dreams to new heights, thereby assuring the coming of the Civil War. He imagined the proud and defiant rebels of the liberated slaver *Amistad,* their wrists and feet once again in shackles, being led through the city's streets on the way back and forth from the old court house to the county jail, their ebony demeanor standing in stark, upright contrast to the pallid grays of the port's curious Yankee onlookers.

The flight attendants came through in preparation for landing, hurriedly collecting the last of the diet soda empties, the coffee cups and blue foiled peanut wrappers, and Annie brought her seat upright. She touched David on the arm to bring him back inside the plane and he pressed the button on his armrest, forgetting that his seat was already up. The gum hadn't helped much and his ears felt entirely plugged. He could feel the pressure building in the middle of his forehead, between his eyes. He imagined the monster headache he would have for hours after landing until he remembered that he would soon be seeing his favorite hypochondriac, brother Howard, certain to have the best and latest in antihistamines and head pain palliatives.

He looked out again as the plane broke through the clouds heading east and suddenly he could see the expanse of Long Island Sound, all glittery blue and afternoon sunlit sparkle, deceptively serene from a distance. He spotted Bridgeport and the Housatonic at Stratford and then what had to be Milford, with its smokestacks, erect above the water. Catching sight of the Connecticut Turnpike, its supine length paralleling the coast like some gigantic motorized anaconda, his vision wandered over to its slower-paced companion, that lethargic stretch of U.S Route #1, known by the locals ever since Washington's day as the Boston Post Road, now perpetually clogged by the strip mall traffic of born-to-shop bargain hunters. Scanning the roadway, he tried to spot where Harry used to work selling Fords in the mid 1950s, and that long gone, fly-by-night used car lot where the old man and Mickey had made a go of it on their own more than a decade later.

The plane descended past Orange, a tree filled 1960s suburb, and he looked toward the West Haven shore where Savin Rock, that gem of a grand old amusement park, once stood with its wavy wood framed roller coaster and giant merry-go-round, its White Way boardwalk crowded with Black couples and sunburned working class Yankees, all locked in endless games of chance.

The eye of his memory conjured up the mechanical fun house fat lady in her orchid satin dress, trapped in perpetuity behind her glass enclosure, beckoning to the crowded sidewalk, her nonstop, automated laughter casting an eerie, fearful thrill to the little boys gazing up at her in the twilight.

"H-a-a-a- h! Ha! Ha! H-a-a-h! Ha...! H-a-a-a h, Ha! Ha! H-a-a-h! Ha Ha!"

 He recalled the hot dog stands and the taste of red candied apples, the sticky pink nests of cotton candy, and that omnipresent odor of thick-cut greasy French fries, all long since urban renewed away. He wondered where it went, the time and the landmarks of his childhood.

And suddenly there it was to the north, New Haven harbor, distinguishable with its freighters and oil storage tanks and its recent generation of green-glassed nouveau classical high-rises. He could now make out the downtown, tightly girdled in its bands of 1960s interstate. He squinted to the distance for the familiar and made out the Knights of Columbus tower still standing there along that swath of highway that the planners and developers had sent north and west from the downtown in the 1950s; that fatal urban renewal project that ripped through the worn slums and social fabric of the downtown and tore the heart out of Oak Street and Legion Avenue. And there, with the elms winter bare, he could faintly discern the confines of the Yale campus with gothic Harkness Tower pointing heavenward at its center, aloof and detached as ever from the rest of the surrounding city. Unable to make out any landmarks of the Jewish west side where he spent most of his adolescence, he turned his aerial gaze to the vicinity of those older neighborhoods surrounding the downtown core, the city's wall-less racialized ghettos.

As the plane droned low across the harbor toward its destination, he looked eastward to what had been an Italian bailiwick since the days of the old "new immigrants" and he readily conjured the aroma from the brick ovened pizzerias on Wooster Street, down by what they used to call the "Guinea Green". And there they were, just to the north now, the tired, rust red loaves of West and East Rock, much smaller than he remembered, still holding silent vigil there, baring witness for the Pequots and Quinnipiacs and all that came after, their accusatory fingers pointing to the white Anglo steeples on the central Green.

A moment longer over the water and the jet made its landfall. David watched as a dirty white blur of seagulls and wind-tossed wastepaper leapt into flight at the edge of the gray-green oily marsh bordering the runway. He closed his eyes and tried to relax as the tires chirped down. He peered out, again looking for the familiar, as the jet taxied to the small terminal and a woman's voice, thanking everyone for flying United, monotoned a garbled welcome to Tweed New Haven.

The first thing that came to him as soon as the door opened, as he waited for those in front to file out, was the smell of the ocean and it dawned on him how much he missed it. Blinded momentarily then by the bright afternoon light and stunned for an instant by the stiff wintry breeze blowing off the harbor, he regained his focus and looked toward the terminal from the top of the steps. He saw the two of them, Mickey and Howard, standing there hugging the chain link security fence at the edge of the tarmac. Annie walked down in front of him and as they moved across the pavement, their carry-ons in hand, he touched her on the shoulder and talked to the back of her head.

"Remember two things. I love you and..."

"Yeah, I know. Don't worry," she responded, without turning her head. "I'm already watching the movie."

He sized up the situation as they approached the gate, trying to detect any immediate emergency on his brothers' faces. The two of them were standing there, together, yet separate, like two deflated strangers still crowding the rail at Aqueduct long after the horses had crossed the finish, neither of them holding a winner. Mickey was wearing one of those dressy half-length rust-brown leather coats still popular among the urban east coast boys, wide open despite the chill. His pressed designer jeans, pale blue, were belted just bellow his belly and his sports shirt, patterned geometric grays and blacks on brown, stood open at the collar revealing the glint of a heavy band of gold swag barely visible under a developed double chin.

Howard, short next to Mickey's mass, was standing there in his neatly tailored wool topcoat, fully buttoned with its collar hiked up as if it was snowing sideways, with the over polished toes of his black wing tips peeking out from beneath the cuffs of his suit pants. Focusing in on their balding heads, the only thing they appeared to have in common, David thought about how much older the both of them looked and how much longer it would be before he would lose his hair. He inhaled a deep breath of ocean air and stepped through the gate.

Mickey rushed him, almost knocking Annie aside. Howard grabbed her flight bag and gave her an embrace as the oldest brother threw his arms around the youngest. He finally let go when David told him everything would be all right and that they had to let the people, now stacking up behind them, through the gate. Mickey stepped back, his eyes full of tears, choked up and unable to speak, and placed his large manicured hand on the side of David's face in a lonely, loving gesture of welcome and grief as the remaining passengers scurried by.

Finally catching his breath, he looked into David's eyes, also watering at that point, and struggled with his words.

"He's gone, Davey! The ol' man's gone! I've lost the only friend I got in the world!"

David turned to Howard and he came forward. They hugged as Mickey turned and smothered Annie, caught a little off guard, with a bear hug and a big kiss full on the cheek, a familial welcome to the sister-in-law.

David looked into his middle brother's face. "It's okay... it's okay, I'm here," he said as Howard started to cry. David hugged him affectionately and kiddingly rubbed his shiny pate and they all began to move into the terminal, with everyone blowing their noses, wiping their eyes and laughing uncomfortably as they went. Howard handed out tissues to all, including Annie, now teary eyed as well from the whip of the wind and the public display of brotherly emotion.

His composure back, Mickey turned to her as they stepped out of the terminal and moved toward the parking lot.

"So how's my brother been treatin' yuh? Any babies yet?"

"Oh, he's good," she laughed, clearly a bit embarrassed by his abrupt directness.

"I told yuh when we came out for the weddin' if he ever gets out uh line, you should call me!"

"Don't worry, Mickey. You don't have to worry," she said, being Midwest nice. "I don't think you have to worry about his getting out of line."

"Hey, I'm serious! As serious as fuckin' cancer!" came the bravadoed reply.

David interceded. "All right, Mickey! Enough already! Who's car we goin' in? You didn't both come in the *same* car, did yuh?"

Howard answered first. "I got the Audi today. Richie took the Sable to work. We'll go back to my place and ..."

"But Davey should ride with me!" responded Mickey, turning to his kid brother. "Come on! Let me show yuh my latest toy! The new 'Vette. I just got it, brand new. She can ride with Howard!"

David halted. "Wait a minute! Slow down a second. Hold it right here! Everybody stop. First of all, let's everyone get somethin' straight, from jump street! That *she* you just referred to, her name happens to be Annie! Second of all, she goes where I go. Thirdly, we can't all fit in the 'Vette, so that's out. Both of us are tired so I especially don't want to start runnin' around, neither."

He turned to Mickey and gave him that timeless quick street smart look they both understood, the signal for him to cool it.

"Let me suggest something. How 'bout if me and Annie, we go back to Howard's first so I can get my bearings and both of us can relax a little. I got a nasty-ass headache, as is, from the flight, so I won't be up for anything for a couple of hours, anyway.... Besides, I gotta make some phone calls. Call me later and we'll get together. How's that sound?"

Giving David one of his serious looks, Mickey came back, motioning to Howard.

"Tell yuh what. You go do what yuh gotta do. Rest a while or whatever, and I'll call yuh later. Maybe go grab a bite somewhere. How's that?"

"Good! Then everything's settled," Howard said as he grabbed Annie's flight bag and moved toward his car. David watched Mickey move off toward the black Corvette, and taking Annie's arm, began to trail after Howard. David turned and looked back to see Mickey as he began to squeeze down into the low slung piece of fiberglass and speed. Mickey looked his way.

"I'll talk t' yuh later," David yelled.

"Hey!" shot back Mickey.

"Hey, what?!"

"I love yuh!" he cried as he disappeared down into the red interior, behind the smoked glass of his identity machine.

CHAP 6:

The Shvitz

1923….. EAGER TO GET TO work and put some distance between himself and his father, Harry moved down the sidewalk. The boy quickly made his way by the young men in shirt sleeves and soiled white aprons hurriedly pulling crates and schlepping boxes in off the sidewalk from in front of the vegetable stands, the hardware, grocery and dry goods stores, and the place selling used everything near the corner of Elliot Street. Two old men and an aged babushkaed *bubbie*, their shopping bags parked on the sidewalk, blocked his path in their oversized coats. Parting company for the day but kibitzing and gesturing as if saying good-bye forever, they didn't notice as the boy eased by.

Moving past the fish market, he glanced sideways at the man removing the last few unsold decrepit mackerel and herring from their window bed of watery melting ice. He paused for a brief instant in front of Teitelbaum's as his eye caught the large *Mogen Dovid*, the Jewish star painted in blue on the front window above the red and gold lettering in both Yiddish and English proclaiming the best in quality kosher poultry at always the best prices. He glanced at the last of the day's chickens, pale yellow and naked, skinny and cold, their heads still on and their eyes closed, dangling by their feet behind the glass. He wondered about what was going on between his father and the rival chicken man.

Remembering that work called, he moved by the several well-lit bakeries on the street, all still busy with people buying up remnants from the previous morning's bake, the reduced loaves of rye bread and *challah*, or something to dunk with the tea or coffee in the morning, a half-priced cinnamon *bobkeh,* imperfect and passed over, growing stale on the shelf or an already rock-hard *mandel brot.* Passing to the end of the block where the main street crossed Orchard, almost at the end of the Jewish section where it began to taper off into the largely Italian neighborhood, Harry came to the bathhouse, hunkered down brick solid in the middle of the block.

Built well before the war, when New Haven's Jewish population swelled with the tide of eastern Europeans, primarily Litvaks, the *shvitz* had quickly become a center for community life, second only to the *shuls,* for the men. Part of the money for its construction had come from the benevolent society created by those earlier arrivals, the city's well-heeled, well-meaning, and often condescending German Jews. Part of it came from the city, after the do-good experts from Yale surveyed the district. Built in part to bathe and civilize the unkempt *shtetl* castoffs, and hopefully to stem the threat of diptheria, typhus, and other slum ailments, its first floor contained a large tiled steam room and shower area and a smaller room with several large bathtubs, as well as a locker room. The upstairs, intended initially as a community hall and meeting place, had become a major night time hangout by the time Harry Rabinovich was born.

Not long after the boy's tenth birthday, his father approached one of the insiders who, in exchange for a favor, got the kid his job. Absolutely fascinated with the place since the day he walked in, Harry paused and looked up at the large brick building as if it were a school and he was some eager striving student returning from a long summer break. Going up the three granite steps and through the heavy doors, he moved past the front counter and called to old Spritzik, perched there as usual on his stool behind the huge pile of folded white towels stacked in anticipation of a busy night. Behind him on the wall sat the pegboard holding all the locker keys, each hanging from a loop on a separate numbered hook. Hand scrawled in Yiddish, a sign detailing the different rates for a steam, a shower, a bath, towel included, and mandatory locker rentals, all hung above in case some stranger, a traveler or maybe a bearded greenhorn just arrived, happened in. "It cuts down on the need for talk," Spritzik had explained when the kid started some five months before.

Harry raced up the stairs to the second floor, already filled with the blue-gray haze of cigar smoke, where some of the early arrivals, finished with their *shvitz,* their heads still damp, sat playing gin or pinochle. He moved across the room to a rear table where Chipofsky sat, the usual unlit cigar plugged in the side of his mouth, rustling through a stack of receipts and scratching on a pad with a remnant of pencil.

An untidy, big-bellied man who had seen it all, including his better days, Chipofsky had spied the kid when he came in and without looking up from the pink and yellow papers and notepad spoke as the boy halted at the side of the table.

"Before yuh even get started up here, I want you should go downstai's and mop the walkway from the showahz to the lockahz. Get up all the excess wahtah. I don't need the lawsuit, somebody should slip and fall, God f'bid. Then do the entiah lockah room. Take the bucket... yuh know where it is. Fill it with hot wahtah and put some bleach in, not too much, and do the whole flawh like I showed yuh. And make sure yuh excuse ya'self if somebody in there gettin' dressed, they should complain from the smell. Aftuh yuh finish there, I want yuh should go see Labeleh."

Finally looking directly at the boy, Chipofsky reached into his shirt pocket and pulled out three rumpled dollar bills. "Get two quarts and take care of them like I showed yuh," he said as he handed the boy the money and returned to his paperwork.

Harry turned to go as the boss paused him with his voice. "I gotta step out for a while but I'll make a little inspection when I get back so do a good job. Yuh heah me? And remember, tomorrow's Friday already, the *shabbes,* so I want yuh should be here good and early, as soon as school gets out 'cause everyone'll wanna get cleaned up and otta here before the sun goes down. Remember! Get here good and early t'marruh."

Harry went downstairs, turned and went through the swinging doors with the milk-white glass and the painted letters pointing to the lockers and steam room. Pulling the mop, pail and jug of bleach from the storage closet at the back of the hallway, he filled the pail halfway from the spigot in the storeroom, poured in some bleach, and moving the bucket along as he went, mopped the areas adjoining the steam rooms and the showers. Excusing himself, he worked around the several men, still reddish-pink from the steam, busily getting dressed. He finished the locker area, dumped the dirty water in the closet sink, and returned the mop and pail to their resting place. Wiping his hands on a rag, he went back and gathered up a few discarded towels and threw them into the canvas hamper that sat near the exit. Making his way back out the front past Spritzik, he walked straight down the block and around the corner to his left. There was Labeleh, sitting on his wooden fruit crate, leaning against the wall in his usual Thursday evening spot, already half gone but still doing business.

An only child, Label Grunstein wound up in New Haven after his parents fled from Bialystock during the 1905 exodus. His mother and father had dropped from the diptheria and he came of age on Oak Street after a short stay at the Jewish Home. At nineteen, he ended up getting grabbed by the draft less than a year after Uncle Sam entered the war. Now one of the dispossessed who had returned from France physically intact but somehow irretrievably damaged, he seemed to live entirely on the street, most of the time more pickled than the kosher half-sours submerged in the wooden barrels at Goldman's Deli. He had been a *handler,* a low-level street supplier for one of the local bootleggers ever since Prohibition came in, before Harry could even remember. While lots of people said he was completely *meshugeh,* the boy didn't pay the talk no mind since Labeleh didn't frighten him, even when the man was real gone after drinking up the profits.

"*Vas machst teh,* my little Hareleh, *kleine lantsmann?* What can Labeleh do for you today?"

"Chipofsky wants two quarts," the boy responded, pulling the three dollars from his pocket.

With that, the street peddler glanced up and down the sidewalk and in the same motion pulled open his heavy overcoat just far enough for the boy to see the tops of eight corked pint bottles, each pointing upwards like stiff-necked nested birds from the extra pockets sewn into the lining. Labeleh peered down, and quickly examined each side of the coat's interior.

"Oy! I don' know *vere mein kopf* is today. Who *schlepps* around *qvartz*? Vait..., vait here. I'll come in a second."

Closing his coat, he stepped backwards through the unlocked door of a dark empty storefront, looking both ways up and down the street as he disappeared. He came back within a minute, clutching a wrinkled grocery bag weighted with two large bottles wrapped in old newspaper.

The boy took the sack and handed over the money. "Here...! Two quarts, *dreih* dollar." He turned to walk back toward the corner, as Labeleh's voice followed.

"And Hareleh not a word. If your *vatter,* he should hear I sold to you a bottle, I'll have to leave Nuh Haven!"

"Don't worry, Label, don't worry!" came the now weekly response.

Back in the upstairs storeroom Harry pulled the string to light the bulb above his head and went to work, relieved that Chipofsky had gone out. Unwrapping the quarts, he placed them on the table. Reaching down below, he pulled out a large cardboard box containing thirty or so empty half pint bottles, a bag of corks and a small funnel. He then crouched way down underneath, back by the wall where nobody would look, and came out with the empty quart bottle he had secreted there. Moving back to the spigot, he filled it.

Chipofsky had instructed him to take each quart and break it down into half pints that he should sell to the card players and anyone else for fifty cents each. The idea for his own side action had come to the boy one night not long after he began working there. He had been standing watching the poker players, looking on intently in hopes of figuring out the game, when he noticed that most of the men rarely drank the strong, rough whiskey straight; that most of them poured it into glasses of ice and added water or a spritz of seltzer. Most of them, focused either on the game or caught up in the endless tableside banter, never drank fast, but sipped. The boy noticed that some drank so slowly the ice melted. It was then that it dawned on him how he could pick up an extra buck.

Instead of eight, he grabbed ten of the half pint bottles from the box and lined them up in a row and stood the funnel in the first. Moving as quickly as possible, he opened one of the quarts of whiskey, and careful not to spill, filled the smaller bottles to well above the three -quarters mark. Finishing with the first five halves, he opened the second quart and filled the rest, closely eyeing the level on each the whole time. Using the funnel, he then topped them off with the water. He corked each one, lined eight up on the table next to the two empty quart bottles, now ready for Chipofsky's inspection, and placed the extra two in the box, concealed underneath the funnel and the bag of corks, to be retrieved when things got busy. Gulping down the remainder of the water from the extra quart bottle, he returned it back to its hiding place. He pushed the box back underneath with his foot, pulled the string on the light above the table, and left the storeroom.

It was eight or eight-thirty by the time the boy returned to the haze of the smoke-filled card room. The place had begun to fill up with the regulars, the cronies and shmoozers, the kibbitzers, bullshitters and conners looking for an evening's score. Most of the afternoon gin and pinochle players had filtered out. Some of them had moved over to join the dime, quarter, half poker game that had gotten underway while the boy had gone to see Labeleh. Glancing around the room, Harry moved over toward the poker table and slipped through the loose circle of onlookers that had already gathered to make mental commentary on the play.

Dov, his oldest brother, was sitting there in his regular gray trousers and a sleeveless tee shirt, his muscular round shoulders draped with a towel. His black wavy hair, combed straight back and still wet from the shower, glistened as he laughed aloud, turned his cards face up on the green cloth and raked in the small mound of red, white, and blue chips from the center of the table.

"What a bunch of crumbs, you guys! I can tell already this is goin' to be a night!" he guffawed as he gathered in the pot.

It was Mandelstam the butcher's deal. Passing the deck to the right for a cut, he tossed in a white chip, signaling to the other five at the table that the ante was ten cents. Taking the deck back in hand, he paused a second, thinking about what to play, and decided.

"Seven stud, nuthin' fancy!"

Waiting for his first card, Dov quickly glanced up and saw his little brother. "Well what do we have here! Hello, Harehleh! You come to join the game?!"

Harry watched intently as the dealer flicked cards to each of the players, two down and one up. With his big left hand nearly hiding the deck, Mandelstam motioned to one of the men sitting directly across from him, and called the play.

"King bets! The black king's the kibitzer!"

"Twenty cents," came the response as two white chips joined the ante in the center.

"Kick it twenty," came the bump, two players to the left.

A player folded in between and Dov momentarily stared at the three of clubs up top before peeking at his down cards. He tossed the three over, folding his hand.

"You guys are too *mishoog*! Besides I gotta talk to my kid brother, here."

At that point Harry made his way around the table and nudged up close to Dov and the older boy, eight years his senior, immediately put an arm around him.

"Jesus Christ, who the hell gave you such a ca-knock?!" Dov exclaimed upon noticing the purple bruise on the side of the kid's face. The boy did not respond, and his silence immediately provided the answer.

Dov pushed back his chair and raised himself up from the table, signaling that he was out, at least for the time being. Already in motion, he grabbed up his pile of chips, slid them into his trouser pocket, and motioned to his brother to follow. They crossed the room to an empty space and Dov turned to Harry.

"So what happened?"

"Nuthin'. I..."

"Don't tell me nuthin! Did Poppa do this to you?"

"I... I..."

"He did, didn't he?!"

"Yeah....," Harry said, "but it was my fault. I..."

"Why? What did you do now?" Dov inquired and the little brother quickly told him about the ham in the truck, digressing for an instant to mention the *tuchas* on the woman in the country store. At that point, Dov laughed slightly as he ran his fingers through his kid brother's hair. "So I bet you won't eat *traif* in front of the ol'man anymore!"

"What *anymore*? I didn't get to have a bite, even!"

"You know better than to try an' fool Poppa! He's smart and don't miss a trick and worse, he's mean when he gets mad... 'Specially when it's rainin'!"

"When are you goin' to come home, Dov?"

"I'm not, Harr. I couldn't live there anymore."

"Never? Everyone misses you! Especially Momma and..."

"I see Momma plenty on the street. We talk all the time and I saw Batyah just yesterday. I just can't live in that place anymore. I'm too big now, too old. And Poppa.... Well, Poppa's Poppa. I have to get back to the game. You okay? You need some change?"

"I'm good, but can I ask you somethin'?"

"What?"

"If you ain't comin' home, can I come live with you?"

"We been through this one already, no? Where would I put you? In some *vantz*-ridden rooming house, with a *shmutzik* toilet in the hall and twenty *shnorers* coughin' all night? You gotta be kiddin'! Besides, they don't allow kids!"

"But..."

"What's to *but*?! You gotta stay at home! Momma always looks after you! Just don't break the ol' man's *baitzim,* understand? Besides, you gotta stay in school! You gotta finish so you don't wind up like me, havin' to hustle every day just to get by! I gotta get back to the game!"

With that, Dov turned and started to move back toward the table. Recalling something, he turned. "Harr, did you hear Poppa say anything the last couple o' days about Teitelbaum, the chicken flicker?"

"No, I don't think.... Wait! The other day when we was in the truck, when I went with him for the pick-up, he said somethin' 'bout how Teitelbaum had been where we was, tryin' to buy chickens. Before we got there."

"Thanks, Harr. And don't mention I was askin'."

Dov crossed the room, with Harry in tow. Sidestepping through the onlookers, he eased himself into a vacated chair opposite from where he had been sitting, its seat still warm from the *tusch* of a recently departed loser. Stacking his chips in front of him, he tossed a couple of red quarter chips into the hat sitting to one edge of the table. "I'm in!" he called, as the hand ended and the cards moved to the next dealer.

Harry's eye caught the flight of the chips from the instant they left his brother's fingers until they clacked against the small pile already accumulating in the torn lining of the battered brown fedora. Inching up to the table, he leaned over to get a better guess on the number of red, white, and blue markers, and he found himself thinking once again about his first week at the *shvitz*.

He clearly remembered everything about that first day. How Chipofsky greeted him as if he were a reunited nephew, son of some long-lost brother, the man's fat fingers warm and soft against the back of his neck. How his new boss explained with that feigned disappointment of his how he couldn't pay very much since things were so slow, fifty cents for a shift going from seven in the evening to one in the morning, but that the boy could keep the kitty, what the poker players threw in the hat.

The boy recalled how Chipofsky immediately promised to exchange the chips at the end of the night and that he would hold any cash in a safe place for him so he shouldn't lose or squander it, or get into trouble going home late with a pocket full of *gelt*. He also remembered how Dov had warned him beforehand not to trust Chipofsky, and how the boss laughed and shook his head when the kid said he'd rather take his tips home at the end of each shift. And how the man's tone immediately changed as he informed the boy that twenty-five percent of the kitty belonged to the house. Harry thought back on how he told Spritzik the next day that he needed a locker with a padlock and how he took to stashing his earnings there, keeping but a few cents for his pocket.

He vividly recalled, too, how he proudly, excitedly hurried home after school, oblivious to the rain that Friday, at the end of his first week. How he stopped off at the *shvitz* to retrieve the nearly thirty dollars he had tucked away in the locker. How he dreamed all the way down the street of buying his mother something. He also imagined what it would be like to buy a new pair of shoes, his very own, maybe with some socks even, since the water seeped through the holes in those he had on, the ones that Casreel used to wear. He thought how he might get something for Faygeleh and Neshkeh and the others, if and when he had enough, and how pleased everyone would be as he reached his building.

He remembered how he burned with excitement, the money hot in his pocket as he rushed up the stairs, two at a time, all the way to the top. How he ran down the hallway and bounded through the front door, flushed with pride, barely winded from the race up four flights. How he called out, expecting to find his younger sisters playing in the front room and his mother busy in the kitchen. And how he found only Izzie, sitting there alone, in his thread-bare chair, the bottle of *shnapps* sitting on the table by his side.

"Where's Momma? Where's everybody?" the boy asked.

"Your mother, she had to get some t'ings before the *shabbes* and I sent your sisters out with her, I should have some quiet for a change."

Harry could vividly recall the voice, the question like it was yesterday.

"So-o-o? Nu? You got paid today, no?"

And how, without another word his Poppa got up, came forward and grabbed and pulled him close. Five months had passed and the boy could still smell the sour, stale odor, the mixed scent of damp wool, soiled shirt and whiskey breath as the man hugged him, smothering his face to his belly. He could still recall that brief instant of joy at his father's embrace.

Five months had gone by and he still could remember how that fleeting feeling of pride and warmth turned, in a second, to confusion, fear and then shock as the man tightened his grasp with one hand and began going through his every pocket with the other. He could still feel that rough hand fumbling and probing his pants pockets and how he attempted to scream, but couldn't, his voice muffled against the coarse-vested belly, his arms pinned, overpowered.

He thought about how his father plucked the wad of bills from his pocket and retrieved the change. He remembered how he began to wriggle, to struggle, his face still buried. And then the pain flashed through his memory. The pain, like nothing he had ever felt before, that frightening sensation between his legs that shot through him when his father grabbed and pinched him hard there.

He could remember how he stopped moving and his father let him go then. He could still see his Poppa, silently standing over him in the front room and how the man slowly counted the money, folded it and placed it in his vest pocket, and dismissed him with nothing more than the wave of a hand. And then the clatter of another couple of chips coming to rest in the brown fedora brought him back to the present.

CHAPTER 7:

The Obit

1989... As COULD BE EXPECTED, Howard started to carry on as soon as they got in the car. Deciding to just let him vent, David slowly reached his arm between the front seats and tapped the top of Annie's hand to make sure she was listening.

"You wouldn't believe the scene he made at the hospital."

"Who's *he*?"

"That brother of yours!"

"Why? What'd he do now?"

"What'd he do!? Oh, nuthin', nuthin' at all. Just went fuckin' nuts, completely out of his mind. That's all!! ...When the doctors came out from working on Harry and told us they had done everything they could."

"So what did he do?"

"We were both up there all afternoon. They had him up in intensive care and it seemed things were stabilized. He was all rigged up with all these tubes in his arms, with oxygen up his nose, and all this electronic monitoring stuff taped to his chest and we were just watchin' him when suddenly one of the machines starts to flash and beep. That went on for like a minute and nobody comes so I finally go out in the hall and yell for help. Finally all these nurses and doctors come rushin' in and make us get out. But we could watch them from behind the glass, through the venetian blinds, at least until one of them closes the slats.

"Five or six of them were workin' on him like crazy. One starts poundin' on his chest and another jabbed him with a huge fuckin' needle, like on one of those doctor shows. Then they wheeled in one of those machines, you know, with the electric paddles. That they jolt yuh with. That's when they realized we were watchin' and drew the blinds.

"They were in there for about ten minutes, more maybe, when the head guy, this big *macher* cardiologist, he finally comes out. I knew, just from the way he was walkin' and how he was takin' off his gloves, that it was all over."

"And then?"

"That brother of yours musta seen it coming too 'cause he immediately starts backin' up as soon as the doctor comes toward us, like he was going t' run the hell out of there. He starts raisin' his voice like he does, you know, insisting that they hadn't done everything they could, that they hadn't come fast enough. The doctor, he tells him to calm down, so what does he do? He starts yellin' and swearin' and threatens the guy…."

"Oh this one's getting good. Then what?"

"Well, here's this big-time heart specialist, probably makes two hundred thou plus a year easy, he's standin' there in the hallway and your brother, the *shmuck*, he's goin' off on him! At that point, one of the nurses musta called downstairs 'cause these two security guys step off the elevator."

"I don't wanna know."

"Yep, you got it! These two rent-a-cops, a white guy and a black guy, come up, see him ravin' like a fuckin' lunatic at the doctor, and they start to pull out their sticks. And he tells this one, the white guy, 'Come on! I'll shove that fuckin' stick right up your ass!' He's so out of his goddamn mind, he calls the black cop a fuckin' nigger right to his face! The cops, they didn't know what to do and called for back up."

"Oh, Jeez…"

"So there we were right outside the intensive care, with all these dyin' people layin' in there, and all these nurses and doctors and other people with family up there lookin' to see what all the commotion was, and there he is, your brother…"

"Hey! Don't blame me!"

"Well, he ain't no brother of mine… He's standing there with his back to the wall, ready to take on these two security cops!"

"So what happened?!" came Annie's voice from the back seat, startling David a bit.

"I started to cry. And suddenly this nurse, a tall, heavier set woman… she looked Jewish, but I'm not sure, maybe Italian… I didn't catch her name, she steps between Mickey and the security guys just as four more cops, another hospital security guy and three New Haven uniforms, get off the elevator. She tells him to calm down.

"At first, he didn't recognize her, but it turns out they knew each other. Even better, he tells me later they went together in junior high school, when Mickey went to Troupe or Sheridan. She recognized him somehow and told him who she was. When he realized who he was talkin' to, he calms down like a baby, all teary eyed, all of a sudden. You know how he gets. The two security cops wanted to have him pinched, but the head doctor, the *macher* cardiologist, he talks them out of it. Mickey turns to the black cop and apologizes, sayin' we just lost the ol' man, as if that made everything okay. And we went out."

"And that was that?"

"Oh yeah! I almost forgot the best part! He stops, before we get in the elevator, and like nuthin' just happened, he walks all the way back to the nurses' station and asks this woman, the nurse, for her phone number, like he was in a bar or somethin'."

"And…?"

"And she gives it to him! Unbelievable!"

"What's not to believe? That's Mickey, all right!"

"Yep, you got it. The brother from hell."

"So what actually happened?"

"I'm not lyin'. I just told yuh…."

"No, I mean with Harry. Was he sick? Not feeling good? I just talked to him Sunday night. He sounded okay. The usual coughin' and wheezin' from the cigars, but nothin' unusual."

"I saw him a few days ago. He seemed fine. Like you said, the usual cough, but nothing I noticed. No warning at all. According to the brother from hell, he showed up at the body shop yesterday morning, like usual, about eight-thirty. He stays there for a couple hours and says he was feelin' tired, that he was goin' home for a nap. Mickey said he came back around noon. Apparently, he made the guys in the shop some subs, and stopped off and got some sodas 'cause he pulls into the yard, goes to get out, reaches back in on the passenger side to get the bag of sandwiches and stuff off the front seat, takes a couple of steps, and collapses.

"Mickey says he saw him go down. He yells for Angelo in the shop to call 911 and runs out. He tells me later, up in the hospital, that he got to the old man and got down with him on the ground, tellin' him not to move. Harry told him he was okay, joked somethin' about how he musta made the sandwiches too damn heavy and how expensive deli has gotten, and how he had dropped his cigar and that Mickey should help him find it, and didn't say another word. The ambulance came and they rushed him to the hospital."

"And that was it?"

"Oh yeah, I almost forgot. Do yuh know anybody named Julie?"

"Julie? Julie who?"

"That's what I'm wonderin'. While we were up in the hospital, he was layin' there unconscious. The brother from hell was sittin' there and I was standin' at the end of the bed. Suddenly, it was like he came to for an instant. His eyes opened and I think he saw me there, but I'm not sure, and he motions with his hand, like he wants somethin'. Me and the brother from hell, we both jump up and go close. He whispered something but I couldn't tell what it was, the first time he said it. Neither could Mickey, so he asks him to say it again, to repeat what he said."

"So…?"

"Save me, Julie."

"What?"

"'Save me, Julie.' He said it twice, like he was talkin' to yuh, but he was actually somewhere else."

"Who the hell's Julie?"

"Right away that's what I was wonderin' so I ask Mickey and he then tells me that while they were waitin' for the ambulance, Angelo rushed out with a blanket they kept in the office and when they slid it under Harry to get him off the ground, he kept sayin' somethin' about this Julie."

"Did Mickey say what, exactly?"

"Yeah. He said the ol' man kept on sayin' the same damn thing, over and over. Just 'Save me, Julie. Save me, Julie!'"

"That's a new one on me. Who the hell's Julie?"

"Mickey don't know. Or ain't sayin', if he does. I'm figurin' it musta been one of his girlfriends. Just like him. Layin' on the ground, dyin', and what's he do? He can't even ask for Mommy."

"What time's the funeral?"

"Stevie Velner said we should all be there by eight-thirty."

"Velners' still where it always was, over on George Street?"

"Yep, the same place."

"And did yuh call anyone, his family or anybody?"

"Just about everyone I could think of. I called cousin Harriet in Florida last night and she's on her way. She said she'd call everyone on the Rabin side, Aunt Faye and the rest of the cousins. I was too much of a mess last night to start dealing with all of *them*."

"I don't blame yuh. Did you do an obituary for the morning paper?"

"Godammit! I knew I forgot somethin' and Richie even reminded me last night! I even left a post-it on the fridge, but I was so damn out of it this morning, I went out without eating."

"It's what? Three? Three-thirty by now? As soon as we get to your place, we'll bang one out, and run it down to the *Courier* office. They still over there on Orange Street? We'll call and find out if they can still get it in. How about a rabbi?"

"Yeah, I got Rabbi Feldstein."

"That pompous sonofabitch?! What a fuckin' *shnorrer*!"

"Yep, you got it! A real *shmuck*! He wanted to put the ol' man in the ground today!"

"You know how *they* are. Did he look to put the bite on yuh?"

"What do *you* think?! I told him not to worry, that Mickey would take care of him."

Soon on the Connecticut Turnpike, the car made its way from the east side, across the harbor overpass, and through the downtown via the Oak Street Connector. Forgetting that Annie had been there before, David pointed out various landmarks as they got off the highway and moved away from the coast. Skirting the west end of the Yale campus, they drove out past the automobile row on Whalley Avenue, and north and west into Jewish Westville. All too familiar and timeless for David, they passed the junior high school and the unchanged streets that he and his oldest friends had aimlessly cruised until they ran out of gas or out of town.

Finally climbing up out of the city to the northwest, they entered the tree-thick confines of Woodbridge, that former Yankee bastion now, since the early 1960s, home to many of the city's *arriviste* Jews and other affluent white flight émigrés. As they moved along, David noticed the occasional clapboard colonial standing there close to the road among the leafless hardwoods and wintered mountain laurel. He thought of how out of place and time they now seemed, strangers in their own neighborhoods, sitting there among the pretentious set back split-levels. He mused on how old Connecticut seemed in comparison to his adopted Midwest. He found himself thinking about how well Howard had done for himself, how hard he had worked to move on up to a place with no sidewalks and mailboxes at the side of the road. He recalled how the brother driving next to him used to promise Esther, when they were kids, that he would someday build her a big house, a mansion, he would say, in Woodbridge. The whole while, Howard talked to Annie through the rearview mirror, rattling off the going market values of each of the substantial homes along the way as if he were some eager real estate agent trying to sell the wife on the quality and status of the neighborhood.

Turning into a narrow lane and then a long, wide curved driveway, Howard hit the garage remote on his visor and they glided to a stop in one of the spaces beneath an end of the large, well-terraced cedar-shaked split-level. No sooner had they climbed out and grabbed their bags, than the yapping started, distinct through the interior door. Howard immediately began yelling in his authoritarian dog command voice as the door swung open.

"Be QUIET!"

The two Shelty collies, paying him no mind, scurried around everyone's legs, frantically circling and barking and wagging and jumping non-stop as they all climbed a flight to the main level and entered into the expanse of plush carpet, low slung chrome and glass tables and off-white leather of the "family room".

David passed a quick glance at Annie, standing there now with a disoriented look of disbelief at the racket. The shrill barking pierced right through the both of them, compounding the pain in his sinuses, and he winced aloud.

"*Oy!* Enough already!"

Taking what he assumed to be his cue, Howard screamed at the top of his lungs. "Seamus! Lucy! Go to your rooms!" and both dogs, measuring his tone and decibel level, suddenly louder than their own, retreated to their stainless steel cage in the mudroom alongside the kitchen.

Richie came down from the upstairs, a little heavier in the middle and thinner on top than David remembered. He immediately embraced Annie, and the two of them exchanged a shared smile of mutual sympathy and humored commiseration. He then turned to David and the two gave each other a brief brotherly hug.

"How are yuh, Richie? You're looking good. How's that brother of mine been treatin' yuh?"

"Oh, fine. When he's not bein' a *shmuck*."

Howard interrupted. "I'll show yuh a *shmuck* in a minute! Don't start today,

Richie. I don't wanna hear it. Not today!"

Humoring him, Richie parried, "For krissakes, don't be such a *kvetch*."

David closed his eyes and placed two fingers to the middle of his forehead. Familiar with the sign language, Richie took the lead.

"Howard, your brother has a headache! Why don't you give him something! Do you want something, David?"

Howard, already standing at the sink of the well-applianced copper-toned kitchen, filled a glass and turned to David.

"Here, drink some water. Did yuh notice? We got a new filtration system. Brand new. It takes everything out, the chlorine, all the heavy metals, the ground contaminants, everything, you name it. Twenty-four hundred. We just had the well tested. That cost me another thou. The guy said everything's good. No Atrazine or nuthin'. But you never can be too sure. What do you got? One of those sinus headaches from the flight? I've got some good antihistamines, or would you prefer a Percodan.... Oh wait! I almost forgot! The doctor, he gave me this new scrip for Percocets. I just got it filled today! I figured you'd have one of those headaches yuh get when yuh fly. I don't get them anymore as long as I take a couple of antihistamines on the way to the airport..."

"How about some plain aspirin? Aspirin will do. Or maybe some ibuprofen."

"Richie, do we have any aspirin? Wha'd'yuh want aspirin for?" Opening the amber plastic bottle, he walked over and handed two pale blue pills to David.

"Here, take these. They'll work."

David swallowed the pills without resisting or asking. He took a sip of water and placed the glass down on one of the glass end tables and Howard immediately picked it up and slid a napkin underneath.

The phone rang. For Howard, he motioned that it was business and Richie took the opportunity to take his in-laws upstairs to one of the guest rooms on the second level, a sizable rear bedroom with a large window looking out on the wooded lot, its own well-outfitted bath, a queen-sized high posted bed and a domed Plexiglas skylight cut in the ceiling. Richie, always the simpatico host, quickly excused himself and closed the door. David just flopped backwards on the bed and looked up at Annie.

"Do you believe this place?! What a mad house, with the dogs barking like that and Howard yelling! And his incessant yacking! He didn't shut up once, the whole way here! My head's killing me! I gotta lay down for awhile!"

"You can't."

"Wha'd'yuh mean, *I can't?*"

"You have to do the obituary."

"Oh shit, you're right! I almost forgot!"

Pulling himself up, he approached Annie, gave her a hug and a peck.

"How yuh doin'?"

"I'm okay. They're pretty nuts, those two brothers of yours. And the dogs?! I thought I was going to go out of my mind with the noise. But I'll be fine. Richie's okay. He seems kinda sane."

"Don't let any of them fool yuh. Yeah, they're all okay, in a twisted kinda way. I just have trouble listening to any of them. The way they constantly concoct and fabricate. I never know who's telling the truth. What's what. Yuh gotta take everything they claim with a grain of salt. I listen, take mental notes, and figure things out, the reality, the truth, whatever the hell that is, later, usually much, much later."

"Don't worry about me. I'm just watching the movie."

Knowing she needed the reassurance, David kissed her on the cheek, hugged her and told her he loved her, all pro forma, and turned and went downstairs.

Howard was off the phone, sitting by himself on one of the sofas in the den. He said he had called the *Journal Courier* office and that they had a little over an hour and a half to get the obit in, and suddenly began to cry and laugh at the same time.

David sat down next to him. Fighting the tears himself, he took his older brother in his arms and rubbed his shoulders and head. Reaching over to the box on the coffee table, he handed Howard a tissue and took one for himself. They both wiped their eyes, simultaneously blew their noses, and laughed.

"Yuh know," Howard sniffled, "after all the years of bullshit, him and me, we finally began to make friends. He even hugged and kissed me when I gave him back the watch. I couldn't remember him ever giving me a hug before. I told Richie he was getting senile."

"Don't worry. He probably was. What watch we talkin' about?"

"You know. The one Mommy gave him. The gold one."

"The one the three of you carried on about all that time?"

"Well Mommy really didn't want him to have it. But I got so tired of listenin' to him and wasn't about to let that brother of yours have it. I just gave it back, figurin' I should make some effort, like you suggested."

"So you made a gesture? That's good. And it paid off, *no*? At least the two of you made some peace before he went."

"Yeah, I know. And I even got the watch back."

David smiled. "How'd you manage that one?"

"He showed up at my office one day last week. Out of the blue. I didn't even think he knew where I worked. He comes in and gives me the watch. Says somethin' about being afraid it would get ripped off from his apartment. He gives it to me and leaves."

"Yep, that's him all right."

"Yuh think he gave it to me 'cause he knew it was time to go?"

"*Now* you're gonna try and figure him out? Let's get the obit done."

The two of them went down to the basement office next to the garage and Howard sat down at the computer and clicked it on.

"So what do you think?"

"I dunno. We just have to write the basics, I guess."

"No, no. I mean about the machine. It's a monster! Has everything. An eighty meg hard drive, dual floppies, 8 meg of RAM, a letter quality twenty-four pin printer, and an internal modem. I can connect directly to the terminals at work through the phone. The latest, twelve hundred baud. It even has a chess game, 3-D! Got a pretty good deal on it. A guy I know through work. And the best thing is, I'll be able to write it off. For home office use."

"Can it write for us is the real question? Does it have a word processor? Show me the basics, quick, and we'll bang something out."

Howard got up and David took his place, readjusting the height of the office chair. After a minute or so of basic instructions, he thought for a second and turned to Howard.

"Wha'd' yuh think?"

"I don't know. They're always the same, sorta like ad copy, unless you're somebody special."

"Yeah, the *Courier* ain't the *New York Times*. Short and to the point."

David began to type and the lemon letters instantaneously popped up on the green terminal.

"A service will be held today for Harold "Harry" Rabin, 76, lifelong resident of New Haven, who died Tuesday from a case of malpractice and professional incompetence on the part of the staff in the Intensive Care Unit at Yale New Haven Hospital...."

"You can't write that!" Howard exclaimed, a bit of mischievous, humored amazement on his face.

"Oh, I know. Just seein' how this machine works, and if you were payin' attention."

Deleting the phrase about the hospital, David tapped the keyboard again and another one appeared.

"Beloved husband of Esther Kuhn Rabin, deceased."

He stopped typing, paused briefly, and moving the cursor back, deleted the "beloved," without turning to his brother. Standing over him, Howard placed a hand on his shoulder, and the clicking of the keyboard resumed. The when and where of the service at Velners' and the name of the cemetery on Fitch Street. Date of birth and names of parents; the names of the siblings, alive and departed. Mention of "affiliation" with the "auto sales industry" since 1954.

David typed that Harry was the father of three sons, four grandsons, and three great grandchildren. It was then that Howard stopped him.

"Uhh... I think we got a little problem."

"What's that?"

"Well, uh, you got the count wrong."

"Wha'd'yuh mean?" He thought of Mickey's oldest son. "Did Jimmy have a kid? How the hell could he have a kid? He's still in the joint, ain't he?!"

"No, he didn't. And yep, he's still locked up."

Mickey's second oldest came to mind. "Josh? Joshie has a kid?!"

"Not that I know of. For that matter, he's been so fucked up lately, high all the time, he wouldn't know either."

"Then who, then?"

"Uh, Mickey."

"Angela had another? How come I don't know this! Why doesn't anyone tell me anything any more?"

"Uh, no, it's not Angie."

At that point David turned around. "Look, stop with the guessin' games. We gotta get this done. What are you tryin' to say?"

"Well, Mickey had this other boy. With his current girlfriend. You know. Gina."

"That one he dragged to my weddin'? You gotta be kiddin'! Does Angela know?!"

"Yeah, and boy, is she pissed. She's threatnin' to leave him entirely, this time for good, but she knows she won't get a dime out of him. Matter of fact, the two of them, Angie and this Gina, they somehow ran into each other in some mall parking lot somewhere in Hamden. Back a few weeks ago. I guess it was a real scene. There was somethin' about it in the *Register*. They both got into it, scratchin' and pullin' hair, rollin' around on the ground. Both of 'em got arrested. The baby was in Gina's car so the cops had to place him in some kind of protective care or something. A real mess. Mickey had to bail the both of 'em out. And that ain't all. You'll never guess the good news!"

"What!? There's *good* news?!"

"Well, of course. They'll both be at the funeral, I imagine."

"Oh, great! That should certainly cheer things up, the two of them pullin' each others' hair out in front of the coffin. Enough with the bullshit. Let's get this finished before, you should be so lucky, lightning hits your house and zaps the computer!"

"Hey, I'm insured. I guess it wouldn't hurt to say five grandchildren."

"Five it is!"

David resumed pecking the keyboard, but paused after a few strokes. Feeling his brother's gaze, he stopped and turned around.

"Now what? Get it out."

"Umm, uh... well, there's something else I think maybe you should know."

"How could I possibly think you were through?"

"Well, I don't know how to tell you this, but..."

David pivoted in the computer chair. "Shit! You know how much I hate it when you preface anything with that one!"

"Well, I don't know. Where do I start?"

"Let me suggest something novel. How about at the beginning!"

"Okay. It's like this. I was on my way to Bridgeport, this is about a year ago. I'm goin' down the Turnpike this side of West Haven, when I come up on the loaner the ol' man was drivin at the time, this black Eldorado. I recognize it immediately from the dealer plates he was usin'."

"This better be good."

"Have I ever let you down, baby brother?"

"Go on, already."

"Well anyways, I pull up behind him, right on his ass, and give him my horn and blink him with my brights. He don't respond. Just keeps on goin' and speeds up a little. But I know he sees me 'cause I can tell he's looking in his rearview. There's someone else in the car."

"Who's the someone else?"

"Let me finish. I pull out and come up alongside him. At first he pretends like he don't see me. Like I ain't there. I look over and make out this female, but I can't see her too good because we're movin' and the Caddy got tinted glass. I honk my horn, and the ol' man starts to take off. But I'm drivin' the Audi and he soon realizes the shit box he's drivin ain't goin' nowhere. So I come up alongside him again and motion for him to pull over. By this time, we're well into Orange. Almost t' Milford. He finally gives up and pulls off on the shoulder, right on the interstate, just before Milford Plaza. I pull up behind him, get out and walk over to his car. Cars and semis are flyin' by. It's blowin' like crazy. He rolls down his window and I ask him what the hell's goin' on. I bend over and look in. There's this young girl sittin' there!"

"A *young* girl?"

"Yeah, my first guess was she was maybe eighteen, nineteen..."

"Tell me he wasn't!"

"No, that's the first thing that came to my mind! Jesus H. Christ, the ol' man's really lost his nut and gone out and got himself a teenage hooker! At that point, I'm leanin' in, starin' at this girl. She's starin' back, with this puzzled look. He inhales and ashes his cigar out the window, like there's nuthin' unusual goin' on, and looks straight at me. And guess what he says?"

"That he's out takin' *her* for a *test drive*?"

"That's funny! That's exactly what *I* figured he was going to say!"

"So what did he claim, already?!"

"*Howard,* my son, allow me t' intraduce you to *your sister!*"

"Get the fuck otta here! Now I know you're bullshittin'!"

"Why should I bullshit? Her name's Alexandra. She's actually like twenty-three, almost twenty-four now and she's our half sister!"

"Unfuckin' believable!! Where'd she come from?"

"Well, she lives down state somewhere, maybe Greenwich."

"That isn't what I mean!"

"I know! I know! Give me a chance. I'm gettin to that! You remember when Harry and Esther had that big falling out? What? About sixty-four or sixty five? When he had that affair down near Darien or wherever. You remember any of that?"

"Just vaguely. It's been a long time. I think I musta sublimated everything from that period, all the shit from back then... I do remember this one time Mommy made me take a ride with her late one night down there somewhere, lookin' for his car."

"Well, this one was the result of that particular fling. He later told me she showed up in New Haven back several years ago. She decided to find him and somehow tracked him down. The scariest thing is she looks just like him."

"*That* bad?! You gotta be kiddin'!"

"No! No! I mean in a good sorta way, maybe what Harry would've looked like all made up in drag, when he was younger. She even got his nose."

"She got his *shnoz*?! This I gotta see! She must be a *real* beaut!"

"No, seriously, she's actually kinda cute!"

"Enough already! Where are we going with all this?"

"Well, she's his daughter, right? Do we include her in the obituary or don't we?"

"I don't know. What do you think?"

"You're the one with all the advanced degrees. I was hopin' you'd have the answer. I was thinkin' it couldn't do any harm."

"But it might. Lots of Mommy's friends and family will be there, or at least see the paper. And there's his sister and the rest of the Rabins. And how do we word it, anyway?" Davey paused for a second and turned back to the keyboard and typed as he spoke.

"Wait! I got it! '...And, oh yes, in addition, an illegitimate daughter named Alexandra from down state somewhere.' What's her last name?"

"I don't have a clue!"

"Her mother ain't named Julie, by any chance?"

"How in the hell am I supposed t' know?"

"I got an idea. We'll flip a coin. Heads she's in, tails she's out!"

David reached into his pocket and pulled out a quarter and tossed it in the air. Howard leaned in as it came to rest on the desk top. "Tails it is. I guess she's out."

"Yep, written out with the flip of coin!"

"You're the historian. I knew you'd figure something out."

The two of them finished and sent the file to the printer. David tore the sheet off and quickly proofed the meager third of a page. Howard offered to run it downtown, but David insisted, saying he needed some air. They went back upstairs and David called for Annie as he pulled their coats from the front hallway closet and grabbed the keys to the Sable. He took the opportunity to fill his wife in on the newest additions to his rapidly extending family as they drove back into New Haven.

CHAPTER 8:

Flight

1923.... Dov HOPPED THE FIRST street car of the morning and
rode it out Congress Avenue to the end of the line. From there, he walked well
into West Haven along the Post Road, his thumb out the whole way, before he
finally caught a ride in a canvas-topped eight wheeler. It wasn't until after he had
climbed in and the thick-fisted teamster asked him where he was headed that he
actually began to think about it.

"Uhh, west. New York, I guess. The city. Yeah, New York'll do," he
responded.

The trucker must have sensed that his passenger didn't want to talk much so
they rode along with hardly a word until the only sounds became the whine of
the old truck's tired engine, rubber on pavement, and the occasional high-pitched
squeal of a worn fan belt. Not having slept, but now feeling relatively safe and out
of harm's way for the time being, Dov began to replay the images of the previous
afternoon in his mind.

It somehow seemed so long ago already. It all happened so fast and he
certainly hadn't gone looking for any trouble. He pondered what occurred as he
stared out his side window at the worn industrial scape, the railroad tracks with
their sidelined freight cars, the old brick factories backed up against the right-of-
way, tinted an orange rust red in the morning light, and the row upon row of tired
gray houses. He suddenly felt a tinge of relief, pleased that he was passing them
by, finally getting out. His thoughts drifted back to the events of the previous day
as the city drifted away and the country space of dark hardwoods, sleeping corn

fields and occasional apple orchards unfolded.

He was minding his own business. Hoping to take a couple of dollars from some of the regulars, he had just settled in for the usual early afternoon penny pinochle game upstairs at the *shvitz* when Charlie came rushing up the stairs. He knew immediately from the look on his brother's face, even before the kid could stammer a winded word, that something was wrong. He instantly knew, just from the look, that it could only be Poppa, not Momma or one of the kids, and the first thing he thought was that the old man must have had a heart attack. But leaning in over his shoulder and whispering as if he was excitedly kibitzing about the game, Charlie told him what he knew at that point. The oldest excused himself and quickly got up and the two hurried out and down the street.

Rushing into the small stall of a shop with its smell of sawdust and stale chicken shit heavy in the air, the boys found their father sitting in front of the counter, hunched over elbow to knee on a couple of empty crates, the front of his shirt all spattered with blood. His left eye was swollen nearly shut, and he was holding a chunk of ice, wrapped in a red-stained cloth, to his mouth. When he moved it away, Dov saw that both the man's lips were puffed and split, and that part of an upper tooth was gone.

"What happened Poppa? Who did this to you?"

"That *vilderkindt,* Teitelbaum's son!"

"Yossie Teitelbaum?! Why? What for?!"

"Why d'yuh think?! I had some words *mit* that sonofabitch, that thievin' father of his at the market this mornin'. Surprised him good when I pointed out what should have been some of mine birds was sittin' there on *his* truck. That no-good, stealing from me like that! He didn't think I would catch him!"

"What do you mean, stealin' from you?"

"Taking bread out my mouth! And the mouths of your brothers and sisters. Dat's what I mean! Grabbin' up birds from where I buy from, from all my regular stops, the farmers out by Wallingford and Guilford. Hornin' in and buyin' up all the plump, quality birds. He didn't t'ink I would figure it out!? Like I wouldn't recognize particular pullets...? As if hens from different farmers, I can't tell them apart!?"

"You still ain't said what happened."

"What d'yuh t'ink happened?! We get into some words, that t'ief callin' me names like you wouldn't believe in front of all the others, and before you know it, the *meshugeh,* he starts pickin' up his hands to me. He gives me a little poke in the chest with that bony finger of his and as soon as he does that, I hit him such a *zetz,* boy, I t'ought maybe his eyes would pop out from that wooden skull!"

"You hit him first?"

"Nobody picks up his hands t' me! Nobody! I don' care who it is or how big!"

"So what then?"

"Nuttin'! The men in the market, they broke it up."

"So how'd yuh get hurt? You said Yossie hit you. How'd he get involved?"

Izzie wiped his upper lip and continued. "The son, he shows up here, not even an hour ago. Comes in, immediately with a *pisk* on him like you won't believe. Like a crazy man. Starts yellin' and hollerin' about how it was me was the no-good. That I was the one was a thief and a liar. You know me, boy! Me of all people, I should take such talk from such a *pisher,* 'specially in mine own shop? I started out from behind the counter. But before I could do a thing, he comes at me. Didn't see what, but he musta had somethin' in his hand, a piece of metal or somethin', and he hits me in the face a couple times, before I could make a move. His father must have sent him! Believe you me, I know these things! The son, he wouldn't come on his own, without a word from the father! Hear what I'm tellin' yuh!"

Dov crouched down to inspect his father's lips and the broken tooth more closely. Taking the compress from the man's hand, he gently dabbed the upper lip to clear the blood, now slowed but still flowing lightly from a deep gash.

"How's it look?" asked the father.

"The top lip, it could maybe use a stitch or two. We'll get Mrs. Epstein, the seamstress...."

"He caught me pretty good, the bastid!"

"You'll be okay, Poppa. But don't you worry," Casreel intoned from over Dov's shoulder.

Standing upright again, Dov paused for a second. Then telling Izzie to stay where he was, he turned to his younger brother. "Come Charlie!" he barked and stormed out of the store.

"Where we goin'?" Casreel asked as they moved down the busy sidewalk.

"Where do yuh think?! Gonna pay this son of a bitch and his asshole son a little visit!" came the response as the brothers hurried along.

Old man Teitelbaum was there alone in his shop, and he told them to get out before either of them could say anything. Dov, feigning a conciliatory ignorance, attempted to get a word in, and it was then that the butcher picked up the meat cleaver from its resting place on the edge of the chopping block and started around from behind the display cooler.

"What! You can't hear!? I already told you once and I won't say it again! Get the hell out!"

As he stepped toward them, the two teens, fearful not so much of the man, but wary of the blade in his hand, began backing up.

"Do you know what your son did, Teitelbaum? Where is he? Where's Yossie?!" Dov asked.

"How should I know? You think maybe I can see t'rough *walls*? Or maybe he's hiding in the walk-in, shivering in the cold, afraid of the likes of you! Go have a look for yourself."

"He musta been here 'cause you wouldn't get so excited the minute we walk in, otherwise. Did you send him?! Tell him he should get my father!?"

The man gestured with the cleaver. "And what if I did?! What are *you* going t' do? I'm not sayin it again!" he hollered, cutting a lateral slice through the air to emphasize his words as he drew closer. "Get out of my store!"

Charlie's back was already to the closed door when Dov, now wedged between him and the oncoming blade, made his move. Throwing a quick diversionary jab with his left, he caught Teitelbaum square on the chin with his clenched right and grabbed the wrist of the blade hand before the man could parry. Taking his cue, Charlie simultaneously pushed forward and took hold of the same arm. The man was strong as an ox, but the brothers' combined weight and youthful quickness swept him across the shop and forced him backwards over the chopping block. With the two of them still holding the arm with the cleaver, they managed to restrain him for an instant.

"Let me up before I kill the bot' of yuhs!" Teitelbaum bellowed.

Dov came back. "You ain't gonna kill nobody! And you ain't gonna send nobody no more to do your dirty work!"

"What?! Like your father, he was never involved in any dirty work!? He never stole from nobody?! He deserves whatever he gets!"

Straining then with all his might against the weight of the two boys, the butcher suddenly lurched upwards and almost succeeded in throwing them off. In the same instant, the brothers, now thinking and acting as one and using their full strength, slammed the man's forearm against the edge of the wood block and both of them felt and heard the snap of forearm bone as the cleaver fell to the floor. Now spitting with the rage of pain, the man shot upright again and Charlie, losing his grip for a second, stumbled backwards. Teitelbaum was almost fully to his feet when Dov reached to the floor and came up in one motion with the cleaver, slapping him full to the side of the head with the flat of the blade. The younger brother recovered his hold and the two forced the man back down on the block. Dov, by that time out of control, didn't hear his younger brother cry, "Dov, stop! Don't!" as he brought the blunt back edge of the blade down hard against the man's skull. Teitelbaum, blood gushing from his deeply lacerated scalp, fell as limp as the pyramid of freshly plucked chickens lying nearby and it was only then that the brothers became aware of the horrified screams of the woman standing there behind them in the open door.

"Murderers! Murderers! *Mein Got!* Murderers!"

Taking a quick instant to feel the side of the man's neck and not feeling any pulse, Dov reeled for the door. With his brother close on his heels, they dashed out past the woman and down the avenue as her shrieks sirened out onto the street.

"Murderers! Murderers! Help! Somebody! Please!! They've *kilt* Mr. Teitelbaum! Help!"

The two darted off the avenue as soon as they could and wound their way in silence through the long-familiar narrow alleyways and backyard tenement passages, running until they were thoroughly winded. Walking further until they felt they had put enough distance between themselves and Teitelbaum's, they finally paused to catch a breath among the uncut headstones behind Lichtenstein Monuments.

Leaning against an uninscribed slab of red granite, Dov turned to Charlie.

"I think I killed him," he panted, still hardly able to breathe. "I really think I killed him!"

"How d'yuh know?"

"Believe me, I know. I felt his neck. I didn't feel a thing. He's dead, for sure! Even that woman, Mrs. What's 'er name, she could tell!"

"Mrs. Wasserman?! What could she know?! It was an accident. You didn't hit him on purpose! You was defendin' yourself. And me! He was comin' at both of us with that cleaver. Woulda cut us both! Old lady, Mrs. Wasserman, she musta seen!"

"Who knows what she seen! Besides, it don't make no difference. It's all my fault!"

"Wha'd'yuh mean?"

"I screwed up real bad, that's what."

"How so? Wha'd're yuh talkin' about?"

"It was me…! How else d'yuh think Teitelbaum coulda found out about Poppa's route, his pick ups!! It was me! I told him!"

"This, I don't believe! You shouldn't kid about such things!"

"Why would I kid?! It's true! We was playin' cards at the *shvitz* back maybe three weeks ago and I got t' losin' pretty good, several hundred. Old man Teitelbaum, he takes my marker and everything seemed fine. Then he comes to me a couple days later. Tells me I can forget about part of the money if I do him a little favor. The cards, they've been off for some time, so never thinkin' it would become such a big t'do, he asked and I told him."

"You told him where Poppa gets his chickens from? That's how all this got started?! *You,* of all people, you told Teitelbaum Poppa's route?!"

"It ain't like I haven't made the trip a hundred times. Who'd uh thought it would cause this much *tsooris*!?"

"Yuh better *hope* Teitelbaum's dead, boy! 'Cause if Poppa finds out…!"

"I know. Believe you me, I know! I'm almost better off turnin' myself in! But I ain't about to go back to the pokey, neither!"

"So what are yuh gonna do?"

"It's about time I get the fuck otta here! That's what!"

Not knowing what to say on that note, the younger brother did not respond and the two continued to catch their breath in silence for a minute or so. Thinking the whole time, Dov then turned to his brother.

"Here's what yuh gotta do. Don't go home, but go straight away downtown and turn yourself in. They'll go easier on yuh if yuh don't make them look for yuh. Tell them you was in a fight with Teitelbaum and yuhr afraid. But don't give them the blow-by-blow even if they get rough with yuh, which they're liable to. Just tell 'em you want to see Poppa. When they ask about me, tell them yuh have no clue. That we split up right away. Do yuh understand?"

"Yeah."

"Yuh musn't tell Poppa what you know."

"What do yuh take me for?"

"Good. One more thing.... You got any money on yuh?"

"A little change, maybe."

The younger brother emptied his pockets and the two hugged quickly and parted, making their way out opposite ends of the alley without looking back. Dov thought for a moment about venturing back to the rooming house to retrieve some things, but decided not to take the risk. It had already begun to get dark, and his thoughts turned to where he might lie low until morning.

Harry heard the wailing and terrified, pleading screams well before he reached the mist-filled stairwell. He immediately knew where the sounds were coming from and rushed up the steps. The noise grew ever louder by the time he reached the top of the seemingly endless stairwell and raced down the fog shrouded tunnel of a darkened hallway. He found the front door strangely ajar and the hysterical, frightful cries shot through him as he stepped into the cramped flat. The crack of the strap snapped like the firecrackers that the older boys tossed from the rooftops to the street below on the Fourth of July and he turned in the direction of the sound to see his father like he had never seen him before.

The man's lips were puffed and bloodied and his eyes were fire red with alcohol and rage. The thick leather belt, spiraling from an upstretched arm, momentarily paused as the man selected his next target and Harry's eye darted to the source of the screams, his four cornered sisters, cowering there in their night clothes, absolutely frantic in their attempt to shield each other from the sting of the leather. Izzie resumed his attack, flailing at them again, *thwack! thwack!* as their high pitched frenzies echoed through the walls.

Harry, feeling dizzy, looked around the room for help and it was then that he saw Rivkah sitting there at the kitchen table as if no one else was in the room. Moving in a trance-like slow motion, she silently bit into a piece of pumpernickel thick with butter and picked up her knife and fork to cut into the pickled herring piled high with onions sitting in front of her.

"Momma! Momma! Do something! He's hurting them! He's hurting them!" the boy yelled.

Oblivious, she proceeded with her meal, resignedly taking a moment to wipe her lips with a folded cloth from her lap.

"You know not to bother your father. Here, *zunehleh*, come sit and have a *bissel* herring with your poor mother," she beckoned. "You haven't eatin' at all today, I can tell, and it's so good and fresh, you should get some before it's all gone."

Utterly terrified to panic proportions by her indifference, the boy flung himself at his father, clutching him around a thigh. The man, undeterred, continued to lash out at the sisters as the boy joined their pleading for him to stop. The strapping just continued so Harry, in sheer desperation, bit as hard as he could into the man. It was then that Izzie seemed to take notice of the recently arrived hitchhiker attached to his pant leg. Swatting the boy away with a quick backhand, he now shifted his attention away from the four in the corner.

"What's this!? Bite your father without saying the proper *brocha* first!? Not in my house, you don't!!"

Moving just quickly enough to dodge the strap as it whipped by his face, the boy darted for the back rooms.

"Here, my Hareleh! Come! Let me show you what your Poppa has for you! A little surprise I thought maybe you should enjoy!" the man called and the boy, as if frozen in place, looked back as his father stepped across the room to the front closet. Reaching in and down, he came out with what appeared to be another belt. But this one was attached to something. It was then that Harry recognized the snarl, even before Izzie could pull Portovsky's black beast of a watchdog, all ravenous growl and gnashing teeth, from the recess. The dog lunged forward and missed with a snap as the boy, now in a place beyond terror, bolted for the rear hallway. But a step ahead of the animal, he somehow made it into the bedroom and slammed the door behind him. Frantically wedging a chair up under the doorknob, he stumbled backwards onto the bed. Trembling uncontrollably, he pulled the blankets up over his head, hoping in his fright that he could hide there undetected until Izzie and Portovsky's dog went away.

He could hear his father's footsteps coming ever closer and the dog, now just outside, still snarling and gasping at the end of its tether, scratching the door with his large claws. The footsteps stopped. And then came the pounding. Once. Twice. Three times. And the voice, loud like thunder, "Harehleh! Open up...! Don't make me break the door! Open up, I'm tellin' yuh!"

And suddenly, the dog went quiet and the knocking and voice grew softer, ever softer until it sounded like a distant far-off whisper. And then came the different sound, the tapping, like the sound of summer rain on the window, and Harry opened his eyes, surprised by his father's strange shift in tactics.

"Hesch! Heschie! Open up! It's me! Let me in!"

"No! No! Go away!" the boy cried.

"Wha'd'yuh mean 'Go away'? It's me, Dov! Open the goddamn window already!"

The boy cautiously peeked out from beneath the tangle of tattered bedclothes and his fright. Still bleary-eyed with sleep, he squinted through the silent pre-dawn darkness of the bedroom, and finally made out his big brother, tapping there on the other side of the glass. Not sure whether he was dreaming or awake, but relieved to see Dov there outside on the fire escape, he quickly hopped out of bed and undid the latch and the youth climbed in.

"Dov! I'm so glad. It's Poppa, he's..."

The older brother took one look and immediately became concerned. "Boy, look at you! You're soaking wet, all perspired! You havin' one of those dreams, again?" He reached over and rubbed his little brother's head.

"I guess I was."

"And what kind of dream was it, put you in such a place?"

"It was nuthin. Just a dream."

"Poppa, again?"

"What are you doin', comin' in the window? It's not even light out yet."

"I like the window. You know that. Where's Charlie? Did he come home last night?"

"No... I don't know. What's goin' on?"

"I've come to say good-bye, Harehleh."

"Good-bye!? Why? Wha'd'yuh mean?"

"I can't stay around here no more. That's all."

"'Cause of what happened with Teitelbaum?"

"So you know already? What did you hear?"

"Nothin' 'cept you and Casreel got in a fight with him after Yossie hit Poppa, and Teitelbaum, he's in the hospital."

"He's in the hospital? How's Poppa?"

"Okay, I guess. Looks kinda funny with his lips all puffed up, and that eye. He got good and *shikker* last night, after Mrs. Epstein, she came and sewed up his lip. He's alright, though. I think he's worried about you and Charlie, more than himself, for a change."

"That'd be different! And Momma? What about Momma?"

"She's real worried. Thinks the both of you will go t' jail."

"And Charlie?"

"I don't know 'cept Poppa had to go downtown to the police station last night and I heard him sayin' something to Momma when he came back about they would have to pay for a lawyer, but how she shouldn't worry about the money."

"Look, Hesch, I came to ask you somethin. I gotta get otta here. Between Poppa and everything else that's going on, I'll end up dead or in jail for killin' somebody yet. I gotta go."

"Take me with you!"

"Now don't start in on that one again. You know you gotta stay and look after your sisters and Momma. And besides, I already tol' yuh you gotta stay in school so's yuh don't end up like me and a million other flophouse *shlemiels*."

"Where will you go?"

"It don't matter. I'll come back, when things quiet down. Right now, I gotta ask yuh to do me a little favor."

"But what can *I* do?"

"Do yuh have a few dollars maybe, from the *shvitz*, I can borrow?"

Without saying a word the boy got off the bed and lifted a corner of the mattress, back toward the wall. Reaching underneath he came out with a small fold.

"All I have is maybe twelve, fifteen dollars. I don't bring all my money home anymore 'cause Poppa, he always takes it, but I started keepin' some here, just in case."

"Well, my little *vantz*, baby brother, this is exactly one of those just-in-cases!"

Placing the money in his trousers, Dov reached into the top of his shirt, open at the collar. Removing the fine silver chain from around his neck, he took it and placed it down over his little brother's head.

"Here, I want you to hold on to this for me. Wear it until I get back. And don't let Poppa get it."

Harry looked down at the silver crafted *mezuzah* now hanging around his neck and took it in his hand. The two hugged and the little one began to sniffle and weep. Dov pulled himself away, making for the window. As he raised the sash, he turned to his brother.

"Remember, Harehleh, take care of your sisters and Casreel. And stay in school, or I'll come back and you give such a *beatin'*, even Momma won't recognize yuh."

"Oh, yeah!" Harry sobbed.

"Yeah...! And one more thing.... Tell Poppa that I love him, too, despite everythin'. That I just couldn't stay."

Dov leaned over again and kissed Harry on the forehead, and without saying another word, stepped through the window and climbed down the escape. Holding the *mezuzah* in his hand, Harry went to the window and watched until his brother reached the pavement below and disappeared at the end of the alley.

CHAPTER 9:

Pigeons

1989.... Mickey had just pulled out of the airport and was nearly on the ramp to the Turnpike when his beeper went off. Holding the wheel with his left hand, he unclipped the contraption from his belt and brought it up to eye level. Recognizing his parole officer's number, he swore to himself. "This fuckin' guy! He just has to go and break my balls today!"

Committed by that time to the westbound lane going toward New Haven, he accelerated across the harbor overpass and exited as soon as he could. He found a pay phone a couple of blocks over at a corner gas station and punched in the numbers from the beeper's display. The by now all too familiar voice answered.

"Sansone here."

"You call me?!"

"I might have. But give me a hint. Which *me* might I currently have the pleasure to be talkin' to?"

"It's Mickey. Mickey Rabin. Did you beep me jus' now?"

"Did you not read this number on your beeper?"

"Hey, com'on. I called yuh right back. Wha'd'yuh gotta give me a hard time for?"

"Me? I'm not givin' yuh a hard time. You'd know if I was givin' yuh a hard time. I just want you should come down and see me right away. That's all."

"Wha'd'yuh mean by *right away*?"

"Let me see, now. What can the words possibly *mean*? Right away? Right away? How about like *now*, as opposed to a week from now?"

"Can't yuh cut a guy some slack? My ol' man died yesterday afternoon. I gotta bury him t'marruh. I was just on my way to… "

"Yeah, I heard about your father, and I'm sorry, but I can't help that. You have t' come in *right now,* like I'm tellin' yuh."

"What the hell's this all about? Ain't I been a good boy?"

"Yeah, you haven't caused me no headaches and I hope, for your sake, we keep it that way. But if you're not here in my office within half an hour, then there's definitely going to be a problem."

Mickey began to go off. "I don't believe this bullshit." He then caught himself, not wanting any unnecessary heat. "But, hey, all right, you call the shots and you're sayin' I ain't got no choice."

"That's what I like about you, Rabin. Always quick on the uptake. Where are yuh right now?"

"I just got off the Turnpike, the N'Haven side of the harbor."

"Oh, so you're close. Why don't you make it fifteen, instead of half an hour? It's gettin' late already and I don't wanna hang around the rest of the day waitin' for yuh."

"Jesus Christ!"

"Didn't you just now say you were bein' a good boy, or was I hearin' things?"

"Yeah, but..."

"Yeah, but what?!"

Mickey caught himself again. "I'll be there right away."

"Now that's what I like to hear!"

He hung up and stood there staring at the pay phone for a moment, as if he was still talking to someone. He thought how he should have told Sansone off, how he would have under any other circumstances. It was then that Harry's voice came to him, counseling him like always, trying to talk some sense, reminding him that it was no time to pick a beef with the P.O..

"How many times do I gotta tell yuh! These guys, they can yank yuh for spittin' on the goddamn sidewalk, bust yuh for jaywalkin', for krissakes. Why look to get revoked for some petty bullshit?!"

He again wondered about what he would do, now that the old man was gone, and then refocused on what he had to do immediately. Picking up the receiver once more, he reached in his pocket for some change, plunked it in the slot and pressed the seven digits.

"How yuh doin?"

"And what do you care, how I'm doin'?"

"Aw, com' on Angela, I just called t' see..."

"T' see what? If I knew your father died? Yes, I know. Your Aunt Edie called last night. Howard called her. I had t' hear it from the both of them."

"Can't yuh lighten up for a change, just once? Did yuh tell the kids?"

"Oh, so now yuhr concerned about the kids, all of a sudden?!"

"Look, I ain't got time for this!"

"So what are yuh callin' for? Wha'd'yuh want?!"

"I just called to find out if I can come and get some things. I ain't got no dress clothes or shoes with me and I need some for t'marruh, for the funeral."

"So go out and buy some! Pick up a suit. I don't even want yuh here!"

"Aw com' on, I ain't got the goddamn time, and you know I ain't got the money."

"You got plenty of money for that whore of yours!"

"Look! I'm sorry I fuckin' called. All right!? All I wanna do is grab some things so I got somethin' t' wear t'marruh. Is that okay with you?!"

"Come and get your goddamn clothes, all of them. Take everything, for all I care! I jus' don't want yuh hangin' around, upsettin' the kids."

"Yuh comin' to the funeral?"

"Why you askin'? You concerned I'll get into it again with that bitch?"

"Aw, c'mon, already…"

"I suppose she'll be there. She better not even look at me 'cause I'll fix her good this time!"

"So you're comin'?"

"What's wrong with you?! Of course, I'm comin'! But don't think for a second that I'm doin' it for you! He was the kids' grandfather, and he was always good to them, and t' me!"

"So yuhr bringin' the kids?"

"Wha'd'yuh think?! They're his gran'kids. The legitimate ones, I should add! Is that bitch bringing your love child?"

"Boy, you don't let up for a second, do yuh?"

"Let up? I haven't even gotten started!"

"For cryin' out loud! I told yuh I ain't got time! That asshole P.O. of mine, he just beeped me. I now gotta go run and see him, today of all days. I'll stop over there after I finish with him."

"Don't make it sound like you're doin' me any favors! Just don't show up here too late, wantin' to see the kids and expectin' t'get anything from me."

The phone clicked.

Mickey returned to the car and tossed the beeper on the passenger seat as he eased himself in. Without thinking about it, he reached down and lifted the lid on the console between the seats. He studied the Beretta, the nine millimeter resting there, its full clip alongside. He wondered if he'd be needing it as Harry's voice came to him again.

"Believe you me, Sonny Jim! Without me, you're a dead man."

He thought for a second about having to keep Angela and Gina separated at the funeral, and automatically began to mull over asking Harry what he would do. It was then that the realization hit him and he just sat there, alone, truly alone like he hadn't been in years. He looked up in the rearview mirror, as if trying to spot something in the distance already gone past. Staring at himself for a long while, eyeball to red-eyed, tired eyeball, he all of a sudden found himself gazing at his father's image in the glass, the face old and gaunt. It was then that it dawned on him.

"How the fuck would this asshole Sansone know you was dead? It ain't even in the paper yet?"

He came back and glanced down at his watch. Quarter to three. Hoping that the P.O. wouldn't take too long, he figured on getting over to Angela's to retrieve his clothes, going back to Gina's and grabbing something to eat and maybe a little nap before going out. He thought how he'd maybe grab Davey and go somewhere for a couple, brother to brother. He started up the engine, brought it into gear, turned into the traffic flow and headed uptown, accelerating just fast enough at each stoplight to keep ahead of the other cars and slow enough so he wouldn't get pulled over by some rookie traffic cop looking to fill his daily quota.

Lucking out, he found a meter on Church Street, right alongside the New Haven Green, across from the new municipal building. He parked and walked around the front of the car to feed the meter. Something made him pause for a second as he pulled out some change, and he gazed across the open expanse of ice-patched yellowed grass there at the center of the downtown. A flock of pigeons, startled by a small kid running toward them, suddenly took to the air from where they had congregated around some old-timer tossing them yesterday's bread. Mickey watched as the thirty or so birds, winging as one, curved in a wide ascending arc and passed over his head on their way to the red sandstone seclusion of the widow's walk atop the old City Hall. He flashed for a second how Esther's mother, the one he always called Bubbie, now long gone, used to bring him down to the Green, to that identical spot, when he was little. He saw himself there, and remembered when he used to feed and chase the birds; how he used to watch as they made their way to that same sheltered safe haven above the city.

"When the hell was that? When was it?"

Thinking of the pigeons brought it back to him then, the story Harry used to tell. The one about the immigrant, the Portuguese guy who used to wash windows on Legion Avenue. How the guy worked for years, all the while wantin' to become a citizen. How he finally started going to night school to learn English and to study for his citizenship test, and how the guys from the smoke shop conspired. Mickey had heard the tale so many times, refined and embellished to perfection with each telling, that he could hear his father recounting it as if they were standing there together feeding popcorn to the birds. He closed his eyes and listened.

There was this Portogie greenhorn, yuh see, this refugee. He use' t' do everybody's windows. Jeez, it's been so long, I can't even remember his name. Well, anyway, this guy, this Portogie, he wants t' become a citizen, get naturalized. So he starts goin' t' night school, studyin' English and takin' classes, 'cause in those days you had t' go before a judge or whoever and answer questions about history and how the government works. Civics, they use' t' call it.

So me and some of the guys that used to hang around the smoke shop, some of the ol' cronies, we tell this Portogie he don't need no night school, that we'll take turns helpin' him with the history and civics. That besides, the test was a breeze, and he would end up savin' a few bucks this way.

Of course, we didn't let on that we had these connections downtown at City Hall in those days. We was all connected through Benny Malvin to the old Democratic machine. So we told him we would take turns preppin' him for the test, teachin' him history and stuff, and that we knew the answers 'cause everybody had to do the test and it was always the same.

We got ahold of the little booklet they handed out to help yuh prep and different guys sat with the Portogie over coffee and crullers late every mornin', havin' him write down and memorize the answers. And this goes on for a few weeks.

In the meantime, Benny Malvin, he was on the rise in the Democratic Party back in them days, a precinct captain or something, he talks to somebody downtown and the whole thing gets set up. We take this Portogie to City Hall and we're all sittin' there in the courtroom where they held the exams, and they call his name and he gets to go up before old Judge Halloran.

Malvin had set it up, yuh see. He let the judge know beforehand that the window washer was already connected in our ward, but he doesn't let on that the fellas from the smoke shop had tutored the guy... I don't even know if he was wise to it.

Well Halloran, this Shanty Irishman, he had come over himself as a kid from the Old Sod, as he woulda called it. He came up the hard way, and takes this whole citizenship thing, becoming an American, real serious. Well, they call the Portogie's name and he walks up to the bench.

He's standin' there in his best clothes, all cleaned and scrubbed, with his cap in his hand. Malvin had even taken one of those carnations he always wore in his own lapel as a boutonniere and he sticks it in the Portogie's.

So he's standing there and Halloran tells him, "Look, I'm gonna ask yuh some questions about this country's history and government and you have to answer them. Do you understand?"

The Portogie says yes and the judge proceeds, not wantin' to make it too hard, 'cause after all, he knows the guy's with us.

"Okay then. When the President of the United States dies, who gets the job?"

The Portogie, he turns and looks at all of us sittin' there, with this great grin on his face, like this is all gonna be a snap. He turns back to the judge and says, "You' 'onor, itsa the undertake who getsa the job."

Of course, at that point we're all sittin' there bitin' our lips, the whole crew fightin' not to crack up. We just contain ourselves and remain straight like nothin's up.

The judge tells the Portogie that the answer was wrong, but that it was okay, there was no problem getting one wrong; that he still has an opportunity, and he comes out with the next question.

"When did George Washington die?"

The Portogie, he looks back at us again, turns to Halloran and says, "I didn't even know he was sick," and just stands there grinning at the judge, figurin' he got that one right.

Well, of course at that point some of the guys start to crack up a little, but me and Benny, we motion for everyone to cool it and the judge resumes, this time voicing some concern.

He tells the Portogie, "Look, the courtroom is no place for levity. And citizenship brings big responsibilities, nuthin' to be trifled with, yuh see. And you've answered two questions incorrectly now so I'm gonna ask you one more, which you must get right. Do you understand?"

And the Portogie, now beginning to fidget a little, he nods, "Yes, you' 'onor."

Well, Halloran by this point, he realizes something must be up 'cause of the way we're all sittin' there, but also knowin' the Portogie's connected, he figures he'll make it easy, cause he really wants to pass the guy, yuh see.

He pauses for a second and says, "What's on the very top of this building?" meaning the American flag, of course.

Now this was the judge's own question, so the boys hadn't prepped the Portogie. He just stands there for a moment, scratches his head. He then looks up at the ceilin', still thinkin'. And then back at us and back at the ceilin'. He looks straight back at Halloran and smilin' wide so everyone can see these two gold teeth he had in front, he says, "That's easy, you 'onor. The pigeons."

Well, the whole room went wild, everyone crackin' up, even this big fat Mic bailiff. Halloran, now realizing the whole thing's a set up, he gavels us quiet, and flunks the Portogie. He then threatens the whole crew, all of us, with fines, and had the bailiff take our names. He demands that we take the poor guy back to the Avenue and instruct him in the proper functioning of government and American history. Says that he could have another chance, but if he failed the test again, we'd all have to pay the fines. You better believe the Portogie passed with flying colors the next time 'round. As a matter of fact, he did so well, a few years later he went on to become one of Malvin's lieutenants and eventually became an alderman.

The revving of a car engine brought Mickey back and he looked at the young pimply-faced kid sitting there in neutral in an old, souped-up Chevie, a '62 Impala, waiting for the light to change, his gum chewing girlfriend close on the seat next to him. Looking over at the 'Vette, the kid revved the overstocked engine again and the mere sound of it transported Mickey to another place. As the light changed, the kid eased the five-speed into gear and drove off as Mickey's imaginings shifted.

He saw himself again in his own early hot rod days, back in the late 1950s. He could place the exact year by the make and model he was driving at the time and recalled practicing his dead start takeoffs, that split-second coordination of clutch, gas, and stick, by trying to hit the pigeons feeding in the narrow street behind the family's place in the projects. It came to him then, how he eventually figured it out and finally got a couple that one day, ran them right the hell over, after luring a bunch of them down off the roof with half a loaf of Wonder Bread scattered on the pavement. Memories of feathers flying everywhere and the panicked survivors, scattered out of formation flying every which way, fleeing back to the safety of the rooftops. He could still feel the momentary thrill of that now distant success, and how he had to pick one of the birds out from his grill work.

"Pigeons, fuckin' pigeons."

A sudden gust of wind whipping across the Green slapped him in the face and brought him back once again. Quickly glancing at his watch as he crossed Church Street mid block through the traffic, he entered the silver-gray glassed New Haven Municipal Building and took the elevator up to Sansone's office. Harry's voice came to him again just as the bell rang and the door opened.

"Hear what I'm tellin' yuh, Sonny Jim, without me you're a dead man."

He realized it wasn't just routine, that something serious was up, as soon as he was shown into Sansone's interior office and saw the two familiar suits standing there. The P.O. could have dispensed with the introductions but proceeded anyway, motioning to the first.

"Mickey, this here is Special Agent Boyer...," and then to the other, "and this is Special Agent Svenrud. FBI."

"Yeah, I know," Mickey responded. "We've met before."

Sansone at that point simply retired to the side of the room, folded his arms and leaned his back against the door as Boyer took the lead. Motioning to the chair in front of the P.O.'s desk with his open hand cordially extended palm up, in part to show his good-cop face, he looked straight at Mickey with that trained, no bull earnest pose all the Feds loved to strike. Mickey sat down and the agent started in.

"Look, Mickey, we're terribly sorry to cause you any inconvenience on a day like this, sorry to have to bring you in, and we don't intend for this to take too long knowing you probably still have things to look after, but we thought it wise to speak with you today."

Mickey reflexed. "Oh, so you guys know about my ol' man, too!"

He then looked at Sansone, leaning there against the door in that perpetual wash-and-wear shirt, those worn gray slacks and same dull tie he always wore and it suddenly came clear how the P.O. knew Harry was gone.

"Of course the Feds would know," he thought.

Boyer continued. "As you know, Mickey, Agent Svenrud and I are with the Tri State Organized Crime Task Force."

"Oh yeah? Which side you on t'day? Lookin' to catch some bad guys for a change?"

"Well, yes, that's what we do!" came Boyer.

"Well, in that case lemme guess, bein' you ain't got nuthin on me 'cause I've been squeaky clean... Sansone can tell yuh. You're here 'cause J. Edgar fuckin' Hoover can't make it to the funeral himself and sent you guys with his condolences."

At that point Svenrud interrupted. "Let's get out of here, Boyer. I told you we'd be wasting our time. I don't even know why you make the effort with such smart mouthed low lives like this, who can't even show respect for the dead."

Boyer feigned a quick stern glance at his partner and then turned to Mickey.

"You'll have to excuse Agent Svenrud. His father served under Mr. Hoover for a number of years."

"Now I get it!! My old man just dies, so you guys had me come all the way down here so you could talk to me about respect for the dead! The lifers at Sommers, some of the old cons doin' serious time, they used to talk a whole lot about what *serving under Mr. Hoover* meant. That ain't no big secret, at least from what I hear. So let's cut the crap. What the hell you guys want!?"

"Actually nothing. You might find this hard to believe, but we actually came to share some information with you."

"Oh yeah? Wha'd'yuh mean by *information*?! And for what? What's it gotta cost me?"

"Just some cooperation."

"Hey, I cooperated with you fuckin' guys before and where did it land me? Back in the fuckin' joint. I'm through with that noise. I happen to prefer where I'm sleepin' these days."

At that point Sansone chimed in. "Hey Mickey, you better listen to what these guys got to say."

"So what is it? Wha'd'yuh want from me? Am I under arrest? Do I need a lawyer? If so, tell me. And if not, I'm walkin' the fuck otta here, 'cause every time I get near you guys, there's nuthin' but trouble. And I really don't need any additional bullshit, especially today or t'marruh, or anywhere else down the road."

"So you don't want to hear *why* we brought you down here?"

"What the hell can you guys tell me, I don't already know?!!"

"How 'bout we just tell you what your father has been sayin' for the past several years? What was it, he'd say? 'Without me, you're a dead man'? What was that name he called you? 'Sonny Jim'?"

"When did yuh hear him say that?!"

"When didn't he say it? He also always used to talk about how the walls have ears! He was a smart man."

"So wha'd'yuh want?!!"

Boyer took the lead. "Look, Mickey, you're well aware that we have our sources. Reliable ones. One of our contacts informed us today that the word's already come down. They've put a contract out on the street for you."

"Now I know you're full o' shit...! Yuhr playin' some kinda game!"

"Why would we fabricate something like that? You've been square with us in the past and we feel obligated. As a matter of fact, we're required by Bureau regulations to let any of our former assets know whenever we become aware that they may be in jeopardy."

"So you come down here, have my P.O. drag me in, to tell me I might get whacked?! Why can't I believe yuhr doin' this out of some civic duty? It ain't cause yuhr feelin' guilty, all of a sudden. What d'yuh want from me?"

Svenrud piped in. "You know as well as we do that your father provided a buffer. He was your shield, your insurance policy. That they would never dare come after you as long as he and the big man were around. But the big guy is away at Danbury, and won't be out for some time. We made sure of that. And now your father is gone. So all these wise guys you've known for how long, some of 'em since you were a kid, maybe? One of 'em will now come up to you, probably the one you least expect. He'll give you a hug and a kiss, extend his sincerest, heartfelt condolences over your father's passing, and put a bullet behind your ear."

"So when's this supposed to go down?"

"We don't know. Our source couldn't say. Soon, more than likely. Maybe tomorrow. We really don't know."

"So what do you think I should do?"

"Well, you could protect yourself."

"And do what?"

"We can offer you immunity. Get you into that witness protection program we offered you before. You just have to be a little more forthcoming, that's all."

"So let me get this straight. You're tellin' me there's a contract on the street for my ass. That I might get whacked at any time, you don't know when. But if I roll over and cooperate with you assholes, then you'll protect me?! And all I gotta do is tell yuh what you wanna hear, what yuh prob'ly already know and then drop everything and leave N'Haven and go who-the-fuck-knows-where. Is that what I'm hearin'?!"

"Well, Mick, we could only offer you the Bureau's assistance if you were willing to testify."

"Testify! Testify to what?! You must really be out of your minds altogether! Even if I knew what yuh think I know and gave it up, yuh think they wouldn't find me?! One of yuhr own people, probably, would lead them right to me!"

"We felt obligated to warn you, and yes, to make an offer."

"Hey! Yuh know where yuh can put your offer! How do I even know y' guys are bein' straight with me? Why should I trust any of yuhs?!"

"What choice do you have?"

"I'll take my chances on the outside. At least if one of those assholes comes at me on the street, I'll have a chance!"

"Again, Mick, we just wanted to let you know that..."

Mickey turned to Sansone. "Are we through here? Can I go now?!"

Boyer nodded to Sansone and the P.O. motioned to the exit with his upturned thumb. Mickey got up and moved toward the door and was just about to reach for the knob when Sansone's voice stopped him.

"And one more thing, Rabin. Don't get caught packin'. If you're found in possession of a firearm, I'll have to yank yuh and it'll be a long time before you see the street again. Trust me on that one. Don't even think about it."

"Hey Sansone, you gotta do what yuh gotta do, right?! Just leave me the fuck alone long enough so's I can bury my ol' man! Is that too much to ask?!"

It was then, with his hand on the door knob, with the door partly opened, that Mickey paused for a second. He turned and faced the Feds. "Yuh know if you guys really want my help, then yuh gotta be a little more... What was that word yuh used? Uh... *forthcoming*? Yuh gotta do somethin' for me."

"What is it, Rabin?"

"I wanna bring my kid Jimmy, the one in the joint up in Vermont, to the ol' man's funeral. You could arrange that, couldn't yuh?"

"It's not impossible, I suppose."

"I tell yuh what. You arrange it so my kid can get down here for the ol' man's send-off, and then, maybe then, I'll consider."

Svenrud interrupted. "And now who's playing a game?"

"Hey! Everybody plays some kinda game, no?! You do me one for a change, and I'll see what I can do."

Boyer answered. "You would have to understand, of course, that while we might be able to arrange something with the Vermont authorities, we have no contingency funds for such an operation. There would be some fees, some costs involved."

Mickey, well accustomed to the con, smiled at the thought of the possible shakedown before responding. Almost instinctively, he reached down and felt the wad through his pant leg, the money retrieved from Harry's.

"Do what yuh can and I'll cover what it takes. Get my kid down here and then we'll talk."

He let himself out and Svenrud turned to his partner as soon as the door closed.

"Do you think he bought it?"

"I don't know, but we certainly turned up the heat on him. That's for certain."

"Yes, but will he crack?"

"We'll have to wait and see. He'll be so wound by the time the funeral takes place that anything could happen. Maybe he'll end up going off. Maybe take a couple of his pals with him in the process. Save the taxpayers a lot of money and us a lot of paperwork."

Sansone joined in. "Do you think he'll be armed? If he is, I can revoke him right away."

Boyer responded. "No, we don't wanna do that. We want to give him enough rope. Enough maybe to hang himself, and hopefully tie up the whole sleazeball crew, in the process."

"And what about this request, the thing about his son? Can we bring him down from Vermont?" Svenrud asked.

"We'll have to do it to assure him we're on the up and up."

"I'll make the call."

"While you're on the phone, you might want to find out what time the funeral is. Where do these Hebes hold their funerals, anyway?"

Sansone chimed in again. "Try Velners'. On George Street."

Svenrud looked at Boyer. "You thinking of goin'?"

"I wouldn't miss it."

Mickey moved back across Church Street and got in the car. Wondering what to believe, he sat there for a minute. "Just what I fuckin' need," he thought aloud, and it was then that Harry's words came back to him.

"*Without me, Sonny Jim, you're a dead man.*"

Quickly looking around in his mirror for unexpected company and not finding any, he opened the console. He picked up the Beretta, and shoved the clip home in its handle. As he slid the gun back down between the seats, Harry's voice came to him once again. One of the old routines.

"*Ladies and gentleman, it gives me great pleasure to intraduce that renowned star of stage and screen, Walter Pigeon, joined this evening, in a special apprearance by his brother Stew, the noted informer.*"

He thought about how much the old man hated even the thought of a stoolie. Starting the engine, he pulled away from the curb as he wondered where to turn.

CHAPTER 10:

Jakey

1989.... D<small>AVID DOUBLE PARKED ON</small> Church Street, already congested with the evening rush, and ran the obit into the *Journal Courier* while Annie, on the lookout for the traffic cops, sat behind the wheel with the engine running. They quickly switched seats upon his return and he drove the few blocks over to Lucibello's, one of the old-time Italian pastry shops still there on Grand Avenue. Annie's unaccustomed eyes widened when they went in and she saw the selection and they left, grinning like a couple of school kids, with four custard-filled treasures nested in a string-tied bakery box. The carton did not stay closed long and they licked the cream from the ends of their chocolate chip *canollis*, brushing away the powdered sugar and crumbs as they rode in silence back toward Howard's.

The car moved across town following Chapel Street all the way from where it began at State, on past the New Haven Green and Yale's "Old Campus" and then northwest to where the street finally widened into the comfortable middle-class neighborhood beyond Edgewood Park and Yale Bowl. He normally would not have taken that route back toward Woodbridge, especially in the late afternoon traffic, but went along as if the car, on automatic pilot, knew the route itself. It wasn't until he saw the solidly-built homes with their nicely-kept yards bordered with shaped English hedge and tamed laurel, and the winter-bare dogwoods, magnolias, ornamental fruit trees, and remaining elms with their graceful naked arms arching upward over the streetlights that it suddenly became clear to him why he had gone that way. It was as if his father's old friend had beckoned.

Annie looked over at him somewhat surprised when he turned into the driveway of the gracious slate-roofed mock Tudor and he quickly reassured her as the car glided to a stop. "There's someone I want you to meet."

It had been years, at least six or maybe even eight he figured, but time collapsed and memories flooded back as they got out of the car. Guiding Annie, he automatically, out of habit, made for the side door still sheltered underneath the aging grape trellis, and he saw himself sitting there in the shade as a summertime kid, taking in the iced tea and the talk.

He pushed the doorbell and they waited. He rang it once again, waited some more and took Annie's elbow, ready to turn away, when they heard the footsteps and the dog bark, and the man opened the inside door.

He was wearing a misshapen pale blue cashmere cardigan, his winter worsted around-the-house slacks, and those comfortably old, fleece-lined leather slippers and David, experiencing a kind of *deja vu* upon seeing the aged but handsomely lean, upright figure through the storm door, whispered to his wife.

"Timeless. *Absolutely* timeless."

The golden cocker spaniel at his feet barked in protective bluster as the man paused an instant to focus through the winter-fogged glass. Then realizing who it was, he smiled welcomingly. Softly commanding the dog to get back and go lie down, he opened the door.

"I figured you'd come. Knew you'd show up as soon as I heard."

"So you know."

"This town ain't all that big, in case you might've forgotten. I got a call this mornin', first thing."

Not waiting for an introduction, the old man turned to Annie. "This must be the wife I've been waiting to meet. Married what? A little over a year now, I suppose. Let me see what we have here... Jeez, Davey, yuh done good. I can tell just from a quick once-over."

She smiled and extended her hand and name and when the man reciprocated she noticed the softness of his touch, a gentleness in his hand as he took hold, welcoming her into his home.

"It's a pleasure. Even under such circumstances. Most people know me as Jacob Hirsch, but since you're with this one, you can call me Jakey. The old crowd, this one's father and the whole bunch, they used to call me 'Hershey', and everything else related that you might not care to imagine, but the chocolate bar thing didn't wear well when I became respectable. Besides, yuh can't joke about bein' chocolate-covered anything anymore. People immediately take it the wrong way. Immediately think you're some kind of racist or something."

He ushered them through the subdued yellow kitchen to the unpretentious living room done in cherry, American maple and warm New England colors. Offering them seats on the roomy, comfortable sofa and taking a moment to poke a bit and place another log in the fieldstone fireplace, he retired to his large leather easy chair. Davey took a moment to look around as if caught in some old reminiscence as he eyed the framed prints on the walls, the family photos on the mantel, and the full wall of hardbound books shelved at the far end of the room.

He noticed the already-read *Times* in its usual place on the hassock and his eye moved to the *New York Review* and the *Nation*, both newly arrived, sitting on the coffee table. The spaniel came in and took its usual place on the Persian throw rug at Jakey's feet as Annie watched and the old man gazed at her through his worn but wise eyes.

"His name's Burt. He's my closest friend these days. Everyone else is gone. Evelyn... that's my wife... she's been gone almost twelve years. Can yuh believe it, Davey? Twelve years, already? And the kids, my two girls... that's their picture when they were younger, the one above the fireplace..., they've been out of the house longer than that. All the old cronies, they're mostly dead, or worse, moved to Boca Raton. So it's me and the dog. Once in a while the girls come with the sons-in-law and the grandchildren.... I got three.... Usually on the holidays. But mostly it's me and my pal, here."

David interrupted. "Yuh look good, Jakey. Yuh haven't changed a bit."

Jake looked at Annie as he motioned with a dismissive wave of his hand toward David.

"Pardon my French, young lady, but your husband has acquired a knack for... How should I put it? 'Throwin' the bull,' shall we say? Clearly inherited from his old man, your recently deceased father-in-law."

His gaze moved back to Davey. "I look like hell and feel worse, so don't start with the con job like you're talkin' to some of your academic cronies. When'd' yuh get in?"

"Earlier this afternoon. We're stayin' up at Howard's, in Woodbridge."

"That makes sense. Can't imagine the two of you stayin' with Mickey. How they doin'?"

"They're both alright, I guess. Kinda hard to tell. Haven't really talked to Mickey yet, and Howard's Howard."

"What a pair, those two. The funeral t'marruh?"

"Yeah. At Velners'."

"And where else?"

"Do yuh see Louie at all?"

"Not really. I don't go out much. I used t' see him plenty enough at the funeral home. I'd see your father there, too, back when everyone around us seemed to be droppin' like flies. But even that's slacked off. I'm not goin', by the way, in case yuh were wonderin'."

"C'mon, Jake, there's no way around it. Everybody's got to go sometime."

"That isn't what I meant, and you know it. I'm not goin' to the funeral."

"Did I say a word?"

"Just makin' sure, so's we don't have to go through some lengthy rigamarole."

David glanced over and caught the puzzled look on Annie's face, and started to explain.

"Jakey and Harry, they had... shall we say... some *unresolved* issues."

"Unresolved, my *tuchas*! What's unresolved? I ain't goin'. That's all!"

"Yuh mean to say, after all these years..."

"That's exactly right! After all these years! I made a promise, that's all. You and your brothers, you were always welcome here. You, especially, I treated like one of my own. And your mother, she should rest in peace, what she went through. Nahh...! I can't now. It would just be too much."

The man paused for a moment, lost in some distant thought, and then directed his gaze over at Annie again.

"I'm sorry. I apologize. Here you are, the recent wife of one of my favorites, we hardly meet, and you get dragged into the middle of some old business. I'm not being too good of a host, now, am I?"

"It's quite all right."

"No, it's not. I haven't even offered you anything. Evelyn would have my hide. Would either of you care for a drink? There's whatever yuh want. Some scotch. Or maybe a glass of wine. I even got a beer or two, I think, tucked away in the back of the fridge, for when the sons-in-law show up. That's what they drink out where you are? Beer? No?"

Annie said she'd have a glass of red and David thought about the scotch but settled for a brew and Jake excused himself and went into the kitchen with Burt, now up again, following close behind. David took advantage of the moment and returned to the book shelves and spoke to Annie as he perused.

"He's something else, isn't he?"

"Yes, I like him. He seems so different."

"Different? Not really. Just a little more refined perhaps, better educated. He's still old school though."

"So why's he so mad at your father?"

"I'm not quite sure, and he's never been clear about it. I don't think it was any one thing, even. Just a culmination of years of who-knows-what, most of which happened before I can even remember."

"So if he's been estranged from Harry for so long, then how'd the two of you become so close?"

"He's just always been there. Since I was a little kid. I can remember coming here with my mother. Or he'd stop by and see us, when the ol' man wasn't around. I figured out later that he must've helped my mother out, now and then. When there was no money in the house. I realized later that he probably had a thing for her. Yuh could tell from the way he looked when she was in the room. Then when I got older, when things got weird at home between me and the old man, starting in junior high and then when I was in high school, I would just come over here sometimes and hang out. Looking back on it, I guess I must've picked up some of what I know just by coming here and hanging around. I didn't come to fully appreciate them, he and Evelyn, until much later, after I was in college."

"What was she like?"

"She was something else. Always treated me like one of her own. Would never let me get away with anything. Always challenging. One of the adults, when I was growing up, who made yuh think about stuff. Always thinking and talking about the larger world. Civil rights and Vietnam. Politics. Not your typical mom and housewife, that's for sure."

Jakey returned with a wooden breakfast tray in hand, the dog now wagging and swirling around his feet in anticipation of a treat. Setting the tray down on the coffee table, he poured a glass of domestic Cabernet for Annie. Handing it to her, he pointed Davey to the bottle of Michelob and the glass.

"You, I don't have to pour for. There's some Gouda here, and some Triscuits, if yuh want. Nuthin' special. I don't get much company, so it'll have to do."

The man tossed a piece of cheese toward the expectant spaniel. The dog caught it in midair and they both returned to their spots, Burt to the throw rug and Jakey to his lounger, ready to resume.

"So now that I've played the dutiful host, where were we?"

Annie took the lead. "So what happened?"

"What happened with what?"

"With you and Harry."

"The things that go on with old, childhood friends. Who knows? Yuh spend so much time together, inseparable when you're kids that yuh never stop bein' attached, at some level. A kind of bonding takes place, I guess. And then life takes its course. Yuh just go your separate ways, take different directions, that's all. We were all alike, yet different, even when we were kids, me and your father-in-law, and Louie Velner.... Have you met that one, yet? All the rest, almost all of 'em dead and gone now, a whole generation. Hard to believe. It's just me and Louie, now that Harry's gone. Getting down to the last of the Mohicans. It looks like he'll get to bury all of us, just like he used to say. I'm gonna fool him, though."

"How's that?"

"I already left word. I'm gonna be cremated."

"How'd you turn out so different?"

"I don't know as I'm any different. In part, maybe it was family. What's the word they use these days? Parenting, I think they call it. Who knew from 'parenting skills' on Legion Avenue? While Harry had no one really, his father, Izzie, always busy with the chickens and that rage of his, his own *mishigas*, and his mother trying to raise all them kids on what little they had, I at least had some mentors, some guidance...."

"Guidance?"

"My father, and my mother especially, though both old country like everyone else, impressed on me that I had to stay in school, that education was key. And of course, 'cause my ol' man received some breaks and did a little better than many, than Izzie Rabin, say, I didn't have to work as much when I was a kid and could concentrate on school.

"Luckily I got into Hillhouse, the academic high. Most of my friends, your father-in-law included, and Velner, those that stayed in school anyway, they went to Commercial, what became Wilbur Cross. But me, I got accepted to the college track. And then I got into Yale. It was a big t' do, back then. After all, they took very few Jews in those days, especially working class youngsters like myself. They used to take a few kids, a handful each year from New Haven in some shallow display of civic mindedness. They never paid a penny to the city in property taxes, but they always took a handful of kids. Some people at Hillhouse pulled for me, an early kind of affirmative action, yuh might say, and I got accepted. My older brothers, they helped out, of course, especially during the lean years, and everyone contributed, even my sisters."

"Your sisters helped?"

"Sure. They took jobs in one of those sweatshops on State Street making ladies' undergarments or whatever to help out with the family so's I could keep to my books and not have to work. My younger sister, if I remember right, she worked in the same factory with Esther, your deceased mother-in-law, *alevashalom*. They worked sewing fancy neckties, for those that could afford them. And that was during the Depression, mind you! What they did, I never forgot. They all wanted I should become a doctor or a lawyer, but that's another story. The whole thing made me very class-conscious, comin' off Legion Avenue and suddenly bein' tossed among all those Yalie blue bloods. I acquired a different vantage point, a different outlook, shall we say."

Davey interrupted. "Jakey used to be a Red. Probably still is, though he'll deny it. Was in the Party."

"A youthful indiscretion."

"You were in 'til when? What? Fifty-six?"

"Okay, okay, so it took awhile."

"A while? Yuh get recruited into the party as a college student in what, the early-mid-thirties? And yuh stay all those years, despite all that Stalin..."

Jake turned to Annie. "Your husband, he studies a little history, and gets some politics, a sixties Johnny-come-lately, one of those know-it-all New Lefties, and he acts like he's got a grasp on all the complexities. And then he turns around and expects simple explanations!"

"Don't mind him. Finish what you were saying. Please."

"Yeah, I was political. Was always on the Left, even before I knew what it was. A few of us picked it up as if by osmosis, from the culture, the streets. How we grew up, the poverty and all. There were always reds around, socialists, communists, even some old-style anarchists. A few that came over on the boat already political and even more that got radicalized once they reached the promised land, the *goldene medina,* they used to call it. Sure, I joined the Party when I became conscious. What else was there to do? What with the Depression on and the fascists on the move in Germany, and Mussolini... And then there was Spain. By that time, it musta been thirty-seven, I wanted to go fight Franco but couldn't. I was in my mid-twenties and married already, so the Party said I couldn't go. They kept me plenty busy right here."

"Doing what?"

"Yuh gotta understand New Haven at the time. The city had become a center of light manufacturing. Aside from Winchester's, there were lots of small garment producers, shirt companies and ladies' wear, that moved here before and during World War I to escape the attempts at unionization and the labor strife in the New York needle trades. At first it was wide open, no unions, with a plentiful supply of cheap labor, lots of poor Italians and Jews. But wha'd they used to say? How the ol' class struggle, it never disappears? We had our hands plenty full, what with the Depression and New Deal, and then the War. And even after that, for some time. Until the reaction set in, with that goddamn Truman and Taft-Hartley, then McCarthy."

"Tell Annie what yuh did during the war."

"What's to tell? I did my part, that's all. It was a war against fascism. Can you imagine if they had won? Those of us that understood, we did what we could, that's all."

"He didn't have to go 'cause he had a wife and kids. They even said he was too old."

"Old, hell! I was in better shape than guys ten years my junior at that time."

"He lied about his age. Said he was younger. Fought in North Africa and Italy. Went ashore at Normandy. Got shot, wounded twice. Promoted several times. Was a decorated hero."

"Hero, *shmero*. A lot of good that did me."

"They came after him later on, during the fifties. HUAC. One of the later Smith Act trials, right here in New Haven. In fifty-six. Everybody in the party that they could get their hands on. Imagine! The same year as Hungary, the year that Khruschev denounces Stalin, and the party's flyin' apart from its own internal contradictions and..."

"Hoo-Haa! *Internal contradictions!* Boy-o-boy, you certainly landed yourself a smart one here, young lady! I can now rest easy, glad to know that someone finally got it all figured out!"

Annie smiled at the two of them. "So let me ask, what did happen?"

"With the party? I got out, that's all."

"No, I'm sorry. I mean with Harry. When did the two of you have your falling out?"

"There was no abrupt falling out. I just couldn't take it anymore."

David joined in. "But something specific happened, no?"

"Wha'd'yuh want I should tell yuh? Your brother Mickey was born in, what? Musta been the fall of 1941. I can remember because it was not long before Pearl Harbor. I think maybe Harry and Esther, like everyone else, figured it was a matter of time before the country would enter the war and the word was goin' around back then that men with families would be called for the service only after single guys or those with no kids. If I recall right, they had been married for about five years before he was born, pretty unusual in those days. I don't know what that was all about and neither of them ever talked about it. But anyways, they lived on Asylum, just off Legion back then, and Harry went to work drivin' a truck for Wonder Bread so's he could keep out of the army, get his deferment. And what's he do? He makes a ton of money during the war dealing in the black market. He uses the truck to make deliveries for Asa Goldman, you know, from the old grocery on Legion. Goldman had tons of stuff hoarded, everything imaginable, and your father would make the deliveries while making his bread drops.

"He worked like crazy during the day and havin' a few dollars in his pocket, well, I don't have to tell you about the ol' man. He'd be out runnin' around at night, hardly ever at home. So there Esther was, pretty much raisin' Mickey by herself. He pissed a lot of money away in those days. I know, 'cause he was still on a roll after I got home from the war and I helped him blow a good chunk of it. Cards, whiskey, the track in New York, the fights. Hell! You name it! I even got called on the carpet by the local party apparats once or twice, accused of what they euphemistically referred to as 'rank and file deviationism'."

"Deviationism?"

"Yeah, their way of sayin' I liked to party and drink too much. But they excused it, attributed it to what they called my war-time trauma, my just gettin' home, and all. Wha'd'they call it now? Post-traumatic stress?"

"Then what?"

"Your mother, God bless her, what did she know from raisin' kids at that point? What did anybody know? By the time Mickey was five or six, we used to see him runnin' around the neighborhood... after I got back from the service. Always on the street, tailin' after the older kids. He learned fast, I'll tell yuh."

David interrupted. "Yuh still haven't said anything about what happened with you and the ol' man."

"Let's just say we went off in different directions. He somehow managed to hold on to some money, God knows how, and opened that first deli, the big one, that beautiful place on Whalley. But then something happened and he lost everything, in a flash. It took him a while to recoup, but he got some more money somehow and that's when he opened the place on Legion, the luncheonette on the corner of Elliot. That musta been about the time you... it was a little earlier... about the time that Howard came along. Me? We had the girls by that time.... The oldest, my Paula, she's a year and a half older than Mickey.... So I turned to making a living. Went back to school on the G.I. bill and learned accounting. Dashed the hopes for a lawyer in the family, but everyone eventually recovered. Plus I had my work in the party, until that ended. Your father took up with a new crowd. And that was that."

"A new crowd?"

"Yeah. I suspect he wanted to expand his horizons. We just drifted apart, that's all."

Annie interupted. "But I don't understand, or did I miss something? Why is it you're so angry, to this day, that you won't go to the funeral?"

"That's water under the bridge. There's no point now. And I'm not angry."

The couple exchanged a look and without speaking decided to let the matter rest. David changed the subject by asking Jakey what he'd been reading lately. They talked about Bush and the economy and that led to some talk about how Reagan had gotten off unscathed, weathering the whole Iran Contra business. They chatted a little bit about what was going on in the Soviet Union and Eastern Europe, about Gorbachev and the meaning of "perestroika" and "glasnost" and Jakey went on for a while about how he thought it could only lead to things positive. Their attention turned to the domestic scene, to the state of the labor movement in the Northeast, and the Democrats in New Haven. They would have gone on considerably longer, but Annie glanced at her watch when Jakey offered her a third refill on the wine. She reminded Davey that they had promised Howard they wouldn't be long and that it had already turned into well over two hours. They politely got up as the dog stretched and yawned and their elderly host retrieved their coats from the brass hooks by the back door.

Knowing better, Davey didn't raise it again but as they were about to leave, the interior door already open, Annie turned back to Jake. Shaking his hand and quickly giving him an adieu peck on the cheek, she thanked him for his hospitality.

"It was really a pleasure meeting you."

"Don't be silly. The pleasure was all mine."

"I do hope you'll rethink your decision."

"What? Yuh mean about the funeral?"

"Yes. If whatever happened is water under the bridge, like you said, then you'll come."

Still the host, Jakey smiled, and motioned to Davey. "See! I was right! As soon as I laid eyes on her, I saw she had something on the ball. A real keeper."

"Hey, tell me about it!" Davey responded. "That's why I married her!"

The couple stepped to the outside and turned to wave through the storm door at the old man and the dog, its front paws posted against the now frosted glass.

It was then that something triggered David's memory and he stepped back toward the door as Jakey opened it partway.

"What? Yuh forget somethin'? You weren't wearing a hat when you came in."

"No. I just remembered. Something I wanted to ask yuh."

"You ain't gonna start, too, are yuh?"

"Nahh, it ain't that. I was just wonderin'. Do you know somebody named Julie?"

"Julie? Julie who?"

"I don't know. That's why I'm askin'. Howard told me that before the ol' man died, like with his last words, he asked for somebody named Julie, said something like, 'Save me, Julie.'"

Jakey paused for a moment as if thinking back, then responded.

"Beats me. I wonder who the hell that can be."

"I was hopin' you might know."

Annie and David got in the car, their breath visible in the shivery evening air, and he started it and backed out. It was then that they simultaneously remembered and hurriedly reached for the bakery box and the last *cannolli*. Davey grabbed it first and made like he was about to injest it whole, but paused for a second and broke it in half, and the two of them finished the pastry, again wiping away the powdered sugar as Davey silently steered the car back toward Woodbridge. He hadn't even turned on the car radio and Annie, unaccustomed to quiet, finally spoke.

"I really like him."

"Yeah, I do too."

"Do you think he'll come?"

"Come?"

"Tomorrow. To the funeral."

"Nah. There's too much history."

CHAPTER 11:

Hermina

1989... IT SUDDENLY DAWNED ON Hermina that the room was entirely dark and she reached over and turned on the lamp next to the easy chair where she had been sitting all those many hours, unable and unwilling to move. As her vision adjusted to the light's intrusion, she gazed down at her hands, the color of strong coffee lightened with but a touch of cream. She unconsciously fingered the darker age spots that had come to dot them, standing out now like some tropical archipelago on the once unblemished surface, and she again thought about how she seemed to be getting blacker, a spot at a time. Her seen-it-all watery eyes, now milky with the attritions of age, fixed on the charm bracelet around her full left wrist as that hand's fingertips brushed back and forth, over and over again across the bumpy surface of the gold rock nugget on her opposite ring finger, both once the gifts and now but the mementos of her dead companion.

She had spent the night, it being Monday, over at his place. He had picked up some jumbo shrimp, a half pound of nice-sized scallops, a couple of soft shell crabs, some plum tomatoes and fresh basil and had set to work in the kitchen making what he called Linguini Fra Diavolo, one of those Italian dishes he loved to make for her. Flavored with dry sherry, the right amount of garlic, "never-too-much," he would say, and that generous touch of cayenne, it always made her think of the dishes passed down by the generations of Sea Island women on her mother's side. She thought about how he laughed when she called it Jewish Italian jambalaya and they ate it with fresh brick-ovened Italian bread, vinegary olive oiled lettuce and tomatoes, parmesan that he bought and grated fresh, and glasses of sharp Chianti.

She remembered marveling as she watched him eat. How he could still put it away, ingesting just about anything that caught his fancy as long as his upper plate wasn't bothering him, and despite the doctor's incessant warnings, the bouts of gout and phlebitis flare-ups, the recurring urinary inflammations, the prostate swelling, periodic kidney stones, and ever present heartburn. How he would dodge and rationalize when she tried to caution him and become irritated if she dare say anything about his diet while they were eating. She could hear him now, clear as if they were in the middle of dinner.

"Would yuh just let me eat in peace, already!?"

They had gone to bed early, not long after he finished the dishes and his daily litany of complaints about Mickey, and he had fallen asleep with his arm around her as usual after she removed the unlit cigar from his drowsing fingers. She now recalled how she had listened to him wheeze and cough in his sleep and how she hadn't thought anything of it. She tried to remember if she had heard him during the night when he went to use the john and light his cigar for a few puffs as was his habit, but couldn't recall. She remembered hearing him get up, as always before it was light out, his morning cough and toilet sounds, and the smell of the fresh-lit cigar coming from the bathroom. How he had muttered on about having to do something with Mickey, a closing on a Cadillac or something or other as he got dressed, and how she had barely listened through her interrupted sleep. She now imagined him tying his tie in front of the bedroom mirror as his lit cigar, perched next to him on the edge of the dresser, spiraled smoke toward the ceiling. She recalled how he leaned over, fresh shaven and smelling of Old Spice, and gave her that usual morning kiss on the cheek, the last one, it turned out, and said something about seeing her later that night.

It had been late afternoon but still light, sometime after three she figured, when Mickey called and told her. It was now totally dark out, well beyond early evening she imagined, and she thought about getting up to find out what time it was, but decided it really didn't matter.

Finally giving in to the mild burning pressure of her bladder, she gradually lifted herself up and slowly padded into the bathroom. Making her way back to the chair, she eased on down. Now bothered by the unwelcome company of the light, she reached over and pulled the chain on the table lamp and settled back into the comfort of the dark.

She thought back to when they had met and could still vividly recall the first time he walked into the lodge. She had just come in from one of those endless foot-aching shifts behind the service counter at the phone company and had been sitting at the bar, in those days one of the few ladies who frequented what was still a largely all male preserve.

It was one thing at the time for women to mark their right to have a drink and socialize, but something else entirely for a white man to come up in there in those days, especially after King had been shot, and all eyes in the place, some of them immediately hostile, took notice when Harry walked in with Bobbie Tyrell. He and Tyrell eased up alongside her and Bobbie introduced him to Houston, the barman, loud enough for everyone within easy earshot to hear.

"Brother Houston, I want you to say hello to my *main man,* Harry Rabin, him bein' the *whitest* black man in all o' New Haven, and a future brother of *this here* lodge."

That settled most of the turf concerns almost immediately as everyone, with the exception of some of the younger brothers, knew what kind of clout Tyrell had and respected him. Harry shook Houston's hand and with the back and forth horizontal wave of his index and middle finger moving as one over the bar, ordered a Dewars with a soda back for himself and the same for his host. Without hesitation, he motioned for the bartender to get the lady to his right whatever she was having and Houston placed a red plastic chip on the bar next to the drink she had working, a marker for the one to come. At that point they turned and faced each other and Bobbie made the introductions.

"Harry Rabin, allow me to introduce you to one of the few *sistuhs* that you'll definitely have to get to know if you wanna be welcomed up in here. *This* is Hermina DeCheneaux."

Harry extended his hand. "This is *the* Hermina? The one I've been hearin' so much about? Well, it certainly is my pleasure."

Already long tired of all those men, white and black alike, years of them, who immediately assumed too much because she happened to be sitting at a bar by herself, she corrected both of them.

"That's Her-MEE-na, with a long E, rather than Her-MY-na with a long I. I ain't to be confused with no vagina! You should know better than that, Bobbie Tyrell! You bes' not be tryin' to fool with me!"

Harry countered apologetically, "The pleasure is still mine, Miss Her-MEE -na, with the long E. I'm sure Bobbie didn't mean no offense."

Tyrell continued without losing a beat. "Harry's my *main man.* He works with me over on the Avenue... I suppose I bes' say I work for him... He's the general manager. Closes all the deals for me. A real pro! I was just tellin' Houston, and you may well have overheard, that he's the *whitest* black man in all New Haven."

"I do hope he's just really light," she quipped, "'cause he really can't be all *that white* if you're gonna be bringing him up in here! You *hear* what I'm sayin', Bobbie Tyrell?!"

She paused a moment and looked the stranger up and down, secretly admiring his natty dress, his double-breasted, wide-lapelled black blazer with its brass buttons and yellow silk peeking from the breast pocket, the pale yellow cotton button down and complimenting paisley tie, his flared gray slacks, and well-shined black tasseled loafers. Eyeing his dark wavy hair, neatly oiled and combed, she figured him for his mid-fifties, maybe six or eight years her senior, and picked up where she left off. "He certainly don't *look* like no *black* man I've ever seen, *whatsoever.* He gotta be *all white.*"

Extending his hand, Harry smiled as he took up the challenge.

"DeCheneaux? And what's that? French? You certainly don't look like no French woman I've ever seen before, neither. Unless, of course, you're somehow related to Josephine Baker. Now that I think of it, I do see a vague resemblance."

Recognizing the bull and accepting the compliment, she smiled and took his hand and thanked him for the drink that Houston had just refilled. Harry gestured a toast with his glass, and they simultaneously sipped. And that's how their twenty-year relationship began.

It was early 1970, she could all too easily recall. She was still grieving at the time though she had not realized it, still lost over the loss of her only boy, her baby, the year before, just turned eighteen and gunned down one night by some skittish white rookie on New Haven's force. Shot for being black and young and in the wrong place, out at the wrong time. The papers suggested that it had somehow been drug related and that's how most people, including lots of the folks she knew, had come to view it, even after the official inquest, largely unreported, labeled it a "regrettable accident," another case of mistaken racial identity. There had been some protests and well warranted charges of "white-wash" from some of the more militant younger brothers and sisters in the community, but the case all became overshadowed by the city's Black Panther uproar later that year, and most people quickly lost any interest. And by that time, she was too tired and spent to pursue a civil suit, despite the urging of some. She couldn't take what she regarded as blood money anyway.

Harry, too, was lost at the time they met, uprooted by the tragedy and scandal surrounding Mickey's first arrest and prison stint, and the two of them quickly recognized the mutual look of loss, an emptiness in each other's eyes, long before they discussed their separate worlds.

Their relationship started out simply. The only commonality they shared besides their grief was their taste for middle-brow scotch, his always chased with soda and hers with a touch of milk. When they finally got beyond the early small talk of discovery and the initial excitement and physicality of their first intimacies, they bonded in a way that was different for both of them, different than anything either of them had experienced before. They would later laugh about it sometimes and explain it in terms of age and experience.

She now reflected on all they had been through. The battles and the affections, the arguments and lies, the hard truths and stripped away honesties. She recalled those early years, all the subterfuge and sneaking around. Those years when he remained with his wife and how he would always leave in the middle of the night after a wonderful evening, making the whole thing feel cheap. And the interim years, after his and Esther's separation, after she found out and asked him to leave for the final time, about the same time he finally lost his job at the car dealership. How he had hemmed and hawed and made excuses about not moving in together, and how he took a room instead at that SRO motel, not having the money for an apartment, and got mad when she refused to visit, never mind stay for the night, in such a place.

And then there was the long period after Esther died. She thought about how heartsick he was, and how he came to her initially trying to conceal his grief and how it all came pouring out after a few drinks. How he sobbed and cried and how she held him during those long worst nights, unable to console.

She now sat there in the dark thinking about all the rest, the latter years, more than a decade together. She thought about his color thing, about how it changed and evolved over the course of their relationship. How she called him on it numerous times early on, his being so unconscious of the myriad subtle intrusions of race, his own ignorance; and how he had really taken strides to deal with his prejudice, and how she had begun to think he had really started to go color blind.

And then she thought how it never really went away, that *white thing*, how it would slither out, unexpectedly, in all sorts of ways. The fact that there were certain places they wouldn't go, to which he refused to take her, always irked her though she rarely said anything. It didn't matter that he would never dream of asking her to any function where one of his family, on either side, might show up and how that kept her from attending the weddings, bar mitzvahs and the increasing number of funerals of his Jewish world. And it didn't bother her when she found herself excluded from his Italian circle, those nights when he left her alone or showed up really late after partying, gambling and drinking and who-knew-what-else with his Fair Haven *goombahs*. She didn't ask, and he never offered. She never felt comfortable around those people anyway.

What bothered her most was how they always ended up at the same places, which eventually primarily meant the lodge on a Saturday night, and maybe an occasional Thursday or Friday. Once in a while dinner out at some out of town hideaway. It bothered her that they always stayed in, alternating between his place and hers, the same weekly routine as if they had become staged TV characters never leaving the set. And it now bothered her still that she had come to accept his infinite explanations, the excuses. That he didn't feel like going out because he was tired, or broke, or it was too cold or too hot, or his feet, or his gums, or his chest or his gout were bothering him. She thought about how easy it had all become and how old habits were so hard to kick, especially those grounded in the compromised comforts of aging companionship.

She began to wonder about how she was going to get to the funeral and thought about maybe calling a cab, but then realized that there would have to be some brothers from the lodge that would be going. At the same moment concerned about not putting anyone out, she pondered over who else she might get ahold of that had a car. She thought for a second about calling Mickey and ruled that out, not wanting to be seen as somehow connected to him in front of all those people who would probably be wondering who the hell she was anyway.

Wondering further about who might be there, she for some reason thought of David, the one Harry always talked about when his mind wasn't infected with all the bickering and carryings on of his other two. She could see him now, as plain as day, though she had only met him once. She felt like she knew him like a relative after all those years of listening to Harry tell the same stories over and over. She thought back on how proud the man was when his son finally finished his degree, and how happy he had been when his youngest finally got married. She could hear him now, the man going on and on, talking in the same breath, one instant about "My little one, the baby!" and the next about "My son, the professor!"

"What was it in? History or somethin'. Where was it?" she thought and then remembered. "It musta been Wisconsin 'cause that's where you went that time for the weddin' and we had that big fight 'cause you didn't want me along. Didn't even ask if I felt like goin'." She found herself reflecting back on that one time she and Davey had met and on the exchange that went on that evening.

Harry had called to explain that his "Son Number Three" had come for a visit, had shown up unexpectedly, and would be staying for a couple of days, but that there wasn't a problem; that the two of them would still have dinner as usual and relax for the evening at the apartment. That made it a Monday, or maybe a Wednesday, possibly a Friday, she recalled.

He picked her up and they stopped off for some groceries, the man so excited that his favorite had come that he spent way too much in the Stop and Shop, piling all kinds of stuff that he would never eat into the cart. When they got back to the apartment, Davey was sound asleep on the sofa. He stirred slightly when they walked in and Harry called to him as he placed the groceries on the kitchen counter.

"You still look bushed, sonny boy. Go back t' sleep and I'll give a little holler when dinner's ready."

The man cooked and woke his son just before placing the food on the table and Davey, still out of it from the long trip, sat up and scratched and groaned. Nowhere near awake nor aware of her presence, he started a bit when Harry called from the stove, introducing them.

"Hey, lover boy, say hello to my friend, Her-*MEE*-na, with a long E! Hermina say hello to Davey, my youngest."

David reached over for his glasses on the end table. Putting them on, he glanced over to where she was sitting, barely said hello, and without saying another word, picked up the remote from the coffee table and clicked on the TV.

The old man, distracted at the stove and preoccupied with the thought of sitting down to eat, must have sensed something when he turned and saw Davey wasn't seated yet. His chef's apron still on, he moved to the entry of the kitchen, placed his hands on his hips and looked directly over at the couch.

"What's the matter, Lub, arn'tchuh gonna eat? I cooked special. Made one of your favorites. You know. The mostaciolli with red clam sauce. *Al dente,* as the *paisans* say. I bought some fresh Italian bread from Rossitani's like you told me you can't get out there. I also fried up some hot sausage with peppers and onions. For later, in case yuh should feel like a little snack. There's some fresh deli, some pastrami, a caraway rye like you like, some potato salad and some nice sour tomatuhs. For t'marruh, I figured, but yuh can have some now instead, if you want. I don't want yuh should go hungry! Come! Com'on and eat!"

Excusing himself, saying something about how he was still tired, a little out of it, and that he would have something later on, Davey didn't move and just stared straight ahead at the screen. Harry made another attempt.

"Whatsuhmatter? You not feelin' good? Come on, I cooked special figurin' you'd have an appetite from all the travelin'!"

Davey just sat there so Harry, shrugging his shoulders and shaking his head, dished up the macaroni, placed the bread and a bowl of salad on the table, and sat down and filled his plate. Dishing himself up some salad, he forked some out for Hermina and without looking, made another attempt.

"Yuh know what I always say, sonny boy..."

"Let me guess," came the reply. "If you're bashful around here, you'll starve."

At that point Harry laughed as he turned to Hermina. "Tell me he ain't just like the old man! Tell me who he takes after!"

"God forbid," came the low voice from the couch, just barely audible above the TV, but just loud enough for Harry's ears, still sharp.

"You got somethin' to say, Davey?! Then say it! Did I fuckin' do somethin'?! Everything was fine th'safternoon. What the hell's eatin' you, all of a sudden!?"

"Nothing's wrong! I'm just really out of it. Tired, that's all. I just wasn't expecting company."

"Company?! *Who's* company?! You mean Hermina? *She's* not company around here. Maybe you forgot, but this is *my* place. If anyone's company here, it's *you!*"

"Look, I didn't mean to start..."

"Nobody's startin' nuthin'! I come home, glad you're here. I shop, buy out half the goddamn store. I cook special. I have Hermina come over for dinner like her and I often do. Tell her I have a special guest that I want she should meet. I was lookin' forward to the two of yuh meetin', figurin' you'd hit it off. And *this* is how you act?!"

"You're makin' a big t'do about nuthin'. I'm just tired, that's all. And I apologize. The two of you go ahead and eat. Don't worry about me. It's not like I'm a baby yuh gotta feed. I'm thirty-five years old, for krissakes!"

With that, Harry shook his head, swore silently to himself, poured himself a glass of wine, and motioning with the bottle to Hermina, filled her glass. He plunged into the bowl of macaroni, tearing chunks from the Italian bread and dabbing it in the sauce as he went, not to be deterred from his supper any longer.

Hermina, knowing he was aggravated, decided to let it rest. Not saying a word, she sat there and watched as the man shoved forkfuls into his mouth. Thinking about how he would pay for it later, she automatically turned to make sure that the large plastic bottle of Tums was in its usual place on the kitchen counter. Her gaze then turned toward Davey, sitting there looking at the tube, and she pondered his icy coolness, why he remained aloof, hardly saying a word. She wondered what it was between the two of them, the father and son. What was it, rooted deep in their history that she was unaware of? She then wondered if it was her presence. And which her? The other woman? Her blackness? Both? Neither?

She mulled it over as she nibbled at her salad and pasta. It troubled her the rest of that evening, even after David lay back down and dozed off again, and well after Harry finished eating, did the dishes, and dropped her off at home, saying he wasn't feeling good.

She found herself still pondering the same questions as she sat there motionless in the dark. She thought again about how she was going to get to the funeral. She found herself wondering about how Davey and the rest would respond to her presence and how she would find it in herself to say good-bye in front of all those strangers she already knew.

CHAPTER 12:

Embalmed

1989... LOUIE RETURNED TO THE prep room, the two bottles of scotch and the cigars in hand, as soon as Mickey left. Setting them down, he quickly glanced over at the corpse, now bluish gray, to see if his son had set its facial features. Seeing that he hadn't, that the dead man's mouth now stood slightly ajar, he suddenly remembered and turned to see if Steven had left the already opened bottle on the cart. Not surprised at its disappearance, he tore the red ribbon off one of the boxes without missing a beat. He silently thanked Mickey for the good fortune as he eased the fresh fifth of Red Label from its Christmas carton and unscrewed the cap.

The voice came from behind just as he raised the bottle to his lips. He pivoted and there sat Harry, looking just a bit more decrepit, poised upright on the edge of the embalming table.

"What the hell yuh doin' Louie? You're already good and *shikker!* Or is this how yuh gotta get before yuh can work?!"

"What?! You lookin' to start again? Why can't yuh just lie there and be quiet like everyone else, and leave me do my work? I got plenty t' do and yuh ain't makin' it any easier."

"What are yuh gettin'? *Senile*?! I'm sittin' here deader 'n dick and you're talkin' to me like we're playin' a hand uh gin. You ain't makin' it no easier on yourself, with all the booze. And since when did you take to drinkin *alone*?!"

"*Alone*? Alone, he asks! Who the hell's left I can drink with?! Wait...! Aha...! *Now* it comes to me. It took me a while but now I catch on. All of a sudden, of all people, Harry Rabin, he's gonna become *my* conscience? Set the moral standard and tell *me* how much *I* should or shouldn't drink? What *I* should or shouldn't do!? Don't this take the cake!"

"Hey Louie, you know me. I don't give a damn what yuh do on your own time! But right now you're workin' for me."

"So I'm workin' *for* you now, is it?! How 'bout we just say I'm workin' *on yuh,* and leave it lay!"

"That's my point! You ain't doin' that neither and I'm gettin' colder 'n hell layin' here with nuthin' on. Pretty soon I'll be stiffer than you. What do I gotta' do? Raise a stink around here? Yuh want I should do everything my goddamn self?!"

"This I gotta see. Go ahead! Embalm yourself.... Or maybe when you're good and ready, yuh can do the makeup and get dressed on your own. How the hell you gonna climb in the box?!"

"See! You're not listenin'! I need yuh to take care of things, and if yuh continue at the rate you're goin', they'll have trouble figurin' out which one of us is the stiff. They'll have to cancel t'marruh's main event so's yuh can sleep it off. Everyone'll have t' come back next week!"

"Main event! Christ, that reminds me! Did you ever tell your kids what happened that time with Julie and afterwards... mention it to them?"

"Who the hell brought that up?"

"That son of yours, Mickey. He asked me. Wanted t' know if I knew anything about somebody named Julie. Apparently you opened your mouth for a change and said something just after yuh had the heart attack, and again in the hospital before yuh checked out..."

"Yuh didn't say nothin', did yuh?!"

"Hell no! Who am I, not to let dead dogs lie! Besides, I gave yuh my word. Why would I go back on it now, after all these years? Lemme get t' work, would yuh?"

"Who's stoppin' yuh? Just keep that mouth of yours shut, and stop with the *shnapps,* already!"

"That's just what I was about t' do."

"Yuhr gonna stop with the drink?"

"Me? Hell no! I'm still the live one! I'm just gonna shut *your* mouth!"

With that, Louie took a long pull. Then pausing a second as if to collect his thoughts, he screwed the top back on and turned and placed the fifth on the cart next to the unopened bottle of Dewar's and the cigars. Without looking at the corpse, he removed his suit jacket and pulled on the long plastic work smock. He thought about the surgical mask, decided he didn't need it, and pulling on a fresh pair of rubber gloves, moved over to the table where Harry lay, silent once again.

Now ready to work, he leaned over close and examined the facial features. Sticking an index finger in the mouth, he checked and found what he was hoping for.

"Good! At least nobody swiped your choppers at that goddamned *gehenna* they call a hospital!"

He then moved to the enameled surgeon's chest behind him and opened the narrow top drawer. Drawing out a large spool of dark surgical thread, he snipped off a twelve inch length. Relying now on all those years of experience, with the automatic placement of the fingers he effortlessly, almost instinctively, on his first try passed it through the eye of a slightly curved two inch needle.

"Pretty good for an ol' man, close to blind," he thought. "Still got the ol' touch!"

"Impressed the hell otta me," came Harry's voice as Louie turned back to the corpse.

Pinching the man's bottom lip between the thumb and index finger and folding it down, he peered in as if to examinine the lower gums. Harry's head jerked to the side in protest.

"What the hell yuh tryin' t' do? Tear my goddamn lip off? What's with the needle!?"

"Somethin' I've been wantin' to do for seventy damn years! Finally, I get to shut you up!"

Taking hold of the now still body's nose and tilting the head slightly back to improve the angle of approach, Louie passed the needle into the left nostril and gently but firmly pressing downwards, directed it through the tissue. Then raising the upper lip to check its course as it pierced through, he worked it down further between the back of the top lip and the cadaver's upper plate. Pulling the lower lip forward with his free fingers, he deftly guided the needle past the bottom set of dentures and through the fleshy membrane, the frenulum he called it, at the front, inside base of the lip and gum. Doubling back, following the same route and again raising the top lip as he went so that he could guide its progress, he worked the needle upward so that it finally poked out the same nostril. Easing it up and out, he fashioned a quick, practiced surgical slip knot and carefully drew the loop tight as he pressed upwards on the chin with the thumb of his other hand, easing the jaw closed. Tying off the knot, he snipped and discarded the loose ends and examined the nostril to make sure his handiwork wasn't visible.

At that point, Harry again tried to say something but the voice came muted, inaudible from behind the sutured mouth. His eyes, now somewhat panicked, pleadingly begged his old friend but the undertaker would not be deterred. Playing then with the facial muscles, the cheeks, sides of the mouth and lips, Louie fixed the facial features. Taking a moment to glance over at the nearby whiskey bottles as if contemplating another drink, he reached over and placed the cadaver's arms across its body, resting right hand on left just below the diaphragm. He again talked to his friend.

"Just stay still now, otherwise you'll screw everything up."

Uncoiling the strands of plastic tubing from the embalming machine, he extended them up towards Harry's head, and then paused for a moment as he thought about his own condition. Not wanting to make a mess of things he opted for another entry point and wheeled the pump halfway down the table. He paused again for a second, gathering his memory, and with both hands, spread the body's thighs ever so slightly. At that point Harry lifted his head and Louie, now nonchalant, caught the absolute look of terror in the dead man's eyes.

"I shoulda known! Just like all the rest, for krissakes! Everytime I do this. Right away scared to death I'm gonna do somethin' with your *shmekel* or your *baitsim*? What's to worry, for cryin' out loud? It ain't like they're worth anything... like yuh need 'em anymore."

Louie paused once more, and realizing that he had skipped a step, addressed the body.

"Let me get those eyes of yours taken care of. At least then I'll be able to work in peace!"

Reaching back to the drawer, he grabbed a pair of eye caps. Opening the left eye, he laid one of the small nickel-sized disks, barbed at the edges, over the pupil, catching the lower edge under the bottom lid as he did so. Taking hold of the eyelashes, he then folded the upper lid down and hooked it on the cap, sealing the eye. His hand moved over to do the second eye but had trouble opening it. He again addressed the corpse.

"Yuh always had to make everything so damn difficult, didn't yuh? Just relax and let me do what I'm supposed t', here."

The eye resignedly eased open and Louie inserted the cap. That job done, he moved back down the table and reaching over, retrieved a scalpel from the collection of instruments spread atop the surgeon's chest. With a quick, practiced motion he cut a five inch incision to the inside of the right thigh perpendicular to the groin. Working swiftly, he then dissected the tissue, exposing the femoral artery and vein. Reaching to his work table, he retrieved the canula and inserted the sharp-tipped hollow tube, its hose running to the embalming machine, into the artery. He then attached the drain tubes to the vein, and checking to make sure the clamps were secure, opened and closed the small plunger attachment to check on the slight flow of blood that had already begun to seep from the hose. Closing the plunger, he reached over and started the pump and watched as the first bottle of rose-tinted formaldehyde and phenol mix began to empty. With that first liter nearly gone, he reopened the valve on the drainage tube. Again checking that the flow was right, he watched for an instant as the darkened blood, pushed by the pressure of the pump and the arterial entry of its replacement, began to pulse from the end of the open tube into the nearby runoff drain. He watched as the ears and back regained more of their natural color and temporarily closed the drainage tube to force additional embalming fluid more deeply into the recesses of the body. Connecting another bottle of the embalming fluid as he worked, he looked at his old friend.

"Yuh know, it ain't all that easy, havin' yuh here this way. I never really thought it would come to this. So just lay still so's I can finish gettin' yuh ready."

He sat back down as the monotonous hum of the pump did its work. The sound and the whiskey suddenly began to lull him and he began to drift. He drifted to another time.

CHAPTER 13:

War Work

1943... L OUIE HAD ALREADY BEEN waiting there for almost an hour and the late November chill had really started to get to him, so he began walking in place, his hands deep in the pockets of his overcoat, to force some warmth into his numbed toes. About to give up, he had just begun to mutter to himself when the white paneled bread truck, distinct with its red lettering and hand-painted multi-colored balloons, finally pulled around the corner from Legion onto Elliot. Figuring he'd surprise his pal, he crouched down behind a faded green pre-war Buick parked at the curb and watched as Harry drove past, slowed, and came to a stop just beyond the alley. He waited until the vehicle began to inch backward then quickly scooted down the sidewalk.

Watching in his side view mirror, Harry nudged the stick into reverse and had just begun to ease the ass end of the van between the brick walls on either side of the narrow alleyway when he caught some peripheral movement from the corner of his right eye, someone ducking low and moving fast around the nose of the truck. Not quite sure what he saw, but constantly on guard for hijackers and the cops, he quickly, almost instinctively reached for the taped blackjack cradled between his seat and the gearbox. But he wasn't fast enough, and Louie leapt up on the running board before he could make him out.

"Hey!" Velner blurted as he grabbed hold of one of the struts holding the driver's side mirror, "Where the hell yuh been!?"

Harry jumped. "For krissakes! Yuh scared the hell otta me! Yuh had me reachin' under the seat, already!"

"A lotta good that uh done yuh!"

"How many goddamn times do I gotta tell yuh, these *bullvons* they got drivin, some of them could be packin'. How the hell'd yuh know it was me and not somebody else?!"

"Aww! Go on! I saw it was you as soon as yuh come aroun' the corner. Between that beak of yours and the cigar, who 'n the hell could mistake that profile?! Who else would be lookin' to back up in here, anyways? And who, in God's name, would wanna knock over a Wonder Bread truck to begin with? I knew yuh'd show up!"

"What? Yuh think I'm the only one with a little side action? Get the hell off the truck! Yuh already fucked up my mirror. Go help me back in!"

"Yuh through for the day?"

"Nah, I got some stops yet. I called earlier and Goldman says he's got another delivery."

"So what's one more run?"

"I'm already in a hurry as is. Shoulda had this crate back by now. That Mic foreman of mine, he's gettin' too goddamn curious, a little suspicious. He's gonna look to put the bite on. I can feel it comin'. Get the hell off and help me back in, like I asked! I can't see a goddamn thing with yuh standin' in my way!"

"I'll take the ride with yuh after we finish up here, help yuh with the run."

"Yuh know I can't take anyone on the truck. All I need is for some *shmuck* to see me givin' you or anybody else a ride and I'll blow everything. I ain't about to risk my deferment for some petty bullshit."

"And you won't lose it if they find out what you been up to?"

"Hey, if they find out, it won't be the service I'll be worryin' about. Com' on, already! Quit bein' such a pain in the ass and give me a hand here. Go on back and make sure I'm clear of the barrels. Get me up as close to the back door as possible so's nobody can see what's what from the street."

Louie jumped down from the running board. Squeezing sideways along the wall until he cleared the truck, he walked backwards down the alley until he could see Harry, with that cigar of his sticking out of the side of his mouth and his cocked trucker's cap, framed in the side view mirror. Waving with the beckoning backward motion of his upstretched hand, he signaled for his friend to come on back and the truck inched up to within a foot of the swollen pickle barrels huddled against the wall to one side of Goldman's rear door.

"Ho!!" Louie yelled, and Harry clutched and placed the truck in neutral and pulled up on the emergency brake. Leaving it idle, he jumped down and quickly entered the back of the grocery. His friend followed and they made their way through the rear storeroom and crammed passageway leading to the front. Slightly parting the curtain that concealed them from whomever might be in the shop, Harry peered out to see who was there.

Asa Goldman was in his usual spot, sandwiched between the glass-enclosed counter and the wall stacked floor to ceiling with jars and canned goods at his back. Watching the old timer, Harry once again couldn't help to notice how this guy he had worked for ever since high school, standing there with his usual unlit half-chewed stub of a stogie resting at home in the corner of his mouth and that jowly bulldog scowl of his, had come to resemble some shirtsleeved, *shtetl*-style Churchill.

Wiping his hands on the bottom corner of his store apron, the grocer pulled a long length of twine from the spool sitting on the anchored dowel to his left. He quickly wrapped it around the package several times in one direction. Pivoting the parcel a quarter turn on its axis, he then made several more passes with the string, and finished off with a quick practiced knot. Pulling a scissors from the jar kept next to the register, he snipped the twine and slid the bundle across to Mrs. Markowitz, standing there counting her change. The woman took the package and placed it in her cloth shopping bag. As she tucked her purchase away, Goldman instinctively gazed back at the curtain, as if guided by a sixth sense. Noticing Harry, he signaled with a quick cautioning eye to stay put and returned his attention to the old woman.

"And remember, Beccah... uh... Mrs. Markowitz, give my regards to your sister when you see her. Tell her she should come and see me, she shouldn't be such a stranger!"

Mrs. Markowitz set her bag down on the counter and tightened the ends of her *babushka*. "I will, don' you *vurry*. I've *alvays* known, all these years, that you had a soft spot for her, *ven ve vas yunk* even. I'll tell her you *vas askink'. Dun'* you *vurry*, Mr. *Goltman!*"

"*Zeig geh zindt*, Mrs. Markowitz."

"The same to you, *Goltman, geh gezund t' heit!*"

As the bell above the front door jingled and the woman exited, Harry stepped from behind the curtain, with Louie on his heels. Goldman came out from behind the glass case, again wiping his palms on his apron.

"Boy oh boy, such a *yenteh*, that one, you wouldn't believe! She's been trying to fix me up with her sister, this one that godda be the queen of Legion Avenue *mieskeits*! For over thirty goddamn years, she's been tryin', like I ain't been married almost that long and I don' got two kids!"

"Tryin' to fix *you* up?! There's *mies*, and there's *mies*, but can the sister really be that ugly?"

"Don't be so smart! Nobody likes a wise guy! Where 'n the hell you been? Mrs. Welstein, you know, the ritzy one.... What's she call herself now? Wellstone? Anyway, she and this guy that works for the husband, the one I tol' yuh he must be *shtooping* her, they were here early this mornin'. Took a big order. She's gonna pay cash, no ration books or stamps. All prime stuff. I told her I'd send you with the delivery. You here with the truck?"

"No, I'm here with my *zehdeh's* horse and wagon! Where's it gotta go?"

"Alden Avenue, off Fountain, by Westville. One of those big apartment houses, you know, across from the Cat'lic church there. Her husband, the necktie *macher*, he got some big war contract making somethin' for the Army. Shirts, or maybe *gotkes*, who knows what. Anyway, he's gone and set her up pretty good up there in her own place, from what I hear."

"You gotta be kiddin'! I can't make that run now. It's what? Eleven? Eleven-thirty? I've been out since five. They're beginnin' to get suspicious already, askin' why I'm always out so long with the truck."

"What? All of a sudden, the money's no good? How many times do I have to tell yuh? Yuh gotta spread some of it around. Don' be penny wise and dollar foolish! Who's given yuh the hard time? That *Irisher* foreman? The dispatcher? What was it that anti-Semite used to say, you know, the one from where was it? Louisiana? What did he used to tell all them rubes before they bumped him off?"

"You mean the Kingfish?"

"Yeah, you know where I'm goin'. You gotta share the wealth!!"

"Share the wealth?! I knew they'd get yuh someday! You're startin' to sound like one of them Reds sellin' papers on the goddamn corner!"

"Red, shmed! Your *tuchas* will turn red before I do! Start throwin' them *shnorrers* a few bucks, that's all...! Give 'em a *bissel geshmekt* each week and they'll back off. Hear what I'm tellin' yuh!"

"It's your stuff I'm haulin', you're makin' a bundle, but I don't see you goin' in your pocket!"

"*I* should *pay*?! Knowin' you, with all the action out there, you're probably makin' more than me, just drivin' that *fahrshtunkeneh* bread truck around all mornin'!"

"So now you're my bookkeeper? Let me get the boxes and get the hell o'tta here. What with the baby not feelin' good, Esther's probably worryin' already how come I ain't home by now!"

"Good! Back to work, where you belong! That's what I like to hear! And you, Velner, standin' there, up to no good as usual."

"What did I do?"

"Who said you did anythin'? Go up by the front and keep an eye. Make some noise if anyone looks to come in. Let 'em in, but don' let nobody come in back. Pretend like you're already some successful undertaker and you're greetin' some grievin' relative! Be a gentleman, for a change. Like you work here. And if they ask for me, tell whoever it is I'm indisposed, you know, and I'll be right out. Not 'he's in the toilet,' like yuh said last time! Come, Hareleh!"

With that, Goldman stepped through the rear curtain and reached up on the narrow shelf hugging the wall in the passageway. Pulling on the release secreted behind a row of dusty canned peaches, the aging grocer, still strong as an ox, slid the shelf sideways with his shoulder and stepped into the concealed storeroom as Harry followed. Reaching up, he pulled a string on the overhead fixture, lighting the secreted vault as Harry glanced around the six by eight foot chamber, what he and the boys had come to refer to as "Goldman's Grotto".

His boss usually pulled the loaded boxes into the passageway or set them by the back door, ready to go, so it had been some time since the old man had allowed even him into the *inner sanctum*. Marveling at what he saw, his eyes moved up and down the well-stocked shelves lined with nothing but the best -- the array of processed meats in their oblong tins; the stacked cans of albacore, pink salmon, and imported kippered herring; the rows of five and ten pound bags of sugar and packages of baker's chocolate, worth their weight in gold. His eye caught the several crates of Chivas Regal, Crown Royal and C.C. sitting in the middle of the floor and his mouth began to water with the sight of the large Hershey almond bars. He imagined someday snatching a box of premium Cuban cigars for his own enjoyment.

It came to him then for an instant, the memory triggered perhaps by the hum of the small deli cooler filled with bricks of butter and flats of fresh eggs or maybe just the smell of the place. The slap. As startlingly sharp and clear as if he was ten once again, sitting there in his father's the old truck with the rain tapping on the roof and an enraged Izzie there at the wheel. The time he hid the slice of ham and caught a good backhand and a ride home in the rain with the chickens for his trouble. He laughed to himself at the memory as his boss, focused elsewhere, pointed to four cardboard boxes sitting on the floor.

"Yuhr not payin' attention! The address is here, on top of the first box, along with the bill. This one, she's gonna pay when you get there. C.O.D.. And don't take no for an answer. She said she'll have the cash, and she's good for it, believe you me. Just remember, no stamps. And get the payment in full! No nonsense!"

Harry knelt and picked up the first box as Goldman continued. "And handle the boxes with care, you shouldn't drop anything. There's eggs and butter and chocolate, and some glass jars, strawberry preserves and such, and five bottles of Canadian and V.O, so whatever you do, be careful. She even bought a pair of silk stockings that I traded from Gandelman. The women, all they can get is nylon right now. Boy, I'm tellin' yuh! You shoulda seen this one, the way she touched them to her face, it made my old *petzel* tingle a little. I thought she was gonna faint! I'm going back up front. I'll have your friend, the mortician, come give you a hand. And remember, get the money on delivery. We're talking over a hundred dolluhs here!"

"And when do I get my cut? This makes four stops I made for yuh today. That makes twelve since the beginning of the week and I'm walkin' around broke!"

"Who you talkin' to, Hareleh? *Broke*? *You're* broke?! You forget you're talkin' to the master? You gamblin' again?"

"Naw! I just need a little extra, that's all."

"I tell yuh what. Take what Mrs. Welstein... I mean Wellstone, take what she gives yuh. Deduct it from what I owe and I'll get the rest to yuh later in the week. And make sure you slide the panel back and secure it before you leave!"

Goldman moved toward the front of the store, but turned for a second before passing through the curtain.

"And by the way, before I forget, tell this one she should remind her husband I got gas coupons, more ration books, if he still needs. He mentioned something last week. And don't forget to slide the door shut."

Louie stepped into the storeroom and picked up one of the remaining boxes and the two of them lugged the cartons out back. Wedging his box against the truck, Harry opened the back door and they slid the contraband inside.

"So where we goin'?" Louie asked.

"You never stop, do yuh? I already tol' yuh, yuh can't ride on the truck!"

"So how long yuh gonna be?"

"At least another hour now, before I get back to the plant. Asa got me goin' all the way over to Alden Avenue, and I gotta make another stop."

"Where at?"

"What are yuh? My partner, all of a sudden?! Does Macy's tell Gimbel's?!"

"Since when ain't we partners?"

"Look! What yuh don't know, won't hurt yuh! I got some other action to take care of, that's all!"

"Oh-h-h-h! So now yuhr such a big *macher* all of a sudden, you forget your best friend?"

"I ain't got time, okay? Help me load the other boxes before I get a hernia, here! I'll catch up with yuh at the smoke shop later th'safternoon."

The two of them went back in, retrieved the remaining boxes and slid them into the van. Harry closed the doors and turned to Louie as they made their way to the front of the truck.

"You okay?!"

"It just so happens, I'm a little short."

"So *nu*?! How did I know you wasn't waitin' for me just to say hello!"

"Hey, yuh're hurtin my feelin's! Lemme hold a double sawbuck. I'll give it to yuh when my brother, the hunchback, straightens out."

Reaching into his pocket, Harry pulled out a neatly folded wad, peeled off a twenty, and handed it to his pal.

"When am I gonna see it?"

"You'll have it next week."

"When, next week?"

"Next week's next week! Don't worry about it!"

"Yuh definitely gonna be at the club later?"

"Yeah, sure. Butter said he's got somethin' on for us. I'll see yuh there, about nine, say."

Harry climbed up into the driver's seat. Checking the side view mirror again, he reached over to the ashtray and retrieved his cigar. Adjusting his cap as he looked in the mirror, he released the brake, shifted into gear, and pulled forward out of the alley. Louie watched him drive off. Then coolly sliding the twenty into his pants pocket, he hiked up his collar and made for the avenue.

It was almost one by the time Harry finished with the order at the Wellstone's. He had hoped to use the dumb waiter, but it was out of order, and he wound up having to shlep the boxes, one at a time, up the four flights. Neither the paramour nor her husband was around and the lady of the house, with little on but a powder blue kimono, a pair of white fur slippers, and a slight martini buzz, was clearly suffering from a mild case of the mid-afternoon lonelies. She flirted with him some and threw him an extra ten spot for his efforts after he brought the last box up and collected for the order.

He had hoped to stop downtown and place a bet on the hockey game at Montreal, but figuring it was already too late, he decided to get the truck back. As he drove down lower Whalley, he thought about Mrs. Wellstone, how her robe fell partly open, giving him a little peek, when she handed him the money. He wondered if it was intentional, or just the gin, or both, and he thought about what it would have been like.

"One of these days, boy, one of these older women with lots of dough, a quickie in the afternoon, it couldn't hurt."

His thoughts then turned to how much he had to do, and how much was out there, waiting to be had.

"No time to be screwin' around," he concluded as he pulled around onto Goffe and wheeled the van into the Wonder Bread yard.

He immediately noticed Mallory, the foreman, on the loading dock with his hands on his hips, his leather flight jacket wide open, his gray teamster's cap cocked back, standing there in his usual pissed-off pose. Harry no sooner came to a stop and stepped down out of the truck when the guy, coming at him, started in.

"Where the hell yuh been, Rabin?"

"Where do yuh think I've been?"

"You tell me! Since when's it take a guy almost eight hours to drop off a truck load of bread and pick up some day olds?!"

"It don't!"

"Then how do yuh explain where you was so long?"

"It's simple. I finished up what I had to do, and I stopped off to see the wife and my kid. I already tol' yuh the kid ain't feelin' good... Since when's that a crime?"

"It ain't. But how long did that take yuh?"

"Hey Mallory, ain't you married? Or don't you Cat'lics ever get it on when it's light out?! I went home and spent a little time, you know, with the wife, and caught a few winks. That's all."

"You're a lyin' Sheeny fuck! I got a call from one of my buddies two hours ago. He seen yuh drivin' in Westville this mornin', way off your route, and I know you ain't gone and moved away from Legion Avenue."

"So now yuh got spies out checkin' on us drivers!? What's the big fuckin' deal?! I went to visit a friend for a minute!"

"There's no big fuckin' deal, 'cept we know what you've been up to, usin' our trucks to haul your contraband shit all over town. Wha' do yuh take me for? Some kinda asshole?!"

"Hey, if the shoe fits..."

"You little Jew fuck, I ought t' beat your ass right here and throw you out in the gutter! I got two brothers fightin' in the Pacific this minute and a cousin of mine bought it in North Africa! For what? So you can drive around profiteerin' on the black market!?"

"Cut the shit, Mallory. I ain't seen you run to sign up! You gonna try and tell me you ain't on the take like everyone else around here?! The only difference between me and you is I don't look to hide behind some patriotic 'pullin' your weight on the home front' bullshit. Let's me and you cut the crap."

A voice came from behind them. "You think it's bullshit?!

Neither of them had seen the guy before he spoke, and they both turned and fell silent as soon as they saw his uniform. It was as if he had appeared out of nowhere, standing there with his dress army coat draped over his shoulders, his bandaged left hand, immobilized in a white sling, protruding from underneath.

The vet turned to Harry. "Did you hear me? I asked yuh, do yuh think it's bullshit? The war. Guys fightin' and dyin' for what we got over here?! D' yuh think it's bullshit?!"

"No, but…"

"But what, then?!"

"Tell him, soldier!" Mallory interjected.

"Who the fuck's askin' you! It looks to me like you ain't never left this fuckin' yard, and yuh sure as shit don't strike me as no hero. Take a fuckin' hike!"

In a fluid practiced motion, the soldier came out from inside his coat with his good hand and flicked the stiletto open, bringing it up to Harry's chin. Looking straight into Harry's eyes, he addressed the Irishman without turning his head. "I thought I told you to take a fuckin' walk!"

Half backing up, Mallory got the message, smiled, and disappeared around the truck and up the stairs of the loading dock. The soldier paused for an instant, the knife still close to Harry's face. Harry broke the silence.

"Where the hell'd you come from!"

"It don't matter. It look's like I showed up just in time."

"When'd yuh get back?"

"I landed in New York yesterday, and hopped the train this mornin'."

"It's good to see yuh, Gambi."

"Yeah, it's good to see you to, Harr."

"You gonna put the blade away?"

"I don' know. Thought maybe I'd give my old *lantsman* friend a little trim. Maybe take some off , what the *mohel* mighta missed!"

The soldier folded the knife, slid it back into his pocket, and the two men hugged.

Giuseppi Gambardella, or Gambi as they called him on the street, waited by the back of the truck until Harry finished his routine in the dispatch office. Leaving the yard, the two crossed the street to Harry's beater of a Chevy and the soldier threw his duffel in the back as they got in.

"So where to?" Harry inquired as they pulled away from the curb.

"Back over by the Avenue. Figure I'll stay with my cousin on Orchard Street. I ain't even seen Mama yet. Gotta gear up 'cause she don't know I was hurt, and she's gonna go otta her friggin' mind when she sees the sling and bandages. She's liable to give pop another heart attack, for sure."

"Whatever you wanna do, but how long you think you can put off gettin' over there? Somebody'll see yuh, word'll get back, and you'll end up with the both of them madder 'n hell at yuh for not comin' home right away.'"

"Don't worry. I was plannin' to see them tonight or first thing in the mornin'. That's what I come t' N'Haven straight away for, rather than stoppin' off in Fair Haven."

"I wish I could be there to see Mama's face when you walk through the friggin' door!"

"Yeah, it'll be somethin', boy. What's with this *scungilli* foreman of yours?"

"Yuh shoulda seen his face when I went back in the office to check out. The asshole looked genuinely disappointed, like he was hopin' not to see me in one piece, still alive! He's just lookin' to put the bite on, that's all. Jealous 'cause he gotta hang around the loadin' dock all day and can't get in on the action."

"You guys union?"

"Yeah, Teamsters."

"Good. That's what I was hopin'. T'marruh or the next day, after I see my mother and the ol' man, I gotta run over to Fair Haven and see some people. You know..... Pay my respects and whatnot."

"You goin' back?"

"What else am I supposed to do? Placing the tips of his thumb and index finger on his good hand nearly together, he gestured to Harry. "I was this far from bein' made when I went away. And now, with my war experience... hey, yuh know. What do I gotta tell yuh, yuh don' already know? Yuh interrupted. I was sayin' as soon as I get over there, I'll arrange to have a couple of people pay this asshole a visit, give him a little talkin' to. He won't bother yuh no more."

"That's good, 'cause I certainly don't need him bloodsuckin' me dry."

"Don't you worry 'bout nuthin'. In a day or two, believe you me, he'll be payin' you to keep the truck out late! And the word'll come down from the fuckin' union, t' boot. Just steer clear until we straighten his ass out."

Harry paused a moment, and looked straight ahead as if the road had suddenly caught his attention. He then continued.

"So how bad is it?"

"How bad's what?"

"Your arm."

"Nothin' serious, it'll heal. They said it just takes time, that's all."

"What happened?"

"Nothin' much. Took a chunk of shrapnel in the shoulder and a piece in the upper arm. My hand was good and fucked up, but it's okay."

"Where?"

"Salerno."

"Salerno! Boy! I read about that one in the papers. That musta been a bitch!"

"I don't wanna talk about it. Someday maybe."

"What was it like in Italy? Did yuh get to see where your mother and father came from?"

"Naw, we was on the other side, above Rome. I felt real funny about it at first. You know, bein' in the old country, worryin' about having to shoot some *paisans,* but that wore off pretty quick. Besides, the only real opposition we saw was all

Kraut units."

"Did yuh get any?"

"What you mean? Like broads?"

"What's uh matter? You ain't been laid in a while, or what?! I'm talkin' Nazi bastids!"

"What did I tell yuh, before I went over? Didn't I promise yuh, if I got the chance?"

"Boy, it musta really been somethin'!"

"Let's drop it, okay? Let's just say I seen enough dead and dyin' to last awhile."

Harry took the hint and just drove. Wheeling across Broadway and onto Howe Street, heading south toward the harbor, they soon reached the intersection where Oak Street and Legion sliced in at an angle. Turning right, they slowly made their way up the congested avenue and finally turned left on Orchard. Pulling over in front of the walk-up where the cousin lived, Harry placed the car in neutral, and turned to his friend.

"How you doin'? Yuh sittin' okay?"

"Ahh, you know... the fuckin' Army, they're always in a hurry for yuh to die, run on up on some beach somewhere and get shot, but yuh gotta wait for everythin' else, with them. At least I'm out now. Paid my fuckin' dues."

Without saying another word, Harry leaned to his left and reached into his right pants pocket. Coming out with his wad, he unfolded it and peeled off four hundred dollar bills. He reached over and placed the money in his friend's hand.

"What's this?!"

"What's it look like?"

"I can't take this, Harr. Christ! This kinda dough! I wasn't lookin' t' set yuh back!"

"Hey, Joe! Yuh been away awhile, right? You have no idea what the war's meant here on the street. You ain't settin' me back nuthin'! If yuh don't want to take it as a gift 'cause I'm glad to see yuh back home, alive and well, then consider it a loan. Let's just say you owe me one, that's all. Someday, maybe..."

"You're too much, Harr. Always been!"

"Cut with the bullshit and get the hell out. And go see your mother! Tonight, for cryin' out loud...! Before somethin' happens to your other arm!"

Gambi laughed and reached over with his good hand and touched his friend's shoulder. He got out of the car and crossed the street and Harry watched as he went up the steps and through the door of the tenement. Easing the car into first, he headed for home.

CHAPTER 14:

The Truck Stop

1989… DAVID FIGURED MICKEY HAD gotten lost somewhere and had just begun to marvel at how his big brother had come to resemble Harry on that count when the phone rang. Howard hollered from upstairs to pick up and Davey looked over at the clock on the mantel. After ten. He had already begun to doze off on one of the large sofas in front of the big screen TV but halfheartedly got up, grabbed the phone from its spot on the kitchen island, and immediately began to pace with the receiver to his ear, as was his habit, as soon as Mickey's voice started in.

"What's doin'?"

Knowing full well he would still be listening, David called to Howard to hang up, waited a second for the click of the upstairs phone, and responded.

"Nuthin'. Just layin' here, starin' at the set."

"What's he doin'? Worried he might miss somethin'?"

"Nothing changes."

"I gotta talk to yuh. Can yuh meet me?"

"Sure. You okay?"

"Yeah, I'm alright. Just thought we could hang out for a while, that's all."

David grabbed a note pad from the counter and scrawled the directions. Hanging up, went up to tell Annie he was going out. Already feeling somewhat closed in by the strangeness of it all, the unaccustomed chaos and alien, frantic commotion of her husband's home world, she immediately jumped at the opportunity to get out for a while and leapt up from the bed and the novel she had brought along. She insisted on going and Davey, sensing her state, offered no resistance.

The two of them were just about to turn down the stairs when Howard poked his head out from his and Richie's room.

"What's he want at this hour?"

"Nuthin'. Sounds pretty down, that's all. Figure'd I'd go see him for awhile. I sorta promised earlier."

"Where's he want yuh to meet him?"

"Somewhere up north of Wallingford. Some truck stop off 91. Sounds from his description like it's almost to Meridan."

"That figures. He's livin' out there somewhere with the latest one, Gina. Have you had the privilege?"

"Yeah. He brought her to the wedding. Don't yuh remember?"

"Why'd you have to remind me? Now I'll never get to sleep… He's been livin' somewhere in Wallingford with her, at her mother's, I think. Stayin' out of N' Haven pretty much, from what I hear. Must owe somebody 'cause he's really been scarce…."

"Look, I gotta run. We'll probably be awhile, knowin' him, so don't wait up."

"Okay. I'll see yuh in the morning. And don't let him get to yuh."

"Don't worry! He won't."

It took them nearly an hour to reach the truck stop. The sting of sharp wind swooping across the misnomered "oasis" whipped into the two of them as soon they opened their car doors, and Annie immediately fled across the lot for the shelter of the all-nighter. The Connecticut Yankee wind with its silent memories of distant winter nights grabbed her husband in the meantime, and he paused for a moment as if frozen in place and time. Turning with his back to the restaurant, he gazed up at the stars, near-full moon, and blue-black sky, all crystalline clear. He looked off at the outline of hardwooded hills looming above the interstate valley, dotted here and there with rural home light. Unconsciously raising his collar, he paused to wonder what it all might have looked like before the intrusions of concrete and steel and incandescent light. He inhaled a winter breath tainted with the taste of diesel and the fumes pulled his vision toward the chromed and pinstriped Peterbilts standing out among the double row of slumbering, long-haul giants huddled at one side of the plaza. Pausing a second longer, he listened to their night-rest yellow-lit rumblings until the rhythmic rattling breath of their engines snapped the cold night spell and prodded him back on course. He hurried across the lot, looking to spot Mickey's Corvette as he went.

Catching his reflection for a second as he passed through the double glass doors, he stepped into the eye-stabbing florescent and neon of the Union 76. He found Annie waiting there, already staring back into the asphalt night, her shoulders hunched up from the cold, her hands in her pockets, wondering where he had disappeared to. They stood there just inside the door as his vision adjusted to the overlit interior and his eyes scanned the room, the counter and tables busy for the hour with a grab bag of over-the-road wanderers and New England nighthawks.

A pink-polyestered graveyard waitress coffeeing the tabled truckers and flotsam of caffeine junkies caught sight of them through tired and indifferent second job eyes and gestured for them to sit anywhere. Davey automatically knew where to look and he immediately spotted his big brother sitting there alone in a usual vantage point spot, a far corner booth away from the windows, his back to the wall, facing the door. They acknowledged each other across the place with their timeless brother to brother nod and David directed Annie down a narrow aisle toward the raspberry vinyl booth.

Mickey, from short distance, appeared weary in the eyes, overtired. In front of him at center table amidst several crumpled napkins sat a half full ashtray and two emptied restaurant plates, one smeared with pepper flecked ketchup and the other streaked with a missed trace of chocolate cream pie, his long-time favorite. As they reached the booth, he got halfway up and offered them both a quick automatic greeting hug and furtive smile which David read from the start. From the style of the welcome and a certain nervousness barely concealed beneath the visible grief, David knew something was up. He shelved any comment, knowing full well that whatever was on his brother's mind would eventually find its way out.

The couple eased into the worn bench opposite Mickey as he retrieved a recently lit Salem from the ashtray and took a long drag, collecting a thought. David watched as his brother drew the smoke in and the way in which he warily surveyed the room as he exhaled, and knew for sure that something else besides Harry was on the agenda. Knowing Mickey would take the lead, he remained silent.

"What's she doing here?"

"Who's *she*? You mean Annie? Didn't I let you know before that you shouldn't refer to her in the third person in her presence? The name's Annie! Get it!?"

"Hey! I ain't one of your college educated friends so cut with the third person crap. I just thought you were comin' by yourself, that's all. There's some stuff I gotta talk to yuh about, you and me."

Annie interrupted. "If you wish to talk in private…, if there's something you'd rather not have me hear, I can go sit at the counter."

David turned toward Annie, "No, you ain't goin' nowhere." He then turned to Mickey. "This might sound odd to you, but Annie's family. There's nothing you can say in front of me that you can't say in front of her! What's uh matter?! Yuh think she's wearing a wire or something?!"

"Hey, lighten up! I didn't mean nuthin'. I was just surprised to see her…, uh Annie. I thought you were comin' by yourself, that's all."

"So now that we got that straightened out, next case. How yuh doin'?"

"I ain't stopped since long before I saw yuh, th'safternoon. One goddamn thing after another. Right after I left you at the airport, I get called down to see my P.O."

"What'd he want?"

"Nuthin. Just lookin' to bust my chops. You know. I then had to run home and pick up some clothes, and..."

"To Gina's?"

"No, home. To my place."

"Was Angela there? How's things with her?"

"The usual bullshit."

"And the kids?"

"They're alright. They'll be there t'marruh. I then had to run back downtown to police headquarters and shell out four hundred for a rent-a-cop, a New Haven uniform for t'marruh."

"For tomorrow? For what?"

"For the funeral."

"What the hell you expect? Gun play?"

"Hey, it ain't no goddamn joke. The shit's serious!"

"What are you talkin' about?"

"Fuckin' Gina and Angela, the both of 'em."

"You don't mean you're still fuckin' the *both* of them!?"

Mickey laughed. "Com'on. Don't play games. Yuh know that ain't what I meant! They're both comin' t'marruh, to the funeral, and they definitely gotta be kept apart. They got into it real bad once before at this shoppin' mall... in Hamden back a couple of weeks ago. Scratchin' and kickin'. Pullin' hair and whatnot."

"Yeah, Howard mentioned. He also told me I got a new nephew."

Mickey grinned a proud father smile. "Yeah, he looks like me!" He then regained his train of thought. "So anyways, I paid for this cop to keep an eye on Gina. If either of them start anything, he's under orders to arrest both of 'em or anyone else who decides to get stupid."

A waitress in a tight brown uniform, in her late thirties perhaps, Italian-looking with pinned-up black wavy hair, came over, coffee pot in hand. Overly made up but somewhat attractive in a night diner kind of way, she smiled and looked at David as if Annie did not exist. "What can I get yuh, hon?"

Mickey interrupted. "Loretta, let me introduce you to my kid brother David, visitin' from Wisconsin, and his wife."

Annie quickly extended her hand and the two women shook. "Hi! My name's *Annie,* and I'll have a BLT and a glass of milk."

The woman placed the coffee pot down, pulled a pen and pad from her black cocktail apron, and scrawled the order. David asked for a coffee and an English muffin as Mickey continued, facing Loretta.

"You wouldn't have no way of knowin', but my father died yesterday. I woulda called yuh, but I was busy. Yuh know. With the arrangements and all."

"Oh, hon, I'm so sorry."

"Hey, it's all right. The funeral's t'marruh at nine-thirty at Velners' in N'Haven. Yuh know where it is? On George Street? I'd appreciate it if you could make it. While you're at it, yuh might as well bring me another piece of pie, the usual. And come join us when yuh get a chance."

David and Annie exchanged a quick why-am-I-not-surprised kind of look as Loretta moved off. Mickey smiled one of his coded "what-the-hell" grins at his brother and resumed.

"Where was I? Oh yeah! You won't believe this! I received word that they're lettin' Jimmy come down for the funeral. I heard earlier tonight."

"How in the hell did yuh arrange that one?"

"Hey, you know..., some connections the ol' man had. He knew a lot of people, boy. They're bringin' the kid down from Vermont. He might even be on his way by now. I had to pay for two escorts, a couple of Vermont state troopers. That's costin' me another twelve hunnert, but I figure what the hell, this way everybody can get to see him and he'll be at the funeral. After all, he was the ol' man's first grandson, right? The money don't mean shit, anyway."

"So let me see if I got this straight. You're layin' out four hundred for the New Haven cop to keep Gina and Angela away from each other. And you're shellin' out twelve hundred more to bring Jimmy down...?"

"Hey, that ain't nuthin'! I got into it with that faggot brother of yours at the funeral parlor today, before you got in. He immediately starts runnin' his mouth to Louie Velner about this and that, how I owe him from who-the-hell-knows-when, so I says to him, 'Howard, just t' show yuh I ain't got no beef, I'll pick up the entire tab for the ol' man. So there!' I can be a *mensch* too, yuh know. He thinks he's so goddamn smart with his fancy suits and that house of his in Woodbridge, all the phony friends and those cars he pays too much for! I tol' him, boy!"

"So where you gettin' the money?"

"Does Macy's tell Gimbels? Don't worry about it, little brother. I know yuh ain't got it right now, but someday you can take care of me. Don't you worry."

The waitress returned with their order and as she eased the piece of pie down in front of Mickey, he slid his big left hand around her and casually, affectionately placed it on her hip, pulling her closer in a show of familiarity and ownership, looking to impress. In the same motion, he took a big gouge of chocolate cream with his other hand and shoveled it into his mouth. She didn't flinch, clearly accustomed to the moves of this one customer, and his arm rested around her as he talked through the pie filling, taking a second to wipe his lips.

"So you gonna try and make the funeral t'marruh?"

"I don't know. I don't get otta here till five-thirty, and gotta be back at three. Workin' the split, and I'm pretty beat already."

"See what yuh can do. I'd appreciate it."

"Will the wife be there?"

"Yeah, the whole family, everybody."

"Then I don't know if I should..."

"Hey, that won't be a problem. Believe me. I'm just askin' yuh try and make it. That's all."

As Loretta moved away, Mickey shifted his gaze back across the table. Grinning at his brother, he resumed.

"Kinda nice lookin', don't yuh think? Where was I? Oh yeah. So I shelled out some serious cash today. Big fuckin' deal. Yuh can't take it with yuh. Even the ol' man couldn't figure that one out, and if he couldn't, no one will."

"Lemme ask yuh somethin'."

"Go ahead, shoot."

"What else is goin' on with you, I mean besides the ol' man?"

"Nuthin'. I'm alright. It's just that it happened all so quick. One minute he's here, carrying on like usual, and the next..."

"Who you talkin' to, here? You tryin' to tell me I don't know when somethin's goin' on with my own brother? You're chain smoking. And anxiety eating, this late at night. The second hunk of pie was the dead give away. And yuh keep looking around the room like you're expectin' company. What else is going on with you?"

"Nuthin. It's just the ol' man."

"Okay. Fine. Let me phrase it differently. What *else* is going *on*?"

Mickey turned to Annie. "Ain't he incredible, my little brother? He don't let up, once he catches the scent. Never misses a trick! Reminds me of my mother. You woulda liked Esther. She always knew when somethin' was wrong. She didn't miss a beat, neither."

Countering the attempted dodge, David reached across the table and took his big brother's right hand in both of his. He removed the fork and placed it on the pie plate, and stared straight across, eye to eye.

"Talk to me, Mickey."

And with that contact made across the booth, the charade ceased. Mickey's tone changed and he looked, suddenly sad faced, into Davey's eyes.

"I got a serious fuckin' problem. Maybe your wife... sorry, I mean Annie... she shouldn't have to hear."

"It's okay, believe me. Like I said, she's family. What's goin' on?"

"Well, remember earlier I told yuh I had to stop and see my PO? I went down there and there were these two Feds, FBI, in his office lookin' to talk to me."

"What'd they want?"

"Nuthin' really. Just lookin' to bust my chops. Wantin' to turn up the heat a little."

"Yeah, so wha'd they *want*?"

"They claimed the people from Fair Haven, you know, they got a contract out on me. That the word went out yesterday."

"You mean..."

"Yep."

"When's it supposed to go down?"

"They don't know. They're talkin' maybe t'marruh. Maybe next year. They couldn't say."

"Why?"

"Some old bullshit. Nuthin' you gotta concern yourself with. They said the ol' man was providin' a buffer, a shield, but now that he's gone, it's a whole new ball game, all bets off, as far as I'm concerned."

"So what the hell'd you do?"

"Like I already told yuh, it don't matter. Some old business."

"So what now?"

"What's t'do? The fuckin' Feds, they're lookin' for me to roll over. Testify and go into some witness protection program. There ain't no way that's gonna happen. Besides, I don't know if they're bullshittin', just lookin' to pull my chain. It could all be a setup, and I got no way of knowin'. I can't take no chances."

With that, Mickey placed his left hand inside the lapel of his leather coat and moved it aside just enough to expose the handle of his Beretta, holstered inside. Annie, calmly observing everything in silence up to that point, suddenly nudged Davey to let her out of the booth, softly saying something about having to use the ladies' room. He got up, let her out, and sat back down and the two brothers just faced each other for an instant as she disappeared.

Mickey broke the silence. "She alright? Did I say something wrong?"

"She'll be fine. Just not used to seein' nice Jewish boys with guns, that's all. Into gun control."

"Who the hell'd you end up marryin', here?"

"You know if they grab you with that, you're immediately goin' away again."

"Hey, I don't care. In? Out? What's the difference?"

"The last time I visited you in the joint... Where was that? Rochester or Sandstone? You seemed to know the difference."

"Look, I just don't care at this point! I feel sorry for the next one that looks to fuck with me. They better be prepared, 'cause I'll shoot the first sonofabitch that thinks about comin' out of his bag. I don't give a fuck who it is."

"Now you're talkin' crazy! What do you think you're in? Some gangster movie? I hope you ain't fixin' to shoot up Velners'. This thing's already costin' way more than what the ol' man would've spent on any of us. And the wife's really gonna be pissed if we gotta shell out to put you in the ground, or worse, you end up gettin' me shot."

"Cut it out! It ain't no laughin' matter. Besides, you don't gotta worry. If anything's gonna go down, it won't happen at the funeral. They'll all be there, you watch, the whole crew, like there ain't nuthin' wrong. But nothin'll happen. You can count on it."

"And how do you know that?"

"'Cause the big man's still in charge. The old-timers, from the old school, they still got some class, live by the code. He ain't about to let anything go down like that."

"We're talkin' about Gambi, right? The old man's connection? He's still away, isn't he?"

"He's due out pretty soon, about now from what I hear. The word on the street is he ain't doin' too good. Either way, he's still in charge, and wouldn't let anything happen at the ol' man's funeral."

Annie came back and David caught the look on her face as she eased back into the booth.

"What's wrong? Somethin' the matter?"

Giving him one of her you-must-be-nuts-for-asking expressions, she then turned to Mickey.

"Do you see the guy directly behind me, straight back, sitting at the counter?

The one with the straw cowboy hat and the washed-out denim jacket."

"Yeah, what about him?"

"I think he's watching us. I noticed him when we came in. He followed me when I got up to go to the bathroom and pretended like he was talking on the pay phone when I came out."

"I already was on to him, noticed him before, but I figure he ain't nuthin. Just some nosey dirt ball. Some trucker. No cop or self-respectin' hitter would dress like that. He probably thinks yuhr cute, that's all. Wanted to catch a closer look when you went to the can."

"But there's something about him."

"Hey, Davey, tell the wife... uh Annie... not to worry. If this mother follows us outside and tries to get stupid, I'll show her how this Beretta works and stuff his ass in Howard's trunk!"

"I'm drivin' the station wagon."

"What? That piece-of-shit couldn't let yuh take the Audi?! Don't you mind this rat bastid over here, Annie, dear. Like I said, if he comes out in the parkin' lot, I'll send him home with the two of yuhs, layed out nice and neat in the back of the Sable, a little present for brother Howard."

With that, Mickey picked up the check and assessed the damages. Getting up, he reached into his pants pocket and pulled out a thick neatly folded money-clipped wad. Stripping a twenty from the middle, he tossed it on the table with the check that Loretta had left, his silent signal that the gathering was over. Davey and Annie looked at each other and got up. They followed him toward the front and watched as he slowly moved by the denimed cowboy at the counter, checking him out from behind.

Mickey turned and waved to Loretta, busy with a tray of pancakes, eggs and white toast sandwiches. He called for her to try and make it to the funeral, "for the ol' man," as if she and Harry were old friends, and the three of them, Mickey, David and Annie, moved back into the night wind freeze.

"I'll see yuh t'marruh," Mickey said as he turned and gave Annie a hug.

"Thanks for the warnin'!" Davey quipped, recycling one of Harry's old lines.

The two brothers silently embraced for an instant and Mickey moved off toward his Vette, now streaked silver with a glaze of road dirt and frost.

"I'll see yuh t'marruh!" Davey called.

CHAPTER 15:

Fricassee

1943... HARRY HAD ALREADY BEGUN to talk to himself well before he pulled into the cramped block for the third time. Cursing everyone in the neighborhood for the way they parked, he almost missed Sergeant Linehan, the cop from across the street, as the man moved toward his car. Coming to a stop a car length back in the narrow one-way, he watched the man squeeze that blue uniformed bulk of his behind the wheel of the black patrol car. As he waited for the car to pull out, he again wondered about how the cop could rate.

"How's this fat Mic sonofabitch get to take a squad car home? He must make out pretty good, I bet, shakin' down all the stiffs on the goddamn night shift."

Linehan finally drove off without a wave or even a nod of acknowledgement and Harry pulled ahead and backed into the spot. He killed the engine and just sat there for a few seconds as he checked his inside mirror for any oncoming cars. Then taking a quick glance at the side view and straight ahead to make sure no one was walking his way, he slowly leaned forward and reached down under his seat. Feeling around for an instant, he retrieved the small rumpled grocery bag, reached in and pulled out the roll, removed the rubber band, and placed the money in his lap. Going into his jacket pocket, he took out the smaller wad, the couple of week's side action he had been carrying around for show. Estimating a count as he went, he took about two thirds of the fold, mainly the big bills - several tens and twenties, the two fifties and the remaining hundred he hadn't given Gambardella - and placed it with the cash from the bag. With one eye moving from the side view mirror to the front the whole time, he curled the money into a tight dowel, rewrapped the elastic, and placed it in the sack. Dropping the bag on the floor, he slid it back with his heel and took a quick peek to make sure it was out of sight. He took the remaining cash and rearranged it, leaving three singles folded separately on top. Placing the money in his right-hand pants pocket as he got out, he quickly peered around, almost locked the door but caught himself just in time, remembering not to send a message.

"Who in the hell locks their cars around here? Don't be stupid, Harry!"

Closing the door, he walked diagonally across the street, silently laughing to himself as he went.

"There ain't a crumbum in the entire neighborhood that would even dream of going near a car parked in front of Linehan's. They'd have to be out of their friggin' mind."

He thought about the day he had had already and the fact that it still wasn't over and began to speculate on the possible evening action at the smoke shop as he beelined for the aged gray wood-frame.

He recognized the aroma as soon as he entered the narrow dingy hallway and his mouth began to water as he moved by the wooden railed stairway leading to the upstairs apartment and passed the locked door that opened into the front room, the one they kept closed when it was cold. Placing the key in the door at the rear of the darkened passage, he turned the knob and stepped into the kitchen of their small flat. Not immediately seeing his wife, he called with his usual, "Hello? Anybody here?!"

Esther replied from the back bedroom. "I'll be right out. Supper's almost ready!"

Quickly kicking off his shoes, he hastily placed his driver's jacket on the back of one of the kitchen chairs and slid across the waxy worn linoleum to the stove. Lifting the lid off the stew pot, he savored the steam rising off the simmering fricassee, and finding it impossible to resist, reached in and cautiously plucked out a piece of piping hot carrot. Pinching it between the nails of his thumb and index finger, he blew on the hot morsel a few times before popping it into his mouth.

Esther must have detected a familiar sound, perhaps the ring of the lid on the stew pot, or maybe she just knew her husband that well after living with him a good seven years already and she called from the bedroom.

"I said it'll be ready in a minute! Keep your hands out of the pot!"

Fighting that same sensation he had as a kid, as if he had once again been caught red-handed snitching penny candies in one of the groceries or an apple from one of the fruit stands on the Avenue, he quickly gulped the carrot, swallowing it so fast that he could feel it burn all the way down through his chest.

"I'm not in the pot!" he cried.

It was then that he sensed the movement at his feet and looked down. There was Mickey, bare legged, with nothing on but a diaper and a food-stained tee-shirt, clutching his nearly empty baby bottle in one hand and his favorite blanket, the worn, ever-present pink one with the tattered satin trim, in the other. Their eyes met and smiled, and Harry turned and picked up his little one, just turned two.

"And how's my *Mickehleh* today? Still stuffed up?"

Pulling a rumpled handkerchief from his rear pants pocket, he placed it to the boy's tiny nose.

"Blow, Mickey. Come on, blow your nose for Daddy."

The puzzled child just stared at his father, barely able to breathe from behind the white cloth covering his face like a wrinkled, old bandana. Harry tried again.

"Come on, blow your nose, I said. Will yuh blow already, yuh little *shtunk!*"

Esther's voice came from behind the two of them. "I've been tryin' all day. He just doesn't get it. How do yuh get a kid that age to blow their nose?"

"Wha' do I know? Yuh just gotta keep tryin', that's all. He's gotta learn. It's just so aggravatin' 'cause he's still all clogged up."

"Do yuh think we should call the doctor maybe?"

"Nah. I'll rub some Vicks on his chest after supper, before yuh put him t' bed. It'll help him sleep better. He'll be all right."

"Yuh know how I hate taking any chances."

Placing Mickey back down on the chilly linoleum, Harry half turned to his wife. "There's nothing to worry about. I'm tellin' yuh. I checked his forehead and he ain't got a fever. He's got a little cold, that's all. No need to pay for a house call. When'll dinner be ready?"

"'When's dinner ready?!' Is that all you ask? Not even a 'How are yuh?' or nothin'? Your wife doesn't get a hug or a kiss, not even a hello, anymore?"

"I yelled hello when I came in."

"Some hello!"

He leaned forward and gave his wife a quick peck. Satisfied, she turned back toward the stove.

"It should be ready. We could eat now if you want. Did yuh remember to bring a bread?"

"Aw, Jees, I forgot. I was so goddamn busy today. Had another beef with that friggin' foreman. It got so *meshugeh* that..."

"So what's his story now?"

"The usual. He wants me to work more hours, do some additional runs. I tol' him I couldn't without some more money and he got all huffy. Gives me some bullshit about how I should know there's a wage freeze, like I don't know there's a friggin' war goin' on."

"Speakin' of which, d' yuh have some money? There's hardly anything in the house. I spent the last of what you gave me on the chicken, and the baby's almost out of milk."

"Don't worry, I should have some cash t'marruh."

"Tomorrow? You'll be gone early and I won't see yuh 'til afternoon. How am I suppose' t' feed the baby during the day? And what about t'marruh's supper?!"

"All I got's a few bucks. Wha' d' yuh need to hold yuh over, 'til I get paid?"

"Well, like I said, the baby needs milk. And there's no bread. Yuh could at least remember to bring home a couple of loaves from the factory. Some day olds, if yuh can't get fresh."

"Yuh know I can't eat that *drek*."

"Who's talkin' about you? There's no meat left... or vegetables. No eggs. Nuthin'. Not even cereal for the baby. Yuh could at least bring some butter from Asa's, like you said. I was hopin' to get over to the avenue and..."

"Look! Yuh ain't listenin' to what I'm tellin' yuh! All I got on me is a few bucks. I wasn't talkin' 'bout a big shop!"

Fingering the money in his trousers, he pulled out the singles he had set aside.

"Here! I got what...? Three dollars. That should hold yuh, no? Get some bread and milk and whatever else. We'll shop later in the week. I promise!"

"But *last* week you promised."

Harry raised his voice. "Why's everything have t' become such a big t'do with you!? Yuh think if I had it, I wouldn't give it t' yuh?! I told yuh we'll shop already! I'll have some money t'marruh!"

"But tomorrow's Friday, and the stores could all be closed for the *Shabbes* by the time you get home."

"Yuh can always pick up a few things at one of the Italians'. Get what yuh need to hold yuh over at Gallucci's or wherever and I'll shop Sunday, when everything's open!"

Mickey, now sitting in the middle of the kitchen floor, began to cry and Esther bent down and picked him up.

"See! Now yuh made the baby cry!"

"Me?! Wha'd I do!? Yuh start with me as soon as I walk in the goddamn door, and now it's my fault! Wha'd I fuckin' *do!?*"

"Nothin' Harry, nothin' at all. Yuh never do anything.... And yuh don't have to use the F-word in front of the baby! Just sit down and eat before everything gets cold already!"

Grabbing a dish towel from its spot next to the sink, he tucked it into his collar as he moved to the small wooden table and sat down. Esther picked up his jacket from the back of his chair and placed it on its hook by the door. Moving back toward the stove, she retrieved the stew pot with a couple of pot holders and carried it over to table. She served her husband first, ladling out several of the larger pieces of chicken, loose on the bone, some potatoes, carrots, pale green celery and several big spoonfuls of gray-brown gravy. She then bent over, and with a slight groan, picked her chunk of a little boy off the floor and placed him in his high chair as she rubbed his pudgy legs. Lowering the tray over his head so he couldn't squirm out, she retrieved his tin enameled dish from its resting place near the sink.

Turning back to the table, she scooped a steaming drumstick from the pot and placed it on the baby's plate. She gingerly pulled the meat away with her fingers, carefully feeling for bone and gristle and blowing on it the whole time as she did so. She half-mashed a couple of pieces of potato and a carrot with her fork and spooned on some gravy. Blowing on it all once again, and touching a piece of the chicken to her tongue to make sure it was cool enough, she slid the dish in front of the child. He immediately picked up a piece of potato and placed it in his mouth, inserting two fingers along with it before she could hand him his tiny fork. Already too tired to bother with another attempt to get him to use the utensil, she sat down and dished herself a helping, a wing and a back and some carrot, and stared at her husband's plate, already half empty.

Harry, noticing her gaze, said something about how good the fricassee was, and how she was right, that it would have been a whole lot better with some bread. His way of apologizing. She watched him eat for a moment more, knowing full well that any further money talk would only worsen things. She quietly poked at a few bits of the chicken and thought about how he would probably lie down for his usual snooze as soon as he finished. She again gazed at him there across the table, eating too fast, as usual, as if someone might take his food away from him or he was in a hurry to get somewhere.

"Where's the fire?" she inquired.

"I was hungry, that's all. I ain't had nuthin' to eat all day."

"You eat too fast. Then you'll be complainin' later you got heartburn."

"Don't worry about it. I'll be all right," came the reply through a mouthful.

She listened to the sounds he made as he inhaled everything except the bones, hardly chewing as he made his way to the bottom of the dish. She looked at Mickey, his face and the front of his shirt already covered with gravy, contentedly cooing through the congestion as he ate. She glanced around at the plain, dull kitchen, the faded yellow paint on the walls, the tired linoleum and aging stove, the worn refrigerator and ancient oil heater and her thoughts began to wander.

For some reason, she found herself thinking about her father. She could see him at the dinner table at their home across town, sitting there with her sister and brother and mother, the rest of the family, seated together at supper, quietly eating without her. She glanced over at the clock above the stove. "Six-thirty. They're probably done just about now," she figured, and thought about going upstairs to borrow the phone and calling home after she finished. She suddenly found herself thinking about what a different place she had come from. But a very short distance from Legion Avenue, it now seemed like a world away.

Harry, saying he was finished, interrupted her daydream as he got up and did just what she figured. Saying something about how he would be going out later, but that he was feeling "a little bushed" and needed to lie down for a while, he made his way to the bedroom and was snoring soundly within minutes. Taking Mickey down out of his high chair, she cleared the table, scraped the plates, and set the dirty dishes and utensils in the wash tub to soak. She emptied the remnant of fricassee into a small soup bowl, covered it with a plate, and placed it in the icebox. She then filled the pot with warm soapy water and wiped the table with a damp dishcloth, toweling it dry as she went. Figuring it wasn't quite time yet, she sat down at the kitchen table again and watched Mickey occupy himself with a couple of toys that he had already dragged in from his small room. Talking softly to her boy as he sat there on the kitchen floor, she waited another ten minutes. Then, motioning to him to be quiet with an index finger held up before her lips and a soft *"Shoosh"*, she got up and quietly eased in to where Harry lay sound asleep.

With an eye on her husband the whole time, and moving as stealthily as an alley cat on the path of some as yet unaware nocturnal prey, she slowly, cautiously picked his pants up from across the chair where he had laid them, making certain to catch the belt buckle and his change pocket to muffle any sound. Quietly tiptoeing out of the room, she quickly pulled out what she was looking for. Half counting to get some idea of how much he actually had, she peeled off a twenty and tucked it into her apron. Then refolding the wad, she returned it to its pocket, and again moving silently back into the bedroom, placed the trousers across the top of chair as she had found them. Stepping back out into the hallway, she nearly stumbled over Mickey, who had waddled after her, curiously watching from behind the lesson he had already seen and would come to memorize. They looked at each other and the mother smiled.

"He never knows how much he has," she whispered as she knelt to pick up her son.

They returned to the kitchen and Esther sat again at the kitchen table with Mickey on her lap. She soothingly talked to him for a moment or so, knowing full well that the boy, like his father, would soon be fast asleep. As he began to doze, she thought about what she would buy tomorrow, and suddenly remembered the Vicks.

Posting the child on her hip with one arm, she quietly got up and reached over on the shelf above the sink for the blue jar. She placed the child, now almost asleep, on the table. Deciding not to let him sleep in his dirty undershirt, she pulled it up over his head. He hardly budged or whimpered a complaint as she fingered a glob from the jar and rubbed it on his chest and the vapors seemed to immediately deepen his sleep. Realizing he was out, she scooted into his room and returned with a clean T-shirt. Sitting him up, she worked it down over his droopy head and pulled his baby fat arms through the tiny sleeves. She then lifted him up and sat back down at the table, gently rocking him with a hum. Her thoughts again began to wander as she sat there in the soft light of the evening kitchen and she once more imagined him sitting there in his overstuffed chair, drawing on his evening pipe.

"Tell us the story, Poppa."

"And what story might that be?"

"The one of how you came to America, how you met Momma."

"But you've heard it so many times. And it's already getting late."

"Please, Poppa, please. Then we'll go to bed."

She listened to the quiet and could hear his voice as he started the old tale, the one of how they came to be. The words came to her clear.

"Your mother, Julishkah, or Julia as she came to be called in this country, this America, she had come as a young girl, just sixteen, all by herself from the eastern Magyar lands close by what was the frontier of the Ukraina. It was 1912 and she had set out on her own from the small Jewish enclave in the town of Kishvarda. She traveled by train, first north and west to Vienna and then north again to Hamburg where she boarded the ship crammed with others, mostly young people uprooted like herself, headed for the promise of an uncertain future.

"Fleeing not long after the troubles of 1905, her two brothers had come before. Both of them were Socialists already, long before they came over, and had come to realize what they used to call the class struggle was about to catch up with them. They had ranged as far as Kiev and Odessa, where they worked in some kind of factory. Several of their comrades were picked up, beaten and held without trial or a word to the outside for several weeks, simply for talking strike. Your uncles had already been fingered by company spies and seriously threatened, so they figured their days in the old country were numbered. But one step ahead of the secret police, and certain that they would soon face jail and forced labor and who knows what else, they opted for a passage to America"

"What happened then, Papa?"

"Little did they expect, but, as they say in this country, from the frying pan into the fire they went. Using the same train route and shipping line their sister, your mother, would eventually travel on, they made their way to New York. After but a few days wandering the 'goldene medinah' on Lower East Side, they were lured by some lantsman, a labor agent who spoke Hungarian, and soon they found themselves in Pennsylvania, at work among a sea of Serbs and Croats, Czechs and Slovenes and Poles, all of us 'Bo-Hunks' now, that flowed to and from the mills and foundries around Braddock."

"What's a foundry, Poppa?"

"A place like hell on earth, but only hotter and more dangerous. Where they make steel. Don't interrupt if you want me to finish.

"Your uncles, Alec and Pauleh, they were careful then about their politics and the three of us, ever too aware of the endless banter among the others, always in different tongues, but always the same, about 'the Yids', we kept to ourselves. The two of them, your uncles, they worked like dogs, twelve and fourteen hours a day, six and sometimes seven days a week, and spent only what they needed to, for the rooming house and food, and work clothes and boots from the company store when the old ones gave out. On occasion, they'd splurge on a Sunday, a little schnapps and some tobacco. They'd buy the occasional labor paper or nickel pamphlet. And that was it. The rest they tucked away until they finally did as they had promised and sent for your mother.

"Momma made it out just before the War closed the shipping lanes, slamming the door shut for those still wanting to come. Somehow, with the help of distant cousins on your grandfather's side, already settled, she made it through New York. Your grandmother had sown a handwritten address on a yellowed piece of cloth to the inside of her coat, and she somehow, probably with the help of the cousins in New York, found her way to the train that carried her to Pittsburgh, and then to Braddock.

"I was there on the platform, standing there off to the side when I saw her for the first time amidst all the tumult, the hugging and crying, and carrying on. You uncles, Pauleh and Alec, they of course had already described her as a beauty, and I had previously seen a picture, but I can honestly say I was struck immediately. They nearly forgot about me in all the commotion, but your Uncle Alec, he finally pulled me into the family circle. Your mother and I were

introduced and it didn't take long in those days. We were married within weeks and you were born within the year. Your mother had just turned seventeen."

"And what about you, Poppa? Tell us about you."

"But I already told you...."

"Please, Poppa, please."

"Me? I came from another place. My family at the time was considered relatively well-off. My father came from a line of handlers with a two hundred year history, generations long buried by the Prague shul.

"I had everything to look forward to. I was well educated, and could already speak five or six languages by the time I was to matriculate. And that was only the beginning as my universe soon went well beyond the confines of the Jewish quarter. After I was accepted to Charles University, each day I walked the baroque span across the Mltava as if it were a bridge to the future.

"And while my father made plans for me to follow in the business, he came to realize, in his estimation, that I was a dreamer, a romantic, with no head for the cold calculus of commerce. And he was right, at least on the business end.

"As it turned out, I wasn't immune to the radical ferment, the democratic hopes that swirled through the student cafes and dreams of the city's youth. I thought myself an intellectual. As things would have it, this one evening I had been drinking late with some of my student friends in one of the favorite haunts, a pub halfway up the Prague steps to the Hradchanie castle. One too many pilsners and an extra shot of slivovitz and the politics of the pub took over. Standing up among my companions, with my pivo raised high, I declared my total unwillingness to submit to the draft, the conscription, and the demands of any state. That, of course, put an end to my Old World aspirations, for the walls of the old city had many ears and it wasn't long, just days in fact, before someone, an officer friend, came to my father, warning him. I found myself having to flee, but one step ahead of the authorities."

"Then what, Papa?"

"I had originally thought of Vienna or Paris, maybe Berlin. But that wasn't to be. The New World always held an attraction, and it's now hard to explain, looking back, but I soon found myself drawn first toward Rotterdam, where I bribed my way aboard a freighter. The first time I saw New York, and then Philadelphia, that was it. I had no idea, of course, what it would take, and that all became too clear once my money was gone and my father stopped helping. It was when things began to get somewhat desperate that I ended up going to Braddock after I told this man doing the hiring in Philadelphia that I could speak eight languages."

"And how'd we come to New Haven?"

"Your Uncle Pauleh, he came first, led the way. We had heard through the grapevine, someone who knew someone or maybe he read it somewhere, that there was good money to be had here, better than what we were making in Braddock. At Winchester's, during the war. Besides, the conditions in the mills and where we had to live would have been the death to all of us. We had to get out. So Pauleh, he came to look see, got work and sent word. After a short time,

we all came. That's all."

Mickey coughed ever so slightly, just loudly enough to rouse Esther from her memories and she returned to her chores, the end of the day doings that needed to get done so she could head for sleep.

Harry got up around eight. He washed and dressed, kissed Esther and the baby good-bye and telling her not to wait up, left the apartment and quickly headed for the smoke shop. Louie was already there and gave him the word that Butter wanted to see the both of them.

The jowly older man excused himself from the game in progress as soon as they entered the back room and he motioned them further back to the former storeroom, his makeshift office. Taking his seat behind the old scarred library table that served as his desk, he faced his two underlings.

"What's the story?" Harry asked.

"Story? What makes yuh think there's a story? Where yuh been?"

"Aw, com'on, Butter. I stopped home for awhile, grabbed somethin' to eat, took a quick snooze and came right here."

"It's gettin' on toward nine already. You shoulda been here forty-five minutes ago. What d' yuh think this is? Wonder Bread?"

"Aw, com'on, would yuh…?"

"I don't know how many times I gotta tell yuh, but if yuhr gonna work for me, yuh gotta be on time. Enough already. There's this big crap game we got set up, down off upper Howe Street. I got the address here."

"Upper Howe? Where? By the campus?"

"Yeah. Some Yalie blue bloods. Serious *goyim*. Apparently a regular weekly game. Novices with plenty of daddy's money, looking for some new action. Good for a few hundred on a regular basis, from what I've been told."

"So how'd we come to them?"

"One of the kids, he's already into us. Started showing up here early in the fall, at the beginning of football. He runs up a tab pretty quick and blew a bundle on the Harvard game. Missed the spread by a point. An arrogant prick, figured he could negotiate, and mentions this weekly game. Obliging like I am, I of course suggest we could possibly manage to cut him some slack if he could figure some way, with all his expensive education, to work us into a game or two with his Ivy League friends. He immediately offers up that him and his buddies might be interested in some craps and I tells him, 'No problem. We'd be happy to assist anyone interested in the fine art, a lesson or two.'

"You, Hareleh, you'll be the teacher. Take Louie with yuh, just in case this Yalie and his classmates, they should decide to get smart all of a sudden. Play it straight, stay consistent with the rules."

"Then how we gonna get 'em?"

At that point Butter pushed his chair backward slightly and opened the drawer at his belly.

"Here, give a look," he gestured, and his two disciples leaned forward to view the small rectangular box in his hand as the man dumped the matched pairs of different colored dice onto the table.

"I got these special from New York. There's six sets, all the regular colors, weighted to throw losers every time. Let them use their own dice, if they want and then match the colors. Make the switcheroo only when it's worthwhile. We don't want 'em catchin' on, yuh hear? Remember, you ain't playin' with no total dummies here, and they're liable to be suspicious to begin with, with two Yiddels from the Avenue suddenly showing up on the Old Campus. So whatever yuh do, be careful. We ain't lookin' for a single score here. I wanna keep these fish on the line as long as possible. So let 'em eat. Don't get too greedy all at once and remember we want 'em to swallow the hook. And mind what I'm tellin yuh. Be careful."

Initially lost in the maze of courtyards concealed behind the gothic archways and ivied walls, it took the two of them some time to find the right place, even with the address written down. Accompanied by Harry's distracting banter and employing that practiced sleight of hand picked up from one of the old-timers, a hanger-on at the shvitz, Louie played them like a pro. Somewhat suspicious but not quite able to catch on, to figure it out, the Yalies went along like willing sheep to the slaughter. An easy score, and they invited the pair back for more.

It was well after one by the time the game broke. Hoofing it with their heads down and their collars hiked up from the night cold, the two of them had just exited the college portal onto York when they nearly plowed right into Sergeant Linehan and another cop, blocking their way on the sidewalk.

"Well, well, now look who we have here. If it isn't my good neighbor from acrost th' street. Mr. Rabin, isn't it? And what is it the two of yuhz might be up to this fine evenin'? A little late night study at the library, a couple of conscientious students like yourselves?"

"We ain't done nuthin," Harry responded. "Just on our way home, that's all…."

"A long way from home, you certainly are. And what was it you were doin' in the college, there? There ain't no reason for yuhz to be in there, except for no good."

"We wasn't doin' anythin'. Just havin' a look see… Thought we might enroll in the fall."

"We've been havin' some reports of some thievin' goin' on on the campus here. Yuh won't mind, we have a little look see, would yuh?"

The two cops had them turn and face the brownstone wall and the junior officer frisked them both, beginning with Louie. It didn't take long for him to find the wad of cash and the set of dice tucked away in Harry's trousers. He handed his find to Linehan and the Sergeant stepped forward.

"Yuh know I ought to run the both of yuhz in, right now."

"For what? For carryin' some cash and possesin' some dice?"

"How about we take yuhz in and figure out the 'what f'r' later on. Give me a good reason why I shouldn't have Officer Boyle here take yuh downtown right now."

"How 'bout cause we're neighbors and you're concerned about the harmony on the block?"

"Now harmony, is it? I have plenty of that in the neighborhood. There ain't no one gonna bother the tranquility of John Linehan's hearth and home. Of that, I'm sure. You're gonna have to do better'n that, a smart young man like yourself. Perhaps you could figure out some way of returnin' a little courtesy if'n I let yuh go."

"And how might I do that?"

"Yuh know, Rabin, I ain't one for eatin' too much Wonder bread. My kids eat it up, but it doesn't set well with me. No texture to it. But maybe the good missus Rabin, she could find it in her heart to come across the street, say in the next day or two, and pay my wife a little visit. Maybe bring her a couple pounds or so of that nice dairy fresh butter. That'd be a wonderful gesture and it would sure help me soothe things on the home front, if yuh know what I mean."

"I'm not sure's I do. Where in the hell is my wife gonna get two pounds of butter?"

"Aw, come now, Rabin. I figure you as bein' much smarter than that. I imagine the next time you're over on Legion, maybe the next time you pull your bread truck in behind old man Goldman's grocery, maybe you could ask him for an extra couple. You could always buy it yourself, if need be, or maybe nab a pound or so from one of the orders you've been runnin'. You always struck me from a distance as a resourceful fella and it don't really matter where it comes from, as far as my missus is concerned."

"You want some butter, I'll get yuh some butter. But I don't need my wife involved in anything, askin' questions and gettin' concerned."

"That's fair. I can understand, knowin' how the women can talk. Maybe the wife shouldn't be visitin' my Mary after all. I tell yuh what. I notice yuh come home everyday nearly the same hour, about the same time I leave for my shift. Let's say we plan to meet in passin' t'marruh and you bring me a little package."

"Naw. That's too suspicious, me handin' you somethin' on the street. How 'bout I just walk up and ring your bell and leave it with your wife. After all, I am a delivery man."

"I knew there was somethin' about yuh, Rabin. I knew yuh had somethin' on the ball. Now get otta here and take yuhr friend here with yuh, before I change my mind and have the both of yuhr Sheeny arses hauled in!"

CHAPTER 16
Jimmy

_____

1989... JIMMY STILL COULDN'T BELIEVE it. It was well after two in the morning and he had finally fallen into a deep sleep with the pillow stuffed over his head to muffle the noise on the tier when the screw banged on the bars and told him to get up and get dressed. He asked what was up but the guard didn't answer, just telling him to get his clothes on and to hurry his ass up. They escorted him down to the warden's office where he was greeted by two Vermont state troopers, one of them carrying a semi-automatic rifle. The assistant warden covering the night shift told him Harry had died and that it had been okayed; that he was being taken to New Haven for the funeral. With no further explanation then, the staters and the acting warden signed some papers and they ushered him out through the gate into the night cold. And there he found himself, his wrists and ankles shackled, riding in the back of this police cruiser as it glided south through the New England winter.

He still couldn't believe it. He couldn't believe they had woken him up from such a sound sleep, the first he had had in weeks. That Harry was dead came as no big surprise, but he couldn't believe they were allowing him to go to the funeral. He kept wondering who could have that kind of pull, the reach to manage that one, and couldn't figure it out. But there he was, on his way to New Haven, sitting there in this cop car, in his gray prison jumpsuit, the orange penitentiary parka with "PRISONER" stenciled across its back thrown over his shoulders, his feet and hands linked together with a length of stainless chain looped through the thick reinforced belt at his waist.

The red glow of a cigarette dimly lit the interior as the driver inhaled. Jimmy strained forward, sat up and raised his knees so he could tap with his cuffed hands on the Plexiglas above the front seat. The puffy faced trooper riding shotgun turned and looked at him as the driver glanced back in the mirror.

"Wha'chuh want, Rabin?"

"Could I bum a smoke?"

"Wha' do I look like, a vending machine? You know no one's allowed to smoke in a state vehicle."

"Could we maybe stop somewhere soon? I really gotta piss."

"We're scheduled to stop in another half hour," the driver responded. "Just tie it off. And whatever you do, you better not piss in the car."

Used to it by now, accustomed to the head games after nearly eight years inside, he resigned himself to the ride and slowly reclined backwards on the seat, careful not to increase the pressure on his wrists or his bladder. He glanced out, trying to make out some of the countryside, but everything was pitch black. He stared for a moment at the green reflection of the dashboard's lights on his window and caught the red mirrored image of the cigarette as the driver once again inhaled. He thought about Harry, the guy he used to call "Grampa", and his father, Mickey, and how he couldn't wait to see him.

"That son of a bitch… That no-good fuck!"

Catching his own reflection on the window, he tried to remember the last time he'd been in a car. He began to think back to that miserable night at the gas station. And what came after.

He had jammed himself up pretty good, but Mickey hadn't helped. And while he knew the bid he was doing was certainly of his own making, he still hadn't come entirely to terms with how his father had roped him in. He apparently had inherited the family propensity to blame everything bad on someone else and the easiest one to blame was Mickey. The thing was, he wasn't fully off the mark.

He and his baby brother Josh had come up real hard. Mickey went away for the first time when Jimmy was four and Joshie was just two. Connie, just turned twenty-two at the time, was left alone with no means of support and no high school diploma, so she gradually worked her way into an assembly line job turning a high speed metal lathe at Winchester's as she slowly turned to the bottle.

There was her sister Charlotte, abandoned by her husband, with four of her own to look after. She helped out when she could. The only other one that could help was Esther, and she did her best, but really couldn't handle the two kids for anything more than an occasional afternoon or morning. And at that point, during the first couple of years Mickey was away, Connie remained defiantly proud. Afraid of being labeled "white trash", she refused to go on welfare. She remained even more afraid, having been that route herself after her dad disappeared, that the state would come and take the boys and place them in some foster home. So she worked long hard shifts with as much overtime as she could get in and took to soothing the ache in her heart and her raw, machine tooled hands with long nights of blackberry brandy at the kitchen table and the company of various guys from the plant. The boys were pretty much left to their own devices, and they caught on at an early age. Growing up in that era before anyone heard about "latch key kids" and all the public uproar about youth crime, they took to the streets and soon became both criminals and victims.

Connie divorced Mickey at the beginning of his second year in the can and married some guy. Into her new life, she soon had the one thing she thought she always wanted, a daughter. She found less time for the boys, who she soon took to claiming "were no good, just like their father." And when Mickey got out on parole after five, he soon married Angela, already pregnant with her first, and found no time whatsoever for the boys. It wasn't that he might have or could have been a parent, or ever provided some guidance. And it didn't really matter since "those fuckin' kids", as he generally referred to them, were pretty much on their own by that time anyway.

They started out small. Trouble at school when they still went, followed later on by petty theft and scams for adolescent joy money. Underage drinking and reefer, inhalants when they were broke and pills when they could score. Jimmy took to downers, while Josh found his way to smack. By the time they were in their mid-teens, they developed their own artful hustle. Posing as boy prostitutes, they took to shaking down the gays who frequented the late night diners, bars, and bookstores along Chapel Street on downtown New Haven's near west side. They got quite good at it, and even worked up enough nerve on several occasions to take a shot at the big time, a trip into New York.

They used the money for what they needed most, whatever it took to momentarily escape. Street smart and careful not to cross the line, they paid close attention not to overstep any bounds with the heavy hitters, the connected dealers and pimps. They somehow managed to steer clear of the law, aside from the occasional misdemeanor run in, driving while under the influence or some petty possession in those days before the drug laws tightened up. As cunning and opportunist as two youthful hyenas, they lurked at the edges of "victimless" crime by preying on the vulnerable. They rarely if ever got physical and avoided the big bust. And that went on for several years. At least until that night when it all caved in for Jimmy.

Mickey and Harry had started up that used car yard and body shop on Route 1 in East Haven when Mickey got out after his second stretch. Early 1979. In part to get Connie off his back, in part so he wouldn't have to listen to Harry go on about it, and partly out of some misplaced momentary desire to do something for the kids he hardly knew, he took the two of them in to work around the place, washing and waxing cars, running for parts, and jockeying back and forth from the auto auctions.

They both did okay at it, when they showed up on time or at all. Josh even showed some potential as a detail man. And things went as well as could be expected for a while, despite the usual arguments over money. That is, until Jimmy took one of the Cadillacs off the yard one night and totaled it by bouncing off a stretch of guardrail on the Connecticut Turnpike while doing Seconals and seventy-five. Mickey had several grand and a couple of weeks' labor tied up in the car and was just about ready to take it to the Jersey auction at Bordentown. He absolutely blew his top and threw Jimmy out after some heated screaming and yelling in front of the joint. "Tired of both their bullshit," as he put it, he canned Josh as well when the younger one opened his mouth in an attempt to chill things out.

So the two boys returned to the street where Jimmy took his own nasty slide. He and Josh had some argument about the split on a particular shake down and weren't talking to each other. Nothing odd or unusual about that. But Jimmy turned around and hooked up with Victor, one of the downtown street weasels "from around". Their primary goal became staying high, and they managed to do just that well into the fall of '81.

They were out driving around late one night, out of pills and next to broke, cold and coming down with no place to go. Already concerned about how they were going to make their next score, they pulled into this gas station to grab some gas and smokes. It was then that they checked and realized neither of them had enough money. They both glanced through the store's windows. One attendant. No one else around. They looked back at each other and Victor produced the twenty-two from under his seat. Without hesitating, Jimmy pulled on the pair of leather gloves lying on the console between them, grabbed the pistol, and told Victor to keep the car running.

He hopped out and went inside, walked right up to the guy behind the counter, pointed the gun at his chest and told him to empty the drawer. The attendant, a big guy in his early sixties, just stared at him for an instant and then started to reach down below the register. Jimmy fired three times and the guy crumbled. The kid jumped behind the counter, emptied the drawer and ran out. Flying high on the roller coaster cocktail of adrenaline and a residue of relaxants, he raced to the car, got halfway in and remembered what he had forgotten. Cursing to himself and yelling to Victor to get ready, he raced back inside. Going behind the counter again, he stepped over the cashier, lying there, still alive, gazing up at him. He thought about shooting him again but grabbed a carton of Newports instead, signaled to Victor, and pushed the button that powered the pumps. Victor filled the tank and they sped off just as another car pulled in behind.

Sensing something was wrong, perhaps from the way they took off, the incoming driver made a mental note of Victor's license plate. They picked him up almost right away, within hours. Not only that, but the attendant, a retired cop, it turned out, wasn't dead. Not yet, at any rate. He described Jimmy. Victor was still high off of what they had scored after the robbery, and immediately rolled over on his partner when the head detective came out with the description. They found him exactly where Victor said, passed out in the low-rent motel room out by the Merritt Parkway. Telling him that the guy from the gas station had died, they took him into custody. They took him downtown, booked him and said he could make a call. He responded that he had no one.

It was after three in the morning when Mickey's phone rang. When the cop voice on the phone told him they were holding Jimmy, he responded by giving his usual response.

"What the fuck yuh botherin' me for? Just keep his fuckin' ass there. Let him rot till morning!"

But the cop told him it was real serious and that he better come down. That he had better bring a good lawyer. It was then that he knew it was bad, something more than the usual bullshit. Muttering something to Angela about "these fuckin' kids of mine", he threw on some pants and a sweater and drove down to police headquarters.

The whole way downtown, he felt it moving in. That trapped, hemmed in sensation that descended whenever everything seemed to be going from bad to worse. He thought how he had just about had it with all of them. The whole bunch. Not just with Jimmy and Josh, but Connie and Angela, the both of them always looking to put the bite on, even when the cars weren't moving. He thought about how even the new girlfriend, Gina, was becoming a pain in the ass. How she and Jimmy had been carrying on behind his back, the both of them getting high together and doing who knows what, as if he wouldn't find out. He imagined, for an instant, what it looked like, his own kid doing the girlfriend.

His thoughts turned to Harry and having to listen to him everyday, always complaining about this or that and always wanting a bigger piece of the take, even when there wasn't any. And the guys in the shop, the mechanics and the body man stealing parts and supplies, their never doing anything right and his having to pay to redo everything, and their bitching if the payroll was a day late. That forced him to think about his silent partners, Harry's connections, always wanting their weekly vig without excuses, no matter what, and the fact that he was now three weeks behind. And then there was the P.O., always looking to yank him, and the Feds constantly breathing down his neck, wanting him to roll over, waiting for him to pop.

"And now, some new, who-the-hell-knows-what-kind of hassle with Jimmy," he thought. "If it ain't one fuckin' thing, it's another."

He began to wonder how he might cut down on the aggravation and eliminate a few headaches. He began to fantasize about how he would someday just take off. Maybe go live in Wisconsin with his brother David. By the time he pulled around the corner to Orange Street and police headquarters, he was talking to himself.

"I should get the fuck otta here. Just leave, and fuck 'em all. Just like Davey did."

He pulled into the reserved parking zone in front of the station and was just about out of the car when he heard the familiar voice. Someone yelling from across the street.

"Hey! Yuh can't park there, goddammit. Those spaces are reserved for police department personnel only!"

It was then that he spotted Vinny Carbone, Lieutenant Detective Vincent Carbone as he was now known, standing there directly across the street under the electric peach glow of the streetlights, looking like some bad imitation movie sleuth.

"What!? You gonna give me a fuckin' ticket now? At this time of the mornin'?! Go ahead! I give a shit!"

The two approached each other in the middle of the street as if it was some kind of neutral zone. Exchanging a silent "what's up" nod-of-the-head recognition, they made their way out of the light to the sidewalk across from the station.

"How yuh doin', Mick?"

"What can I tell yuh, Vinny?"

The two of them went back a long way already, back to when Carbone's grandfather had the grocery and the best Italian ices on Legion Avenue. Back when they had run together as little kids on the street, with the rest of the gang, playing cowboys and Indians and pretend cops and robbers.

"I figured I should catch yuh before you went in."

"So what's the story?"

"That was me, woke yuh up. I recognized your kid right away when they brought him in. He didn't even want to call yuh, so I figured I should. He's lookin' at some serious trouble, Mick."

"I was dead to the world but I thought I recognized the voice. What kinda serious we talkin'?"

"He shot a gas station attendant, out by the Turnpike. A retired cop. Hit him three times in the chest with a fuckin' twenty-two."

"A cop! You gotta be fuckin' kiddin'! The guy gonna make it?"

"He died not long after they got him to Saint Raphael's."

"Tell me you're bullshittin'."

"Believe you me, Mick, I wish the hell I was."

"So what's it look like?"

"You know I can't talk about it, Mick, but the kid's lookin' at felony murder. He could end up doin' some serious time."

"Hey! I know what the fuck it brings these days! What?! Twenty-five to life in this fuckin' state! That wasn't what I was askin'."

Carbone drew closer, took a quick drag on his smoke, looked around, exhaled, and lowered his voice.

"Look, Mick. We've always been straight with each other, you and me. Let's just say you owe me one, and you didn't hear this from me, but we ain't got shit on the kid. This West Haven cop he popped, he gave a description before he went, but the way the report reads, he coulda been describin' any one of a thousand junkies from here to Providence, and God knows how many more, workin' west. And the guy's dead. We picked up the kid's partner from an I.D. some good Samaritan made on his marker."

"Tell me it wasn't that scumbag, Victor."

"You got it. A real *scungil*, this one. He rolled over right away."

"You gotta be kiddin'..."

"Hold on a second. Let me finish.... The thing is, it's his word against your kid's. The fuckin' security video in the place wasn't workin'. No tape! And there was no witnesses. Your kid was apparently wearing gloves 'cause the only prints they got were from the partner, that the asshole left on the gas pump. We don't got the gun yet. All we got at this point is the car and Victor's story and his prints, and some vague I.D. from a dead man. We talked to the kid, but he's no total dummy. He hasn't given us anything yet. He could walk, but he's gonna need a good attorney. He been in trouble before?"

"You ain't seen his rap sheet?! Didn't yuh look at it? Just some minors, the usual bullshit. Nuthin' serious. He musta been high as a kite!"

"He sure was when we grabbed him at the motel. Still is, probably. They musta used some of what they grabbed at the gas station to score somewhere and stashed the rest. There was no cash at the motel."

"Can I talk to him?"

"Yeah, I imagine we can do that. Let me check. You might wanna call your lawyer."

"Naw, what time's it now? What? Four? Four-thirty? I call Stevie Sieger now, the mother fucker'll end up costin' me triple just for wakin' his ass up. What time they gonna bring him down?"

"The arraignment won't happen till after nine, at best."

"I'll call the lawyer later. Get me in to see my kid."

"Whatever you wanna do. And remember, you didn't hear nuthin' from me. And yuh owe me one, *capiche?* Just wait a couple of minutes before you come in."

Carbone went back across the street, up the steps and through the thick glass doors. Mickey lit a Salem and exhaled in long, slow, tired breaths of frustrated resignation. As he stood there alone in the chill under the frosted streetlights, he felt that hemmed in feeling as it crept in again. It enveloped him like some thick, icy winter fog. He began to think about the additional expenses in time, money and new levels of aggravation that he was now looking at. He thought about Jimmy fucking Gina, and could hear Angela complaining about throwing more good money after bad. Toying with the keys in his jacket pocket, he looked over at his car and thought about getting in and driving away. Instead, he took another drag, exhaled, and tossed the smoke as he crossed the street and went in.

He walked up to the front desk, stated who he was and that he understood they were holding his son. The Irish desk sergeant took his driver's license and told him to have a seat, that it could be a while. He returned to the cold oak bench by the entryway. It came to him then, as clear as the chill through his pants as his ass hit the seat. He knew what he had to do. It was time to alleviate at least one source of aggravation.

Jimmy, of course had no clue what went down and only began to piece it together later on, much later. After he had the beef with Victor in the maximum at Sommers, before they shipped him out of state, to Vermont. And now, as he sat there in the back of the cruiser, by this time having to pee real bad, he thought about how he couldn't wait to see his old man, just to tell him face-to-face, cops or no cops, that he knew. That he had figured the whole thing out.

Some of it still remained vague and some of it had grown distant. He could clearly remember going into the gas station and pointing the gun at the guy. The rest was still a blur. He had no memory of pulling the trigger or going back in to turn on the gas pump, but somehow remembered the carton of Newports. What remained etched in his memory was the conversation he had with his old man that morning before he copped the plea.

They had brought him down, still cuffed, and put him in some bare room with a table and chairs and one of those two-way mirrors. He sat there for a while, figuring they were watching and that they were going to question him again. That's when Mickey walked in. He could remember their talk like it was yesterday, like it just happened.

He turned on his father right away.

"What the fuck you doin' here?!"

"No, asshole, you got that all wrong," Mickey shot back. "The real question is what the fuck are *you* doin' here?!"

"I don't need your help, that's for sure!"

"Oh yeah? Yuh think yuhr so smart? Who you gonna call? Your mother, maybe? She'll be in good shape at this hour. Or maybe you wanna call your friend, Victor. He's already rolled over on yuh."

"I don't believe they brought you down here!"

"Hey, I'm the only one you got at this point and yuhr lookin' at some serious fuckin' charges! So you better cut the bullshit and listen 'cause we ain't got much time. Did yuh know that guy yuh whacked was an ex-cop?"

"Ex-cop, my ass!"

"Oh yeah! The guy was retired from the West Haven force! Do yuh know what that means?! They're definitely gonna look to throw your ass away for the rest of your miserable life! So right now, yuh better wise up for a change and just this once, listen to what I gotta' tell yuh."

"And what can you tell me, I don't already know?"

"Look, I've been there and back already. Yuh think you're gonna play smart on this one?"

"I didn't mean to do it. The fuckin' guy was goin' for a gun, and..."

"Hey! Are you fuckin' off your nut altogether?! Otta your goddamn mind?! They can hear every word yuhr sayin'. And don't think they ain't listenin'! Just keep your mouth shut and listen to me, 'cause I'm gonna tell yuh what you gotta do. And for once in your life, I hope yuh can hear me."

"Oh great! All of a sudden you, of all people, is gonna start bein' concerned. When the hell'd you become my father?!"

"Hey, look Jimmy, I don't have t'stand here and take your shit. I'd just as soon go home and climb into bed with the wife and put it where it's nice and warm and not give a fuck about you or anyone else. But you're my oldest, and where you're headed, possibly for the rest of your life if you don't smarten up, there ain't no warm beds. The only one you'll be snugglin' up with, you don't even wanna think about. Now I can talk and you can hear what I gotta tell yuh, or I can walk right the fuck otta here and wash my hands of the whole goddamn mess. It's up t' you!"

At that point they just paused and stared at each other for a moment, and Mickey turned and started for the door. It was then that Jimmy made a major mistake.

"Wait a minute. Don't go. I... I need yuh."

Mickey turned back. "Then you gonna listen to what I have t' say? Without interruptin'?"

"Yeah."

Mickey came back and sat down with his hands and forearms gesturing across the table.

"They got you dead away. The guy in the gas station, he lived long enough to finger yuh. They showed him your fuckin' picture at the hospital and he I.D.'d yuh right out. And your pal Victor rolled over on yuh as soon as they grabbed his sorry ass. Said the whole thing was your idea from jump street. That you planned it. He told them up front you were the shooter. They'll end up cuttin' him some slack, put him on the stand to testify against yuh and he'll get off with a wrist slap, draw a couple, five max. Some guy pulled in behind yuh when you were leaving, some fuckin' Yalie do-gooder. He got Victor's marker number, and says he can identify yuh."

"But he couldn't even see me. I was already in the car. He drove up right when we were leavin'."

"There yuh go, openin' your mouth again! When yuhr talkin', yuh ain't listenin'. It don't fuckin' matter where you was! They put him on the stand after some promptin' from the D.A., with you sittin' there in the court room, who the fuck's a jury gonna believe? You or some Yalie professor? Between him and Victor, where yuh gonna look to go at that point? You tell me!"

"How do yuh know all this?"

"I know somebody here. A connection. From the street. They already filled me in. Square business."

"So what are yuh sayin'? What d'yuh think I should do?"

"Yuhr lookin' at felony murder. Twenty-five to life. Yuhr fuckin' lucky they ain't got the death penalty in this state. Yuh gotta get out in front on this one 'cause if this shit goes before a jury, and they find you guilty, and you can bet your sweet ass they will, then you gotta get the max. But if yuh come clean right away, then you got some room to maneuver. Throw some of the shit off on Victor, how it was his idea. That it was his piece."

"But it was."

"Good! Tell them that! Tell them, maybe, how the both of yuhz went in. How yuh was scared and high and didn't mean to do it. You'll draw ten, possibly fifteen. With the situation in the joint now, the overcrowdin' an' shit, you'll end up doin' three to five."

"How do yuh know all this?"

"That's how it works. My lawyer'll tell yuh the same thing. Trust me on this one."

"Trust me on this one...." The phrase still sounded in Jimmy's head eight years later. It seemed to echo through the cruiser even after it started to get light out. Even after they stopped at the rest stop on the Mass Pike and the staters escorted him inside to go pee, and the cop riding shotgun let him stretch his legs a little bit alongside the car and finally gave him a smoke.

"Trust me on this one...." It was all he could hear, even after they crossed the Massachusetts line into Connecticut and he slowly began to distinguish the suddenly familiar hills and red brick river towns as the police car moved down through the upper Housatonic Valley.

"Trust me on this one...." All he could hear was Mickey's voice. It got louder and clearer the closer they got to New Haven.

Mickey had gone out and the detectives and an assistant from the District Attorney's office finally came in. Jimmy told them he was willing to talk. They had him sign a piece of paper waiving his rights to counsel and had him talk into a recorder and videotaped the whole thing. He told them what went down, embellishing Victor's role in order to make sure they got him real good. Even talked about how the two of them had gone inside together and how Victor was the actual shooter. About nine o'clock, they took him across the street to the courthouse, where he had a couple of minutes' talk with Mickey's lawyer, Stevie Sieger, who assured him everything was on the up and up; that they were talking fifteen, out in five. They went before the judge and copped a guilty plea. Remanded over, he was sentenced two weeks later, with Connie, Josh, Mickey, Harry and his Uncle Howard sitting there in the courtroom. Twenty-five to life. Boom! Next case!

At first, he just couldn't believe it. He initially thought it was just the judge reneging on the agreement. At least that's what Sieger said, the one time he came to visit, talkin' some nonsense about a hearing before the state sentencing board. A slight suspicion began to gnaw at him when Mickey kept promising to visit, but never showed up. And then it was only a matter of weeks before it all came clear, when he finally crossed paths with Victor in the D Wing at Sommers.

They had Jimmy mopping floors and he didn't even see it coming, it happened so fast. Victor and his *bulvon* of a cousin, Malestraro, doing his own bid on felony assault and extortion, grabbed him from behind and pinned him against the wall, a piece of honed steel to his throat. Victor was spitting with rage.

"You no-good cocksucker! Yuh rat *me* out!? I gotta kill yuh!"

Jimmy struggled back. "You ain't gonna kill nobody. You ain't got the balls. And who the hell ratted who out first?!"

"Who ratted on who?! I didn't say a fuckin' word until they showed me your live fuckin' video performance. What the fuck you claim I was in the gas station with you for?! You're the one shot the fuckin' guy!"

"My ol' man said...."

"Your ol' man!? Your ol' man!! You still don't know what went down, do yuh?!"

That fuckin' Vinny Carbone, that no-good Guinea rat bastid! He was laughin' about it later on! He's probably still laughin'! I heard him tellin' some of his cop *goombahs* about it when I was waitin' that mornin', before they took me across the street. Fuckin' braggin' how he got that ol' man of yours, that stupid fuck, to do his work for him. How it was the easiest case he ever done."

"You're a fuckin' liar...!"

"I'm a fuckin' liar? You got some balls after what you and that fuckin' ol' man of yours did! Let me show yuh how much of a fuckin' liar I am! I told yuh I was gonna kill yuh!"

Jimmy turned and ducked just quickly enough so that Victor missed his throat. The blade swiped across the back of his head, nicked off a small piece of his right ear, and opened a seven inch cut across the scalp and down the side of his neck. The next slash, in the struggle, missed its mark entirely and sliced Malestraro's arm. By that time it was over, as four guards fell on them with sticks and a stun gun. Jimmy ended up getting forty stitches and the transfer to Vermont as part of some regional prisoner exchange program. For his own safety, he was told. He also got a new clarity about the workings of the world. And a new yearning to get close to his old man. They moved him to Vermont on his twentieth birthday.

CHAPTER 17:

The Fedora

1947... IT WAS LATE ALREADY, long after dark, when the stranger walked in and sat down at the counter. Most of the regulars had already eaten and gone, with the exception of the three elderly reds camped out in one of the pale green booths, huddled close in some animated political dispute over their empty plates. An additional remaining straggler, the lanky mid-thirties loner from the small, independent print shop down the street, lingered on one of the stools, hunched over a final cup of coffee and part of the sports page from the morning's *Daily News*. It was late enough that Harry had started to clean the grill at the back and the threadbare, aging Irishman, the one they affectionately called "Yonkeleh", had already finished scrubbing most of the larger pots and pans at the deep service sinks mid-counter.

With his back to the place, busy scraping the cooked-on grease from the steel plate atop the stove, Harry hadn't noticed the newcomer when he came in, but Yonkel intentionally coughed to get his boss' attention and nodded toward the counter. He turned and not recognizing the late arrival, thought about telling him the place was closed, but caught himself, remembering how the noontime rush had been less than hoped for and that the dinner crowd hadn't panned out, either.

Moving down the counter, he addressed the outsider.

"Can I help yuh?"

The weather-featured man, large framed and dark, the collar of his overcoat hiked up as if he was still outside, stared at the grill and responded from under the down-turned brim of his worn, gray fedora.

"I was sorta hopin' for a 'burger and a coffee but it looks like you're gettin' ready to close. Could yuh manage somethin' simple for a hungry traveler?"

Harry gestured toward the stove with the metal scraper still in hand, "Yeah, you're right. The grill's closed down. The dinner specials are all gone, but I still got some turkey, fresh made this mornin', and a bit of roast beef left. There's some egg salad or tuna. Otherwise, you're hard out o' luck at this hour."

"The turkey'll do, if it ain't too dried out."

"I wouldn't serve it, if it was. How 'bout on rye, with a little Russian and coleslaw? Some tomato and a nice thin slice of Bermuda?"

The man nodded his approval and removed his hat and Harry retrieved the glass coffee pot from its hot plate and poured the stranger the last of the dinner hour brew. Turning then to the stainless steel prep table, he paused and wiped his hands on his apron as he thought for an instant how something about the stranger seemed distantly familiar. He had caught it for a second, something about the way the guy looked when he took off his hat, but couldn't put a finger on it. His attention turned to filling the order and he quickly proceeded to fashion one of those thick deli sandwiches for which he was known.

Retrieving two remaining pieces of rye from their white bakery bag and fingering them enroute to make sure they weren't too stale, he laid them on the worn maple cutting surface. He smeared one slice with the Russian dressing and pivoted to the once-proud, foil-covered corpse of a bird. Carving several evenly cut slabs of remaining breast from the hulk of a carcass, he layered them on the dressed piece of bread and without any loss of motion hurriedly reached over and scooped a clump of coleslaw from its resting place and spread it on with his bare hand. Wiping both hands with a nearby restaurant towel, he deftly sliced several discs of tomato and some onion, added them to the growing stack, and situated the remaining slice of bread in place. With his steadying left hand atop the whole time, in quick practiced motion, he cut diagonally through the mound, slid the flat of the blade underneath, and agilely hoisted the sandwich onto a thick white dinner plate grabbed from a column of dishes to his right. Tossing on a half-sour pickle wedge and a red cherry pepper, he slid it to the stranger and watched for a moment as the man raised one half in both hands, opened wide, took his first bite, and smiled appreciatively.

Harry had already made the guy for a *lantsman* as soon as he laid eyes on him. He now began to wonder what his story was as he gazed at the man's broad shoulders and dark, copper-browned features, the lined face and hardened hands toughened by what must have been years spent working outside in the sun. He pegged him to be somewhere in his early forties, not quite forty-five, and figured him from someplace down south, maybe Florida, or maybe out west. Now curious, he engaged the stranger.

"Everythin' all right?"

The man responded with a slight, indistinguishable accent, somewhat European, but somehow different, alien to Harry's ear. "Yeah, plenty good. I ain't had such a *gehshwoleneh* sandwich... it's gotta be... God-knows-how long. Yuh can't get somethin' like this from where I come from now."

"I make everything fresh, from scratch, first thing every mornin'. Everyday 'cept Sunday, a twenty-pound turkey, a roast beef, at least two pastramis, fifteen pounds of corned beef, and a baked ham I keep off to one side... you know... for the *goyim*. Case you're wonderin', I also make all my own pickles and sauerkraut, the coleslaw and potato salad, you name it. No garbage. Nuthin' but the best so's all my customers, they shouldn't leave disappointed. Where'd yuh say you was from?"

The stranger split the cherry pepper with his fingers and removed the green stem and clump of yellow seeds.

"I didn't."

Harry got the signal. "Sorry for askin.' I don't want yuh should have t' rush or nuthin', but I been here since five this mornin' and I gotta finish up back here yet and be back, the same time t'marruh. That'll be seventy five cents, when you get a chance. The coffee's on me. It's been sittin', the last of the pot."

Turning back to the prep table, he moved quickly to cover the perishable leftovers, the meats and salads and spreads, and placed them in the double-doored fridge sitting next to his work area. Returning to the grill, he slowly poured a glass of hot water across the surface and listened for a second as it hissed and steamed on first contact. It partially evaporated as he methodically scraped the metal clean, from front to back with rapid, even strokes. He turned off the range and carefully removed the grease trap from beneath the grill. When he turned to dump the scrapings into one of the pails underneath the counter, he noticed that all that remained of the stranger was an empty plate. A buck and a half sat alongside the cup and saucer.

"Some people!" he thought out loud. "Not even a thank you, or nuthin. But I should complain? At least this sport, he knows to leave a tip!"

Taking that as a hint, the printer asked for his check, left a dime alongside his empty cup, and exited with the last of the store's newspaper under his arm. The old-timers sitting in the booth, caught during a lull in their recountings, suddenly realized it was time to go and they too pulled on their coats and made toward the door as Yonkel cleared the last of their plates. Saying good night, Harry closed and latched it behind them. He paused a second to pull the string on the red neon "Rabin's Lunch" in the window, and turned the "Closed" sign hanging on the door to the outside. Making his way back behind the counter, he opened the till and began tallying the day's take by the light of the small brass lamp mounted above.

Yonkel had finished the last of the pots and pans and stray utensils, now pyramided next to the large double washbasins to air-dry. He watched Harry move around to the register and took that as his signal. Coming out from behind the counter, broom and dustpan in one hand and a damp towel in the other, he wiped down the table tops and swept out the four booths and from between the line of stools. Finishing the floor, he returned the broom and emptied the dustpan. Eyeing the dulled linoleum one more time, he decided it didn't need mopping and with what seemed like years of accustomed motion, pulled the plug on the pinball machine and jukebox and fingered the coin return on the cigarette machine as he made his way to the rear of the luncheonette. He looked to see if everything was all right in the lone bathroom, and coming back, switched off the long, double row of overhead fluorescents. Retrieving his tattered tweed topcoat from its hook near the back door, he checked the rear dead bolts and returned to pause at the middle of the counter opposite the seltzer spigots where his boss stood, still facing the cash drawer.

The old rummy of an Irishman feigned another cough to get his boss's attention and Harry stopped his count in the middle of a stack of singles and looked up to face his lone employee through the wall mirror behind the register.

"For krissakes, Yonkel, either you should do somethin' with that damned cough or try talkin', for a change. Yuh made me lose count, again. Now I gotta start over. Yuh want yuh should get paid, I suppose?"

"I didn't mean to disturb yuh while you was addin'."

Harry turned and counted out eight singles on the countertop, started to pivot back, but paused for a second, and added two more ones to the pile. Then walking around to the customers' side, he made for the door as the old-timer picked up his day's pay and followed.

"You can take off. I'll finish up, myself. Just remember I want yuh here good and early t'marruh. Five o'clock, no later. And don't think I didn't notice yuh didn't mop. The floor's gotta get done before we open. So don't' go gettin' *shikker* t'night, just 'cause I gave yuh a couple extra dolla's. Yuh hear what I'm tellin' yuh?"

Yonkeleh muttered the routine response and a good night as his boss told him "Good night" and let him out. Harry latched the door and returned to the register where he resumed his nightly tally, recounting the ones, and then the quarters, dimes, the nickels and pennies, scrawling the totals on a scratch pad next to the till as he went. Finished, he took part of the day's take and folded it into his pants pocket, and placed the rest in a zippered canvas bank pouch. Taking a quick look through the front windows to make sure no one was watching, he tossed the bag into the wastebasket. Alone then, he could hear his father's voice, clear as if Izzie was standing there, still alive.

"What kinda t'ief in their right mind, I ask yuh, would ever t'ink t' look in a garbage pail?"

Tossing a newspaper in to cover the deposit and leaving the register drawer open and the lamp on, he walked to the rear and checked the back locks. Grabbing his coat from its hook, he made his way to the front and looking both ways up and down the now empty avenue before opening the door, let himself out.

He had just turned the corner onto Elliot and hadn't gone twenty yards when they grabbed him from behind. He immediately counted at least two from the sets of strong hands gripping his arms but he didn't get a chance to see a thing as the thick burlap sack came over his head and shoulders. The distinct feel of the barrel at his side immediately convinced him not to struggle or to cry out and he softly invited his assailants to take what he had, that his money was in the right front pocket of his pants.

The thickly accented unfamiliar voice to his right responded, "We don't vant your money. Keep your mout' shut and you von't get hurt."

The men twisted his arms behind and he could feel the pinch of the handcuffs as they squeezed closed, tight on his wrists. They lifted him up, his feet just barely touching the sidewalk, and hustled him toward the curb just as he heard squeal of a truck's brakes and what had to be the sliding door of a delivery vehicle. The two half lifted him again, forcing him to step up, and jostled him forward. He stumbled slightly and came down hard and the echo that his body made as it thudded to the bare metal floor confirmed for him that he had to be in an enclosed empty van, similar in sound to the one he drove during the war. He listened as the men climbed in. They yanked him upright, relieving the cuff's pressure on his wrists, and positioned themselves on either side as the truck began to roll.

"That makes three," he thought to himself, and he spoke to the dark. "What gives? What the hell's goin' on?"

The same voice from before, now sitting to his left, cautioned him again with a warning smack to the back of his head.

"I t'ought I told yuh to keep yuhr mout' shut!"

The vehicle moved off of Elliot and turned right onto Sylvan and he tried to keep track of its course, drawing a map of the memorized streets in his head, but soon lost all sense of direction. He listened to the breathing of the men silently situated to either side of him and noted the slight, wheezy cough of the one to his right, the one that hadn't spoken. In a resigned kind of way, more curious than frightened for the time being, he thought about who his captors could be. He tried to recall everyone he owed and any outstanding gambling debts that may have conveniently slipped his mind. Running through the amounts in his head, he couldn't conceive of anyone that would go to such extremes for a few hundred dollars, spread here and there, four or five, maybe six maximum all around, excluding what he owed at the bank and to the landlord and utilities. He thought it strange that his kidnappers handled him the way they did, not really playing rough, not even knocking him over the head, and that led him to figure everything wasn't lost. He pondered for an instant if the whole thing was some kind of mistake, that they had the wrong man. Deciding to test his hunch, he again spoke, this time softly to the dark.

"You got the wrong guy," he murmured, and the silence of his two abductors told him what he didn't want to hear. He again began running through the list of everyone he owed, wondering who he might have missed.

The truck eventually came to a stop after what seemed to him like a good half hour, maybe more. He listened as the driver's door opened and closed and heard the distinct rattle of steel chains like those on a large overhead warehouse or factory door. The driver got back in and the van moved forward a number of yards and stopped and Harry could tell from the sounds that they were inside someplace.

As soon as the vehicle came to a halt, the driver turned off the ignition, got out, banged his door shut, and walked away. The two alongside him climbed out the rear, closing him in like one in a tomb as they slammed the doors.

What seemed like an hour, maybe but a few minutes, passed, and for the first time he began to feel a genuine fright, a slight tinge of terror, brought on by the total darkness, the absolute silence, the suddenly suffocating, stifling mildew smell of the burlap, and the added variable of being left, totally abandoned.

A few more minutes went by and he heard the approaching steps. The truck's back doors opened and he made out the presence of two men, the one with the cough and the other. He recognized the strength in their hands as his captors brought him to his feet and silently guided him to step down from the rear of the vehicle, forcing him to duck so he wouldn't hit his head. They walked him a few yards then silently prodded him to sit, guiding his shackled arms around the uprights of what felt like a curved-back wooden chair. It was then that he sensed the presence of another party in the room, someone other than the driver, even before he spoke.

The accented voice came from directly in front of him.

"Remove the hood."

One of the men standing at the back of the chair lifted the sack and as his eyes adjusted to the light, the first thing Harry saw was the stranger, the gray Fedora with the turkey on rye with Russian, the big tipper.

"What the hell is this? There gotta be some kind of mistake! Who the hell are you?"

"Relax, Harry. There's no mistake and there ain't no sense getting yourself all worked up!"

"Worked up!? A couple of *bulvons,* they grab me right off my own street, kidnap me and bring me God-knows-where, and some guy I don't know from Jesus, he tells me not to get worked up!! Who the hell are yuh? How do yuh know my name?!"

"If yuh calm down, I'll have the boys undo the cuffs."

Harry turned his head and glanced over his shoulders at his abductors for the first time, two rough-hewn *lantsman*. A fourth character, who Harry made for the driver, stood off to one side with his arms folded.

The Fedora moved forward to within a yard and straddled a wooden chair, its back turned toward his captive. Now at the same level, he gazed straight across into Harry's eyes and smiled slightly.

"That was quite a sandwich yuh made, but I coulda done without the onion. Or the cherry pepper."

"What?! You went to all this trouble to tell me yuh got a little heartburn?! Yuh couldn't come back t'marruh and complain like the rest?!"

"All we want to do is talk to yuh for a little bit. That's all. Make it a whole lot easier on yuhrself and make it so the boys, here, don't have to play rough. Just relax and they'll undo the cuffs."

Harry assessed the situation and without a word slumped down submissively on the chair. The Fedora nodded and one of the men unlocked the bracelets and he brought his arms around, rubbing his abraded wrists.

"We just want to talk to yuh, that's all. We think you could be of help to us."

"Me? Help? What kind of help?"

"We got word that you're one to be trusted."

"Word? From who?"

"Let's just say an old friend, for now. All we want is for yuh to run a couple of errands for us, that's all."

"Yuh got some helluva way of askin'! What kind of errands?"

"What d'yuh think of what's been goin' on in Palestine?"

"Yuh mean with the Jews and the British? Them not lettin' the survivors in?"

"Yeah, what d'yuh think of all that?"

"What's t' think? All I know is what I see in the papers."

"Yuh ever hear of the Irgun?"

"Yuh mean the guys who blew up that Hotel in Jerusalem, killed that bunch of British?"

"Yeah, that's right."

"What's that got to do with anything? I don't understand."

"What d' yuh think…? Of what they been doin'?"

"The Irgun? Some of the guys that come in the store, they say they're nuthin but a bunch of *shtarkers*…. You know, gangsters. We got enough bad guys right here in N'Haven. It don't concern me, what goes on over there. I got enough *tsooris* of my own."

"And our people, they shouldn't have their own home, a homeland, after all that's happened?"

"Who said they shouldn't…? But that ain't my concern just now. I ain't political, okay? I got plenty of customers, they believe what they want and support this or that cause. I give at the *shul* when they collect for the refugees, and my wife, she cleaned out a whole closet for the clothing drive. I vote Democrat like everyone else… That's it."

"Oh, so you voted for that Roosevelt, even when he closed the doors on our people trying to escape the Holocaust?"

"I heard talk of that, but wha' do I know? Yuh gonna tell me Truman's bad for the Jews?"

"Another anti-Semite."

"I got a feelin' yuh didn't bring me here for some civics lesson. Yuh still ain't tol' me what yuh want."

"We need someone to act as courier."

"A courier? You mean like a delivery boy? I'm through with that."

"We ain't talkin' about a new career. Just an occasional run, that's all. All you'll have to do is once in a while drop off a package, that's all."

"Yeah. Of what?"

"Money."

"How much? And what's in it for me?"

"Serious money. Life and death money. You'll be taken care of."

"And what's it for?"

"For guns bought right here in New Haven, otta Winchester's and wherever else we can get 'em, otta Connecticut."

"You gotta be fuckin' otta your minds! For who?"

"For us. For our people. For what will soon be Israel."

"The Irgun? I already tol' yuh, I ain't political. I don't get involved. I managed to stay otta the war somehow. I got a wife and kids, a new baby. And a store to look after."

"And lots of debts, from what I hear."

"Who tol' yuh that?"

"We have our ways. We hear everything."

"I don't get it! Why me, if yuh know so much?"

"'Cause we can't operate out in the open any longer. The Brits already got wind that we're over here and they got the Feds lookin' for us right now. I personally took a risk even comin' to see you this evening."

"So yuh want I should get involved in a Federal rap? Of all the goddamn crumbs and do-gooders in New Haven, why me? And what's t' stop me from goin' right to the law? It ain't like I came here of my own free will! And I seen who all of yuh are!"

The Fedora got up and closed distance between himself and Harry. He said something in what Harry now realized had to be Hebrew and the two underlings standing behind moved forward as well. Grabbing his shoulders and upper arms, they braced their captive against the back of the chair. Harry, anticipating a punch to the face or the back of the head, prepared himself for the blow. Instead, the Fedora, now towering over him, slid his large hand down into the seated man's open collar and pulled out the mezuzah by its silver chain.

"I think you've held onto this long enough."

"DOV!?"

"Hello, Harrehleh."

CHAPTER 18:

Troubles

———————

1989...   THOSE SAME PRE-DAWN DARK hour sounds that woke him almost every morning had already come and gone and Mickey just lay there staring up toward the ceiling, oblivious to the tears moving down across his temples. The distinct metallic whoosh of the cell door, sounding for an instant like a high-speed night train as it rushed through its runner in the floor, had come first and ended, as always, with that reverberating clang of iron against iron as the cage crashed shut, closing him in. That ever present dream state intrusion had once again succeeded in jolting him from some few moments of sound sleep and it took him several seconds to realize where he was.

The fabric softener scent on his pillow and the sleep sounds from Gina's motionless form tipped him off, told him he was safe, and he soon closed his eyes and slid off for a while longer. And that's when the more nightmarish, yet familiar roar of ripping steel and the clattering rain of falling metal and glass debris, the conjured imaginings of the explosion, jolted him awake once again.

He rolled over and squinted at the clock at the side of the bed and his waking thoughts turned first to what day it was, and then upon remembering, to Harry. And that's when he began to weep. Secluded there in the darkness, with both Gina and the kid quiet and still for the time being and with no one else around to see, he let the tears flow as images of the old man rushed in.

The first thing that came to him were all the Wednesdays and Sundays, the nearly eight years' worth of long, endless mornings that seemed to stretch forever into early afternoon as he waited for word of Harry's arrival. He imagined him now, the old man, making those regular hauls up I-91 from New Haven, driving undeterred like some legendary mailman through the summer heat and autumn blanket fog, the zero visibility rain, treacherous winter sleet and above-the-ankle snows. He could see him then, at times making the trip with no one else in their right mind out on the road, going like clock work twice and sometimes three times a week, every week, all the way up and back beyond Hartford to the joint at Sommers.

He listened to the dark and could still hear the ring of the wall phone in the prison kitchen, that anxiously-awaited overdue call down to the chow line where he worked during those first hard-time years. His mind's eye watched as the bulk-bellied guard picked it up and the ear of his memory heard the "Yep... yep... uh-huh..., uh-huh" and the anticipated signal.

"Hey, Rabin! Yuh got a visitor!"

He watched himself then, as if it were yesterday, as he dropped what he was doing, peeled off his stained apron and hurried off, pass in hand, down the long stretch of corridor and through the maze of gated checkpoints to the visitors' room.

He thought about the many visits, so often the same, the endless attempts by the old man to make amends and belatedly become a father, all the easy-for-you-to-say advice about being smart and keeping the mouth shut, the too-little-too-late words of wisdom on who to talk to, who to get next to and who to stay away from. He recalled the promises made on the upbeat days, all the talk about the various people being talked to, this one or that one who knew somebody who had this here or that there connection. And the letdowns that would invariably follow, Harry's telling him how things moved slowly and how he just had to be patient. He could see the old man sitting there now as if they were still facing each other across the table in the visiting room, at times talking in little more than affected whispers as he ran through the news from the outside, from New Haven. The redundant routine of family headaches, the occasional word of this or that old-timer now gone, the old man always playing his cards close to his chest, always withholding the really bad news for the good of everyone involved. And now, nearly twenty years down the road, he once again found himself hearing the words and wondering about what his father actually meant, the multiple meanings of that advice which invariably passed from the old man's lips at the end of every visit.

"Hang in there, sonny boy. Hang in there."

His thoughts shifted as he rolled over on his side and there it was, the interior of the prison shop, the garage where they finally set him to work repairing the state-owned vehicles, the patrol cars from the State Police barracks. The scene came rushing back as if he had never left and he could see each and every one of them, the "side jobs", as they rolled across the assembly line of his recollection.

The whole thing started off slowly, as an occasional "favor" for the captain. The patch job on the dinged-up Camaro or Malibu that some guard's ol' lady or kid heading nowhere in a hurry had whacked, or the torn-up Charger in need of some nose work belonging to some screw lieutenant's brother-in-law. Visualizing every detail, the bodywork on each and every one, he counted them now as if counting sheep. But sleep wouldn't come as the image of each car led to the what-if calculations, the money lost and the time paid.

Thoughts of the scam carried him back to Harry and how crazy the old man had become when he finally caught wind of the so-called "rehab program" run by the captain-in-charge and who-knew-who-else, higher up. He could see him there now, how he fumed that day when he found out, sitting there in the visiting room, when Mickey explained how the bastard had to be taking down a serious piece of change with his little in-house body shop for the friends and relatives of what seemed like half the corrections officers in the state. It didn't matter to Harry, of course, that Connecticut's taxpayers were footing the bill for the Bondo, paying for the paint and primer, the sanders and spray guns, the buffers and the rest. But that his son was overseeing the entire crew, supplying the skilled labor and all the finishing touches, the detail work, and not getting something on the side, that really got him going.

Mickey's thoughts wandered further and he recalled how the captain, Manion was his name, reluctant to watch his moneymaker walk, delayed parole twice by handing out extra "tickets", demerits for bullshit infractions, and how the guy, out of spite, forestalled the final release for several days by burying some key paperwork.

Gina moved ever so slightly in her sleep and Mickey, jolted back to the present by her motion, got up to pee. Not wanting to face himself, he thought about leaving the bathroom light off but clicked it on anyway and leaned into the mirror after finishing at the bowl. His eyes were tired and bloodshot, and the long wisps of remaining hair, usually combed over but now in night-time disarray, accentuated his baldness. He focused for a second on the faint dotted line still visible across his upper forehead, those spots where they had placed the plugs after he volunteered for that experimental trial-run transplant during his first stretch. Then eye caught mirrored eye and the saddened face staring back reminded him again what day it was. Remembering that he wouldn't have to go to the shop, but to the funeral home instead, he returned to bed, not so much to go back to sleep but more so just to have some quiet time to himself, some peace before Gina or the baby finally woke up. He lay there thinking about his earlier conversation with the Feds. He wondered about what they had told him, the word about the impending hit and, if it was real, when it might come down and from whom. He thought for an instant about seeing Jimmy and what that would end up costing and thoughts of money led to what he had to shell out for the rent-a-cop to keep Gina and Angela from going at each other at the funeral. He then remembered the twenty-five hundred that he had found in Harry's shoes. Thought of the day's forage led him to wonder about Harry's watch and its whereabouts, and in turn carried him to thoughts about Howard and then David. He wondered for a bit about who Julie was. He tossed and turned as images of the old man kept intruding and he finally closed his eyes in an attempt to hold back the new tears.

It was Martinelli's distinct gravelly voice, recognizable immediately, the songster-guitar player's laugh, that rousted him. He opened his eyes as the whole room turned electric white with a sharp fluorescent glare and he found himself gazing across the crowded scene inside Chuck's on Whalley Avenue, that once premier place to grab a late bite on a summer Saturday night.

Looking around for a familiar face, his eyes surveyed the jam-packed red and white black-trimmed interior, the full tables and booth loads of boisterous Jewish *noshers*, the *shmoozers* and hangers out, the array of regulars lined up on their usual counter stools, the gamblers seated over toasted bagels and black coffee or half-eaten American cheese omelets, their faces buried in the sports pages of the just-arrived New York papers.

He paused and listened and above the din could pick out the under-the-breath chatter of the Puerto Rican bus boys and the constant back and forth banter between the regular customers and the Irish waitresses. The calls through the opening to the kitchen caught his ear and carried his gaze toward the overweight caricature of a broken-nosed sandwich man and the Black short-order cook now hollering above the heat and commotion for this one or that one to pick up from the stack of orders piling up under the heat lamps. His mouth began to water from the sight and smell of deli spread everywhere.

One of the harried partners, caught short handed and doubling up as cashier and host behind the front register, took a moment from his quick, nervous tally of the waitresses' receipts to ask if he would mind sitting at the counter. But Mickey had already spotted them. With nothing on but his T-shirt, he raised himself off the edge of the bed and moved toward the couples jammed into one of the candy apple corner booths, barricaded there behind a mound of deli combo platters, corned beef with chopped liver, turkey clubs, melted Swiss pastrami specials, and side order heaps of coleslaw and fresh cut French fries.

Martinelli again called to him from halfway across the place as he approached.

"Hey, Mickey, come! Come have a seat. Your Uncle Charlie's here, the sport. I'll embarrass him intuh buyin' yuh a raz-lime. Come! Come grab a seat by us!"

And there he was and he couldn't figure out exactly how, but it was suddenly 1959 or 1960 and he was eighteen or nineteen again and oh, so cool, still out at nearly one or one-thirty, showing up at the spot in search of some of the guys and in hope of scoring a roast beef on rye. Now there somehow, and invited to sit with the oldsters. Standing youthful tall and handsome in front of the table, his eyes scanned the quarter circle of vinyl bench.

"Yuh can sit here, but just until your father gets back," instructed Martinelli, pointing to a curve-backed wooden chair on the aisle. "He musta gone to the john."

His full face blushed with the taint of alcohol and lack of sleep, a silk blend summer suited Uncle Charlie suddenly appeared. "Yeah, I just left him. He's in the little boys' room, playin' with his *petzelleh*."

Belching softly as he affectionately laid his huge arm across his nephew's shoulders, Charlie turned to the table.

"Yuh know just about everyone here. My dear sister, your loving Aunt Faye, I don't have t' intraduce. Martinelli yuh obviously know 'cause he's the one who spotted yuh and invited yuh over in the first place, I bet. This is his lady friend, Betty, who yuh probably don't know. Betty, say hello to Harry's oldest, my nephew, Mickey."

Mickey glanced across the table at the two women, both in their early to mid forties, seated in the middle of the booth in their Saturday night finest, the one called Betty in a black spaghetti strapped sheath with a silver-sequined top pushing up breast and holding in midriff; the other, his Aunt Faye, in a turquoise summer chiffon with a brocade bodice of fine glass, all light blue, white, sparkly clear with glints of gold. Each wore one of those hand-stitched, beaded Italian evening sweaters draped over their shoulders as protection from the air conditioning and he caught the glitter of their fashionable fifties clip-on earrings, the gold charm bracelets and diamonded fingers, their reddened lips, mascaraed eyes, and the glint of the rhinestoned glasses retrieved to give him the once over. He felt their smiling eyes on him as they both unconsciously toyed with their teased bouffants, identically frosted and sprayed in place, and he suddenly found himself wondering what it would be like with an older woman.

Faye started. "Hello, my Mickey! Where yuh comin' from, out so late?" she asked as she fingered the overripe sour pickles in the stainless relish bowl at center table, feeling for one that wasn't too soft.

"Just out. On my way home. Figured I'd stop and get somethin' t' eat."

His mouth still watering, he glanced down at the table full of deli and it was then that he caught Martinelli's latest girlfriend, the younger and distinctly more attractive of the two women, staring at his unconcealed privates. His *putz,* suddenly conscious of the attention, leapt up uncontrollably and poked its head out from beneath his undershirt as she intently watched. Then, with one motion she placed her turkey with chopped liver down on its plate and taking an instant to swallow and napkin her lips, reached out clear across the table as if to shake hands and grasped it in her hand.

"Everything's just delicious" she suggested, smiling up directly into the kid's eyes the whole time. "Yuh really should get somethin' to eat."

"Maybe I will," he half-embarrassedly grinned, as Aunt Faye again grabbed the conversation.

"Whatsuhmatter, Mickey?! Me, your loving aunt, you're ashamed t' intraduce your friend there to?"

Not wanting to go in that direction with her, at least not with Uncle Charlie standing there, he glanced at the entire crew, still sizing them up as he responded.

"So where yuh all comin' from?"

"The big summer shindig. You know.... The annual formal at the beach club," replied his aunt as Charlie talked over her.

"Yeah. Everybody and his cousin was there. Quite the turnout. Arnold Most and his Orchestra played, and everything. But wait, I haven't finished with the intraductions. What's wrong with you? Yuh don't say hello to your mother?"

Mickey's attention turned to Esther, suddenly appearing there, scrunched in on the end of the bench next to Aunt Faye. Like the ladies to her left, she too was dressed in her finest, but Mickey immediately noticed that something wasn't right. He took another second and realized that her dress just hung off her, way too large, and it was then that he focused in upon how old and ashen she looked, how wrinkled and shrunken in comparison to her companions.

What at first sounded like a muffled laugh, in actuality a soft, breath-catching wheezy sob came from the old woman in the oversized evening dress and he pretended to ignore her condition as he spoke.

"Hi, Ma. Yuh here by yourself? Where's the ol' man?"

"How should I know? Like I ever know where he is at this hour?"

"Whatchuh cryin' for?"

"Me? I'm cryin 'cause you're gonna go' away and yuh haven't even begun to figure it out yet. I'm cryin' for your kids and your wife, and for all the years I tried. And how you wouldn't listen…."

"But ma, I wouldn't even be married yet. And I sure as hell didn't have any kids back then. At least none that I know about. Josh and Jimmy aren't even born yet. Nothin' was your fault, anyways. And besides that, who 'n the hell cries in Chuck's on a Saturday night? Everyone's suppose' t' pretend like they're happy. You're suppose' t' go out and have a good time and not worry about nuthin'."

"Good time? Yuh expect I should have a good time? How can I when I can already see what's coming?"

"What are yuh talkin' about? What's comin'?"

"The one that'll turn out far worse than his father ever was, he asks what's comin'."

"But ma, I already tol' yuh a million times, I'll never be as bad as him."

"Oh, please, Mickey. Stop, already! Yuh sound more and more just like him, everyday."

"Where the hell is he, anyway?"

"Yuh think I know or care?"

Uncle Charlie interrupted once again. "I already tol' yuh, before. He's in the shitter."

Mickey turned and looked toward the men's room door visible at the rear of the luncheonette. Trying to be polite, he gently unwrapped Betty's fingers, still firmly holding on down below, and as he did so, his eye met his Aunt Faye's knowing look as she bit into a soggy piece of sour pickle, her head now tilted slightly back to keep the juice from dribbling down onto her bodice.

"Go, my Mickey. Go see why that father of yours is takin' so long. Your mother shouldn't have to sit here by herself."

Reaching down, he retrieved half an unclaimed corned beef and tongue with Russian as Martinelli, clearly posted to stand watch over the sandwich, protested, "Just help yourself, why don't yuh!" as Betty countered. "Leave the kid alone, can't yuh see he's a growin' boy?"

Ignoring the two, Mickey grabbed a bonus of French fries off one of the plates and devoured them as he moved toward the men's room, sandwich still in hand, while the entire late-night crowd, suddenly noticing his unclothed, erect state, looked on in a now-I've-seen-it-all silent stare of astonishment. Passing through the door, he looked around the empty black and white checkered wash room, to the vacant urinals and lone sink, but Harry was no place to be seen. He half way turned to leave but pausing, took a second to peek down below to see if the single stall was occupied. Recognizing the patent leather loafers, the ones with the black bows, he opened the door. And there sat his father, naked to the waist, a pallid scarecrow of an old man in suspendered tuxedo pants and cummerbund, reclining there on the crapper, chin on chest as if he was already sleeping one off.

"Dad... Hey Dad! Wake up. Your food's on the table."

"Yuh mean yuh forgot about me already? I can't wake up. I'm deader 'n dick. *Tote!*"

"But yuh got to! Your sandwich's gettin' cold."

"It don't make no difference. I ain't got no appetite anymore, anyways. Besides that, how in the hell'd yuh get in here with no pants on? Nobody in their right mind's gonna serve yuh, dressed like that...! You'll end up gettin' everybody busted, t' boot. The cops'll shut the whole damn joint down, for krissakes, and I'll never hear the end of it!"

"Don't worry about it. Nuthin's gonna happen. Nobody even noticed. Ma's wonderin' where you're at for a change and I told Aunt Faye and Betty and the rest you'd be right out."

"My sister?! She's come from Florida? And Betty?! She's here? I can't have her messin' up the funeral! Who in the hell invited her?"

"Martinelli, I guess."

"Hear what I'm tellin yuh, sonny boy. I know yuh ain't gonna listen, but stay away from that one! She's nuthin' but trouble, no goddamn good!"

"But there ain't nuthin' goin' on. I was just..."

"Listen to what I'm tellin' yuh or before yuh know it, she'll end up leading yuh around by your Johnson, there. Doin' her biddin'. Hear what I'm tellin' yuh! Take it from the ol' man. Believe me, I know!"

Mickey shot upright and as his head began to clear he just sat there with his legs over the side of the bed, thinking about it all. "Betty! Fuckin' Betty!"

She was really something, that one. A real spirited beauty in her prime, she had already long departed on her descent when she first latched onto Mickey, her downhill slalom to the bottom propelled by way too much money, alcohol and diet pills, three out-of-control kids, and her husband Elliot's abuse. Already well-known for her spit and vinegar vindictiveness, she spelled certain trouble from the beginning, but it didn't matter to the kid. It didn't matter since he couldn't read the warning signs anyway, especially after she began introducing him around to her lady friends, her immediate circle of fashionably-outfitted new wealth Woodbridge women, that klatch of lonely golf widows, young divorcees, and husbandless workaholics' wives.

He certainly liked it while it lasted, at least until it turned ugly. The mere scent of those older women, the allure of their money and easy sex, the thrill of suburban secretiveness and clandestinity, the rush of running around, all of it, all of it intoxicated him and he couldn't resist. Even when Betty began to use him and ask him for favors.

It started out simple. The occasional ride with her past the downtown Chapel Street night spots, the late night prowl for her husband, the both of them riding in Mickey's car so Elliot wouldn't spot them. The money, the availability of plenty of it, served as the main lure and he readily grabbed every penny as if it had no strings. He needed it then, what with Connie at home with Jimmy and already pregnant with Josh.

With his hand in her purse and hers on his *putz,* she guided him, prodded him, moved him along to a place that he had never imagined. And when the ante went up with each degree of difficulty in her requests and demands, he found it impossible to say no. She wouldn't let go, anyway. Her investment had already cost too much.

The problem was that he actually had developed a weak spot for her, especially after those occasions when Elliot smacked her around, bruising and battering her, blackening her eye that one time, when she came to Mickey with her guard down for an instant, vulnerable. He couldn't resist, nor did he want to, when she called him to come pick her up and she would climb into his blue T-Bird, all beaten up and frightened, her makeup streaked black down her swollen face from the tears. So when she offered the additional money to sweeten the pot, it all seemed too easy. He had his game to play, as well, it turned out.

She figured he would just go ahead and do it when she finally asked, especially after she offered him the ten thou. "Get it over with," she urged him on. "A simple job for a guy like you... Or don't yuh care about me? All you gotta do is climb down and cut the cable and the hill out of Woodbridge will do the rest." So when he failed to carry out the brake job as he promised and went Dixie with the payoff, and Elliot survived to come at her again and again, she placed Mickey near the top of her payback list.

Most of New Haven, its middle class, at least, was shocked and somewhat horrified when it heard about the blast, the explosion which thundered through the residential quiet of that Westville morning when Elliot went to go to work and started his El Dorado. And none were more shocked than the city's comfortable west side Jews. After all, they thought, their people didn't do such things. But those in the know, those either with a longer perspective, some memory of the old days, or those with some inside line on the story knew otherwise and their suspecting eyes turned immediately toward Betty.

The cops grabbed her up right away. Exhausted by the disappointment after they told her Elliot had lived, she rolled over quickly and they picked up Mickey that same morning.

The entire city just assumed the obvious. After all, Mickey worked with cars and was involved with Betty and her circle. Who else would or could plant a bomb for her? The whole thing seemed so cut and dry that few people even bothered to fully read the stories emblazoned across the front pages of the *Register* and *Journal*

Courier. And the few of them who came to know the truth, or those who read far enough, seemed to quickly forget as their short-spanned media attentions moved on to the next sex scandal, the next bit of juicy gossip or true crime diversion.

After all, Mickey's picture had been on the front page right next to hers above the fold. Everyone just assumed he must have done it. The point was, he had nothing to do with the bombing. Betty had handled that differently, hiring out-of-town hitters from Providence through a country club friend with connections in Newport.

But when the detectives came knocking, she delivered him up right away. She wasn't one to forget, especially when a serious piece of change was involved. So when they came to pick her up, she produced the tape, the recording of the conversation between her and Mickey, the whole deal over the phone sweetened by the offer of ten grand in cash, the agreement made three years earlier to cut Elliot's brake cables which Mickey, the money long-spent, had already forgotten about.

They grabbed him, played him the tape, and charged him with conspiracy to commit murder and there he appeared, that miserable mug shot of his right next to hers on the front page, imprinted in the public's mind as the patsy who dynamited the husband's car. Trapped and conned pretty good by the detectives and an ambitious D.A. eager to get some good press off the publicity surrounding a "quick resolution" of the case, Mickey spelled out what he knew about Betty and further incriminated himself in the process. The end game came quickly. Under bad advice from his low-rent attorney, he copped a plea to a conspiracy charge for the brake job hustle. Originally told he could be looking at three to five as part of a "deal", he ended up drawing eight to fifteen.

The bombing hurt a lot more people besides Elliot, of course. Badly mangled and nearly pronounced dead at the scene, he lost a foot and the use of part of his right side, but survived through sheer will and the skill of the well-paid, top-shelf surgeons and specialists at Yale New Haven. He eventually went on to do all right for himself once again.

With Mickey away and left with the two little ones, Connie all but freaked out. She divorced him during his second year in the joint and the two kids eventually took to the streets. The scandal and the embarrassment all but put an end to what was left of Harry and Esther's marriage as well, as they both blamed each other, in some way, for what happened.

Harry, after all, had provided the initial connection. It was Elliot who gave him the start in the car business, after he lost everything, the luncheonette on Legion Avenue, the whole works, in the mid-fifties. Mickey, of course, never understood that it was the resultant guilt, a kind of over-the-road penitence that prodded the old man to make those twice-weekly drives to Sommers all those years.

The whole affair, when combined with all the other hurts and disappointments, wore most heavily on Esther. It contributed to her decline since she, too, felt somehow responsible. After all, it was she who had first reached out and taken Betty under wing, feeling sorry for her when Elliot used to smack her around. Set up by her motherly concern and soft-touch sympathies, she had left her oldest unprotected and defenseless and she never forgave herself for not saying something at the time, for not putting a stop to it when he began running around with the woman.

The reverberations from the blast never stopped. They continued to ripple through people's lives long after the debris from the Cadillac was cleared away and the publicity from the case died down. It went on long after Elliot recovered. Even after both Mickey and Betty got out of the joint. The bombing and the pain from its aftermath, combined with all the other disappointments, ultimately killed Esther. And therein lay the most tragic part of the story, the silent epilogue that few people ever thought about.

As for Mickey? He wound up spending half of his twenties in Sommers, "goin' to college", as he later described it. It was there that he perfected some new hustles and ended up going to work in the prison's impromptu body shop. It was there, as well, that he first began having those predawn nightmare imaginings of the bombing and what it must have been like, that roar of ripping steel and the clatter of fiery metal and glass debris raining down on pavement, ever present in his dreams, distinct to his ear as if he had been there that fateful morning.

As he sat there now on the edge of the bed he unconsciously wiped the remaining trace of tears from his face with a corner of the top sheet. He glanced over at the first hints of daylight that intruded in a faint glow through the window shades and he realized it was time to get up. He lifted himself up from the bed with a slight groan and the noise must have disturbed Gina, stirred her from her own dream world, and she asked where he was going so early, her eyelids still closed.

"I gotta go bury the ol' man," he replied as he made his uneasy, morning-clumsy way toward the bathroom.

CHAPTER 19:

Cards

1947...   THE AVENUE HAD PRETTY much closed down for the day by the time Harry locked the door and started across to the smoke shop. Non-stop busy from before the breakfast rush until after the dinner crowd thinned out, he barely had time to think. But now, as he stepped off the curb, something, perhaps the plain simple hush of the empty evening street or the chill breeze at the back of his neck, triggered the images. It all came rushing back from two nights before. His getting grabbed from behind, the gun barrel in his ribs, his being strong armed across the pavement to the waiting truck, the musty suffocating smell of the burlap over his face, the crosstown ride and the wait in the dark. The fear. The larger than life image of his long gone brother, Dov, suddenly looming there above him grasping the mezuzah, the sudden recognition, leapt from the shadows as he approached the hangout.

From mid street, the small tobacco store looked dark and deserted but he knew better. As he reached the far curb he made an effort to refocus his attention toward what momentarily mattered most, the weekly serious game, his once-a-week shot at coming out a little ahead. The gangly teen posted as a lookout unlatched the front door just as Harry stepped into the entry and with his hopes already up, he slipped the kid a quarter. Guided by the crease of light from under its door, he beelined for the converted storeroom.

Well settled in, the usual crew was already at it. The only thing that remained to be seen was the cards and they hadn't been there for weeks. Not for him, at any rate. It didn't matter what, they just wouldn't come. Gin or pinochle, especially poker, he couldn't remember such a bad streak. Confident that his luck would change, that it eventually had to, he stayed at it anyway. Things had gotten so bad that Louie and some of the hangers on at the shop had even begun to rib him about it and shake their heads in mock pity, while Jakey made the attempt, tried to get him to back off and take a little break. He couldn't and wouldn't listen.

Oblivious, he couldn't even see that he had pretty much scraped away any residual topsoil as he dug himself deeper into the hole with Butter. As wise in his ways as some ancient Talmudic graybeard and with street survival instincts honed as sharp as those of an old king sewer rat, the establishment's proprietor was always willing, as part of what he described as his "God given calling", to extend credit. Up to a point, that is, and he already had his hooks well into Harry.

Little over an hour and a half had passed since he sat down and it looked as if it would be turning into another one of those nights. It didn't matter what he picked up. Two pair and someone would have trips or a hidden straight. He'd turn over a flush and Butter or Louie would flip over a stronger one or a boat. Barely eleven and he had pretty much worked through the store receipts for the week, maybe four hundred. That on top of the additional six that he already owed Butter. But he remained optimistic, certain that the cards would turn.

The bookie had been on a tear since before Harry sat down and those malevolent quirks of his had already surfaced. That gloating, badgering banter; that you're-all-a-bunch-of-suckers scoff of a laugh each time he raked in a pot. So Harry should have known better, should have read the cautionary signs, the aggressive attitudinal tells in Butter's play.

Calling straight seven as he shuffled, Louie dealt and Harry waited to see his top card before peeking at the bottom two. A jack and ten, hearts in color, with another ten flipped up. The best start of the night, he thought. His eyes made their way around the table as Louie called the play.

"The queen of diamonds talks. Your bet, Sidney."

Sid Berman, from Legion Hardware up the street, sitting to Harry's left, bet a buck. Jakey and then Louie called, with nothing on top, and Butter, showing an eight, raised one, making it two to Epstein the butcher. Playing it tight, conservative as usual, he folded and that brought it around to Harry. Fingering his dwindled wad, he paused, thought about raising but simply called. Berman saw the bet, as did Jakey. Louie pushed his cards toward the center and resumed the deal.

Coming around, he tossed Harry another jack. Berman drew a king to accompany his queen up top. Jakey bought a nine to go with a visible seven, and Butter caught a four. Berman, high on board, bet two dollars. Jakey called and Butter, sitting there with an eight and the four showing, raised two more. Happy to see the jacks over but not wanting to give anything away, Harry paused as if pondering some lousy cards. He looked across at Butter.

"What the hell yuh got, yuhr so proud of? I bump another."

Berman called, Jakey folded, and it came back to Butter, who looked over at Harry.

"What? Yuhr so smart all of a sudden? Lookin' to play with the big boys? Make it another three."

Again not wanting to seem too eager, Harry paused another moment as he looked at the bookie.

"Another *draih? Mit vus?* A skip straight? Two lousy pair, maybe? I call."

He floated the singles into the center and with Berman along for the ride, the pot straight, Louie tossed the next cards up. Harry bought a nine. Berman bought a ten to improve his now probable straight and Butter received another four.

Louie took charge. "A pair of fours bets."

Butter bet five. Jakey folded, Harry called, and this time Berman raised. "I see your five and raise it another." Butter kicked it again, bringing it back to Harry, who now had to study the table more closely.

Out of the hand and looking to move the game along, Louie made the read.

"Com'on, Harr, it's ten to you."

Harry pretended he didn't hear. *"Okay,"* he thought to himself, *"Berman already has his straight. Butter sees him and raises with a pair of fours on board. He's already bettin' with an eight and a four showin'. So what's he got? A boat already, tops?"*

He looked at Butter and then to Louie as he put in the raise. "Ten it is. Deal the cards."

Harry maintained his face as the third jack came. Berman filled in four to the straight with the case jack and Butter bought a three, no visible help. Louie looked to his friend as he resumed the call.

"Jacks over. Your bet."

Harry drew from his cigar, placed it back in the nearly full ashtray sitting to his left, and peeked at his bottom cards as if to remind himself what he had. Quite proud of his full house after six, he bet five. Out of it by that time but not reading the table, Berman raised it five more and that gave Butter, sitting with his probable two pair, a boat at best, reason to pause.

"I should go out, but what the hell, I'll see the ten and go yuh ten more."

Harry figured what that meant, that Butter had the boat, possibly fours over, but more likely eights full. Not wanting to seem too eager, he again puffed on his stogie and hesitated for effect as he blew a gray cloud out over the growing mound center-table. Louie took charge.

"Come on, Harr, we ain't got all night. Some of us gotta work t'marruh. It's a quarter t' you. One more left. In or out."

Taking another second to check his money, Harry set his hole cards down and looked across at Butter, not even concerned with Berman. "I raise a quarter."

Finally realizing what was up, Berman folded. "I guess my straight ain't goin' nowhere, this time o' night."

Butter called and Louie reminded the two remaining players of the house rules as he dealt the final card down.

"Just the two of yuhz left. Fifty's the limit. Jacks talk."

Not expecting to improve, Harry took a peek anyway for effect, glanced over at Butter, and counting the remainder of his cash, pushed it all toward the center.

"I bet forty-five."

This time Butter paused.

"What are yuh? Some kinda wise guy? Yuh think yuhr smart, sittin' there with your possible tens boat, maybe jacks? I don't think yuh got it. I see your forty-five and raise another half."

"Yuh wanna bet intuh me again? Fine. I'll see yuh and raise it another."

"What another?! Yuh ain't even got the half to cover my bump. How yuh gonna raise?"

"I'm goin' shy, that's all."

"Shy?! Whatchuh got to back it up?"

"Yuh worried?! Since when ain't I good for it?"

"Since now. Yuh already owe me what? Six before t'night? How much yuh down here? Another four easy, maybe five?"

"I said I'm good for it."

"I know you're good for it. But I saw my doctor the other day and he gave me some bad news. He says I might not live forever."

Harry looked over at Louie, and then toward Hershey for some backing. Receiving no support from his pals, his gaze turned back toward Butter.

"Wha'd'yuh want? Blood?"

"You ain't my type. How about that watch of yours?"

"Be serious! I can't give yuh the watch. I lose it, I might as well not go home."

"Yuh think all of a sudden I care where yuh sleep? Besides, I ain't lookin' t' keep it. I got a drawer so full of crumb-bums' watches, someone could take me for a pawnbroker. Like I had three balls. Yuh want another advance, a little loan, fine. But yuh owe too much already. It's time yuh gimme some security."

"Wha' d' yuh think I'm gonna do!? Take off or somethin? Leave town?!"

"Put up or shut up!"

Confident in his cards but caught, Harry paused a second, and shaking his head the whole time in disbelief, slowly undid the gold clasp. Sliding the watch from his wrist, he placed it mid table atop the pile of cash.

"The fuckin' thing's worth a hell of a lot more than what's in the pot. Make it a C-note! Another hundred!"

Louie interceded, reminding the two of the house rules, that the limit was fifty bucks. Butter, his bead firmly fixed on his prey, waved him off with an upraised palm as he spoke to Harry.

"What!? Yuh wanna be a wise guy! There's one more left, no? I see your hunnert and raise one more."

"I'm in!" responded Harry, laying his jacks full face up on the table. Butter paused, straight faced for an instant, and then grinned as he laid his cards down. Three eights hidden, four of a kind.

"Do yuh believe this? I bought the final eight! The case goddamn eight on the last card! Unbelievable!"

Harry could feel his guts tighten and the blood drained from his face. Pushing back in his chair, he raised himself up and resignedly stared down at the center of the table, still studying the upturned cards in disbelief, as Butter raked in the pot.

"I don't believe this bullshit. I'm through."

Butter laughed as he raised the time piece to eye level for an up close look.

"I don't believe it neither. What's that make it now? The six from before, plus what you was shy. Let's see. Three hundred tonight. Yuh owe me nine."

Rolling the watch in his pudgy fingers, he paused a moment and brought the piece close to his better eye. He spoke without looking across the table as he squinted at the inscription.

"That wife of yours, Esther, she got pretty good taste.... When it comes to watches, that is. But yuh don't have t' worry, it ain't goin' nowhere. Yuh'll get it when yuh bring me all of what yuh owe."

"Jesus, Butter, yuh ain't gotta hold on t' the fuckin' watch. Yuh know how I kill myself every day across the street. It ain't like I'm goin' anywhere, for krissakes!"

His look suddenly serious, the bookie's tone changed.

"Wha' duh I look like, here? The Salvation Army? I have to tell yuh, like yuh don' know how it works? This way yuh got a little incentive and I get a little security. That's all. Nice guy that I am, t' show you what kind uh friend I am, I ain' even gonna charge yuh the interest. No vig. How's that? I just want what yuh owe. And I want it soon. That's all."

Hoping for some help, a mediator perhaps, Harry again looked across the table at Louie and then to Hershey, the two of them sitting there detached, expressionless. He then turned back toward Butter.

"Yuh'll get your goddamn money."

"When?"

"When I get it. Okay!?"

"Yuh got two weeks. How's that? No watch 'til yuh pay me. In full!"

"You're one helluva guy."

"I'm not likin' your tone."

"Tone?! Yuh don't like my tone!? How 'bout this then? Yuhr a no-good son of a bitch, Butter!"

"Is that any way t' talk?"

"Yuh had no business stayin' with the eights boat, and yuh know it. Not with my two pair showin'."

"Let's just say I had a feelin'."

"Feelin'? Go fuck yourself with your feelin's!"

Harry turned for the door as the bookie hollered to his back.

"Nobody talks to me like that! Not in my own place. You're banned, eighty-sixed! Don't even think about comin' back in here 'til yuh bring me my money! Yuh hear me!?"

"Yeah, I hear yuh, and I hope yuh go t' hell!"

Half dozing at his post, the kid at the front jolted upright off his stool with the slam of the rear door. He had already worked there long enough to tell from the hour, the sudden commotion, and especially from the way Harry moved as he came out of the back, that a tip was out of the question. He silently undid the dead bolt and held the door open anyway as the disgruntled player exited without so much as a word.

Replaying the last round in his head as he crossed Legion Avenue, feeling slightly sick to his stomach, and already wondering what he was going to concoct when Esther asked about the watch, he didn't even notice as the van crept up from behind on the opposite side of the street. Its lights out, it stalked him for a moment as he made his way down the dark, empty side street and finally came up alongside him in the middle of the block. He turned and recognized Dov's man at the wheel, illuminated by a streetlight, just as the guy signaled with a thumb to get in. Harry hesitated at the curb for a second. Then realizing that it was just going to be one of those nights, he paused for a second to shake his head and resignedly crossed over. The rear door swung open and he climbed in.

The big one with the rough hands and the cough, the one they called Shmule, pulled the doors closed behind and motioned for him to sit on the floor.

"Yuhr brudder, he wants t' see yuh."

"Well, I'm sure glad he could send the chauffeur and valet."

"No more *talkink*. Here, put dis on."

Harry fingered the coarse hemp of the sack. "It ain't like I'm gonna tell anyone where we're goin'. I can't even see out…"

"You don' listen good. I tol' yuh no more talkink," came the reply.

Once again weighing what amounted to a lack of options, Harry hesitated briefly then slowly pulled the stifling burlap over his head.

As the truck moved off through the neighborhood, he again tried to track the route but soon became disoriented. It eventually came to a full stop after fifteen or twenty minutes and he listened as the driver got out. He heard some steps, the rattle of chain link and the screechy whine of unoiled wheels on concrete, the sound of a large sliding gate. The driver returned and the truck moved forward thirty yards or so and halted. Harry heard a heavy overhead garage door ascend and the vehicle moved another ten yards and stopped.

The rear opened right away this time and he found himself somewhat relieved as he recalled his first visit and that interminable wait, handcuffed, with the sack over his head, enclosed in layers of darkness, alone. Another pair of firm hands assisted the ones with the cough as they pulled him up and guided him down off the back of the truck. He sensed someone else to his left as his feet hit the ground and the trio silently guided him a few more yards before prodding him to sit. A minute or so passed and the hood lifted and as his eyes adjusted to the light, he found himself in a different location, inside what appeared to be a large commercial garage, a repair shop of some sort. There, facing him, straddling a wooden chair as before, sat Dov, his gray Fedora cocked back on his head.

"So how's my baby brother?"

"How should he be?! A ride in such luxury. A guy could get used to it."

"Yuh still have your sense of humor, I see. That, I like."

"And so do your boys. Lots of laughs. Somethin' tells me yuh didn't bring me here for an audition, however. What's the story?"

"So you decided to help us out?"

"What decide?! I get grabbed up and brought here with a bag over my head. Like I had some choice?"

"Choice, there's plenty of. After all, this is America, no? It ain't like we're a bunch of gangsters. Yuh can get up now and get back in the truck and one of the boys'll drive yuh home or wherever... back down to the Avenue. And that'll be that. Nobody's gonna force yuh t' do nothin'."

"Or...?"

"Or yuh can help me, us, out."

"Who's 'us'? What do yuh mean, 'us'? I already tol' yuh, or maybe yuh didn't get the message. I ain't no joiner."

"How much did yuh lose t'night? Wha' d' yuh owe on the street, all tol'?"

"What makes yuh think I lost? And what's it to you what I owe?"

"Yuh left the game pretty early, no? Yuh musta lost good. Otherwise you'd still be playin'. The word on the street says yuh been on a losin' streak."

"How would you know?!"

"Like I tol' yuh before, we know everything. I just figured I could maybe help out my kid brother, like he did for me once."

"So yuh remember?"

"I remembered the mezzuzah, no?"

"Yuh think the ten or fifteen dolluhs, whatever it was I gave yuh when yuh left, that's gonna help? Besides, yuh still ain't exactly said what yuh want me t'do. I can't afford to get jammed up and I ain't about to become somebody's fall guy."

"I already tol' yuh. All we want is for yuh t'make some runs, some deliveries. I can't go paradin' around myself. Things are too hot. I need somebody I can trust. Someone who knows the city. That can make some drops when we need and help direct the fellas here on occasion, when we got a pick up. The whole thing shouldn't take no much more'n a week. Two, tops. Then I'm otta here."

"And what if something goes wrong? I end up gettin' grabbed, squeezed in the goddamn middle?"

"If yuh don't wanna help, yuh can walk right now. Shmule here'll drive yuh back, like I said. I just thought maybe yuh wouldn't be so averse to helping me out. Figured yuh could use the extra cash. That's all. Besides, everything's already been taken care of. There ain't gonna be no trouble."

"There ain't? Then how come you're hidin' out? And what's my take?"

"They're lookin' for me, not you. They don't even know who I am, for real, so they got no way of connectin' me t' you. We'll give yuh two hundred for each run. Cash. Each time yuh make a drop."

The brothers stared eye to eye as Harry paused, calculating whether to take the risk and the offer. He thought about what he owed on the Avenue to Butter and the rest, the growing line of bill collectors, the rent due on the store and the flat, how he could use the cash. He unconsciously rubbed the spot where his watch normally rested.

"And what am I supposed to be droppin' and how often? Doctor says I shouldn't do no heavy liftin'. 'Cuz I got this hernia."

"You won't have to do no *shleppin'*. Just envelopes. A couple right away. A few more after that."

"Yuh gonna fill me in on what's really goin' on?"

"You in or out?"

"I gotta hear more."

"Okay. It's like this here. We got some people on the inside at Winchester's. There's maybe a hundred or so pieces, but we gotta go slow. We can't move 'em all at once. They gotta be brought out a dozen, maybe two, a crate at a time, tops. It's all cash and carry, pay as yuh go. All you gotta do is drop the payments when it's time for a delivery, every several days. Everything's on the up and up."

"And if somethin' goes wrong? I get picked up?"

"The money'll be there. The kids and Esther, they'll be looked after."

"That's exactly what I wanted to hear! Count me out."

"Why?"

"'Cause yuh already got me doin' time. That's why!"

"Relax. Like I said, nobody's gonna get grabbed."

"How is it yuh know my wife's name? That I got kids?"

"Yuhr not listenin'. I already tol' yuh. We know everything."

Weighing the variables, Harry paused another moment as if standing in line at the two dollar window, scratch sheet in hand. Again thinking about the watch and Butter and everyone else he owed, the shylocks and the wholesalers, the landlords, he finally shook his head in resignation and a slight what-the-hell, go-for-it grin crept into his expression. Dov had his answer.

CHAPTER 20:

Gladiolas

1989... DAVID TOSSED AND TURNED and tossed and turned, rolling first on his side, then onto his belly, and then over on his back again, until it finally dawned on him that he shouldn't have had that last cup of coffee at the truck stop, or maybe even the first. The caffeine certainly had not been a concern at the time, sitting there with Mickey, listening to the crazy talk about guns and Feds, a maybe mob contract on the street, and a possible hit at the funeral. It wasn't the content of his brother's ramblings that kept him awake, since nothing on that count really troubled or even surprised him anymore. He just found himself lying there, wondering about truth and reality and where they might reside in Mickey's world. He resigned himself to the fact that there was no telling and turned over on his back once again, tossing aside the uncomfortable foam pillow as he rolled.

He gazed up at the night through the Plexiglas skylight above the bed and turned to check the green digital time on the night table. Two-thirty. He thought about going downstairs to raid the refrigerator and sat up on the edge of the bed, feet on the floor, about to get up. But Annie stirred ever so slightly with his movement as if to remind him and he remembered Howard's warning. The security system, the motion detecting infrared would be on on the first floor. He thought about making the attempt anyway and imagined the scene: the private security cops speeding up, lights flashing, in some heavy-suspension black Bronco. A couple of flak-jacketed SWAT-team rejects, their ninja ski masks barely concealing multiple double chins, jumping out with their high caliber nickel-plated pistols and pump actions cocked, at the ready. A couple of blasts followed by the warning to halt.

The suspected intruder's blood, guts and bone fragment splattered up and down the downstairs hallway and across the den, all because he wanted a glass of milk and a frozen bagel, maybe some yogurt. He could already hear Howard hollering about the cost of the cleanup and repair for the riddled, pock-marked walls and the ruinous red stains in the plush wool carpeting, as well as the impending lawsuit.

Even if he could manage to turn the system off, he figured, the dogs would start barking and wake the whole house as soon as he stepped into the hall. Resigned to the situation, his stomach now growling, he just lay back down and listened to Annie's shallow breath as she slept.

"Trapped, a prisoner in my own brother's house," he mused as his gaze returned to the skylight.

He tossed for a while longer, now too hungry to sleep, and his thoughts wandered to the arrangements. He tried to remember the last time he had seen Louie Velner and he wondered for a bit about who might show up. He imagined Harry all decked out, with a slight bit of contentment, a kind of would-yuh-let-me-rest-in-peace-already smile on his face, lying there in some gaudy casket surrounded by baskets of flowers and several tripodded floral wreaths probably boosted from the winner's circle at the horses. That brought the gladiolas to mind.

It must have been the last time he was in New Haven. Or maybe the time before. He couldn't quite remember. He had gone up to see Esther's sister, his Aunt Edie, now living on the ninth floor of the senior citizen high rise. "Tower One", they called it, the one downtown, alongside the Oak Street Connector near the Yale-New Haven Hospital.

Uncle Manny was out, gone to the store for something and then over to the *shul*, she said, and he knew what that meant. Off to the OTB to take care of his morning Jones, the perpetual dream of some long-shot parlayed pay-off. She asked him if he wanted anything.

"Can I get yuh somethin'? A cup of coffee, maybe? I got some Entenmann's, a crumb cake, to go with."

Grabbing her metal cane, she got up and padded into the kitchen despite his polite "Don't bother. I'm fine. Really, I'm okay" part of the ritual.

He listened and chatted back as she put on a pot and took down the cups and saucers, the plates and paper napkins for the cake, talking the whole time as she *putzed*, the routine questions about the wife, and Wisconsin, and the weather "out there". She returned and eased herself down into the recliner and continued the interrogation. He answered each question as the coffee perked and studied her features as she went on, the loose hanging skin on bone, the wrinkles and aged eyes, now paled by cataracts. He thought about how attractive she was when he was a kid, and how old she had somehow become.

Still clear as a bell, sitting there in her plain worn pastel housedress and slippers, with the accompanying blare of one of those daytime T.V. talk shows competing in the background, she went on about the latest Pacino movie she and Manny had gone to, and the woman down the hall who fell and broke her hip, and the one across the way who just lost her grandson to cancer.

"Young, too. Such a shame. It's one thing, I'm tellin' yuh, to die when you're old already, lived your life. But for a mother to lose a child. That's gotta be the worst."

She caught him gazing over at the tube, inattentive, and drew him back.

"There's nothin' on worth watching anymore. Who needs it? I don't watch. With my eyes the way they are now, I can hardly see a goddamn thing anyway. But your Uncle Manny, he has to have it on all the time. Even when he's not here. So I shouldn't feel lonely, he says. Do me a favor and put it off already. God only knows what he did with the remote."

David got up and clicked off the set as Edie switched mental channels, going from her daughter and "that partner of hers", the both of them long gone from the scene, living poor but happy somewhere up in Vermont to how Howard had been up to visit recently and how he had taken her and Manny out to dinner during the holidays. Her attention then turned to Mickey.

"That one? He'll never change. And his kids? Jimmy and Josh and the little ones? I hear there's another one, too, with the latest girlfriend. It's such a shame, I'm tellin' yuh. But what's to expect? Let me tell yuh somethin' about that brother of yours. He's far worse than your father ever was. It's a horrible thing to say, but it's a good thing your mother, *alevashalom,* she didn't live to see."

She paused and looked toward the kitchenette and he caught the signal. Again, part of the routine. Getting up from the sofa, he unfolded the white enameled snack tray, set it alongside her recliner, and went in to pour two cups as her voice followed.

"Do yuh take milk? I don't remember. The doctor said I have t'stop with the sugar, but there's some up above, next to the stove, if yuh want. I also got Sweet and Low. I take mine black, though I shouldn't do that either, what it does to my stomach and how it makes me wanna go *pish* all the time."

He carried the cups in and setting them down, went back for the cake. When he returned, he noticed she had paused for a second, as if deciding what to say next.

"There's something I've been tryin' to figure out, maybe you can help me with."

"Yeah? What's that?"

"A little puzzle."

"You still do the crosswords?"

"Crosswords? Who can see, for krissakes?"

"You can see to go to a Pacino movie."

"Manny, he watches. Me, I just listen. I can't see, but I'm not deaf, your old *tanteh.*"

"What puzzle we talkin' about?"

"It's the strangest thing, but every time I go visit your mother.... You know... to the cemetery, like on High Holy Days, Rosh Hashanah, or on her birthday or for the *yahrzeit,* the anniversary, Manny takes me and whenever I go, there's almost always gladiolas. Someone leaves gladiolas."

"Gladiolas?"

"Yeah. On the grave. Sometimes they're fresh, like somebody just was there. For the love of me, I can't figure it out, who in the hell leaves gladiolas."

"What, Edie? You don't know? Who d'yuh think would bring her gladiolas?"

"That's what I can't figure out. I haven't a clue."

"You really don't know?"

"Would I be askin' if I did, Mr. Smarty?"

"It has to be Harry!"

"Your father?! What makes you think that?"

"Who else could it be? Look. Yuh remember how he used to go out and shop every Sunday? You probably don't, but I sure as hell do. How he'd go and get whitefish and lox and onion rolls and bagels on Legion Avenue or out Whalley at the kosher supermarket after they tore everything down."

"Yeah, so?"

"After he finished making the rounds, his Sunday *shmooze,* he'd always make one last stop at that little flower stand on the corner, the one by the Boulevard. No matter what was going on between the two of them, he'd always bring gladiolas, when they were in season. Always gladiolas, every Sunday. Without fail, like clockwork."

"But that was when they were still together. You mean to tell me that after all they went through, what he put your mother through, now, after all these years, he still brings flowers?"

"Exactly! Exactly because of what he put her through. I'd bet you anything, that's who it is."

"This, I don't believe."

"What's to believe?"

Lost in thought, she got up and slowly made her way into the kitchen, without the cane this time, and returned pot in hand to refill their cups.

"It was what…? Five years they were separated before she died, and what's it now…? Over twelve she's gone already, my sister, and that one, he still puts gladiolas by her grave? This one, I still can't believe!"

"I'll bet yuh ten bucks, even up, and the rest of the Entenmann's, it's him."

"Please. I got enough *tsooris* with your uncle Manny and the gambling. Yuh think I need your money? The cake's all dried out anyway. Gladiolas. Who would've thought?"

Lying there in the dark, he tried to picture the two of them, Harry and Esther, and what they must have been like when they were young. Before it all soured. He could still remember the tailings of mutual affection from when he was a kid, those rare moments when some of what they once shared appeared through the layerings of fugitive hopes and violated trust. But that had been a long time ago and the only remaining evidence of their mutual joy sat captured in some old photographs that had come to him, the irrefutable black and white proof, now kept tucked away, of the two of them caught in love forever, happy, smiling, mutual in their adoration, embraced in their younger years. Several with Esther in a black bathing suit tied behind the neck, and Harry in a V-necked T-shirt and plaid Bermuda shorts, with his cookout apron and a cigar between his fingers. A picnic somewhere, maybe Chatfield Hollow or what they used to call Camp Roosevelt, way out Route 80. Summer snapshots of the two of them, smiling, proud, holding a pudgy, hand-in-mouth, diapered Mickey, his hair in curly ringlets, between them. David puzzled over their relationship, his mother and father's, and finally slept for awhile. That is, until something, he wasn't sure what, a voice, he thought, stirred him.

Wondering if he had actually slept at all, he squinted over at the illuminated time next to the bed. Three-fifteen. He put his head down and lay there listening to Annie's sleep, that soft rhythmic sound she made, somewhere between a faint snore and a wheeze. He pulled the quilt up over her bare shoulder and rolled over on his back and stared up at the starlit winter blackness beyond the skylight. Closing his eyes, he began to doze off.

Suddenly the voice came again, clear this time, rousting him.

"David! Again I'm telling yuh, it's time to get up! I don't want you should be late!"

He opened one eye partway and reached out in the dark for Annie, silent and motionless, still sound asleep. Unable to place what he heard, he closed his eyes, thought for an instant how distant, yet familiar the voice seemed. He started to drift off again when it came once more.

"I'm not sayin' it again! You gotta get up! Now!"

His eyes closed, he responded. "But I don't f-e-e-l good!"

"You do this every time I let you stay up late! You're not staying home today. I got too much to do. So don't start with the 'I don't feel good' routine. You've already missed too many days! You're going to school!"

"School?!" Not wanting to be late again, he bolted upright and as he fumbled for his glasses on the night table, the realization hit him. He put them on and peered off into the room.

"What? You thought you could sleep on a day like this? You thought I would leave you sleep?" came the voice as his unadjusted eyes tracked the sound back to the table by the window.

There she was, sitting there, silhouetted in the cold blue moonlight.

"Ma…? Mommy?"

"And who else would you be expecting?"

"But… but…."

"Yes, I know. We haven't talked in a long time. And maybe I shouldn't even bother, like you forget and don't bother."

David quickly glanced over at Annie, still snoring slightly, undisturbed. He looked back at the figure.

"But this can't be! You're… you're …"

"I'm what? Dead? Who said I wasn't?"

"But I don't believe in ghosts!"

"And who said anything about ghosts? Let's just say I'm memory. Come and sit by me while I finish."

He got up and walked toward Esther. He couldn't believe his eyes and intentionally caught the inside of his right cheek between his side teeth and bit down hard, a reality check. She motioned for him to sit and he took the chair across from her and stared in amazement.

She was wearing her old pink housecoat, the quilted winter one with the white, lacy trim, which Howard had given her for Hanukah one year. Her tired brown hair, frosted at the ends, was wrapped in a maze of rollers, clips, and scotch tape. Her gray-green eyes, hazel the word she used to describe them, just looked down intently at what she was doing.

In her right hand was a small paring knife. In front of her sat two large kitchen bowls and a rooster-shaped cutting board, the one that he had made for her in ninth grade shop. One of the bowls held grapefruits and oranges. The other was halfway filled with segments, already peeled and sectioned. Their discarded rinds sat in a small pile alongside.

Without saying a word she picked up one of the grapefruits and positioned it in her left palm like a small globe, upright on its axis. Using the knife, she clipped off the two poles. Careful not to cut too deep and slowly rotating it as she went, she then slit the yellow skin from top to bottom, following several imaginary meridians, and peeled away the rind. Then using the blade of the paring knife and her thumb, she scraped away the white remnants of pulp until a pinkish-gray softball shape appeared. She put the knife down and inserted her thumbs where the stem had been and pulled the grapefruit apart, releasing a juicy citrus mist into the air. Separating a single section with her long well-kept nails, she tore the fleshy membrane from its center and picked out the seeds before tossing it in the bowl.

"Fruit salad. You know how the girls like my fruit salad. We're playing here tonight. You can have a little taste, but I'm not cleaning it all so you and your brothers can devour it before they get here. Just a little and then its 'hands out'!"

"The girls? What girls?!"

"Just the usuals. Mabel Yuritsky and Cookie, Evelyn Epstein and Eva Brodsky and maybe a fifth, if Dora that *yenta,* she decides to show up. Do you know anyone else, might be coming?"

She looked at his somewhat puzzled face and answered the question before he could repond.

"Oh yeah, I know. They're all gone now, at least from where you sit. But me? I've been waiting now, for what…? Almost thirteen years so we could get a decent game together. One's passing should never be an excuse to break up a card club, especially as long as we've been playing. We played since high school, you know. And now that everybody's back together, all the girls, I thought we could get in a few rounds of kaluki or a little canasta. Besides, I don't expect your father will come walking in tonight."

"Why are you here?"

"Didn't I answer that before? Where else should I be?"

"But why now?"

Esther reached around and picked up the dish towel draped over the back of her chair. "Boy, I'm tellin' yuh, the juice from the grapefruit, it really stings. My hands, they get so dry and cracked in the winter. They've been bothering me all day, ever since I got up this morning. And do you think for one minute that my friend Dora, she'll appreciate it? Peeling all this fruit. She'll find one seed I missed and she'll let me hear about it, believe you me!"

"Come on, Ma, you didn't come just to *kvetch* about your hands or Dora. Everyone knows she was an ingrate. What's new about that?"

"O-h-h-h! So my doctor son, the Ph.D., the one who thinks he's so smart now, he wants to rush his old mother?"

"Tell me why you've come."

"It's the watch."

"The watch? What watch?"

"The one I gave your father. You know. The gold one with the inscription I gave him. Back when we were first married."

"Oh-h-h-h! *Now* I get it! The fuckin' watch Mickey and Howard have been carrying on about all these years!"

"Such language you use in front of your mother?! Is that what they taught you in that fancy graduate school? My son the doctor with the mouth like his father!?"

"I'm sorry, Ma. But tell me, what's with the watch?"

"It's a sentimental thing. The watch itself, it can't be worth very much, but your brothers have been carrying on forever over it. Ever since I died and Howard got his hands on it. They're absolutely *mishugeh*! It was your father's and from what I hear, where he's goin', he certainly won't want to keep time. You're the one. You have to decide what to do with it!"

"I don't understand."

"Don't worry, you'll figure it out. And by the way, one more thing. I know they're both a pain in the ass, and I know you live far away.... I can tell you did good marrying that one, the *shikseh,* over there, but you should look after Mickey and Howard as best you can."

"But I have my life."

"Of course. Who said you didn't? And I'm not askin' you should feel compelled to go to any great lengths and jeopardize what you've done for yourself. But at the same time, you shouldn't ignore your brothers either!"

"I'll try, but I can't promise."

"Who's askin' for promises? Between your father, you, and your brothers, I figured out long ago that promises are *gornisht*. You know from *gornisht*, my educated son? For nothing. As I always said..."

"Yeah, I know. 'It's what you do, not what you say, that counts!'"

"Oh-h-h, so you actually learned something from your mother, when, after all these years, she thought you weren't listening!"

"Ma?"

"What, my David?"

"I gotta ask yuh somethin'. Somethin' I'm curious about."

"So, *nu*?"

"You know anybody named Julie?"

"Julie? Julie who?"

"Both Mickey and Howard said the last thing Harry did was he called out for someone named Julie. Called out for this Julie to save him. You remember anyone named Julie?"

"Was it a man or a woman?"

"I don't know."

"Dollars to doughnuts, I'll bet yuh it's one of his girlfriends, one of those *kurveh* whores he'd come home stinkin' from! There'd be nothin' in the house for you kids to eat but he'd have plenty of money for his *shikseh* whore girlfriends!"

"So you think maybe it was one of his girlfriends? Was there one named Julie?"

"I didn't say that. I never wanted to know their names then, and I can't be bothered with them, or your father, now. The girls will be here soon and I still got plenty to do yet. Besides, you're gonna be late for school."

"Late for school!" David shot upright in the bed, grabbed his glasses and scanned the night dark room. He checked the time. Almost three-forty. Setting the glasses back on the night table, he put his head down on the pillow and closed his eyes. He rolled over and put an arm around Annie and felt the sore spot on the inside of his cheek with his tongue until sleep finally came.

CHAPTER 21:

Opportunity

1947... HARRY IMMEDIATELY CAME TO like his side job in the New Haven weapons trade. After all, things went smoothly the first couple of trips and he couldn't complain about the money. He merely received a call and picked up what clearly felt like a wad of cash, wrapped and rubber-banded in a sealed business envelope, at a prearranged drop, different each time. Then driving it across town, he did as he was told. Waiting to make sure no one else was inside except the owner, he entered the candy store a few blocks up from the factory complex on Winchester Avenue. With one eye on the street, he pretended to browse the display rack of magazines and out-of-town newspapers by the front until he was certain no one was watching. He then slid the envelope from inside his coat and eased it down behind the upright stack of *Saturday Evening Post*s as directed. Approaching the display counter, he asked the proprietor for an Aspargas, one of those fancy Cuban brands they didn't carry. The password. He bought a couple of Cuetos, his Connecticut Valley nickel specials, and left. The next morning he found an envelope with a deuce inside waiting for him on the floorboard just under his driver's seat. That was it. That simple. That is, until the routine changed.

A week and a half had gone by and he had already made three uneventful drops. So he was surprised that Thursday night to see Shmule waiting for him after he closed, parked there around the corner just up the street from the store. The unshaven hulk of a man, as laconic as usual, silently hand motioned for him to get in, this time in the front, and they drove straight away downtown to the factory off lower State St. As they pulled up to the loading dock, Harry recognized it immediately, by the name anyways, "Bottmacher Garments", painted in two-story tall three dimensional cursive, white, red, and black on the illuminated brick. The name alone, that of one of the city's long established German Jewish families, for the first time gave him some clearer sense of the scope of the operation and he finally felt somewhat reassured on one count. That Dov wasn't handing him a line after all about Esther and the kids actually being looked after if the whole thing turned sour.

A night watchman stepped out of the shadows and greeted them with a knowing nod as they moved up the steps of the dock. Passing through the rear door, they entered into a high-ceilinged shipping area lined with parallel rows of storage racks stacked with banded cardboard boxes. The two workmen busy there hardly looked up as they hand-trucked a bulky steel-strapped bale of what appeared to be rags or used clothing onto a trailer backed into the bay. Without a word, Shmule led him past and through a set of swinging doors to an interior room where they passed three others, including two that Harry had already come to recognize as part of Dov's crew, busy along a large work bench. His eye caught the wooden packing crates sitting off to the side, all of them wood burn branded with the Winchester's trademark. He looked on in passing as one of the men reached in and removed a bolt action rifle from one of the boxes and began wrapping it in pieces of old clothing heaped at the end of the table while one of the others shoved another piece, already swaddled, down into the center of a partially constructed bale positioned on the floor. His guide moved him along.

A swinging steel fire door led them to a narrow corridor where Shmule, without entering, directed him through yet another door leading to an office. There sat Dov and an older, neatly groomed man. The handsome, silver-grayed stranger, well-tailored in a wool suit and silk tie, was seated behind a large wooden desk. Dov came to his feet as did the gentleman and the brother proceeded with the introductions.

"Mr. Bottmacher... uh... Nathan, allow me to introduce my kid brother. Harry, say hello to Mr. Bottmacher."

The older man rose and extended his smooth unworked hand across the desk.

"Please, please. You can suspend with the formalities. Call me Nate."

Harry shook and the man motioned for him to have a seat.

"I was just reminiscing with your brother how I can remember your father from the old days. Back when I was still in high school. How he used to bring fresh chickens to my mother. We lived out Sherman Avenue then. He'd deliver them special, for the *Shabbes* and holidays, in that old truck of his, sometimes with the live birds in crates, their heads sticking out, on the back. I can remember like it was yesterday."

"That musta been some time ago."

"It was, it was. A different era, then. All gone now. I suppose you're wondering why I've asked you to come."

"Let me guess. Yuh found out I could use some shirts t' fill out my wardrobe."

Bottmacher smiled slightly. "No, that isn't why, but we can send you some if you wish, a dozen or so. Oxfords, with the button-down collar like the Yalies wear, assorted colors, whatever you like. My eye isn't what it used to be, but you wear what...? A fifteen? A fifteen and a half, maybe?"

"I didn't know you was also in *shmateh handel*, the rag business."

"Rags...? Oh, you mean this current venture, the men in shipping. Part of the Appeal clothing drive. For the refugees. I do what little I can to help out."

"So what's the story? Why'd yuh bring me down here?"

"We have a rare opportunity, the possibility to move a sizeable shipment, all at once for a change. You don't have to know the details. We just want you to hand deliver the payment. It involves a trip to Hartford."

"I thought you guys were only moving Winchesters, stuff outta N'Haven. What's in Hartford? Colt? Remington?"

Taking a step forward, Dov interrupted. "Let's not ask too many questions, Harr."

But Bottmacher waved him off. "It's quite all right. I appreciate a man with some intelligence, one who can ask good questions. We'll take whatever we can get our hands on. Every gun, every bullet, brings us one step closer to a homeland, to Eretz Israel."

"I don't know if my brother said anythin' or not, but all of that doesn't concern me."

"How can it not concern you? After all our people went through? After so many millions died? It doesn't concern you?"

"I got plenty of my own *tsooris*. Right here in N'Haven. Yeah, it was horrible, the Holocaust. Who could've imagined? I wouldn't hesitate a minute, killin' one of those Nazi bastids, believe you me, but ..."

"And a Britisher? An English soldier in Palestine? Would you hesitate then?"

"They was our allies in the War, no?"

"And so were the Reds. The British and the goyim here in this country, the ones that run the show, they refused to let our people in. Left 'em trapped like rats. Pretended like they didn't know what was goin' on and still do. Turned a blind eye, all of 'em. The Brits, they promised us a homeland back during the first war and now they stand in our way, concerned more with Arab oil and holdin' on to what they got."

"That ain't my problem."

"Not your problem? What are you? Just some mercenary, solely in this for the money?"

"And who's talkin', if yuh don't' mind my askin'? All of a sudden, you're Mr. Philanthropist? Like me and half the city never heard what went on, probably still does, in this here factory of yours.... The women and young girls, Jewish women even, the hours they put in. And what your family got away with paying?"

Bottmacher turned to Dov.

"What did you bring me, here? A Po'ale Zionist? A socialist?!"

Harry responded. "I ain't political. I ain't got the time. I'm in this 'cuz my brother dragged me in. I'm doin' it for him. Plain and simple."

"And that's all?"

"Nothin' comes for free, no?"

"Of course not. And that's why you'll be well taken care of."

"So what's the deal?"

"Are you in or out?"

"I already asked yuh. What's the deal?"

"You know how to get to Hartford, no?

"Yeah, sure, I can find my way."

"Good. Monday morning early, you'll ride on one of the trailer trucks with Shmule. He'll have his instructions, but he'll need some help gettin' there. Your brother tells me you have a hernia so you won't have to do any lifting. Others will handle the loading. All you have to do is make sure Shmule finds his way and that you hand deliver the payment. A little over an hour up, an hour or two to load, the ride back. Less than a day's work. Five hundred."

Harry glared at his brother. "This I don't believe. Now yuh got me ridin' in a truck with a load of stolen guns. For five hundred? Wha'd'yuhz take me for?!"

Bottmacher came back before Dov could respond. "Seven-fifty and no more!"

Thinking how much he could use the money, but not wanting to appear too eager, Harry paused as if at the poker table. He turned briefly and looked at his brother, hesitated a moment longer, and faced the manufacturer.

"I'm in. But I need half my take, up front."

Bottmacher turned to Dov. "He drives a hard bargain, this brother of yours."

"He always did."

Without another word, Bottmacher reached inside his suit jacket, pulled out his billfold and counted out four hundred dollar bills.

"Half of seven-fifty is three seventy-five. I don't have change. Here's four. You'll receive the rest when you return."

Harry tucked the money away as Dov took up the conversation. "Be ready at six-thirty Monday morning. In the middle of the block on Elliot, where we picked yuh up before. Shmule'll come and get yuh. And not a word to anyone. Is that clear?"

"I'll have to find someone to mind the store."

"That's not my problem. Just remember. Not a word to anyone. And be there on time, ready to go."

"I already tol' yuh, I'm in."

Bottmacher returned to his side of the desk and opened the top drawer. Removing a large thick envelope, he handed it to Harry.

"I'm going to trust you with this until Monday. There's too much here to be leaving some drop off like we've been doing. You're to pass it on to the people in Hartford. Shmule will have the rest of your instructions when he comes to pick you up."

"Anything you say, Mr. Bottmacher."

"Just don't lose the envelope."

"Don't you worry."

"I won't be the one to have to, if you do. Do I make myself clear?"

"Yeah, sure, Mr. Bottmacher. Perfectly clear."

"Just call me Nate."

He finally made it home sometime after two. Relieved to find the small flat dark and still, he silently undressed without putting on the light and slowly eased himself into bed, cautious not to wake his wife. Sleep came quickly, barely three hour's worth, before the alarm went off and he had to force himself up into the morning chill.

When he came out of the bathroom, Esther, just barely awake, eased past him without a word or touch and went in. She never got up that early and when she didn't return to the bedroom where he stood before the mirror getting dressed, he knew that he wasn't about to make it out of the house without some words. He began preparing the excuses, the alibis as he finished buttoning his work shirt.

She was sitting there at the kitchen table in the half dawn darkness, robed in her worn out housecoat. Staring out the window toward the house across the alley, she didn't even turn to face him as he entered.

"The landlord called again yesterday. That's twice now since Monday."

"Yeah? What'd he want?"

"Wha'd'yuh think he wanted? He says we're two months behind and the new month's coming up."

"He must be out of his mind. Musta figured wrong. I paid him last month."

"And the electric and the phone company? They all make mistakes?"

"How do I know?"

"Please, Harry. Don't start. Don't look to turn it around on me, neither. The bills aren't getting paid and..."

"Things've been a little slow in the store the last month, that's all. Don't worry about it. It'll all get straightened out."

"And what else?"

"Wha'd'yuh mean?"

"You're gamblin' again. I just know it. How much do yuh owe?"

"What gamblin'? Who's gamblin'? Like I said, everythin's just been slow. Business is off, that's all."

"Yuh don't have to lie to me."

"Who's lyin'? I just said...."

"Yuhr lyin' to me now and it ain't like I can't figure it out. Yuh come home late, and leave early every morning. Your clothes don't smell from drinkin' and who knows what else and yuh haven't given me any money in over a week. There's not a goddamn thing to eat in the house..."

"Yuh lookin' to start?"

"Start?! I see yuh, what? Once, twice a week...? I have no idea when the kids saw yuh last. It's a wonder they remember what yuh look like."

Harry moved over to where she was sitting, but she turned away, her back to him. He placed a hand on her shoulder and she turned her head just slightly to face him from the side. Her tone softened.

"Don't try being nice. It won't work. What's gonna happen if yuh don't make the rent again?"

"Everythin's gonna get straightened out real soon. I promise."

"Don't start with the promises."

"It's just been a little crazy lately, that's all."

It was then, as he reached over in an attempt to make up, that she noticed his vacant wrist.

"Where's your watch?"

"My watch? Aw, I... I musta left it at the store. Probably by the sink when I was cleanin' up last night. Doin' the last of the pots and pans."

"Yonkel doesn't do the pans anymore? You didn't leave him go, did you? Since when do you forget your watch?"

"I dunno. Just musta slipped my mind."

"Yuh didn't lose it, did yuh?"

"Be serious. You know how much that watch means to me. I'm sure it's where I musta left it, sittin' by the register or the sink."

"So what are yuh going t'do about the rent?"

"Don't worry about it. Everything'll get straightened out next week, like I said."

"And the watch? You'll get the watch back?"

"I didn't lose the watch."

"I wanna believe you."

"What's not to believe?"

Pulling on his topcoat, he bent over to kiss her good-bye but still not in the mood, she drew back and his lips just barely grazed her cheek. Unfazed, he turned and made his way for the door.

"I'll see yuh later."

"What time yuh comin' home?"

"When I get there. Not too late. I got stuff t' do."

The morning crowd came and went once again and he waited until the lull following the breakfast rush. Leaving Yonkel to keep an eye and not even bothering to remove his apron, he pulled on his old zipper jacket, the one he kept on a hook in the store, and made his way across to the smoke shop. It was barely ten-thirty but some of the regulars, the old-timers, had already settled in to their late morning pinochle. Aware from the talk on the street, they all turned and silently paused to watch as he walked in. Butter, hunched over the sports page and another cup of coffee at the front counter, had already spotted him coming across the street and didn't even look up from his paper but spoke in a voice loud enough for the others to hear.

"What the hell you doin' in here? Didn't I tell yuh you was eighty-sixed 'til I get what yuh owe?"

"That's why I come."

The bookie lowered his voice as he leaned partway across the counter.

"Yuh got it all? All what yuh owe?"

"For krissakes, cut me some slack. Let me give yuh six right now, that's a half, f'r cryin' out loud. I'll have the rest next week."

"The pastrami specials must be movin' pretty good."

"Take the six and let me have the watch."

Butter lowered his voice still further.

"What's wrong with you? Yuh know I can't do that. Word gets out I cut you a break, then everybody'll want one. Yuh expect me t' jeopardize everythin' I got goin' here? Send it all right down the toilet? Yuh shouldn't even be in here."

"Look, I'm sorry for what I said. All right?"

"I can't do it, Harr. When I get it all, you'll get the watch. That's that."

"Where 'n the hell yuh expect me t' get it all in one shot? How am I supposed t' come up with six hundred more by the end of the week?"

"That ain't my problem, now is it?"

"Yuh ain't gonna take the six, while I got it?"

Butter paused for a second as if reconsidering, looked over at the pinochle players, all of them now pretending to be deaf, and gestured with a quick nod for Harry to come closer. Harry leaned across the top of the display case as the old gambler talked, almost in a whisper toward his ear.

"Look. I really ain't got no beef with yuh. You know that. But yuh put me in a lousy spot here with that friggin' mouth of yours, tellin' me off in front of the players. It's a matter of respect."

"Alright. I was out of line. I apologize."

"Good. That's what I wanted t' hear."

"So you'll take the six and let me have the watch?"

"My word's my word. Yuh know that."

"So what d' yuh want from me?"

"Nuthin'. Just thought I could help yuh out a little so's we can straighten this whole mess out."

"Where's this goin'?"

"Just figured you'd be up for an inside line, that's all. Take the six and place it on the fight t'marruh night."

"T'marruh?"

"Yeah, at the Arena. Julie's fightin'."

"That's t'marruh, already? I all but forgot."

Butter motioned with his hand and Harry leaned in still closer.

"Yeah, yuh gotta promise t' keep this one t' y'rself. Strictly between you and me..."

"Yuh got my word. Go on."

"It's a done deal. This bum Callahan, he's set to go down in the fourth. Yuh know me. I usually don't bet my own money, especially on the fights, but even I'm goin' in on this one."

"Yuh sure? Yuh wouldn't bullshit me now, would yuh?"

"How far back we go? Have I ever steered yuh wrong? I'm tellin yuh it's done. Money in the bank. Besides, yuh make a score, I get what yuh owe me. Plus some consideration for the tip, naturally, say ten percent. Everyone makes out like a *bahndeet*."

Silent, Harry thought about it for another moment.

"Yuhr sure? Absolutely sure?"

"What are yuh? Hard o' hearin'? Would I put up my own money if I wasn't?"

"What's it bring?'

"New York's callin' it close, Callahan in a decision. By a point, a point and a half. It doubles up, yuh take Julie and four t' one on a kay-o if yuh pick the round."

"Take the six hundred?"

"Sure. But just on the bet. Not toward what yuh owe."

"Natch. Understood."

Harry started into his pants pocket, but Butter waved him off with fingers raised slightly upwards off the glass.

"Not in front of the players. I'll get it from yuh later."

"But yuh got me down for six? Julie double on the K.O., four to one in the fourth, like yuh said."

"Don't worry about it. Yuhr in."

Butter resumed an upright position and glanced over at the pinochle game, raising his voice once again as Harry moved for the door.

"And remember, I don't wanna see yuh in here again. Not until yuh get straightened out!"

CHAPTER 22:

The Merry-Go-Round

1989... WHEN HE INITIALLY HEARD the soft, muffled whimper, when it first lifted him out of his own deep sleep just after dawn, Richie thought that it might have come from one of the dogs curled up on the end of the bed. Wondering if they were okay, he stretched a covered foot down and gently nudged them both with a big toe to feel for any movement and sensing none, repositioned the pillows and closed his eyes. He was just about to drift off again when the soft cry, sounding almost like that of an ill at ease child, came again. He raised himself up slightly on a forearm and listened more closely. Now certain of the source but wanting to leave him sleep, he reached over and placed a light hand on Howard's shoulder in an attempt to ease his partner's deep sleep discomfort.

The whimpering returned after a minute or so, accompanied by a slight shudder, and he ever so gently shook the still form next to him until without moving, it muttered, "Not this morning. Let me sleep, will yuh?"

"You were sleeping. That's the problem. Your sleeping was keeping me awake."

"What now?"

"You were crying."

"Cryin'? I musta been dreamin'."

"It musta been a good one! What was she doin' to yuh?"

"What 'she'? Who said anything about a 'she'? I was dreamin' about Harry."

"And what was he doin' now?"

"I'm not sure. Besides, yuh woke me up right in the middle. How d'yuh expect me to remember?"

"You were cryin'. Just like a little kid."

Lost in a drowsy reflection, Howard paused for a moment before responding. "I can't believe it."

"What now?"

"How I let him get to me. I could see it comin' for years already and I promised when he went, I wasn't gonna let him do it."

"He's your father, for krissakes."

"Yeah, right. All of a sudden."

"It coulda ended a lot worse. At least the both of yous made up."

"You just don't get it, do yuh? I wouldn't feel so bad now, if we didn't. But he had to go and give me back the watch. He always had to have the last word."

"What are you talkin' about?"

"His watch. You remember. The one Esther gave him. I had it all those years and gave it back. And then he has to go and return it."

"This, I don't believe! He's dead and you're still carryin' on about that worthless, stinkin' watch? I remember when yuh gave it to him. When did he give it back?"

"About a week ago. He stopped by the office. I didn't tell yuh?"

"When do you tell me anything?"

"Don't start."

"Does Mickey know you got the watch?"

"I tol' yuh not to start."

"Who's startin'? You're the one woke me up. I'm a wreck already and the day hasn't even begun yet. I just wanna get some sleep."

"Who's stoppin' yuh?"

"Yeah right," returned Richie as he removed his arm from Howard and adjusting his pillows one more time, turned over toward his side of the bed. It took a moment but Howard finally realized he, too, did not want to start the day off on the wrong foot so reaching out, he briefly placed a hand on his partner's upper arm in a silent reassuring gesture of affirmation. He then returned to his thoughts, his attempt to recapture the dream.

He had lied to Richie, of course. One of those little white, day-to-day lies that we all make to a close companion, a lover, or a life-long friend in order to spare them and ourselves any unnecessary grief or additional headaches. He had already been awake for over an hour, sobbing silently as possible to himself in the dark, before Richie woke. But when he sensed the movement next to him, when he felt the glide of a foot down the bed to check on the dogs and sensed Richie's anticipated touch on his shoulder, he feigned sleep. With knees tucked up and spine curved, curled there now in his fetal crescent sleep position, he struggled to recapture the dream images.

It was Richie's comforting touch, that ever so slight physical reminder of another's presence, which oddly enough brought back the fleeting fragments. The tactile sensation, the sting of the strap so seemingly present that it almost made him wince, stood out like one of those raised welts on his childhood torso. It all seemed so real.

They were at Savin Rock. That he could remember. From what he could figure, it must have been late spring, that first Sunday afternoon after school let out for the summer and the old sunlit seaside amusement park was teeming with other kids and their families. The ritual promotion celebration.

They were all there, in the dream. Esther in a light summer floral, smiling, happy, with Harry's proud arm around her. Mickey standing close by looking maybe fourteen or fifteen, in his family outing chinos and a short sleeved dress shirt, his wavy hair oiled and nicely combed back just like the old man's. He saw himself standing there with Davey, the two of them as little ones holding hands amidst a crush of other grade school kids, all wild with anticipation and excitement as they waited and watched for the huge merry-go-round to come to a stop.

He watched as the blur of enameled white and gold and red and black, the giant multicolored flying horses whirled by at what seemed like an ever faster and faster speed, apparently propelled by nothing more than the streaming blare of accelerated Sousa coming from the calliope at the wheel's multi-mirrored center. He found himself watching for that favorite pony as it came around again, the one he had already chosen, the great big white one on the outer ring with the gray tail to the floor and thick, wavy mane, pink flaring nostrils, those glassy black defiant eyes and ornate golden saddle.

He looked for it again as the giant hand carved stallions finally slowed, made one more rotation, and came to a stop. Timed perfectly, the attendant finally unhooked the restraining chain and unleashed a mad dash for the best of the ponies. Catapulted by the rush and his desire to get that one special horse, he leapt up on the circular platform and zigzagged through the maze of scampering, screaming kids and wooden beasts now alive in his imagination.

He finally found his choice, already his old friend. Relieved that no one had beaten him to it, he eagerly climbed up on his own and cinched the wide leather safety belt around his waist. He leaned over and patted the pony's mane as they waited for the start and it seemed to take forever until the calliope began and the wheel slowly started to rotate. Remembering his mother's plea to hold on tight, he grasped the pole extending upwards from the front of the saddle with both hands and looked off to where Esther and Harry had been standing. It was then that he remembered Davey, as he spotted him standing there with one curled fist to a tearful eye, crying there, left behind, alone between the merry-go-round and Harry and Esther looking on from behind the spectators' railing.

His horse made another rotation and by that time both Harry and Esther were standing behind his little brother and he could tell from his father's body language, from the way he stood there with his hands on his hips, his head tilted slightly back, his cigar jutting upwards from the corner of an angry scowl, that there was going to be trouble.

He leaned forward and talked toward his horse's ear. "Let's get otta here!" he ordered and the pony bolted off in a mad gallop.

As they came around again, the boy heard a shout and glanced back to see Mickey astride the wooden black Arabian, the one he had almost chosen. He watched as his big brother leaned to the outside and grabbed a brass ring from its holder on the far turn and raced up, motioning, and yelling above the music's din as he came alongside.

"The ol' man's gonna beat your ass when yuhr done!"

"Why? What did I do?" the boy yelled back.

"Yuh forgot Davey! Yuh left Davey behind!"

Howard spurred his mount and the faithful beast reared up on its hind legs before charging off around a turn, leaving Mickey in the dust. The merry-go-round made another revolution and when he looked to where they had all been standing, there was no one. No Esther. No Harry. No Davey bawling alongside. Confused by their absence, he glanced backwards over a shoulder and there he saw him, Harry riding fast and furious, gaining ground and coming up on him. The boy again spurred his horse, but the gelding, suddenly inanimate once again, wouldn't move and Harry rode up alongside, the tip of his cigar glowing cherry red from the wind.

"Wait until I get your ass home, yuh little bastid...!"

Howard again spurred his horse. "Yuh gotta catch me first!"

"Catch yuh! I'll catch yuh, yuh little...! Where's my strap! Get me my goddamn strap!"

He tried to ride faster, to get away, but it was too late. As the two horses raced neck and neck around the back turn, Harry now in a frenzy, tore the heavy safety belt from his saddle and holding on to the support pole with one hand, leaned over and took a swipe at the child. That first swing, ill timed, missed, but the man immediately reared back and let fly again, this time catching the boy full on the soft of an upraised inner forearm. The unbearable sting almost made him faint but Howard somehow held on long enough to undo his safety belt. Wanting to fight back, to defend himself, he yanked at it but it wouldn't come loose from its mount. By that time, Harry caught him again, this time across the back. The leather cut into his shirt as the force from the lash knocked him off balance. Losing hold of the reins and the horse's mane, he screamed as he fell and fell and fell. He woke up.

His shrink had told him to write down his dreams, or at least to remember them as best he could, so he lay there silently rubbing his inner arm as the tears streamed down his face. And while he couldn't quite recapture it all, as the images of the dream world assault receded, he now found himself recalling some of the other episodes.

There it was, indelible, that particular instance clear as if it happened yesterday. He could see himself, sitting there on the living room floor in that sparsely furnished fourplex up-and-down, the two bedroom in those red brick, low-income look-alike projects where they ended up having to move. When they got evicted that time. After Harry lost the luncheonette and disappeared for a couple of weeks.

He could see himself then, a kid, maybe ten. That made Davey seven and the two of them were sitting there on the looped throw rug in front of the TV. It was a Sunday night. It had to have been, he realized, because Ed Sullivan was on and Harry was home, sprawled out behind them in nothing but his V-necked T-shirt and boxers, gazing at the set.

Desiring the lone, worn couch for himself, he had already ordered the two kids off, onto the chilly tiled floor. Huddled there on the rug, they soon began to whisper and paw at each other and received their first warning when their noise level began to compete with the back-up music for the juggling act, the Korean guys twirling kitchen plates on long bamboo poles. They received another as Carmen McCrea came on, when Howard complained aloud in response to a clandestine finger in the ribs from his little brother.

"If I hear another peep out of either of yuhz during this song, you're both goin' upstairs."

"But David started it. He keeps poking me. When you're not lookin'."

Already sensing her husband's mood and knowing full well where it could lead, Esther made her first attempt at an intervention, a move to pre-empt the inevitable. Hoping their eyes would meet hers, she tried to warn the boys with her tone as she got up from her nearby chair and raised the volume on the set.

"Didn't you hear what your father said? Let him watch, already."

But Howard's eyes remained fixed on the tube as he responded.

"I wasn't doin' anythin'! David keeps...."

His eyes glued to the screen as well, Harry interrupted, "I don' give a shit, who's doin' what! I'm not gonna tell yuh again, Howard. The next peep and yuhr goin' t' bed."

"But it wasn't me!"

"Yuhr not listenin', Howard."

McCrea finished and bowed and beamed from the stage, the camera panned the applauding audience as she exited, and Sullivan reappeared, stage left on the black and white screen. "Let's hear it, ladies and gentlemen. How 'bout a great big round of applause for Carmen McCrea!" His shoulders back, his arms folded, he introduced the next act, one of those Borscht Belt comedians, maybe Jackie Mason or Myron Cohen, and Harry issued a clear caution.

"I wanna listen t' this, so don't let me hear a peep out of either of yuhz. Yuh understand?"

The monologue had hardly begun when Davey, disinterested in the comic but mischievous as ever, snuck a hand across the rug and gave his brother a clandestine pinch on the thigh. Howard shrieked just as the stand-up delivered his punch line and Harry, missing the point of the story and catching nothing but the laughter from the audience, sat upright on the couch.

"All right! That's it. Yuh won't let me watch! Get the hell upstairs! The both of yuhz!"

Esther, now alarmed, attempted another mediation.

"Go on. Do what your father says. Besides, its already gettin' late and yuh both got school t'marruh."

Davey protested. "But Ma-a-a-a!"

Howard whined, "I wasn't doin' anythin'!"

And Harry, his blood pressure now mounting, turned to Esther.

"And yuh wonder why I don't come home!? These goddamn kids! I can't even relax in my own house! Where the hell's my strap! Get me my strap!"

Just the mere mention of the word elicited the desired effect and the boys, suddenly silent, headed up the narrow stairwell as Harry issued his last warning.

"And I don' wanna hear another peep outta either o' yuhz or, believe you me, someone's going t' cry!"

Blaming his brother for the early forced exodus as they climbed into the single twin bed crammed into the corner of the tight room, Howard began.

"What'd yuh have to go and start for?"

"I was just playin'."

"Yeah, right. And cuz uh you, I gotta go t' bed early."

"He wasn't gonna let us stay up late anyways."

"Not with you pokin' and pinchin' me during his show, he wasn't."

Howard kiddingly, somewhat affectionately poked his little brother through the blankets.

"You got all the room. Move over, yuh bed hog."

"I'm not a bed hog. You got all the covers!"

Davey tugged at the blankets, uncovering his brother's feet, and Howard, pulling them back, replied with a tap to the head. And before they realized it, they were both enmeshed in one of those sibling kid contests, a game, meaningless yet serious, a power struggle for nothing. A jab, a pinch in response, another attempted parried poke and a counter move, the sneak attack scratch of an extended big toenail under the blankets, and the follow-up retaliatory kick.

They laughed and giggled, oblivious to their increasing noise level, and would have been caught totally offguard if the bottom two steps had not creaked, the warning that he was sneaking up the staircase. Giving each other that knowing look of alarm, they scrambled for safety under the bed, where they flattened themselves up against the far wall just as he entered the room. He turned on the light but all they could see was his two skinny shins and bony feet, the palest of blue-veined pink, white in their sharp contrast against the bare wooden floor.

"Come out from under there, the both of yuhz!"

Trying to be cute as usual and misreading the seriousness of the situation in the process, Davey couldn't resist.

"With our hands up?"

Howard silently motioned to his brother with an upright index finger in front of closed lips and already pleading, frightened eyes as Harry's voice, increasingly agitated, responded.

"Don't make me come under there and get yuh, yuh little bastids!"

Howard, still silent, attempted a quick warning jab with an elbow, but he was already too late. The image of Harry crawling down there under the bed had already struck a funny chord with Davey and he giggled aloud.

"I bet yuh can't."

That did it. Suddenly, the mattress and the box spring, bedding and all, disappeared from above them, lifted and tossed aside as if caught in some hurricane squall. There they cowered in fright, corralled in by the bed frame, trapped against the wall with no chance of flight with Harry towering over them, leather belt doubled up in hand.

Pausing a moment as if to map his route of attack, he knocked away the oak slats, those last obstacles between himself and his target, and began to flail away, as Esther, entering from behind him, tried to restrain him.

"Not the face! Not the face!"

Taking the mandatory quick swipe at the little one's legs, Harry immediately shifted his attention and zeroed in on his prefigured victim.

"What? Yuh think it's funny? I'll teach yuh t'laugh at your father, yuh little bastid, yuh!"

"But it wasn't me! I didn't do anythin'!"

"Yeah, you never do nuthin'! I warned yuh, but yuh wouldn't listen."

The leather belt found its target, immediately raising several red swaths across Howard's back and legs as the child, horrified beyond terror by his father's irrational anger and the fiery sting from the strap, screamed and cried in panic. Now out of control, Harry went for the head but caught the boy across a raised forearm as Esther grabbed her husband's other wrist.

"I told yuh not the face! Enough! Enough already!! What are yuh tryin' to do…?! Are you crazy!"

"I'll kill the little bastid!"

She now placed her body between her husband and the boys. "Yuh wanna kill somebody?! Get it over with, already, and kill me!!"

Reaching around his wife, Harry took a parting, half-hearted swipe at David's legs.

"And that's for you, yuh little instigator."

He then turned from the room and started down the stairs, calling back over his shoulder as he went.

"Now you'll let me watch, I bet!"

Esther turned to the boys now huddled together, crying on the floor.

"Why is it you boys won't listen…? When will you learn?"

"But I didn't do anythin'!" Howard, eyes closed, tears streaming, stammered. "It was Davey."

"It doesn't matter who. Come now, help me fix the bed."

Esther helped her boys up off the floor and the three of them reassembled the bed as the crying gradually subsided. Finished, she tucked them in and turned from the room.

"Now get some sleep. Tomorrow's school and you already stayed up too late."

Davey rolled toward Howard as her footsteps receded down the stairs.

Reaching out, he softly touched the welt, the color of red raspberry, on his still whimpering brother's inner arm.

"I didn't mean it…, honest."

"What'd yuh have to go an' start for?"

With Richie now asleep and the dogs still motionless, lost in their own dream worlds, Howard lay there unconsciously rubbing the inside of his forearm, that very spot where Harry had caught him that one time so many years before. He found himself thinking about Davey's touch. He again began to cry as he lay there in the dark, alone. His mind wandered further and he found himself pondering the same old questions.

"Why me? Why me all the time and not Davey? Why did I have to be the one? Yuh always let him get away with everything. What in the hell did I ever do to you?"

CHAPTER 23:

The Gamble

1947... HARRY COULD FEEL IT there as he got ready for work the next morning. *Shpilkes,* they called it. That nervous knot in the pit of his stomach that tightened up whenever he placed a large bet, that feeling like someone was jabbing him in the guts. But anticipating the win and blinded to even the possibility of a loss, he already had the money well spent, paying off the bills, the rent and all, by the time he got to the store. He even found himself thinking about what he would do with the extra cash.

The Saturday morning routine at the luncheonette always went a little slower since most of the shops on the street, Jewish owned, remained closed for the *Shabbes.* With the majority of weekday regulars in *shul* or at home, he still went in early to prep for what usually turned into a worthwhile lunch crowd, the ritual mid-day *shmooze.* He opened the front door later than during the week, at eight, but remained moderately busy with the scattering of late breakfast short orders - the eggs, buttered hard rolls and coffee for the unobservant and the scattering of Italian and Irish customers camped at the counter.

He had just slid the roasting pan with the lunchtime turkey partway out of the oven. Testing it with a long cooking fork eased to the inside of the leg joint, he was about to lift the bird onto the cutting board alongside the stove to cool when Jakey's voice greeted him from behind.

"Yuh straightened out with Butter yet?"

Harry talked over his shoulder as he turned the oven off and hoisted the bird, rack and all, up onto the board.

"Yeah, I'm straightened out all right, no thanks to you."

"Hey, what d'yuh want from me? If I had the cash, I woulda helped yuh out. Yuh know that. Besides, I tried to get yuh to slow down, but do yuh listen? When the cards ain't there, they ain't there."

"But I had the fuckin' hand. He had no business stayin'."

"You goin' senile, or what? That's *exactly* his business. Yuh think the additional hundred, or two or three, it matters to him? Of course he's gonna take the shot when he's on a roll, up like he was. If, for no other reason than the possibility of stickin' it to someone. Which is exactly what he ended up doin'."

"So let me guess. I don't see yuh in over a week and yuh just stopped in this mornin' to rub my face in it?"

"Excuse me for livin'. Just came by t' see how you was doin'. Maybe grab a bite. That's all."

Wiping his hands on his apron as he turned toward the counter, Harry fully faced his friend.

"Actually, you're just the one I was hopin' t' see. I was just now thinkin' of yuh, wond'rin' if yuh could maybe help me out."

"I already tol' yuh...."

"Nah, nah.... I ain't talkin' money. I need yuh t' give me a hand here in the store. Monday mornin'."

"Why? What's up?"

"I gotta be somewhere, take a day off. I need someone to watch the place, cover for me, that's all."

"What do I know from runnin' an eatery?"

"Yonkel'll be here t' handle what needs to be done. All you gotta do is serve the stiffs and mind the till, clear some plates, maybe, and whatnot. I'll come in early and everything'll be ready, all set up before I go."

"What'suhmatter? Esther can't come in?"

"Be serious. She noticed right away I ain't got the watch. There's no way she'll cover. Ain't no way I'd ask her to. Besides, she'd have to leave the kids with her sister or at her mother's."

"Where yuh goin'?"

"Can't tell yuh. I just need the day, that's all. I need yuh to keep an eye on things."

"Yuh ain't off to the track, are yuh?"

"Without you? Hell no. Will yuh do me the favor or not? It's important."

"What time?"

"The mornin'. Six."

"That early?"

"Yeah, like I said, I gotta be somewhere. Besides, people start comin' in at six. Maybe yuh should make it five-thirty."

Jakey reluctantly said yes just as the front door flung open and Louie burst in as if catapulted by the four or five guys pushing from behind.

"Hey, Harry! Everyone! Look! Look who the hell's here!"

All eyes at the counter turned to the commotion and some of the patrons, indeed most, pivoted on their stools and came to their feet upon recognizing the local hero. More people crowded in from the street to get a look, perhaps a handshake, and the regulars murmured as if slightly in awe of the unexpected celebrity.

"It's Julie. Julie Kogan!"

"Yuh believe this guy?" Louie shouted. "The day of the fight and he's out on the Avenue just strollin' around like it's a Sunday!"

The boxer, Florida tanned and handsome, clean shaven, with his hair well combed and oiled, beamed all around at the fans and old neighborhood faces. A kid from the street grabbed a napkin off the counter and asked him to autograph it as others reached in for a handshake. Taking a few more greetings and pat-on-the-back best wishes, he turned directly to Harry, standing there hands-on-hips proud behind the counter.

The fighter extended his rock solid arm and the two shook over the countertop.

"How's it goin', Hareleh!?"

"Me? Me, things are good! T' what do I owe the honor?"

"Honor? What honor? A guy can't come into one of his old haunts anymore, just 'cuz he throws on a pair of gloves and decks a couple of crumbs?"

"A couple? What's it now...?"

"Fourteen and two!" Velner shouted, still all smiles and excitement. "Fourteen and two!"

"What can I get yuh? A nice turkey sandwich, maybe? Still fresh, just out of the oven. How 'bout a nice egg cream?"

"I'd love t' but I shouldn't eat nuthin' now, the day of the fight. Just out for a walk, some air. Thought I'd see how things was doin' on the Avenyuh."

"At least let me get yuh a nice *glas krepz wasser.*"

"A little seltzer's fine, but please, nuthin' else."

Harry quickly drew a Coke glass full of soda water and handed it to the fighter.

"So yuh gonna beat this bum, what's his name, this Callahan?"

Louie interrupted. "What kind of question is that, the day of the fight? Would he be out walkin' around, unconcerned, if he wasn't?"

Julie chuckled. "Boy, Louie, I shoulda made yuh my promoter. I'm gonna knock this Mick son-of-a-bitch right on his ass. It'll be over in four, five tops!"

"Can we bet on that?" came another voice.

Louie responded. "Another stupid question! Don't you guys know gamblin's illegal in this state?"

Everyone laughed and Julie leaned over the counter as he drained the last of the soda water. Handing back the glass, he again took Harry's hand.

"Again, I'm just out for my mornin' walk. Just wanted t' stop in for a second t' say hello, t' wish yuh some *mazel.*"

"Good luck? Why yuh wishin' me good luck?"

"'Cause I got plenty, and everyone could use some, no?"

Reaching into his inside coat pocket as he spoke, he grinningly slid the eight by ten counterward.

"I almost forgot why I stopped in. I wanted to give yuh a little somethin'. For all those glasses of seltzer and your support over the years."

Harry took a second to study the glossie of Julie caught there in that classic fighter's pose, the right shoulder slightly dipped, its arm and gloved hand coiled and tucked to the side, ready to strike, the left raised ever so slightly, poised as if to parry and throw a quick jab. His eye fixed on the Star of David emblazoned there in sharp white contrast against dark trunks on the boxer's thigh. He looked down at the inscription. "For my good pal, Harry Rabin," signed Julie Kogon.

Almost at a loss for words, Harry thanked the man. Reaching out to shake one more time, the boxer looked eye-to-eye at him and winked. Then, without so much as another word, he turned through the clutch of fans and made his way for the door with the youngsters and some of the crowd that had entered with him, Louie included, in tow.

Jakey, still seated on his stool, turned to his pal just standing there, his hands still on his hips, just staring at the photo on the countertop.

"What the hell was that all about? And what's with you? What are yuh, starstruck all of a sudden?"

"Yuh think he was tryin' to tell us somethin'? Give us an in?"

"You ain't thinkin' about bettin' the fight now, are yuh? Just because he gave yuh a picture and wished yuh good luck?"

"Naw, there's nuthin t' think about. I'm too tapped out."

"Yuh wanna go anyways?"

"I'd sorta hate to miss it."

"Good. 'Cause that's why I came by in the first place."

With that, Jakey reached into his coat pocket, pulled out the pair of tickets and slapped them down on the counter.

"Front row, ringside. Figured you was due."

"Front row! Jeez, Jakey!"

"I finagled 'em, I can't say from who. Louie'll be there, too. We figured you could use some cheerin' up."

Jakey no sooner walked out the front door than Harry called to Yonkel to keep an eye and shot to the back stairwell leading to the basement. Pulling the string on the overhead light as he closed the door behind him, he reached up on one of the storage shelves along the wall and came down with the cigar box. He removed the thick envelope and held it, cradled in his hands for a moment as if it had some magical powers. Reaching into his pants for his pen knife, he unfolded the thin blade and slowly worked it underneath the flap, careful not to tear the paper.

Unwrapping the rubber band that held the wad together, he made a quick estimate of how much was there. As if momentarily stunned by the size of the stack of hundreds, he paused for a second and then slowly recounted to get the exact count as he nervously, unconsciously glanced over his shoulder. He couldn't believe it. More cash than he had ever held in his hands at one time. He counted it again. Five thousand.

Calling for Yonkel to watch things as he finished pulling on his coat, he made for the door and quickly darted over to the smoke shop. Butter was there in his usual spot, a morning cigar at one side of his mouth, leaning over a paper at the display case.

"You back here again? I thought I...."

Harry, his hands still in his coat pockets motioned with his head toward the rear of the shop. Streetwise as he was, Butter realized something was up and the two made their way to the back room without uttering a word.

"I wanna up my bet."

"How much?"

Harry pulled the envelope out of his pocket and tossed it on the card table.

"There's five grand there. Count it for yourself."

"Five G's!? Where the hell'd yuh get that kinda dough?"

"Does Macy's tell Gimbel's?"

"It ain't hot, is it?"

"Nah, it's all legit. I wanna place it on Julie in the fourth."

"Legit! Who you talkin' to here!? You're placin' it for someone else, aren' chuh? And after I went and did yuh a favor!"

"Naw, it ain't like that. Honest. Yuh gotta believe me."

"I don't know's I can handle such an amount."

"Then talk to somebody who can."

"I suppose I could. Yuh sure yuh don't wanna say where yuh got it?"

"Let's just say I worked hard. Saved all the nickels and dimes, the tips from all the big spenders. The ones they left on the counter the past hundred years."

"All right, all right. Sorry I asked. Ain't none uh my business, anyway. I don't wanna know."

"So I'm down for the five?"

"Plus the six hundred from before. That is, if my people can handle it."

Harry reached into his pants pocket and came out with the additional wad.

"Plus the six."

"Five, six. You're in."

Butter watched through the front window until Harry had crossed the street. Returning to the front counter, he reached for the phone then hesitated a moment. For that brief instant, he thought about not making the call at all and swallowing the whole take on his own, but knowing better and not wanting any heat, he dutifully dialed. The voice on the other end listened as the bookie laid out the new situation.

"Yuh remember that fish I tol' yuh about, the one with the six hunnert placed on Kogon....? Yeah, yeah, you got it... That's right. The one with the mouth. Anyways, he just comes walkin' in here and plunks five big ones on the goddamn counter.... That's what I said.... Yeah, you got it, another five grand on Kogon. The same deal.... Yeah, this one's already dreamin' about gettin' straight.... Nah,

nah, I got it all right here in my hand as I'm talkin' to yuh. Up front. We won't even have to lean on him. Just figured I'd fill yuh in, that's all.... Okay, good.... I'll see yuh t'night. I'll bring it with me when I come."

CHAPTER 24:

Alexandra

1989... STILL PERSPIRING SLIGHTLY BUT no longer winded from her morning jog along the shore front, Alexandra had listened to the message as soon as she walked in the door. She had started feeling fat and unattractive so had gotten up early, determined to get back with the program. Putting on that extra layer of silk long underwear beneath her hooded jogging outfit as an added protection against the cold, and wrapping a towel around her neck like some road working boxer, she had gone out to run before six. She got back to her tiny efficiency in just over a half hour and found the red light flashing on the answering machine. She hesitated a moment, figuring it could only be her ex-boyfriend, the one she now referred to as "the slug", wanting to talk. "Who else would call so early?" she thought. But giving in to habit and that insatiable curiosity of hers, she pressed the button and listened.

And now over an hour had passed and she just sat there on the couch by the phone, still in her sweats, her hair a mess, not quite ready or able to move. She realized she had to decide. Whether to call in sick and make the trip, or to just let it pass and feel guilty the rest of the day and for who knew how long afterwards.

"Come on, Alex," she thought to herself. "Make up your mind. Either way, you gotta get your ass up! Go to work or go to New Haven. Either way, you still have to get into the shower, do something with your hair, figure out what to wear, and get moving."

She unconsciously picked at the dull pink polish on the nails of her left hand as she guesstimated how long it might take to get ready and make the drive.

It was Rosie's voice on the tape, the nonchalant sound of it, she realized, that initially upset her. The sound of it, as if her aunt had called just to talk about the weather or to forward some momentary gossip about some neighbor down the street, the usual whatever about somebody's daughter in trouble again, or this one who left that one, or someone else's druggie son.

"Hi, hon, it's just me," the message went. "Just wanted to let you know that my friend Janet just called. You know, the one I keep in touch with in New Haven. Anyways, she called and told me that she saw in this morning's *Journal Courier*... she gets it delivered first thing... that Harry Rabin died. I figured you'd wanna know. Sorry, hon.... Oh yeah, the paper said the funeral was at ten. At Velners', on George Street.... That's one of the ones where the Jews have their funerals.... Close to downtown, if I remember right. You wouldn't want to go, would yuh? Give me a call, later, if you feel like. Love yuh."

Not wanting to have to listen to her aunt carry on and certainly not about to make the trip to New Haven with her, she decided not to call back. She just sat there by the phone, weighing the pros and cons. She replayed the message several times as if it might divulge some hidden meaning, something else not revealed in her life, and she again pondered what to do.

"Should I or shouldn't I?" she thought. "Should I take another day off and make the damn drive one last time? Go to the friggin' funeral? Will anybody there even care?"

Her thoughts turned to the father she hardly knew.

"He didn't even come to Ma's funeral," she recalled. "Why in the hell should I go to his?"

She slowly rose up off the couch and as she padded toward the bathroom, pulling the sweatshirt up over her head as she went, she found herself thinking about the first and last time she had seen him, and everything that had come between.

She had just turned seventeen when she finally convinced Rosie to tell her what she knew. About who her father was. Her mother had died the year before from what the doctors at Greenwich said was an aneurysm, a blood clot that had traveled to the brain, they explained. The girl couldn't get a word out of her about the old man anyways, so on that count her passing didn't much matter. Rosie had taken her in after the funeral and she eventually turned to her mother's sister to find out what she could.

The aunt proved at first to be as stubborn as the mother. She initially denied knowing anything, but the teenager persisted, and the woman's responses changed. "Why?" she would say. "What's to know?" "Why tear a scab off a healing wound?" "Let sleeping dogs rest!" The girl refused to give in and Rosie finally relented.

What Alexandra finally got out of her wasn't much. She learned that her long-secret father lived somewhere in the New Haven area, that his name was Harry Rabin, and that he had sold cars at one of the dealerships on Whalley Avenue. That was it, but it was all she needed, it turned out.

She wondered now, as she stepped into the shower and turned on the hot soothing spray, what had compelled her, what led her to seek him out. She realized that she still hadn't figured that one out and almost seven years had passed since that day she skipped school and went alone, not daring to tell any of her girlfriends. It was during her junior year, spring, she could readily recall. That made it eighty-three.

She remembered leaving the house early and driving from Darien, braving the Turnpike by herself despite the morning rush hour. She took her time and stayed in the right lane the whole way, paying close attention to the traffic, and simply headed east until she saw the exit sign for "Downtown New Haven, Route 34." A guy in the first gas station off the end of the Oak Street Connector gave her directions and Whalley Avenue was easy enough to find, a right-hand turn and just a few blocks up, it turned out.

She pulled into the first dealership she came to, the Lincoln-Mercury franchise a block beyond the Holiday Inn at the beginning of what was then the city's "Automobile Row". She walked into the showroom with its gray slate floor, potted palms, and simulated cherry paneling and asked the slick looking younger salesman with his ass propped against a new Continental just inside the thick glass doors if he knew Harry Rabin. Hungry for a start-the-day-right sale, he had already sized her up as way too young, a waste of time "looker" at best, well before she entered and he didn't even bother standing up straight or to feign the usual customer courtesy smile. The name didn't mean anything to him anyway, so he indifferently pointed her to the back wall and one of the old-timers, a heavy set Italian guy he called "Big Al", seated there at his salesman's desk, morning busy with his coffee, the daily scratch sheet and a call in to his bookie. She could still hear his raspy voice as he told his connection to hold on a minute and could vividly remember the flecks of powdered sugar on his tie and lapel from what must have been a second or maybe a third cruller. She recalled the smart alecky smile that came to his face when she asked.

"Oh, Jeez, miss, who don't know Harry Rabin?! But unfortunately you got the wrong place. What made yuh think he worked at Lincoln-Mercury? Last I heard, he was still workin' up the street. At Chevrolet. Easy from here. Just go straight up three blocks, on the left. Yuh can't miss it. If yuh see the Pontiac place, you've gone too far."

She walked into the Chevie showroom and asked for Mr. Rabin. Another youngish salesman, identical in his well manicured hustler style to the one leaning on the Lincoln down the street, sized her up and down. She felt his eyes on her body as she approached. He, too, pegged her for a looker, too young to be a serious buyer, and directed her to the general manager's office, not wanting to risk snagging one away from the boss.

"Mr Rabin? Certainly, miss. Yes. Just go upstairs here to your right. The first door to your left, at the top."

She could still vividly recall the initial blend of fear and excitement, the anticipation and the nervous gurgle in her tightened gut as she silently climbed the steps. Finally about to meet the man she had always wondered about, she trembled slightly, paused for a second to catch her breath, and slowly turned the corner to gaze at him through the open office door.

There the man sat, preoccupied with a pile of early morning invoices, behind his metal-gray managerial desk, gazing through a pair of half-lensed reading glasses. He didn't notice her and she wasn't quite sure if she should interrupt so she took a moment to study his features - his dark graying hair, silver at the temples, his large nose, like hers she immediately thought, his out of place, fresh-from-Miami tan, his tasteful wool blend spring suit and silk tie. He was bigger than she imagined and older, too, and not quite as handsome as she hoped, but she immediately liked his looks overall. She timidly cleared her throat to catch his attention, and he glanced up over the top of his glasses without raising his head.

"Can I help you, miss?" came the business polite voice.

"Are... are you... uhh.... Are you Mr. Rabin?"

"That, I am. What can I do for you?"

She paused for a second, forgetting everything she had rehearsed on the way. "Well, you see, I don't know how to go about this, exactly, so I might as well just say it."

"Say what?"

"My name is Alexandra Bertolli. I'm... I'm your daughter."

The man blanched slightly and sat there for a moment, still peering up over his black frames. He then smiled ever so slightly, and without saying a word reached for the phone. Hitting nine first for an outside line, he tapped seven digits from memory and motioned to her to stay put with the palm of his upstretched hand as he waited for someone to pick up. The party on the other end finally answered and she listened to one side of the conversation.

"It's me.... You better get down here right away.... Why? 'Cause I'm tellin yuh to, that's why...! Important? Would I be callin' at this hour, if it wasn't...? Just do like I'm tellin' yuh and get over here right away.... There's just someone here I think you should meet. That's all.... Oh, Christ no! They haven't been back in months.... You think I'd set you up... Just let's say it's a little surprise.... I already tol' yuh, it's a surprise!.... You'll find out when yuh get here.... Yeah, yeah, just don't take all day, that's all!"

He hung up and apologetically explained that she definitely had the wrong man. Flushed with embarrassment, she wanted to turn and run out, but before she could, he went on to introduce himself.

"I'm Charlie Rabin. See," he said as he got up and pointed to the name plate on the door. "Who you're looking for must be my brother Harry. Harry Rabin."

She told him she knew. That it was Harry she had come to see. She apologized for the confusion and they both laughed nervously and Charlie told her it was okay. Lots of people, he explained, had confused the two of them throughout most of their adult lives. And not to worry.

"Your real father should be here shortly. Can I get you somethin'? Maybe a cup of coffee, while yuh wait?"

It took him twenty minutes to get there and her new found uncle, not knowing exactly what to say or do, had excused himself. Claiming he was sorry, but that he had some important business to take care of, Charlie brought her a cup of coffee, showed her to a seat outside his office, and disappeared.

So she sat there and waited on a chair, alone in the upstairs hallway as if she had been sent out of class in grade school. She finished the weak office coffee and fidgeted with the empty styrofoam cup, engraving spirals along the exterior with her well kept nails as she fought the urge to flee. She finally heard the footsteps on the stairs.

She recognized him as soon as he turned the corner. And he must have done the same to her. That's how much they looked alike. She came to her feet and they just stood there facing each other, not saying a word. Charlie came out in the hall and looked eye-to-eye at his brother, and then at Alexandra and back to his brother, not knowing what to say, as well, and introductions became unnecessary as Harry broke the silence.

"Come," he said as he took her arm. "Did you have breakfast? All I had was a cup of coffee and a roll, and that was hours ago. There's this okay luncheonette up the street. They got nice, fresh bagels this time of day. Do you like bagels? Come. Lemme get you something... My treat."

And that's what happened each time she came to New Haven after that. They'd go get something to eat. He soon introduced her to lox and eggs with translucent, sauteed onions, fish salty to the taste, at one of the less patronized Jewish delis. And delicious minute steak sandwiches, thick with grilled onions and lettuce and tomato at some inconspicuous downtown joint somewhere close by Yale, where they ate incognito among the proud alumni dads and aspirant sons and daughters fresh from a tour of the *alma mater.* And sometimes, if she drove in later in the day or on a Saturday, he would take her to one of the Italian places off Wooster Square, for clams and linguini, maybe an *abeetz,* as he called it, with anchovies and mozzarella, his choice. Or maybe to the remodeled *Jimmy's* on the shore in West Haven for a buttery lobster roll or one of those soft-shell crabs, deep-fried whole, its legs sticking out from between two pieces of tartar-sauced toast. On Sundays, they'd go Chinese, sweetened spare-ribs dipped in hot mustard and Wanton soup as appetizers, Lobster Cantonese for the main dish. Sometimes they'd drive as far as Branford for a sit down dinner in that redone Route 80 roadhouse, a place belonging to one of his old-time cronies. Prime rib and a baked potato for him and jumbo scampi with pasta on the side for her, for starters that special salad they would share, olive oil and balsamic vinegar and that strong Gorgonzola cheese. They always met over food and she soon came to recognize what he already knew. How eating made it easier for the both of them, since neither had to talk as much and the silences didn't seem as awkward.

As she stepped out of the shower and wrapped herself in a bath towel, she recalled their initial meetings, how uncomfortable they always were. For both of them, she had come to realize. There was so much she wanted to ask and so little he had to tell. She got him to talk about his childhood some, memories of his family, his mother and father, brothers and sisters, and tales of the old neighborhood. The poverty stories, his way of impressing her on how far he had come. And he talked about the car business, how he had worked at various places up and down automobile row over the years since the mid fifties, and how he had managed Chevrolet and made a ton of money for the owners while they took off to become scratch country club golfers during the early sixties. And how his brother Charlie, who he had given a job, ended up replacing him after he got fed up and quit. But the rest remained a mystery, as if he had no adult life, had never grown up.

She untangled the cord from the blow-dryer and plugged it into the outlet next to the sink, and as she began working the heat through her thick dark hair with her brush, she thought about that one evening over dinner at Consiglio's on Wooster Street. It had taken nearly a year, but she finally got the courage over a plateful of lasagna to ask about his relationship with her mother. Now gazing into the foggy bathroom mirror, she recalled how the question stopped him in the middle of a mouthful.

Swallowing slowly, he wiped his lips with his linen napkin, took a sip of the Lambrusco he had been nursing and just sat there, lost in thought, for what seemed forever, in reality a few seconds.

"I knew you'd eventually ask. And I've been tryin' to figure out what to say ever since you showed up and Charlie called me down to the showroom."

"So what happened? Didn't you even care that you had a daughter you didn't know?"

"What can I tell yuh? Wha'd'yuh want I should say?"

"Did you ever wonder about me? About who I was?"

"Of course, I did. But things weren't that simple. They never are."

"Things? What things?"

"Well, for starters, your mother and I had already broken off our relationship. I hadn't seen her for a couple of months, when she called me one day, out of the blue, and told me she had a little surprise…. That you were on the way."

"And what else?"

"My wife. I guess you wouldn't know I was…"

"*Your wife*?! You were *married* at the time?!"

"Your mother knew from the start."

"So that made it okay?! She gets pregnant, and being the good Catholic she was, she decides to keep me, and you were married?!"

"Like I said, me and your mother, we were already through by the time she found out about you."

"And you never made an effort to find out about the baby? About *me*?!"

"Like I told yuh… It wasn't that simple. I sorta wished it was. Your mother, such a good Catholic she was, she made for a holy helluva mess right after you were born by making sure my wife found out. Esther... that was my wife, she usually figured out when I was foolin' around and always took me back for some reason, but that nearly put an end to it."

"*That* meaning *my* being born?!"

"Yes, but I swore me and your mother was finished and Esther let me come back. She never forgave me, though, I don't think. She's gone now."

"Well, that certainly makes me feel better. Not that she's gone.... That I'm glad *I* wasn't to blame for your marriage falling apart."

"Christ all mighty, you're startin' to sound like one of my sons. Don't get too smart!"

"Sons!? We spend nearly a year in almost every out of the way restaurant in New Haven, and you wait until now to tell me you have sons? I have brothers!?"

"Yeah, there's three of 'em. I didn't mention them before?"

"Three?! I suppose they don't know a thing about me!"

"I think my oldest, his name's Mickey, I'm pretty sure he knows, but he's never said anything."

"And the other two? Did you have them with *her*?"

"Now you're gettin' too damn smart!"

"Maybe I take after my old man!"

They didn't talk for several weeks after that. She didn't call him and refused to talk to him when he called, simply saying she needed some time. Then finally he called again and they talked a little. He apologized, explaining how hard it was for him, not knowing what to say, and she finally gave in and took him up on his offer to drive down to Darien and pick her up.

They had lunch that day, nothing special, at a place he knew, a Greek nouveau diner off the interstate on the Fairfield side of Bridgeport. He said it was connected and she pretended she knew what that meant. She had the spinach cheese pie and he devoured a huge Athenian salad as they smiled, and finally laughed and deepened their relationship.

And that's what Alexandra now remembered the most as she pinned her hair up and put on her makeup. That day in the Greek diner, when they started to become friends. Noticing how she had scraped most of the polish off two of her nails, she quickly touched them up. Blowing on them while she decided what to wear, she finally slipped into a full skirted winter floral, subdued reds and black. Tossing the red leather belt that came with it onto the bed, she grabbed a simpler black one from the closet, and in the same moment opted for the pair of dark red pumps, not wanting to appear too somber. Never having been to a Jewish funeral before and not sure if she would need it, she took the black lace scarf, the one Aunt Rosie had given her when her mother died, and placed it in her small black clutch.

Finally pulling on her winter dress coat, she stepped out into the cold and hurried to the car, the used Accord Harry had found for her. Starting it, she retrieved the ice scraper from between the seats and got out. As she cleared the morning frost from the windshield, she suddenly realized that she hadn't eaten a thing. She thought about getting something in New Haven, coffee and a muffin maybe, and then changed her mind.

"Lox and eggs with a toasted bagel and cream cheese on the side. And black coffee. You can run it off tomorrow," she decided. She looked at her watch, and realized she would have to hurry.

CHAPTER 25:

The Loss

1947...   ALONE IN THE EARLY morning darkness, Harry just sat there at the end of the counter, lost in his thoughts. Wondering where to turn, he had lost track of the time and out of habit, glanced at his empty wrist. Reminded about the watch, at that point the least of his worries, he peered up at the wall clock above the register, just barely visible in the faint dawn light. Five-thirty. He thought for an instant about doing the prep for the Sunday crowd, about starting the turkey and roast beef, about getting the corned beef on the stove, and decided to wait for Yonkel to show. Finding it impossible to move from stool, he kept on urging himself to remain calm.

"Everything'll work out," he kept telling himself. "Everything'll work out. It always does."

But the more he talked to himself, the more that panicky feeling found an in. He kept thinking about how quickly it all went down. He pondered for a moment where to turn, the next step, some way forward, but soon found himself replaying the situation.

It had taken forever it seemed, just for him and Jakey to maneuver their way from the crowded sidewalk and through the front entry of the Arena. Funneled through the crush at the turnstiles and past the blue uniformed ticket takers, they finally found their numbered portal and flowed with the rest through the poorly lit passage with its odor of gambler anxiety, discarded cigars and years of spilled beer. Emerging under the bright houselights, they lingered momentarily to gaze out on the scene like two underground explorers just entering some newly discovered grotto, some secret subterranean colony.

The large oval auditorium was already filled to the rafters, standing room only, and it seemed like most of Jewish New Haven, certainly all the men from Legion Avenue and points beyond, had somehow crammed into the old-before-its-time sports palace. Neither of the two could recall seeing so many *lantsman* gathered in one place, even on Yom Kippur, and the pre-fight cacophony of collective chatter, the back-and-forth banter of so many familiar faces filled the space with an electric excitement so thick, so palpable, that it seemed as if the haze of tobacco smoke already suspended below the high ceiling lights had spontaneously risen from the heads of the combustible, simmering crowd. The two friends looked toward the center of the place, what would normally be center ice, now covered by plywood and canvas and rows of folding chairs. Their eyes fixed on the ring, bathed there in its own white overhead light, the still empty epicenter of everyone's anticipation.

An impatient usher moved them away from the mouth of the portal just as Hershey spotted Louie waving to them from ringside, gesturing with two upraised fingers toward the two remaining seats up front. Making their way down one of the crowded aisles, exchanging quick hellos and "how are yuhs" and an occasional handshake to this one and that one as they went, they reached their chairs just as the real commotion began.

They brought Callahan and his handlers in first, accompanied by a couple of off-duty uniforms hired to clear the way amidst the resounding boos and catcalls from the local partisans. The whole place then erupted, the entire house up on its feet, as the hometown hero paraded in, his head towel-covered and his blue silk robe shrouding his taut, muscular frame. Stepping through the ropes, he went immediately to his corner, where he bobbed and weaved in place, throwing a flurry of quick-flick jabs and uppercuts at an imaginary foe to the heightened delight of the cheering fans.

The bell rang, the microphone came down at center ring and the announcer, a dapper, white haired Irishman in black bow tie and worn tuxedo, attempted to hush the hall. Barely audible above the din, he ran through the upcoming events and introductions, and the ref waved the two rivals, still bundled in their fight robes, to mid ring for the prerequisites. Both men retired to their respective corners and Julie removed his robe. As if on cue, the entire crowd went absolutely wild upon seeing the large white Star of David sewn there across the left thigh of his blue trunks. Exuding all the poise and confidence of a champ, Julie, still dancing slightly in place, leaned sideways toward his trainer as if to catch some last second instruction and it was then that Harry saw, or thought he saw, what he was looking for, a clear sign, some indicator.

Certain that Julie had looked straight in his direction, motioned to him and only him with a gloved hand, he signaled his two pals just as the bell sounded and the fighters, their muscled bodies glistening with sweat and oil, moved center ring to begin their dance.

"Did yuh see that?"

"See what?" Jakey yelled.

"He looked over our way. Right at us. Noticed we was here!"

"What the hell yuh talkin' about?!"

"Julie. How he looked our way, just now, right before the bell."

"You must be *meshugeh*!"

That's all he could hear now as he sat there. Jakey's words. "You must be *meshugeh!*" Still buried in his thoughts, he didn't hear the tapping at first, the soft rap at the front door, but the sound soon caught his attention and he turned to see Louie standing there, silhouetted in the morning light. He unlatched the front door and let his buddy in.

"I figured I would find yuh here, but I wasn't sure since the place was still dark."

"I been here all night, since we left the fight. What the hell you doin' out this early?"

"Esther called, lookin' for yuh. She was worried sick, said it wasn't like yuh to stay out all night. That's how I knew t'come lookin' for yuh. Me? I got a couple of stiffs to finish up. Three today and who knows how many more by the end of the week. One heart attack from last night, a die-hard fight fan. I won't be surprised, there's a couple of suicides."

"Yeah, me neither. Or murder, even."

"Everyone took a hurt. Even Butter, from what I figure. How much you blow?"

"Yuh don' wanna know."

"That bad?"

"I'm in serious trouble."

"What's serious? How serious?"

"Like I said... Yuh don' wanna know."

"How bad?"

"Would yuh believe five G's, plus?"

"Yuh blew five grand?"

"Plus."

"Where the hell'd' yuh get that kind of dough?"

"Yuhr not hearin' what I'm sayin'... Yuh really don't wanna know."

"Butter got that kind of reach, he covered that kind of bet?!"

Louie sat still, not saying a word, his eyes wide as his friend finally unraveled the story. Or most of it, at any rate. As if in shock, his mouth partially opened, he just sat there in silence for a moment as if searching for the words.

"Yuh realize yuh don't make good, these Irgun guys'll look to put a bullet in your head?"

"That has entered my mind, believe it or not."

"If yuh ain't got a head, yuh don't got a mind!"

"Not now, alright!"

"Your brother, I don't believe he's back. When'd he show up? Did he ask for me?

"A couple weeks ago… And why would he ask for you?"

"From what I hear about this Irgun mob…, yuh don' make good, he won't be able to help yuh. He brought yuh in, he could end up a dead man, too! And this Bottmacher, from what I hear, he don't mess around neither…"

"Tell me somethin' I don't already know. Who do we know, can help me cover?"

"I don't want no part of this one. Uh, uh. No siree. Count me out!"

"Think. There's gotta be somebody."

"Yuh got me! Ain't nobody I know got that kind of *gelt*. One thing I do know's there ain't no *lantsman* yuh can ask. Yuh tell one single *yiddel* and *ganzeh* Legion Avenue, the entire street'll be talkin' by t'night. And it's still Sunday. Word's sure to get back."

"Like I don't know that already. Thanks a lot."

"For what?"

"I just thought of somethin'."

"Yuh gonna let me in?"

"Yuh already said yuh didn't wanna know."

Without another word, Harry slid behind the counter and turning on the small lamp alongside, opened the small cigar box next to the register. Retrieving the jumble of an old address book from its hiding place beneath the ever growing pile of incoming bills and petty cash receipts, he undid the elastic band holding it together and began poring through the scraps of paper, the penciled names and numbers protruding from its dog-eared pages. Finding what he was after, he beelined for the phone booth at the back and slid a nickel in the coin slot as he closed the door behind, sealing in the brief conversation.

Placing the phone on the hook, he returned to his friend.

"Thanks, again."

"For what?"

"Yuh don't wanna know."

The Sunday crowd had already cleared out by one and Yonkel, not about to say anything about the way his boss just sat there on one of the stools most of the morning, had already begun to sweep out the booths. Nothing had been cleaned up or put away. The grill still needed scraping and some of the cooking pans still sat on the stove or in the sinks from the morning. The leftovers still sat out, waiting for the fridge, and a scattering of emptied plates and crumpled napkins remained abandoned on the countertop. But Harry just sat there, his mind clearly somewhere else. So Yonkel, able to read the signs and knowing better, just silently moved the broom through its usual motions.

The peal of the pay phone startled the silence and jarred Harry off his seat. Dashing half the length of the place, he grabbed the receiver off its hook and sliding the door shut, excitedly spoke, barely able to conceal the urgency in his voice. Yonkel, now curious from tone more than anything, waltzed his broom toward the muffled conversation.

"Yeah, yeah... Hey, how are yuh...? Sorry t' have called yuh so early, especially on a Sunday.... Thanks for gettin' back.... Well, yeah, I got a little problem and was wonderin' if maybe I could come over and see yuh.... If that's all right, I mean.... Sure I'm sure, it's serious. I'd never've bothered yuh, especially on a Sunday, if it wasn't."

Harry once again instinctively glanced down at his empty wrist and slid the door open. Silently motioning for Yonkel to move from his line of sight as he leaned from the booth, he squinted across at the clock. Unable to see from where he was, he peered at his lone employee who gave him the time without being asked. He brought the receiver back to his ear.

"Yeah, yeah, sure, I know where it is. If I leave right away, I can be there in twenty minutes, half an hour, tops.... Yeah, sure, okay. I'll see yuh then. Thanks. Thanks a million!"

Returning the phone to its cradle, he turned to Yonkel, still embracing the broom, pretending that he hadn't heard a word.

"I gotta run otta here, be somewhere in a half an hour. Do me a favor and finish cleanin' up. Put everythin' away."

"Yuh expect me to do it all myself? The place is a mess."

"Do what yuh can. What yuh can't get to, I'll take care of in the mornin'. Just be sure t' lock up when yuh leave."

The old pizzeria, a longtime favorite with the Wooster Street locals, was already partially filled with a mid afternoon crowd. Several extended families with lots of little kids, impatient pops and moms not wanting to cook for a change, black-draped grandmothers and silent mustachioed grandpas in starch white Sunday shirts and dark suspendered dress pants filled the large green booths to one side and tables pushed together down the center of the long narrow space. As he made his way directly back, Harry eyed the several young Sunday outing couples romancing each other over glasses of Chianti and bottles of Rheingold at single tables along the other wall. Thankful that there was no one there he recognized, he ignored the usually irresistible fragrance of pureed plum tomatoes and garlic and broiling sausage wafting from the brick ovens. Pausing at the back counter, the tiled divide between kitchen and eating space, he glanced over at the two older men, rendered thin by decades of open hearth heat, both bleached ghostly white by years of night work and clouds of semolina dust, as they carried on their craft at the large hardwood table center kitchen.

Each worked at his own space, at a separate stage of completion fashioning grapefruit-size dough balls into perfectly symmetrical hand-tossed discs laid to rest atop large, long handled rectangular paddles. Harry patiently watched as one of the guys added a puddle of sauce to the center of his disc and using the back of the ladle, spread it evenly toward the edges with practiced spiral motions. A hand sprinkled layer of grated mozzarella, a dozen dollops of pink raw sausage, a squiggle of golden green olive oil and the man moved the large pie ovenwards. Then, with a quick practiced in-and-out jerk of his forearms, elbows raised, he slid it from its board onto the fire brick platform under the flame. Using the front lip of his giant spatula to lift an edge and check the underside of two pies already underway, he then stood the paddle upright in its rack alongside the oven and turned to Harry, standing there by the register, ignored until then.

"Somathin' t' go?"

"No. I'm here to see the boss. He's expectin' me."

"The boss...? You mean uh my son-in-law? You must be the guy from upatown, Legion Avenyuh ."

"Yeah, that's right."

Without another word, the cook hand-motioned Harry to come around behind the counter and directed him back and up a narrow staircase. The door to what had been a small flat, now clearly an office hideaway, opened just as he reached the top and there stood his friend, welcoming him into the over furnished cluttered space with a smile and the wave of a hand.

Gambi offered a drink but his guest refused.

"Long time, no see, Harr. To what do I owe the pleasure on a Sunday? Yuh said on the phone it was somethin' serious."

"I never would've called yuh so early if it wasn't."

"No need to shoot the bull, then. What's up?"

"I'm gonna need some juice, a serious piece of change."

"How serious?"

"Five grand."

"Jeezus, Harr. Sounds like you got yourself jammed up pretty good."

"I can't begin to tell yuh."

"Anybody we know, somebody connected, I can help with?"

"I'm afraid not. But it's serious people. I definitely gotta come up with the cash."

"Hey, you owed me that kinda dough, you can bet that sweet *tuchas* of yours, you'd pay. When yuh need it by?"

"How 'bout t'marruh, first thing..."

"I'm glad yuh waited 'til now."

"I wouldn't be askin' if it wasn't an emergency..."

"This ain't 'cause of the fight last night, is it?"

"Yuh heard about it?"

"Who ain't? Half uh N'Haven took a hurt on that one. Wish I had a piece of that action. The mornin' paper was sayin' the home crowd was seriously upset."

"Upset ain't the word, but that ain't why I need the dough. I wouldn't come to yuh on some bad bookie bet."

"And yuhr sure yuh don't wanna tell me what went down?"

"Nah. It's somethin' I gotta take care of myself. Like I said, yuh can't help with on that end. I'll pay the points, whatever it costs. The thing is, I need it before t'marruh mornin'."

"There's need and there's need. Why the hard deadline?"

"How 'bout 'cause I wanna see Esther and the kids on Tuesday and there's other people involved I don't wanna see get hurt."

"Yuhr obviously jammed up with some serious people. Yuh sure I can't help? Do some mediatin'. Maybe buy yuh some breathin' space?"

"Nah, like I said, yuh wouldn't know these guys."

"In this state? Who don't we know? I don't get it."

"These are *lantsmen*, Jewish guys."

"So what? They wouldn't be connected through New York?"

"Just spot me what I need."

"If that's what yuh want... Whatever way yuh wanna go."

Gambi picked up his desk phone and dialed. On the line less than a minute, he hung up and turned back to Harry.

"As you can figure, I ain't got that kinda cash sittin' around. Had to call one of my people. I'll go make the run and get back as soon as I can. Five grand even?"

"Yeah, that should do it. I really appreciate it."

Gambi spoke as he pulled on his overcoat.

"Ain't no big deal. I never forgot what yuh did for me. When I got home from the war. How yuh reached in your pocket without battin' an eye."

"That was nuthin'. How's the arm doin', by the way?"

"It was plenty at the time, believe you me. I'll never forget. The arm's good. A little numbness once in a while, in the fingers. It's the memories that take the longest."

"Well, at least you're okay now. About the money, it'll be a while before I can get it back t'yuh."

"Did I say anythin'? It's my turn. To return the favor. I'll have t'make good with the people who I'm goin' t' see, but I ain't even gonna take nuthin' on my end. We'll treat this one outta friendship. I ain't intuh shylockin', anyway."

"Hey, I didn't come here not expectin' to..."

"Don't' worry about it. I'll take care of the points with the people upstairs and you and me, we'll work out the details when you get up and runnin' again."

"Jeez, Giusepp, I don't know what t'...."

"Don't worry about it. I could be gone a while. Yuh want somethin' from downstairs? What kinda pie yuh like?"

The knot in his stomach had already begun to relax and Harry suddenly realized that he hadn't eaten since yesterday.

"How about a small anchovy, not too heavy on the *motz*?"

"Good. Make yourself comfortable up here. I'll have one of the boys bring it up. A beer okay?"

"Yeah, fine. A Hull's or Rheingold."

An immediate wave of relief swept over Harry as soon as the door closed behind his old friend. He immediately began to think about the future. The fact, at least, that it had suddenly reappeared.

Monday's trip up and back from Hartford came off like clockwork. The early morning ride with Shmule silent at the wheel the whole time, the guns, an entire trailer full of Colts, loaded at a warehouse close by the Connecticut River factory after the envelope passed to some tight-lipped heavies, it all went without a hitch. Hardly a word exchanged as if any sound uttered could or would be used as evidence.

It wasn't until the ride back, somewhere between Berlin and Meriden that Harry, sitting there alone in the silence with his own thoughts, began to replay the last several days. It wasn't until then that he realized he maybe should have asked Gambi for more. Rushed by fear and that concern to get out from under the sure bet of *shtarker* peril, he hadn't considered it all. But then, as the truck made its way back to New Haven, he suddenly remembered the outstanding debt to Butter. The rest of it, what he owed everyone else on the street, didn't matter at that moment. What came to him was the watch.

Yonkel and Jakey had everything pretty much in order by the time he made it back to the store. The normally heavy Monday lunch crowd had long gone, leaving but a few stragglers and Harry called to Yonkel as he waved Jakey toward the back with a nod of the head.

"Bring me and Jakey a coffee, and keep an eye while we talk, would yuh, please."

The two friends slid into the booth by the rear door and Yonkel followed a minute later, sliding two saucered cups in between them. Slowly stirring as he added cream and sugar, Harry silently studied the swirl of light brown liquid as if looking for some guidance on where to begin. Not touching his, Jakey just sat there with his forearms resting on the table, knowing full well from the silence that something was up. Finally, his friend began.

"So how'd everything go?"

"Here? No problem. Yonkel saved the day. And you?"

"Everythin's under control."

"Yuh gonna tell me where yuh went?"

"It don't matter. I gotta ask yuh somethin'."

"Like I didn't know that was comin'?"

"No, seriously, I need yuh to do me one more favor."

"Oh, boy, here we go."

"I need yuh to make me a loan."

"I tol' yuh yesterday, I'm tapped out."

"Who you talkin' t', here? You mean to tell me Jakey Hirsch, who I've known all my life, he doesn't have a little somethin' squirreled away somewhere?"

"How much we talkin'?"

"Eight hundred. A grand tops."

"What do I look like to you? Mr. Rockyfeller?"

"Yuh ain't gonna help me out?"

"Why should I bother? How much did yuh blow on the fight?"

"Not that much."

"Then how come yuhr so depressed. I don't think I ever seen yuh like this, the way yuh look. When was the last time yuh shaved?"

"Yuh gonna help me out, or not?"
"Under one condition. That yuh tell me what's really goin' on."

Jakey just sat there, transfixed in disbelief, as Harry unraveled another version of his reality. Taking a moment at story's end, he raised his cup to his lips and took a sip from the already chilled coffee. He then turned his gaze to his friend's eyes, filled with both a pleading and a trapped resignation, staring at him from across the table.

"I don't believe it! When the hell yuh gonna learn?"
"You're right! You're right!"
"Don't give me that 'I'm right' crap! Let me get this straight... Your brother's back. He hooks yuh up with the Irgun and that big wheel, the garment *macher*. They make yuh a runner. Butter tells you yuh got a sure thing on the fight. Yuh bet the whole wad, the Irgun's five grand, and Julie goes down. So you get jammed even deeper, way in over your head. Then, in all your genius, yuh go to Wooster Street?!"
"What d'yuh want I should tell yuh?"
"Yuh think you'll ever get out? They'll ever let yuh out?"
"After this, I'm through! This is it! Done!"
"Done?! Done!? You're so done already, somebody should do to yuh like one of those turkeys yuh make and stick in the goddamn fork!"
"I need your help."
"What do yuh want from me? I thought yuh covered with the juice from Wooster Street!"
"I'm still short on what I owe Butter. Plus I'm behind on the rent. If I don't get straight, especially with the flat, we're gonna get evicted. Besides, I gotta get Esther's watch back."
"Why come to me? I already tol' yuh twice, three times, I was tapped."
"Yuh ain't got any money from the Feds like you was gettin', the payments from when you was in the service?"
"Every penny I get from them is goin' toward school."
"Yuh gotta help me. I'll get it back to yuh. You know that. When have I ever not?!"
"You got one helluva nerve! Brass balls, you got! Don't yuh know me at all? Where I'm comin' from, where I've always been at with these things!?"
"What are you talkin' about?"
"A little action, the weekly poker game or the horses occasionally, that's one thing. And we've all owed a little on some line with one of the bookies...."
"So...?"
"The Irgun! And then the mob!? Which is worse!? What if yuh had been caught with those gun runners!"
"I'm here, ain't I?"
"And this Bottmacher? *Lantsman* or no, he's a real class enemy."
"Don't start with the commie crap."

"Mobsters and bosses! Zionist gangsters…! What's next!?"

"You gonna help me out, or not?"

Visibly perturbed, Jakey got up from the booth. Walking a few feet, he paused, with his back to his friend. Standing there another moment or two without a sound, he finally turned around.

"This has nothin' to do with you, yuh understand. I'm gonna give yuh the money, but it's for Esther. And the kids."

"For Esther! It was always her, wasn't it!"

"What are yuh talkin' about?"

"What? Yuh think I'm blind? Yuh think I never noticed how yuh look at her? How yuh act different when she's around?"

"You're really off your nut. Way the hell otta line!"

"You've never had a thing for her?"

"And what if I did, so what? You should only have what me and Eve…"

"So yuh did! There *was* somethin' there."

"Yeah, sure! And yuh know what? It was mutual. Always was. I just made one lousy mistake, that's all."

"And what was that?"

"I put you and me, our friendship…, it always came first!"

"Fuck you, Jakey!"

"Fuck me?!"

"Yuh gonna give me the money, or not?"

"You're one lucky son of a bitch, boy. Normally you'd be askin' the wrong guy, but I just got my school check from Uncle Sam."

"When can I get it?"

"When can yuh get it back to me?"

"When do yuh need it by?"

"We gonna play games, here? I'm gonna need it soon, yesterday."

"You'll get it. You'll get it. Yuh got my word."

"But when?"

"I said you'll get it."

CHAPTER 26:

The Lot

1989... Up LONG BEFORE THE rest of the house began to stir, David just stood there motionless beneath the hot needle spray of the guest shower as fleeting images of Harry first and then Esther flooded his waking memory. Suddenly, he was a high school kid again and he could hear her calling from the kitchen as if it was last Saturday.

"Go already, hurry up. Take your shower before your father gets in the tub. You know him. He'll use all the hot water and then you'll be shit-otta-luck."

He noticed it after he had toweled himself off and put his glasses back on, as he leaned over to wipe the still steamy mirror. The bottle of Old Spice sitting there by itself next to the sink. He thought it strange, a little bit more than coincidental, then realized that Richie must have left it there as a hospitable touch. Slowly picking it up, he examined the off-white bottle with its blue stenciled sailing ship as if it was something mysterious, a sealed castaway carried by trans-oceanic currents, washed ashore many thousands of miles from home. He unscrewed the top and tipped a few droplets into his upturned palm and the confined space, still fogged with steamy mist, filled with that unmistakably distinct fragrance. His father.

Returning to the bedroom, he slowly dressed, putting on the underwear and socks, the pale blue Oxford shirt. As he pulled on the pants to his one dress suit, the soft brown academic tweed that Annie had picked out, fresh images of old memories rushed in. He could see him plain as day, caught in that moment before he put on his suit pants, Harry standing there before the bedroom mirror in his over-the-calf dress socks and boxer shorts, struggling with the collar stays of his crisp white dress shirt still starchy stiff from the cleaners. The father getting ready for a night out and his son's memory so clear that his eye caught the sheen of the man's well oiled hair. The smell of aftershave lingered in his nostrils as if Harry was actually there in the room.

Finished dressing, he turned back toward the bed, toward Annie, and kissed her gently on the cheek to rouse her. She turned partway toward him, her eyes still closed, just barely awake.

"What's that smell?"

"Smell?"

"Like... like the aftershave my... my father used to wear. When... when I was a little girl."

"That's funny. I don't smell anything.... It's early, yet. I'll call yuh in a little while."

He went down and sat in the soft after-dawn light of the den, alone. He thought about it for an instant, the cologne coincidence, and then just sat there calmly, meditatively listening to the quiet. The old, deep memories came to him then, those distant images of intimate times, those little boy moments when he used to cuddle with his father. Those occasions when Harry, so ravenously hungry for some tenderness, the kind his own father and grandfather never knew and could never give, would smother him with demands for "hugs and kisses". The demand to be loved. He found himself pondering that mystery that must have been his father's childhood.

The others finally came down not long after he absentmindedly called up the stairs to rouse Annie and got the dogs barking. They left the house early since Howard, nervous as he was about the arrangements, had to stop at the deli in Westville to make sure all the food was ready. For afterwards. The three of them, Annie, Davey and Howard, rode in the Audi since Richie volunteered to go and pick up Aunt Edie and Uncle Manny. With Howard remarkably quiet, the other two hardly spoke and even the radio remained silent as the car crept down out of Woodbridge and in toward the city center.

David, raised on all those clichéd Hollywood funeral images, had assumed it would pour throughout the morning and as they left the house, had even thought of asking Howard if they should take along umbrellas. He now just stared out his passenger-side window at the cold winter sun caught napping just atop West Rock's wooded ridge. He imagined for an instant that he was actually home safe in Wisconsin and smelling the crisp air, wondered if it might snow before the day was out.

His focus shifted as they entered the tired, worn city. He watched as the inbound cars with their solitary commuters, the infrequent lone head-bowed pedestrian hurrying for work on the chilled early streets, even the skinny mongrel stray that he spotted, its nose to the ground on a routine morning prowl among the curbside cans, all seemed to move in slow motion.

The parking lot at Velners' sat empty when they pulled in and Davey, wondering for an instant if they had the right place or time and day, looked all around and then turned to glance back at Annie. As if knowing what he was thinking, perhaps from his mildly perplexed look, she silently calmed him with a faint reassuring smile and touch over the top of the seat as Howard's voice fractured the silence.

"Well, I guess I over ordered. There's no one here. Sorta like I expected. But it's okay, I'll freeze the leftovers, the bagels and stuff that'll keep, and send the rest home in doggie bags with whoever shows up."

Davey smiled wryly. "I got a better idea. How 'bout I just help yuh bag what's left and Annie and I take it over to Mickey's."

"Mickey's! Over my dead body! You're not really goin' over there, are yuh? T' Gina's, I mean."

"Yeah, just for awhile. After. T'night, at some point. I figured me and Annie... I sorta promised I would. You know how he gets."

"But I got some friends comin' over later, people I want yuh t' meet."

"And right now I have to concentrate on what matters most and while I'm at it, spend some time with both my brothers. Yuh follow me?"

They no sooner got out of the car when Mickey rolled in next to them behind the wheel of a sleek-riding early eighties Eldorado, a wire wheeled, chrome-detailed silver-blue four-door with light gray vinyl and matching leather. Clean, almost cherry, as they would say in the used car biz. Powering down his tinted window, he halfheartedly flicked a half-gone Salem to the pavement and he glanced up in silence at Davey sandwiched there between the cars. Pausing for a second, he swung his door open and hoisting himself up and out of the Caddy, came nearly face-to-face with his kid brother.

"So wha'd'yuh think?"

"Think? What's t' think?"

Mickey half grinned. "I mean about the car! Not bad, no? Figured the ol' man should go out in style. Left the 'Vette home and borrowed this one. From this friend of mine, this dealer I know. Totally on the cuff."

"On the cuff?"

"The guy owed me. Yuh wouldn't believe what they're gettin' for the rental on a limo these days. Just for a mornin'. I'm tellin' yuh, boy, I don't know about you but I'm definitely in the wrong racket."

Davey shot a quick dart glance from the Eldorado to Annie and then toward Howard, standing close by with that disdainful "My brother, the putz!" look on his face. He turned back toward Mickey and stared at and through him until he finally received some eye contact.

"It sorta looks like... well, what do yuh want I should tell yuh? It looks like... like a pimpmobile."

"Hey, you know me! Nuthin' but the best for the ol' man!"

Still eyeball-to-eyeball with his big brother, Davey stifled an outright laugh and revealed a grin as he shook his head in mock amazement, his way of cutting through the macho bull. And that was all it took. Choking back his emotions with a dry cigarette cough, Mickey lurched forward and the kid brother consolingly hugged him.

"You okay?"

"Yeah, I'm all right. I'll be all right. He just went so fast, that's all."

"Better the way he did than endin' up layin' in one of those nursing homes."

"Fuckin' A. Imagine the nut on that one, what that woulda cost?"

"Remember what he used to say? How, if one of us tried to put him in one of those joints, he'd put a gun in his mouth first."

"He wasn't bullshittin' neither."

"Everything cool with you?"

"I already tol' yuh. Last night. There ain't gonna be no trouble."

"That isn't what I was askin'. I was wonderin' how you're doin'. That's all."

Gina's voice intruded, an abrupt interruption. David hadn't seen her get out of the Caddy and he didn't stand a chance as she rushed him with an insincere hug, a feigned sympathy smile and a quick lipsticky kiss to the cheek.

"Hi yuh, Davey! It's been so long. Really sorry to hear about your ol' man. Your father, I mean. Harry... Aw, you know what I mean."

He wondered what she possibly could have meant as he extended a rote thank you. The girlfriend let go and the other passenger, Joshie, Mickey's second one, drew close. Davey had but an instant to look him over before they embraced. There he was, the once-upon-a-time cute little kid now pushing his mid-twenties, no longer pimply but still pallid, almost ashen in his unbuttoned black leather dress jacket, a pair of cheap gray slacks and a brown open-at-the-neck disco shirt, his black hair slicked straight back in that affected just-got-out-of-the-oily-water look. He embraced his uncle, and holding each other by the forearms, they came eye-to-eye.

"How yuh doin', Uncle Dave? Sorry about granpa."

"Yeah, me too."

Davey smiled directly into his nephew's deep set saddened eyes as the manchild's pupils, perpetually on guard against any open, warm look, the sure sign of a hustle, darted away. He naturally had assumed that Joshie would show up loaded, and now could tell that he apparently wasn't as narcotized as expected, that the kid had decided to maintain and had somehow pulled it together for the funeral. Relieved that he now had one less thing to concern himself with, Davey hugged him again, this time for an instant longer. Clapping his uncle between the shoulder blades, Joshie, too, felt a sudden rush of relief, confident now that he had overcome his first hurdle of the day since Davey hadn't noticed how high he actually was.

Mickey, meanwhile, pressed Annie close in a not-meaning-to-be-so but nevertheless forward, almost sexual fashion, his accustomed way of embracing a woman. He kissed her on the cheek as he gave her a low-keyed, sombered version of his "How yuh doin?". He then turned to Howard and the two of them, each in his own way aware of the customary charade of sibling civility, the bare minimum required by the moment, carefully hugged without allowing their bodies too close.

Then suddenly stilled by the awkwardness of the situation and the impending reality, they all silently paused as if frozen to the salt-streaked asphalt. Howard unconsciously looked at his watch as if he had an appointment somewhere and David took the cue.

"Wha'd'yuh say? It must be about time, no? Shall we go take care of the ol' man?"

With that, they moved as if one toward the front door of the funeral home as other cars, their barely recognizable passengers peering out as if driving by the scene of some sidewalk homicide, slowly filed into the lot. Davey noticed it then, the hearse standing by the side entrance with its engine running, waiting there as if delayed at the drive-up window of some take-forever fast-food joint. Pausing for a second, he wondered if Harry could still be in the back, if the driver was running late or had forgotten somehow and was just now dropping him off. An imaginary microphoned voice came to him as Annie took his hand and guided him toward the main entry. *"Good morning and welcome to Velners'! How can I help you?"*

His brief stutter-stepped pause halted Mickey following close behind. Taking the opportunity, he straightened the pale velour jersey now riding up under his out-of-season silver-gray suit jacket as his urban eyes, first scanning the perimeter of the parking lot, moved across George Street. He spotted them sitting there in the unmarked Ford, the two Feds from the day before, from Barone's office. He thought about tossing them the finger, but decided not to. Josh must have sensed something and he too came to a full stop as his eyes followed his father's gaze across to the stakeout.

"Who th' hell's that?"

"Who else would be seen in a stripped down Fairlane with blackwalls? Gotta be Feds. I don't even have t' see the plates."

"What the hell they want?"

"Who the hell knows? The usual bullshit. A couple of assholes hopin' maybe somebody famous'll show up so they can take some pictures. Maybe write down some marker numbers."

"Lemme take a walk over there. I'll straighten 'em right out."

"Worry about straightenin' yourself out. I don't need no heat. 'Specially t'day."

The entourage moved forward. Joined at the entrance by Richie, Aunt Edie and Uncle Mannie, his yarmulke already in place, they moved inside.

Alexandra had a rough idea where the funeral parlor was. She remembered Harry pointing it out to her during one of their early visits, on their way to some downtown eatery. But that had been some time ago and New Haven's one-way streets always confused her. Already uncertain, somewhat lost and now truly concerned about being late, she pulled the Accord into the big Shell station where Goffe and Whalley merged at Broadway and went up and asked the youngish attendant behind the bulletproof Plexiglas for directions. He didn't know, wasn't quite sure where George Street was, but a customer behind her, an early thirtyish black man with brushed back rust-red hair and a gold front tooth, smiling as if to show it off, interrupted as he stepped around her and dropped his pay-in-advance gas money onto the sliding tray at the bottom of the cashier's window.

"'I'm on pump three, fi'e dollahs... Scuse me, miss, but I couldn't help but overhearin'. You lookin' for Velners', where the Jewish people, they hold their funerals?"

"Yes, I am," she responded, already on guard, presuming some sort of impending hustle.

"Da's easy. No sweat, from here. Go on up Whalley, right here. 'Bout half a mile 'til yuh comes to Sherman. Go lef' and over a couple blocks. Maybe i's one long one. Jus' go to the firs' light after yuh see the Catholic hospital, St. Raphael's. Da's Jawge. Go lef' again. I's right there, over 'bout a block or so."

"Thank you."

"Scuse me, again, miss, but can I as' yuh somethin'?"

"Here it comes," she thought, as she paused for a second and gazed at the man.

"You Italian miss, ain't chuh? Yuh looks Italian."

"What of it?"

"I could tell. The way you is dressed and looks and all. I don' mean no offense or nuthin, but if yuh don' minds my askin', how come you be goin' to a Jewish funeral?"

"Its for a friend. An old family friend."

"My condolences, miss. God bless." He smiled again and turned back toward the gas pumps.

Velners' was right where he said it would be and she saw them as she pulled in. Still wondering why she had even come and suddenly just wanting to watch, she glided past them all, busy greeting each other, and backed into a space toward the rear of the lot. She looked on as they chatted for a moment and finally started toward the front door of the funeral home. She spotted Howard first, recognizing him immediately as if it was still that day when Harry had first introduced them on the Turnpike through the window of his car. Her eye then moved to Mickey, unmistakable by his size, dominating the space there in the middle of the group. Her gaze shifted across to the one she hadn't met. Davey, as Harry called him, the one he always talked about, recognizable from the photos on the top of the TV in his apartment. There they were, her three brothers.

Unnoticed, she watched them as they made their way toward the entry. She looked on as David paused for a second and stared at the building, perhaps at the hearse sitting alongside, until the woman by his side, his wife, she assumed, took his hand and eased with him toward the front door. She noticed as Mickey paused and adjusted the pullover under his suit coat and looked around as if he was checking the lot. Convinced he had spotted her and relieved that he hadn't, she followed the direction of their gaze as the two of them, her oldest half brother and the younger one with him, one of her nephews, she figured, paused for a moment and stared off across the street. Her eyes traced their line of vision and she spotted them as well, the two suits sitting there in the plain burgundy Ford.

"Cops, must be cops," she realized. "A couple of plainclothes cops. Just like in the movies."

She watched as the rest of the family moved through the door. Feeling quite the outsider, not ready to move, she just sat there and looked on as other cars slowly filled the lot and additional mourners filed toward the entry. She watched as the police car, a bronze Caprice with large badge decals on its front doors reading "Vermont Highway Patrol" drove in and parked alongside the building. She pondered why they would be there and looked on as the two patrolmen guardedly got out and escorted their shackled prisoner through a side door. She looked as the New Haven taxi pulled up at the curb and the older black woman, large in stature and dignified in her walk, her head up, slowly made her way to the entrance aided by a wooden cane. She wondered who the woman could be as she checked her lips and hair in the rearview mirror, opened her door, and got out.

She immediately had drawn the Feds' attention when she pulled to the back of the lot and just sat there without getting out. Boyer raised the small pair of surveillance binoculars and peered over at her from the passenger seat as his partner squinted through his sunglasses toward the Honda.

"Who can that be?" queried Svenrud.

"I don't know, but she's certainly a good-looker," came the reply as Boyer lowered the angle of view on the field glasses. Setting them back in his lap, he jotted down her marker number as he continued.

"She looks Jewish, maybe Italian. Could be a family member, but she probably would have got out by now, would have joined the others if she was. This could be one we don't know about. Get a couple of shots of her when she heads for the door."

Svenrud, without taking his eyes off the parking lot, removed his shades and raised the camera off the seat. He started to adjust the telephoto focus but quickly lowered it, interrupted.

"It's our friend, Mickey. I think he's spotted us."

"That's exactly why we parked here. We want him to."

"Turning up the heat?"

"Yeah, like I said before, maybe we can get him to flip if he thinks his world is caving in."

"Yuh think he bought it?"

"The bit about the contract? He's certainly had a whole night to worry about it. We'll just have to see."

"Who's the kid with him?"

"That must be his son, the second one. A list of misdemeanors, a felony waiting to happen. Another piece of work."

"The nut don't fall far, does it?"

"That's what they say. I'm wonderin' about the other one."

"Which?"

"The professor type, with the woman holding his hand."

"One of the sons?"

Recalling something, Boyer checked a page on his clipboard.

"Yeah, here he is. The name's David. Says here he's currently living in Wisconsin. Was a history teacher, a professor or somethin'. The home office had an old sheet on him they faxed over, some minor student radical stuff. During the late sixties, early seventies. Nothing really recent."

"These Jew boys, there's always a Red, ain't there. Who's the woman?"

"Must be the wife."

"They sure walk like they're married."

The two Feds looked on as the group moved inside and each checked his watch as the Vermont patrol car pulled in.

"Right on schedule," Svenrud noted.

"Yeah, some nice cooperation for a change from the Burlington office."

The two watched as the troopers moved Jimmy inside. Svenrud then snapped a few shots of Hermina, an "unidentified elderly black female" as Boyer described her in his notes, and clicked off several of Alexandra when she finally moved across the lot. They had already begun to wrap it up, to clear off the seat between them, when Boyer spotted the late arrival, the Lincoln town car, as it pulled up in front. He raised the field glasses as he spoke.

"Well, well, what do we have here?"

Svenrud, already focusing the lens to his camera and firing away, caught the junior associate as he got out on the front passenger side of the late model Continental and turned and waited to open the rear door. He snapped two more as a second figure, a slightly bulkier sunglassed man, a dark suit with an expensive Italian knit underneath, came around the rear from the other side and positioned himself. The soldiers in place, the first attendant opened the door and Svenrud clicked away as the older man, dressed for the part, raised up out of the backseat.

Boyer's voice briefly interrupted the shoot.

"Well, isn't this nice. If it isn't our old friend, Mr. Gambardella, coming to pay his last respects."

"I thought he was still away..."

"I did too, according to the last reports I had...."

"I don't get it."

"Neither do I."

"And the others?"

"Yeah, let's see. The usuals. Junie DiMichaeli riding shotgun, Raphie "the Rapper" in back. I can't quite make out the driver from here...."

"Testa. It has to be Testa. He's always the wheel man."

"Yep, you're right. All present and accounted for."

The agents watched until the driver parked and returned and the foursome moved inside. Boyer turned to his partner as the two proceeded to pack the rest of their equipment.

"It'll be a while now before they come out. We might as well go grab some coffee."

"Now you're talkin'. I noticed before there's a Dunkin' Donuts just up the street by the hospital."

CHAPTER 27:

The Parlor

1989... POSTED JUST INSIDE THE entry, Stevie Velner stood and greeted each of the family members with one of his consolingly soft, practiced handshakes as a pale, young, gray-suited woman, an attendant at his side, helped everyone with their coats. Mickey spotted the New Haven uniform, the younger white guy with a gun belted below his belly, standing off to the side even before he reached the undertaker. Pulling Gina by the arm before she could even get her coat off, he approached the cop.

"Hey, how yuh doin'? I'm Mickey Rabin. The one who hired yuh. This here's my girlfriend, Gina. I don' know if anybody explained t' yuh yet what yuhr here for, but I want yuh to stay by her the whole time. If anyone looks to start anythin' with her... yuh know... looks to get stupid, don't hesitate t' arrest 'em. I'll definitely press charges."

Mickey gave the silent, unimpressed cop a look as if they were long lost pals and coming out with his money-clipped wad, peeled off a twenty and slipped it to the guy as he continued.

"Here's a little somethin' extra. I especially want yuh to keep her and the wife separated. That's the main thing. They got into it once before and I certainly don't need any extra headaches t'day. Yuh know what I'm sayin'? This one here, she'll point the other one out when she gets here."

It was then that Mickey noticed the cop's name tag.

"Linehan? Which Linehan are you?"

"My father was Jimmy."

"No shit...! Ain't this somethin'! I know your whole family. My ol' man, the one we're here for, we used to live right across the street from your grandfather. Back years ago, when I was little kid..., on Asylum Street, over by Legion Avenue."

"Yeah, I know who you are..."

"Do me a favor would yuh and just stick with the girlfriend."

Davey in the meantime found himself sizing up the younger Velner. Remembering him entirely as nothing more than a little kid, he now noted the fine cut of the nicely-tailored charcoal suit and the conservative silk tie, the alabaster fingers with their manicured nails, the diamond pinkie ring, and soft-toned, well-rehearsed expressions of sympathy, all stock-in-trade. As the two shook hands, he wondered if his father's friend was still around.

"Hello, Steven. It's been a long time."

"Yes, it has. Sorry about your father."

"And yours? Is he...?"

"Oh yeah, he's still here. Apparently has no plans of going anywhere. As a matter of fact, he asked if you could maybe join him for a moment. Before we get started."

Davey quickly introduced Annie, still by his side. Telling her he needed a minute, he excused himself and Stevie showed him into the office. Louie raised himself up and came around from behind the desk and grasped the hands of his old friend's youngest in both of his.

"Davey, Davey. My God! Look at yuh!"

"Hello, Louie."

"Where's it go, I ask yuh?"

"It?"

"The time, for krissakes. One minute, you're a little snot-nosed *pisher* screamin' and runnin' around, raisin' hell like all the rest, and suddenly here you are, a grown man, lookin' like some Yalie professor. The whole get up, the beard and all, the tweed suit. All uh yuhz, all grown up. Where's it go?"

"I was wondering the same thing all the way here."

"Where'd yuh come in from? Wha'd your father tell me? What was it? Minnesota? Wisconsin?"

"Wisconsin."

"Wisconsin, Minnesota, the same goddamn thing. I'm glad yuh made it. The ol' man, he woulda been disappointed as hell if yuh didn't show."

Louie gestured toward his mouth with an imaginary shot glass.

"Yuh care for somethin'? A little eye-opener? I thought maybe me and you, we could have one together. A little toast."

"I don't usually, this early, but I guess.... Yeah. Sure. What the hell. One for the ol' man."

The undertaker moved back around the desk and opened the bottom drawer. Dispensing this time with the silver tray routine, he pulled out a half empty bottle and a pair of plain restaurant water glasses. Pouring a couple of fingers in each, he came back around and handed Davey one.

"Yuh stay in this business long enough and yuh realize it's never too early."
The two clinked as the old-timer led the toast.
"L'chaim."
"Yeah, *l'chaim.*"
"For Harry, *alevashalom.*"
Davey downed part of his scotch and watched as his father's old friend snapped his head back and drained his glass in one single motion. He studied the man's bloodshot, weary eyes, their lower lids saggy with age and alcohol, the deep troubled creases across his forehead, the blood vessels visible in his full cheeks, the loneliness and loss.
"It must be hard on yuh, Louie."
"Hard? What's hard? Yuh know how long I been doin' this? How many I took care of, over the years?"
"I'm not talking about the rest. I'm talkin' about the ol' man. How difficult it must be."
"You gonna look to start, too?"
"Too?"
"Yeah, first I gotta deal with him. And now you?"
"Like I said, it must be hard. He really did love yuh."
"Yeah, I know. And that's the problem. Despite how difficult he made it. I loved him, too. We all did."
"He never made it easy for anyone."
"Yuh lookin' to tell me somethin' new?"
"How far back yuh go?"
"We were little kids together, for krissakes. On Oak Street, what became Legion Avenue. Seen it all. The good times, the bad. Prohibition and the Depression. Christ, you name it. We even survived what they did to this goddamn city. Urban renewal, my ass! I'm talkin' over seventy goddamn years."
"Lots of memories."
"Yeah, too goddamn many."
The door opened and Steven poked his head in. Pretending this time not to notice the glass in his father's hand or the bottle on the desk, he addressed his senior partner.
"The place is filling up. Rabbi Feldstein's here. We're gonna have to start soon."
"How's the turnout?"
"Not bad, considering. More than I figured. We might have to bring in some extra chairs. Maybe open up the second room before we're through."
"Go figure. It's a good thing we didn't have a doubleheader, with the other room booked.... Davey'll be right there."
"You're not coming out?
"I don' know. I think maybe I'll just stay here. Sit this one out."
"Do what yuh want."
Stevie closed the door as he left and David turned to his father's old friend and smiled.

"Well, I guess it's showtime."

"I suppose so. I'm glad we got a minute. You were always real special to the ol' man. He always talked about yuh."

"You were special to him, too."

Davey embraced the old-timer once again and moved toward the door. He turned then, just as his hand reached the knob.

"Yuh mind if I ask yuh somethin'?"

"What's that?"

"Among the guys you came up with, the old crowd, was there someone named Julie? Maybe some woman?"

"You too?"

"Me, too, what?"

"Your brother Mickey, he asked me the same thing. When he was here. Yesterday."

"He did? And you don't know?"

"Not a clue. Haven't the foggiest."

"Just thought I'd ask."

As soon as the door closed, Louie turned back to his desk and eyed the bottle sitting there. He contemplated another drink but this time caught himself. He couldn't figure it out, the sudden quandary he found himself in.

"This, I don't believe! You're layin' out there, all dressed up with but one place to go. And me? I still end up havin' t' cover for yuh. What was the big deal anyway, that I gotta keep your secret all these years?"

Harry's voice came to him.

"That's what friends are for, no?"

"What? It would hurt so much now, to fill 'em in, to tell 'em, your kids, what happened?"

"Yuh gave me your word."

"What's the big deal?"

"Let it rest, I'm tellin' yuh. Just let it rest."

Using the cane her man had given her, the fine old hickory one with the bronze ram's head handle, Hermina slowly made her way from the taxi and moved inside. Unaccustomed to being alone around so many white people, with no other brothers or sisters, not a single soul in sight from the lodge, she kept reminding herself that she had as much right as any of them to be there. Way more than most, she told herself. She found it easy to ignore the pretend distant stares, the way some of the ones congregated in the foyer hushed and looked past her as if she didn't exist when she paused to remove her coat and retrieve an embroidered hanky from her bag. Determined to pay them no mind, she remained at ease, calm and focused. That is until she saw Mickey. Until he nearly walked into her and suddenly realizing she was there, threw his arms around her, engulfing her as if she was some long lost relative, the tears welling up in his eyes. Still holding on, he spoke to her embarrassed ear.

"Ain't this somethin? I was just thinkin' about yuh. Hopin' you'd show up."

"I know you have other things to be doin' rather than fussin over me," she said, pulling back. "You the man now, Mickey. The boss. Just show me where I'm supposed to sit and I'll...."

"You can sit with us. Right up front. With the family."

"Oh no, Mickey. I couldn't do that."

"Why not?"

"'Cause I won't, that's why."

"Whatever. Do what yuh want. You wanna see him before they close the box?"

"No, that's all right. I'll be fine with my memories."

"I was just goin' to get Davey. Did you ever meet Davey, my kid brother? I was goin' t' take him to see the ol' man."

Without making introductions, he turned to Joshie standing there alongside. "Where's Davey? Did you see where your uncle went?"

"Yeah, I saw him a second ago. He was with his wife, goin' in t' one of those rooms on the side." He pointed the direction. "Over there."

Relieved to be left alone again, Hermina simply shook her head as Mickey moved off without so much as another word, his son trailing behind.

David had just left Velner's office and made his way back to the foyer, now crowded with a score of distantly familiar faces, a half dozen first and second cousins, some old family friends and guys from the car business on Whalley Avenue, all of them somehow older than he remembered, staring at him from the sides of the room. Annie was standing there alone and her eyes, wide with suppressed fear, caught his as she rushed toward him.

"What's the matter?!"

"Cops! With guns!"

"Cops always got guns. What are you talking about?"

"Two of them. Two more. They just walked in. With some younger guy in handcuffs. Carrying rifles! They brought him in the side door!"

"Carrying rifles? Jimmy. It must be Jimmy! Where are they?"

Annie motioned toward a side room set back from the now congested entryway and followed Davey as he moved off. His eyes met his oldest nephew's as soon as he turned into the empty side parlor. The two troopers had sequestered him there away from the flow and they immediately came to their feet, their weapons pointed muzzle downwards, just barely concealed at their sides, as Jimmy, his wrists and ankles restrained, cautiously rose up off the narrow side sofa set against one wall.

"Hi yuh, Uncle Dave."

"Hey yuh, Jimmy."

"Sorry about gran'pa, but I'm glad to be here, I guess." He nodded to his escorts as he raised his chained wrists. "Even like this."

"I'm glad you are."

"Is my ol' man here yet?"

"Yeah, we came in together."

"I can't wait to see his miserable ass."

"Why's that?"

"'Cuz I miss him so much. That's why. 'Specially since he ain't been to see me once since I got moved t' Vermont."

"Glad t' hear yuh been thinking about me," came Mickey's voice from the doorway. "I was wonderin' when you'd show up."

Jimmy, still on his feet, tensed immediately and his two escorts, perhaps keyed into body language or the subtle rattle of chain or simply going on that intuitive sense acquired from years spent moving cons cross-country, stepped forward as father and son came face-to-face.

"I know what yuh did," came Jimmy's voice, soft, almost whispered, but with an edge sharpened like a contraband blade.

"You tryin' to say somethin'?"

"You know what I'm talkin' about. I'm just tellin' yuh I know what yuh did."

The troopers, by that time, standing to either side like the seconds at a duel, leaned in to listen as Mickey turned to one of them.

"Wha'd yuh bring me, here? Was he this high when yuh started out? Or did he somehow get wacky on the way down?"

The son responded.

"They wouldn't even let me have a smoke. I ain't high and I ain't crazy and I ain't playin' no game. It took me a while, but I figured it out. You know what yuh did."

Mickey then turned to Davey, still standing there with Annie close behind.

"Yuh believe this?! I go and shell out twelve hunnert to bring him down here, all the way from fuckin' Vermont. For the ol' man and so he could see everybody. And what's he do? Immediately he goes and cops an attitude like I owe him somethin'!"

His son, now sandwiched more tightly between the two guards, responded.

"You don't owe me nuthin'. It's what I owe you. And I ain't stayin' in forever. I will get out."

Mickey looked at the two officers, thinking he could maybe get the upper hand.

"You threatenin' me?"

Unprovoked, still penitentiary cool, Jimmy came back.

"I don't have t' threaten nobody. You know what yuh did and I'll catch up with yuh. Later. That's all."

Mickey turned and took his brother by the arm as the troopers, with just enough implicit threat in their posture and a word or two concealed under their breath, eased Jimmy back toward his seat.

"Yuh believe this fuckin' kid! Com' on. Yuh wanna see the ol' man one last time?"

Davey looked over his shoulder toward his nephew seated there, defiant, his back upright on the stiff-backed sofa, framed by what now appeared to be two loyal centurions posted at either side. Wondering about what he just heard, he was still trying to think of something to say as Mickey pulled him into the hallway.

Now entirely aggravated over Jimmy and not focused on where he was walking, the older one once again nearly plowed into Hermina, paused there in the corridor.

"Hey Davey, before I forget... Lemme intraduce yuh to someone. This here's Hermina. She's been the old man's girlfriend for over twenty years."

The youngest son and the father's companion exchanged greetings and condolences with their eyes as Davey took the woman's free hand in his.

"That's Herm-E-E-na with an E, and not with an I, if I recall."

"Then you do remember?"

Mickey interrupted.

"The two uh yuhz met before?"

Hermina, still face-to-face with Davey, responded.

"Oh, yes... Oh yes, we have."

He spoke into the woman's milky, watery eyes.

"Would you accept a belated apology?"

"For what?"

"For my being such an ass that time. At my dad's place. It was just that..."

"That I was there?"

David paused a second. "Yeah... yeah, that might have been it, I guess."

"There ain't no need to apologize for that, son. Besides, I'm here now, ain't I? How come it don't bother you now?"

"It wasn't because..."

The aging woman brought her handkerchief hand toward her face as if to cough and ended the conversation with an upraised index finger to her lips. Davey got the message and the father's friend turned away.

No sooner did she move off than Howard approached, accompanied by a younger woman, perhaps in her mid to late twenties, someone that Davey didn't recognize immediately but Mickey apparently did.

"You ain't gonna believe this," whispered the oldest brother as the four converged.

Howard faced Davey as if Mickey wasn't standing there. "There yuh are," he began. "I've been lookin' all over hell. I wanna intraduce yuh to someone."

Davey turned squarely toward the woman and no introductions became necessary as he studied the brow, the set of her deep dark intelligent eyes, the slight curve of nose, his father's features clearly imprinted, unmistakable, on the face curiously studying his. Howard continued, regardless.

"Allow me to introduce you to... Well, this here's your baby sister.... Alexandra, this is your brother Davey."

David offered an extended hand, Alex took it, and the two of them just stood there without saying a word for a moment as they studied each other's eyes and felt the smoothness, the guarded gentleness in one another's touch.

"Hello, Davey," came her voice before he could utter a word.

"Hello, Alexandra. I didn't catch the last name."

"It's Bertolli, Alexandra Bertolli. But most people call me Alex."

"Alex, it is then. Everyone calls me David, except for family. You doin' okay? I mean, with all of this?"

"What can I say?"

"I know what you mean."

Not to be left out, Mickey intruded.

"Hey, I got an idea, now that we're all together. Why don't we all go see the ol' man. The four of us. Before they close the box."

Alexandra paused for a moment, clearly thinking about it, before she responded.

"No, that's okay. You all go ahead. I'll see him afterwards."

Davey made the attempt.

"No, please, come with us. You're more than welcome, of course. Jews don't display their dead. They keep the coffin open for a short time, just for the immediate family, and then they close it. If you don't come now, you might not get to say good-bye."

"I don't think he'll be able to hear me, anyway. Do you? Besides, the three of you should go together. Alone."

"But..."

"No really, it's okay."

Prodded by Mickey's impatience, the three made their way down the center aisle to the front of the main parlor. Howard already began to sniffle slightly as they approached the casket and Davey put an arm around him. Mickey began, too, and each found himself fighting back the tears as they reached the coffin.

Howard's repressed sobs turned into a tearful, muffled giggle as he focused in through watery eyes on Harry laid out there.

"Oh my God! This I don't believe!"

Davey, wiping a tear away with a Kleenex Howard had handed him, stared into the box and began to grin, as well.

"Unbelievable. Too fuckin' much," was all he could say.

The two younger brothers automatically turned to Mickey, his chest inflated, standing there proud as could be.

"Somebody had to do it. I mean send him off right."

The three simultaneously turned and looked down at their father comfortably lying there with his hands folded on his chest. As if he was at home on the couch taking one of his early evening prelims for a long night out, a "little siesta" he used to call it. Howard, still wiping his eyes, muffled another giggle and that set off another three-way round of stifled laughter as Davey turned toward Mickey.

"This was your idea?"

"Well sorta."

"I didn't think you could be blessed with such inspiration."

"What? You underestimate your brother? Ahh, what the hey, it was Louie did all the work. He did a pretty good job, don't yuh think?"

Davey took another minute to mentally record a parting still shot. Moving from the slightly contented grin frozen on Harry's face, his eyes moved to the hands resting there mid chest. The left sat relaxed atop the right and between its index and middle fingers, propped upward, rested one of the man's favorites, a Connecticut Valley Top Stone. Davey's eye then moved upwards to the breast pocket of the deceased's gray pinstripe, bulging there with what must have been another eight or ten additional stogies. The half gallon of Dewars slept on its side, its body snuggled between suited rib cage and arm, its neck resting in the crook of his elbow.

"So wha'd'yuh think?" came Mickey's voice.

Davey, standing between the other two, smiled, again shaking his head.

"That should hold him for awhile. Through the afternoon, at any rate. The only thing missing is a dog at his feet."

"Oh, I seen that one a million times," came Richie's voice.

"Seen what?"

"The one with Gary Cooper... Beau Geste. On cable, one of the oldies rerun stations. I love it."

"Yeah, I do too. Harry Rabin, the Jewish Viking."

"You're right. A dead dog would be a nice touch."

Mickey joined in. "Don't think that still can't be arranged."

Howard and Mickey, mindful not to touch one another, placed an arm around Davey standing between them and the three just silently peered into the box. That is until the rabbi, now standing behind them, informed them of his presence with a feigned clearing of the throat.

Davey recognized Feldstein immediately, as if it hadn't been twenty-five, maybe thirty years. He still looked the same. The same pale pink man, somewhat more blubbery and aged, his jowl folding over the collar of his white-on-white shirt, the sloppy Windsor knot of his subdued silk tie still too tightly tied, and apparently the same black wool blend everyday suit, shiny in the seat. The rabbi extended his prosperous pudgy hand toward the youngest of the brothers. They shook and Davey barely got a word out as the man, staring into the coffin, started to sputter and gasp. Mickey, playing the role of the eldest, made the preemptive intervention.

"I don't mean no disrespect or nuthin', Rabbi, but I don't think you should say anythin'."

"But... but I never, in all my life, saw such a..."

"It ain't got nuthin' to do with you. Yuhr just here to..."

"But, but..."

"Maybe you don't understand, so maybe I should make myself clear. Yuhr just here to do what you gotta do, say what gotta be said, the prayers and whatnot. That's all."

"But, but... such a thing, such a mockery. The bottle and... and.... In all my life, I..."

"What?! You never drink?! It ain't like yuh ain't gonna get paid..."

"But... but..."

"I guess what I'm tryin' t' say, Rabbi, is... Lemme put it to you this way so's you can understand. Maybe you should shut the fuck up."

David interceded.

"Our father wanted it this way. A final request."

"Such language. In all my life, I never..."

Now feeling challenged, Mickey moved closer as Howard and Davey, knowing their brother and reading the clear warning signs as yet unintelligible to Feldstein, simultaneously wedged themselves between. The middle brother pivoted the rabbi and began walking and talking him away from the coffin toward the family waiting room.

"I'm terribly sorry, Rabbi. You'll have to forgive my brother. We've all been through so much. The stress and all. He really didn't mean...."

Davey faced Mickey.

"What the hell's wrong with you? What are yuh doin?!"

"Nuthin'. I just ain't about to let some *shmuck* tell me what I can or can't do. Especially today."

"But he's a rabbi. He wouldn't say 'shit' if he had a mouthful."

"What are yuh sayin? Because he got a yarmulke on his head, that makes him special? He don't bleed like other people?!"

"Would yuh quit fuckin' around!?"

"I ain't. And nobody, I don't care who it is, better look t' fuck with me today, either. I'm just tellin' yuh!"

Mickey furtively glanced around the room and opened the left side of his suit coat just enough to show Davey the handle of a thirty-eight, the snub nose strapped in just below the armpit.

"I thought you said there wasn't gonna be any trouble."

"There ain't. But just in case..."

"You losin' it or what?! You gotta be out of your mind, packin' in here!"

"It's okay. Everythin's cool. I got it from the ol' man. A little memento, yuh might say."

At that point, Joshie entered from the back and called to them from halfway down the aisle.

"Hey, Dad, my mother's here. And so's your wife. The other one."

Mickey again turned to his brother.

"Great. Exactly what I need right now. More aggravation. Come. Let's go see your sister-in laws."

"Thanks, but I'd rather have a minute by myself with the ol' man, if yuh don't mind."

"I wish I could get one. There's no reason why you should have to get further upset, anyways."

Mickey headed up the aisle and exited with Joshie as Davey turned back toward the casket. Looking down on his father, he found himself inexplicably focusing in on the makeup job, the cosmetic attempt to cover the man's obviously ashen features. Harry, lying there as still as he was, made him think of his mother. He thought of her and what she went through, the life she had. What she sacrificed. He thought about the old man and the sons, himself included. About what they did or didn't say, the things they did or didn't do; how all of them, each in their own way, sent her to an early grave feeling abandoned, alone and dejected, brokenhearted. Then blocking the memories of the old man at his worst, he moved himself to focus for but a second on the good times, the affectionate father and son moments filled with warmth and the smell of Old Spice. He thought about the finality of it all, the irreversible loss, the irretrievability.

CHAPTER 28:
Family

1989... MICKEY SAW THEM AS soon as he approached the entryway, clumped together by the front door. Angela there restraining the younger one by the wrist and Ray Ray, their fourteen year old, sullen as usual, standing close by. His first wife, Connie, stood there as well as if she and Angela had suddenly drawn close, as if their father-in-law's passing had acted to form some kind of sudden bond between the two of them.

Both women spotted him immediately, before he could duck or disappear and he quickly scanned the rest of the room in hopes of finding some cover, a diversionary buffer. Glancing in one direction, he spotted Gina, the backs of her long nailed hands on hips, obviously peeved, glowering there next to the rent-a-cop. His eye then caught Alexandra chatting to one side with Aunt Edie and Uncle Manny. Bolting toward his half sister, he quickly tore her away from his aunt and uncle without so much as excusing himself and guided her by the arm toward his present and former spouses, making it up as he went.

"Sorry to pull yuh away. Edie and Manny are really somethin', aren't they? I just wanted yuh to meet some people, the rest of the family."

Angela and Connie watched when he darted over to where Edie and Manny stood talking to the younger, attractive woman. Suspicious from custom and decades of combined experience, they immediately assumed the situation as he pulled her their way. As practiced as the two of them, Mickey responded to their expressions before either of them could utter a word.

"Cut it out, the both of yuz. It ain't what yuh think."

Angela started in as she eyed the woman by his side. "It ain't? I was sorta hopin' it was. That maybe you got yourself another one and dumped that other bitch. Don't think I didn't notice, by the way. What's with the cop? She in custody again?"

"Yuh got it all wrong. This... this here's my kid sister."

Connie weighed in. "Are you out of your mind, or what? What do yuh take us for?!"

"No, seriously.... Tell them, Alexandra."

"For cryin' out loud, Mickey, don't you ever stop?" Angela toned.

Mickey gestured with a hold-on-a-second upturned hand as he spoke.

"No, seriously. Let me intraduce yuhz. Alexandra, this here's your current sister-in-law, my loving wife, Angela."

He then motioned toward the other one, momentarily paused there with a still incredulous look on her face.

"And this here's my ex, Connie. The first one."

Alexandra, by this time somewhat confused but not wanting to be impolite, extended her hand.

"I really am a sister. Harry is... was my..."

Perhaps sensing the awkwardness and potential explosiveness, the little one still holding Angela's hand started to squirm. Taking an instant to discipline the kid with a stop-it-already yank on the arm, she lashed out at Mickey.

"This one really takes the cake!"

"What the hell did I do?!"

"It's a good thing your mother..."

"Why d' yuh always have t'bring her into it? I'm tellin' yuh the truth! This here really *is* my sister. My half sister!"

"You're really full of it, Mickey!"came Connie.

"No he's not!" responded Alexandra.

"Whoever you are, you better not look to start. Not with all he's put us through. You better cut the bullshit," came the reply.

At that point, someone tapped Mickey on the shoulder from behind and they all fell silent as their heads turned. There stood Gina, backed up by the clearly confused New Haven cop.

"Not now, Gina," Mickey pleaded.

"Then when?"

"Not now, not ever. That is unless you want to catch a worse beatin' than the last time," intruded Angela as she stepped forward, already hostile.

Gina turned to the officer as he cautiously, hesitantly moved between.

"I want this one arrested!"

"For what?! Wha' do I look like here, a referee? I thought I got hired to do a funeral? Ain't this supposed to be a funeral?"

"I don't even have food in the house, and this one's rentin' cops to protect his whore!" charged Angela.

Mickey attempted a cover.

"He really ain't rented... He's... he's an old friend of the family... His grandfather was a police sergeant, used to live across the street from the ol' man and ..."

Connie again weighed in.

"I don't believe you got a cop for this one! Wha' did that cost?"

"You payin' the bill? Yuh want cops? I'll show yuh cops! Just take your ass down the hall there, the first room on the left and check out the state troopers watchin' your fuckin' oldest one!"

"Jimmy! Jimmy's here!?"

"That's right! I not only shelled out for this one here, but I also paid to bring your fuckin' kid down! All the way from Vermont. Just for you!"

It was then, as Connie rushed off, that Mickey spotted them, just as they came through the door, Gambi and his crew. Seeing his out and checking with a slow cautious hand to make sure his suit coat was unbuttoned just in case, he bolted from the conversation, leaving Gina, Alex, Angela, the two kids, and the cop still squared off against each other. Approaching the four, he first shook the boss's hand and then took a condolence embrace from each of the crew. Turning back to the elder, he leaned in to receive a hand to the upper arm and a word to the ear.

"He was a good friend, your father. Always a good friend. He'll be sorely missed."

"Thank you, Gambi."

"He not only was a good earner, but he really had some class. A good counsel, a true voice of reason and wisdom in his later years. A huge loss."

"I thought you were still on vacation."

"Hey, you know how it works. A couple of phone calls and I got a little furlough so's I could come say good-bye. Your father was like family."

"I never had that kind of pull."

"You ain't me."

"Everythin' cool with us?"

"As cool as a cucumber. "

The younger Velner, by that time nervous that everything was off schedule, had already begun moving the dispersed family members into the waiting room as his assistant directed others into the main parlor. Sighting Mickey, he walked over, politely excused himself and asked the oldest son to join the others in the side parlor. Mickey, of course, wanted to pursue the conversation.

"Yuh sure everything's okay?"

"Why you askin'? You nervous about somethin'?"

Stevie moved him away.

Davey saw Aunt Faye as soon as he entered, sitting there by herself in the middle of an empty row of chairs lined against the front wall of the waiting room. It had been twenty years, maybe twenty-five, but he recognized her immediately, despite how she had aged. She raised her head slightly and looked at him as he took the seat next to her, then resumed staring straight ahead, lost in her memories. He wasn't sure if she realized it was him and was about to say something when the raspy old voice, almost a whisper from the side of her mouth, sliced the silence.

"So when'd yuh get in, Davey?"

"Yesterday afternoon. And you?"

"Last night. Late. Your cousin Stanley, he's here. Did yuh see him? He came to get me at LaGuardia. Yuh can't fly direct from Florida t' New Haven no more. Your wife come? I never met your wife."

"Yeah. She's here."

"You'll intraduce your old *tanteh*, no?"

"Yeah, sure."

The old woman paused for a moment as if searching for the words.

"So that brother of mine, the last one, he's gone now, too?"

"I'm afraid so."

"So, what happened?"

"What d'yuh mean, what happened?"

"How'd he go?"

"What can I tell yuh? From what I can figure, the way I look at it, he just decided it was time. That's all."

"What makes yuh think that?"

"Howard was saying he received a call just the other day. From some short-term quickie loan outfit, one of those money store joints."

"The legalized Shylocks, like they got in Florida? They got 'em up here, too?"

"They're everywhere now. Your brother, he apparently took 'em down for a piece of change. Signed a note."

"For how much?"

"Nothing serious. Twenty-five hundred. Forged Howard's name as a co-signer. Maybe ten days ago. From what I figure, he musta been lookin' to have himself a last fling."

Faye's head whipped around and she faced her nephew with an incredulous smile, her eyes opened wide in humored disbelief, the tip of her nose now twitching slightly, instinctively as if on the fresh scent of a possible score.

"Who the hell gave him a loan?!"

"This one you'll love! The place was called Great Country. Great Country Loan!"

"So you know that one?! How my mother, your grandmother, *alevashalom*, she used to say it. When everything was going from bad to worse, always she would say 'America! America! Great country!'"

"I thought you'd like that one."

"That brother of mine, boy, I'm tellin' yuh. He stuck Howard with the note?"

"Can yuh get blood from a stone? The ol' man, believe you me, he had that one all figured out, well in advance. Howard won't pay it. Ain't no way."

"Good for him. Good for the both of them. A fitting end for that brother of mine!"

"A little poetic, don't yuh think?"

"Poetry, shmoetry. This one I don't believe. Someone really gave him a loan?"

"Yep. I'm just wonderin' now what he did with it."

Gambi spotted him as Mickey departed, recognized him despite the time and distance, standing there way off to the side like some neutral observer. The two made eye contact and signaling his escorts with a hand gesture to stay put, he made his way across and took the hand of the other old-timer.

"It's been a long time, Louie."

"Too long. Wha'd'yuh say, Gambi?"

"Me? The doctor says I ain't got long myself, but I can't complain. Been takin' it easy. They got me stayin' at one of their better rest homes. I can see you've done okay for yourself, as well."

"What? Someone else was gonna do it for me?"

"How you holdin' up?"

"This one's been tough."

"What can I say? We'll all miss him."

"We'll all be there soon enough ourselves."

The two paused and silently shook their heads until Louie resumed.

"This one, he really took the cake."

"Tell me something I don't already know."

"This one, you'll appreciate. His son Howard, the middle one..."

"The *faigeleh*."

"Yeah, yeah..., he brings me some of the ol' man's clothes this mornin'... A suit and shoes and whatnot..."

"Yeah, so?"

"Later on, when I go to dress our friend, I have trouble puttin' on one of the shoes. It won't go... Like there's something jammed inside. I feel around a bit and guess what I find?"

"How much?"

"A deuce!"

"Two hundred in one shoe? Christ, maybe you and me, we should take a little ride."

"Be serious. Yuh gotta figure Mickey's been there already."

"Yeah, you're probally right on that score."

The two paused for another moment, pondering the layerings of loss, until Louie continued. "I gotta ask yuh somethin'."

"What's that?"

"Did Mickey or the other two, David or Howard, ask yuh?"

"I just walked in and talked to Mickey for a second. I don't talk to the other two. Asked me what?"

"About Julie."

"Julie? Which Julie?"

"Julie Kogon."

"The fighter? How'd he come up?"

"Harry. He was askin' for him just before he went. Somethin' about callin' for

Julie to save him. Supposedly his dyin' words."

"Yuh mean like at the fight?"

"So you know about that one?"

"Half of N'Haven was there that night. Everybody knows that Harry story. What the hell brought that up, after all these years?"

"You know better than me."

"What's that suppose' t'mean?"

"Look, I never got the whole story but some of it leaked out in conversation. A little from Harry… and from Butter before he went."

"What story we talkin' about?"

"How Harry placed a bundle on Julie that time. The fight with Callahan at the Arena. How everything was supposedly arranged but Kogon went down for the count and took Harry with him. From what I figure, Harry was in way over his head, playin' with somebody else's money, and you bailed him out. Helped him cover."

"That's news to me."

"Is it? He told me so himself, afterwords, how yuh helped him out."

"You got a problem with that?"

"No. I just always wondered about it. That's all."

"What's t' wonder?"

"That was also right about the time you and Harry became real tight. No?"

"Hell, we knew each other from the street long before that. He helped me out after I got home from the war. Didn't have a dime and he reached in his pocket. Without me even askin'…. I never forgot… That's probably why I'm here. What's it to you, anyway?"

"I don't think he ever got out from under. That's all."

"Hey, Louie, I came here t'day t'pay my respects and t'say good-bye to our old friend. I certainly don't need no headaches. Yuh hear what I'm sayin'?"

"Yuh don't wanna hear the rest?"

"What rest?"

"Like what I got from Butter, or what I pieced together later. How you and him was connected back then. How Butter was hooked up with your people, through the old connections in New York. How Butter snagged him and reeled him in and yuh all fed off the carcass."

"That's what I always liked about you, Louie. Yuh always had a good head on your shoulders. Smart, but not quite smart enough to know everything."

"And what'd I miss?"

"It was Butter's doin'."

"Who yuh think yuhr talkin' to, here? Some Johnny-come-lately? One of your crew?"

"What do yuh want from me? Of course, we knew what was up. So what? All I heard at the time was Butter calls me and says he has some fish on the line for a few grand, some wise guy he was stickin' it to on a payback, and he's runnin' him in the wrong direction. I can remember t' this day even how me and some of the fellas at the old hangout, we laughed about it when he first called. He calls me back a little bit later t' tell me the same guy, I swear to yuh at that time we didn't know who it was, he wants to up his bet by five large. I can remember thinking then only about how loyal Butter was. That was back when loyalty meant somethin'. Back when the code had meaning. Yuh hear what I'm sayin'?"

"So you're tellin' me you didn't know the guy with the five grand was Harry?"

"On my mother's grave, lightnin' should strike me dead as I'm standin' here. I didn't know."

"Unbelievable. And yuh helped him make good?"

"Wha' do I gotta lie for? Both of us are too old. He was my friend. I never forgot how he helped me out."

"And for how many years did he pay for it?"

"What? You buryin' him for free?"

"Of course not."

"Good. I kept him out of an early grave and he paid for it and someone's payin' you t' put him in, well past his due. What's the beef?"

"There's none."

"Okay, then. Next case. He was callin' for Julie to save him? On the way out?"

"From his deathbed. At least that's what his kids said. All of them, with the same question."

"What's that?"

"Who Julie was."

The two stood there in silence again until the old soldier spoke.

"It's funny how life goes sometimes."

"It's even funnier, sometimes, how it ends."

"I can imagine."

"No, yuh can't and yuh don't wanna know."

"I could tell you some, believe you me."

"I bet yuh could. There's one thing that never ceases to amaze me about it all. After all these years."

"What's that?"

"The stories yuh hear in this place."

"It's a good thing the dead don't talk."

"What? Yuh think they don't?"

Chapter 29:

The Return

1989... As THE PLANE BOLTED up out of the harbor and banked to the southwest over the Sound, Davey twisted his head sideways to gaze out and down in an attempt to watch New Haven disappear. It wasn't that he wanted or needed some final fix and he was indeed relieved that he and Annie were finally on their way home. He just couldn't help looking back.

Finally turning to face forward, he lightly tapped on the top of Annie's hand, relaxed there beneath his on their mutual armrest, as if to reassure the both of them that everything would soon be back to normal. She merely looked his way and gave him one of her "I'm okay, don't worry about me" smiles. He closed his eyes and tried to relax.

His ear picked up on it once again, the constant exterior engine hum, and he reached out to feel the low-level vibration on the interior layer of his portal, as if to confirm he was really going back, returning to what he now considered home. He briefly listened to the lulling hiss from the overhead air nozzles before returning to the constant blur of episodic images, mind's eye snapshots of the last couple of days.

The scenes from the previous day flew by in jump-cut motion. The service itself seemed to take but an instant. Rabbi Feldstein, compelled by duty, finally got up before the packed room and said the obligatory *brochas*. Surveying the house, he decided to forgo his love-of-a-lost-one boiler plate *shpiel* and introduced Davey before making a hasty retreat to his seat. Taking his place at the small dais to the right of the coffin, the son spoke without notes, a brief eulogy that everyone later said was "real good".

What came to him now for some reason was the born-again, the small-boned faded woman, wife of the body man from the shop at Mickey's place. He thought about how she had been "so, so moved" as she put it, that she "just had to come up" immediately after. He noticed her then as she patiently waited her turn to timidly step forward and almost apologetically praise him for his "inspired" words, her hands earnestly clasped together across her abdomen the whole time. She explained how she didn't know Harry at all but that she had to come up and tell him that he certainly had "the spirit", and that he was "blessed". He figured her for an abuse victim, though from her husband, her father, her god, or combination of the three, he could only guess.

His cousin Robert's words, hitting the nail on the head, came to him then as he sat there safe in flight away from it all.

"One thing I gotta say about your ol' man, boy."

"Yeah? What's that?"

"He certainly danced to his own tune."

He found himself staring down at the seat belt, its stainless buckle unfastened, straddling his right thigh in mock defiance of the flight attendant's instructions and the overhead warning. That somehow triggered the image of Mickey as he shot up out of his chair, untethered, at the end of the eulogy. How his brother engulfed him, nearly smothering him with that huge emotional hug, full of pride and gratitude, grief and loss. He thought about the brief tinge of embarrassment that crept in as he stood there pinned in that brotherly bear hug hold with the entire room looking on in suspended animation as if waiting and hoping for him to wrestle free. He now mused on what the whole scene would have turned into if the piece wedged there below his brother's armpit had somehow fallen to the floor and discharged during their embrace. He chuckled to himself, just loud enough for Annie to hear, and explained it away with a wave of the hand, saying it was nothing.

She lightly touched his forearm and he must have started, jumped but a bit since she automatically, almost instinctively apologized.

"Sorry... but can I tell yuh something?"

"Sure."

"I just wanted to say thanks."

"For what?"

"For the warning."

"'Bout what?"

"About the movie."

"It was really somethin'. Yuh held up pretty good. "

"Your warning really helped... Someone should write a book."

"Who would believe it?"

"No, really. I'm serious...."

"Can I tell you something?"

"What's that?"

"Never, ever doubt for a moment I love you."

Everyone had milled around for a while longer as those remaining, the ones so compelled moved forward to console and extend condolences. Then suddenly, despite Uncle Mannie's protests, the fact that he considered it a sacrilege, Mickey herded the immediate family into one of the side parlors for a group photo. "Somethin' for Jimmy to have in the joint," he exclaimed as he corralled everyone and Connie, Angela and a cousin or two took snapshots.

The photo op over, Stevie Velner and several assistants ushered them all out the front door as the two Vermont troopers, instructed not to go to the cemetery, escorted Jimmy through the side exit to the waiting cruiser and his trip back. Two other attendants meanwhile wheeled Harry out to the hearse and they all made their way to their predetermined vehicles.

On Mickey's insistence, the brothers left their respective partners to their own devices and rode to the cemetery in the borrowed Cadillac with Joshie, the only one willing and able to drive, behind the wheel.

Davey could still hear his older brother's voice directing the nephew as the car, first in line behind Harry, slowly turned onto Chapel Street and crept westward toward Edgewood Park and the Jewish cemetery beyond in Westville.

"Just watch where the hell you're goin'…. And take your time. There ain't no rush."

"Where d' yuh think I'm gonna go?"

"I don't need any lip today, or you'll end up goin' with the ol' man. And I sure as hell don't wanna get pulled over. Just do what I'm tellin' yuh for a change and stay behind the hearse. There ain't no rush."

Positioned behind the driver, Davey watched Mickey's face in the rearview as the eldest talked with his hands.

"This one's drivin' while under suspension again. It's a matter of time, he gets grabbed. He'll end up with his brother. Mark my words."

What came to him as he thought about the cemetery scene was the initial chaos. People silently, perhaps instinctively, herded together on the cracked sidewalk at the ass end of the graveyard, bunched there, directionless, as if reluctant to enter the old wrought iron gate. As if those unable to read the Yiddish script on the sheet metal scroll above the entry had been denied passage beyond.

That's when Philly Levin appeared, as if out of nowhere. His pal since home room, junior high pulled up, a godsend of sorts, as they were standing there on the sidewalk, before the coffin came out. Speeding down from Boston but delayed by a rush-hour accident on 91, he had missed the service, but zoomed over to the cemetery. "On a long shot," he later explained. "I was hopin' to catch yuh."

And there he was, sitting there behind the wheel of his leased Lincoln, blocking the morning traffic on Fitch Street, his oldest New Haven friend, now an over-the-road New England salesman, there to see the old man off.

The two made quick eye contact and Philly popped it into reverse, pulled to the curb, jumped out and darted across the street. They hugged, oblivious to the rest.

"I knew you'd come."

"What're yuh, nuts? Yuh think I'd miss this one?!"

Clearing a path, Cousin Robert made them move aside and the pall bearers, several first and now-distant second cousins recruited from the crowd, escorted the casket up along one of the narrow walkways to the mound of orange Connecticut dirt. With everyone finally gathered in around the hole, the rabbi hurriedly recited the mandatory *brochas* and they lowered the box. No wailing or carrying on, just a few silent tears on the part of some, the few momentarily facing their own mortality or the thought of others long gone. Each one, starting with Mickey, then Howard and Davey tossed in a handful of dirt. And that was it.

He could hardly remember the ride back, could not immediately recall how he got there, but the scene at Howard's now came rushing in in a flurry of flash-bulbed snapshots. Everyone, the long distant relatives and family friends, crowded into the den and kitchen, highball glasses of VO or scotch for some, black coffee for others, in hand. All of them there except Mickey and his immediate branch, trapped in their parallel universe at Gina's. He could still hear the stifled small talk and handshakes, the ubiquitous "What's to say?" followed by the initial feeding frenzy, the collective anxiety eat.

He thought about the rite-of-passage ritual spread, the huge smoked whitefish with its glimmery bronzed skin and dead iridescent eye, lying in state center-table on its bed of lettuce. His memory surveyed the orange-pink Nova lox sliced translucent thin, the mound of sesame and salt and onion bagels, poppy seeded rolls and *bialys*, the cream cheese, plain and with chives; the plates with sliced Muenster and Swiss, Bermuda onion and red tomato, assorted pickles, the half-and full sours, the black olives and Hungarian cherry peppers, red and green; the sugary *kichels*, marbled *mandel brot* and honey cake, the urns of hot coffee and decaf, with half-and-half and Sweet and Low for those nervous about their weight or "the sugar".

Everything just as if Harry had catered it himself and David imagined him standing there, the center of attention, highball glass in one hand, lox and bagel in the other, laughing loudly, talking with his mouth half full, a smear of cream cheese at its corner. There he was, with the index and middle finger of his drink hand outstretched, emphatic, his face animated with the embellished retelling of some ruse or deception gone awry, the description of some tragicomic character long passed, his captured audience totally engrossed.

She just glided in as if she belonged. Sometime after his third or fourth drink, she just walked in with that fluid walk of hers, made her way through the trees out back and eased herself in through the sliding door to the rear deck. She had been furthest from his mind, buried way, way deep somewhere, so it actually startled him somewhat, took his breath away for an instant, to see her standing there, so out of place, still wrapped in that practiced silence and unreadable smile.

As if clued in to the unknown history or keyed to some intuitive, instinctive sense, his facial expression maybe, or his body language perhaps, the entire room fell silent. Frozen in place, they watched as he made his way across to her. He hadn't seen her since she left him. Approaching what, seven... eight years? He couldn't recall at the moment and none of it mattered, neither the time nor the distance, the old heartache nor the bottomed out bouts of depression. It all vanished as he stood there, face-to-face with her. Again.

"Hello, Mona."

"Hello, David."

"What are you doing here...? What are you doing in New Haven, I mean... I... I don't understand."

"I'm not really back... Just here for a while, a moment, some time off from the City."

"New York? You in New York now?"

"Yes, you knew that. I didn't come to talk about me, however. I'm sorry to hear about your father. I know how much he meant to you... Happy birthday, by the way..."

"You remember?"

"Of course, you silly goose..."

"Come, please.... Come, have something to eat. A cup of coffee? Yuh care for a drink? A scotch rocks, maybe? Yuh still drink scotch, no?

"I really can't stay. I just wanted to stop for a minute. I actually have to meet some friends, downtown. It took me some time to find the house.... I thought I knew where it was. I promised...."

"Friends?"

"You don't know them. People from after you and I..."

"Is he with you? You still married?"

"Yes, he is. And yes, we are. I don't want to be too long."

"I'm married too, now."

"Yes, I heard."

He turned to look for Annie, wanting to introduce her, and noticed that she was nowhere to be seen. Taking Mona by the hand then and immediately wanting, as soon as their fingers touched, to pull her close across all that time, he guided her instead to the bottles arrayed on the kitchen counter. Pouring her a scotch rocks, he turned.

"I don't get it. So how'd you hear about Harry?"

"You know how it goes. We tend to hear these things."

"Okay, I won't ask.... So how's Mona's world?"

"Again, I didn't come to talk about me. I came to see how you're doing. How've you been?"

"What's t' say?"

They just stood there smiling at each other, that mutual, knowing look they always shared; shared long before they ever exchanged a word years before. And then she was off, there for an instant and gone, passing through as if in one of those dreams of his, the ones where she would appear and disappear without saying a word, just long enough to jar his sleep and sometimes wake him up.

What snapped him out of it, or more accurately nudged him out of his daydream, was the quiet, a sudden hush as if the whole room had taken a deep breath. The silence turned him from his view of the deck and the backyard and there they were, Howard and Annie standing there, holding the cake, with everyone else looking on from behind. The room broke into "Happy Birthday" and everyone laughed and joked about his age as he blew out the candles. Some even clapped. Annie sliced and Richie helped with the paper plates, and they all ate chocolate cake with white frosting. All except him, that is. "We hoped it would cheer you up," she later explained.

That wasn't the final surprise of the afternoon, of course. The initial crush had thinned out well before noon and he had just settled in at the kitchen table, another drink in hand, to swap old stories with several of the remaining cousins, Philly and Annie close by, when he heard the doorbell. He paid it no mind, knowing full well someone, probably Richie, would get it. So he was a bit taken aback to suddenly see Jakey standing there looking at him from the entry to the den.

He immediately got up and approached the old-timer as Annie converged to greet him. The scotch spoke first.

"Well look who we have here... If it ain't dear ol' Uncle Ebenezer! Come to join the nephew's Christmas party, have you?!"

"Be nice, Davey," came his wife's understated voice. She turned to the old man and relieving him of the coat already folded over his arm, took his hand and invited him into the room.

"It's so good you could come, Jakey."

"I... I came to apologize," he stammered.

"Apologize? For what? Don't be silly..."

"For being such a selfish old goat. For not coming this morning."

Davey took over.

"No big deal. You're here now, arn't chuh? Can I get yuh somethin? A little V.O. or shnapps, maybe? A cup of coffee? There's plenty left to eat. Come... please."

"Nah, I'm good.... I can't stay.... Is there someplace, maybe, you and I could talk for a few?"

Annie caught her cue, briefly embraced the old man as a way of saying thanks, and left the two. David thought about it for a second and walked the man down the opposite end of the first floor to the spacious living room, now emptied of its earlier round of visitors. The old family friend paused for a moment in front of the large windows as if admiring the country scene. He then turned.

"There's something I gotta tell yuh, I have to admit t'yuh. Remember when yuh stopped by yesterday, yuh asked if I knew anybody named Julie?"

"Yeah."

"Well, of course I did. I knew who yuh had to be referring to as soon as yuh asked."

"So who was she? One of the ol' man's girlfriends?"

"Aw, hell no. He was a guy. The fighter. Julie Kogon."

"The boxer? The one the ol' man always used to talk about? So what's the big deal? All the secretiveness?"

"It's complicated, not that simple. Even after all these years."

"Does this have something to do with your estrangement? Your falling out with the ol' man?"

"Well sorta. Yes and no."

"Yuh gonna tell me about it?"

"I shoulda told yuh right out, but it's not that easy. Like I said, kinda complicated."

"So-o-o-o?"

"As you probably know, the ol' man was a big fight fan."

"That, you don't have to tell me. I can remember when I was a little kid, maybe five or six, before we moved from Legion Avenue, how he used to watch the Friday night fights, how excited he'd get.... The Gillette Cavalcade of Sports... I can still remember the sponsor's jingle, the cartoon parrot and the bell! *Look Sharp! Feel Sharp! Be Sharp!*"

"Your memory's pretty good!"

"I can remember, like it was yesterday. Fighters with names like Willy Pepp and Kid Gavilan. He used t' have me come watch with him in the livin' room, when we lived on Asylum Street... And then after awhile, he'd forget I was there. Just him and the TV. He'd talk to the set, sometimes yell and get mad and tell everybody to shut up if my mother and whoever, her sister, maybe.... Yuh remember my Aunt Edie...? Or my grandmother or us kids, we got too loud in the kitchen...."

"You're just like your ol' man! A guy can't get a word in edgewise! You gonna talk, or you gonna let me tell my story?"

"Sorry. Of course. Let me blame it on the scotch. I hardly ever drink. Just on special occasions. Go on. Please."

"I don't know if I should mention this or not, whether I should bring it up even, but yuh know.... Well, yuh must know, I'm sure. I probably don't have t' tell yuh. Your ol' man was also a pretty big gambler."

"Who you talkin' to, here? Like I don't remember the refrigerator empty, nuthin' to eat in the house? Yuh could always tell when he was on a roll 'cause he'd give my mother some money to shop, or he'd show up with bags of groceries. Or the times when he'd stop goin' out and stay home. Esther would always say that's when she knew he was really broke..."

"Yuh gonna let me finish?"

"Sorry, I...."

"You raise the question, of course."

"Which is?"

"I could never figure it out... how your mother, *alevasholom,* how she put up with it all those years."

"I don't either. Where yuh goin' with this?"

"Yuh know the fights were all controlled back then."

"Yuh mean by the boxing commission?"

"Commission, my ass! Don't you know they were fixed, all set up?"

"Like it ain't a big racket now?"

"Aw, it's different t'day, more sophisticated. Real big money involved, so the Feds and everyone else, the boxing commission, they're always looking in. Everyone's still on the take, of course, but back then, in those days, shit, say back in the forties, I can remember...."

"And?"

"The fights were still real big then, even at the local and regional level. All over New England. You wouldn't believe how people used to pack into the Arena to catch a good bout. Lots of big names, kids on their way up, or the ones who couldn't get out, on their way down, they all used to come through. Before television got big and places like the Arena stopped with the boxing. Before the big-time developers got their hands on the downtown with their "urban renewal". We saw 'em all, Joe Louis even. Some on their way to the Garden, others never quite there, fillin' a local card. It was all controlled."

"Yeah, okay, so where we goin'?"

"Well, there was this one time. Kogon was fightin'. The place was packed like sardines. How old are you now? You wouldn't know from Julie...."

"Like I said before, Harry always used t' talk about him. I remember the photos the ol' man kept. The autographed glossies with the guy posing in those boxing trunks of his with the *Mogen Dovid* sewn on the front."

"You got it. Right off the street, from Legion Avenue. One of us, the Jewish kid from N'Haven, headed for the big time. He could dish it out and take it with the best of 'em, punchin' it out with some of the best and a lot of crumbs, as well. You younger guys today, you can't imagine."

"What's to imagine?"

"How much of a source of pride he was for a lot of people, a lot of Jewish working stiffs, us little guys in those years after the war. What with word of the Holocaust still fresh and all. A lot of anti-Semites, even after the war, they'd make these claims, pass remarks that us Jews got what we got because we were afraid to fight. Back before Israel showed 'em different."

"I'm not a Zionist. Where's this headed?"

"I wouldn't expect yuh would be.... Whenever Kogon fought nearby, in Bridgeport even, or Hartford, but especially in New Haven, there was always a huge crowd. Almost entirely *landsman*. And when he fought in the Arena, boy, it was packed. Right to the rafters. All the *yiddels* in New Haven, those who knew someone that could get their hands on a ticket, anyways, they'd all show up. The scalpers would have a field day."

"Yeah, so?"

"So I remember this one time, this one bout like it was yesterday. The place was loaded with characters, everyone was there, the who's who from Oak Street and Legion Avenue, the old neighborhood. And plenty of *machers,* too, from Westville with their fine suits, some with their fancy *shikseh* girlfriends... The wives never came…. Me and your father and Louie Velner, we somehow finagled some seats ringside, but it didn't matter 'cause your ol' man was on his feet the entire fight, yellin' the whole time at the top of his lungs. Standing so close, he kept slappin' his hand on the edge of the canvas until one of the ring officials, backed up by this big Irish cop, had to warn him to back up."

"What was he yelling?"

"Yuh gotta understand. Kogon had been a contender in his class, actually fought a few in the Garden. I saw him deck a number of guys in the first round. Big, powerful hands and shoulders he got from haulin' crates as a kid down at the produce market, drivin' truck for his ol' man. Long before he stepped into the ring. He had a helluva punch, I'm tellin yuh. Him and his brother, when they were kids, they used to stage fights in one of the yards behind the tenements and charge admission."

"You tellin' a story or writing the definitive biography?"

"What, yuh think you're so smart now, 'cause yuh got some fancy degree? He was fightin' this big flat-nosed Irish guy, from Boston, or Providence maybe. I can't remember the crumb's name. But this Irish kid…, it was something like Callahan, I think…, he was clearly hungry, a rough son of a bitch. He was givin' Julie one hell of a go, movin' him all over the ring. Julie was dishin' out these tremendous shots, I mean *serious* punches, but this kid, he just keeps comin' straight ahead, his hands up the whole time, workin' to the inside, poundin' the body, throwin' jabs to the midsection. The word on the street was Kogon in four, but everyone in the place can see as it gets beyond the fourth, into the fifth or sixth, that the Mic, he ain't the pushover many supposed, and Julie's startin' to wear down from the pounding to his body. And your father, God knows how much he had ridin' on that one, but it musta been a bundle."

"How do you know?"

"Let me finish. The ol' man, he's standin' there, on his feet the whole time, carryin' on like you can't imagine. Like he was the one getting hit. Yellin' at the top of his voice…"

"How do yuh know it was a bundle?"

"'Cause Julie's gettin' knocked t' hell in front of the home crowd, and all you could hear above the din was your old man, yellin' at the top of his lungs, carryin' on like a madman."

"So what happened?"

"What d'yuh think? Julie goes down. Late, maybe in the eigth or ninth. He was dead on his feet and the Irish kid… I still think he got lucky 'cause Julie seemed to let his guard down for a split second, like he lost his concentration, his focus, maybe from exhaustion…. Well this Mic, see, he gets lucky. Catches him with a right hook that came from nowhere. Caught him so hard it knocked his mouthpiece clean out of his head and Julie hits the canvas, facedown, like a ton of bricks. The ref, he steps in for the count and the entire place goes silent like someone sucked all the air out of the joint. You could hear a pin drop. Not a sound. That is, except your ol' man, still carryin' on as if it ain't clear to the entire Arena it's over. The only thing you could hear was the sound of the referee's count and that ol' man of yours. Him just standin' there yellin'. I can still hear him, like it was yesterday. And that's what...? Forty somethin' years ago."

"What was he yellin'?"

"*S-a-a-v-e me, Julie! S-a-a-v-e me!*'"

"Save me, Julie?"

"That was it."

Davey smiled.

"So the fix was in?"

"That's a good question, and it ain't for me to say! It's still a touchy subject, t' this day among some people, I imagine, t'even suggest that Julie Kogan might've gone into the tank. Again, I'm tellin' yuh, he was a source of pride for a lot of people. Besides, I was in close enough to see the shot he took. There was no fakin' that one."

"But you just got through explainin' how it was all controlled back then."

"Did I say that? Let's just say it was, and it wasn't. And besides, what do I know? While it never got as bad as the wrestling, certain bouts were a set up, that's pretty certain. But sometimes, they just let 'em go at each other t'make sure the crowds kept comin' back. Besides, I'd be the last one t' suggest that Julie was crooked. We all was kids together. Off the same streets. The same ones as your ol' man!"

"So what happened?"

"Like I told yuh, as soon as Julie went down, the whole place went silent, like some kind of collective shock set in! And all you could hear was your father, his voice all raspy, half gone, still yellin' as if his life was ridin' on it. Boy I'm tellin' yuh, I've never forgotten the look on his face when the ref counted ten and that bell sounded. It looked like part of him died. Like he was a kid who had just found his dog that one of the neighbors musta poisoned.... That happened to me once, but that's another story.... He just stood there, with this huge crowd goin' crazy, booin', and throwin' beer cups and crumpled up programs toward the ring. Just standin' there starin' at center ring, alone in the world as if the entire place had emptied out and left him behind."

"And you never got the rest of the story?"

"Me? No, I never asked. I just figured he lost a wad. He was down for a while, a week or two, but was soon back on his feet, so I figured it couldn't have been that bad."

"What happened to you and the ol' man after that?"

"We just sorta drifted apart, that's all.... Went our separate ways, I guess. Wha' d'yuh want I should tell yuh?"

"But from what I understand, you and him and Louie Velner were pretty inseparable when you were coming up. Him and Velner remained tight. What happened with you?"

"He's gone now, no? Leave it rest."

"*It*? What *it*?"

"Just a figure of speech."

"What happened after the fight?"

"Wha'd'yuh mean?"

"Yuh said he lost big. Let me guess. He put the bite on yuh, didn't he? Did he burn yuh?"

"You always were the smart one and yuh know him pretty good too, but no, it wasn't the money. Understand me clear, the amount didn't matter. Small potatoes... God knows, I took far worse hits than that over the years."

"Then what was it?"

"What he turned into..., that crowd he ended up runnin' with."

"Crowd? What crowd?"

"Yuh mean t'tell me, yuh don't know? About his Fair Haven pals?"

"That's what got you mad and kept you that way? Got yuh to the point where you no longer talked?"

"That wasn't it really...."

"Then what, then?"

"What he did to your mother and you kids. Hell, it turned my stomach, the money he used to piss away and how you all lived. I wish I had a dime for the number of times she would call or come over, lookin' for help. Even after me and the old man parted company. Long after."

"Yuh loved her, Jakey. Didn't yuh?"

"Nothin' ever happened."

"I wasn't lookin' to suggest..."

"Then why'd yuh ask?"

"Just somethin' I always noticed. I didn't understand when I was a kid, but I do now."

"And what might that be?"

"The way yuh used to look at her. When she was in the room. That same look on your face when you talk about her now. I noticed it the other day, when me and Annie stopped by."

"It killed me, what he did to her."

"It put her in an early grave."

"Aw, Christ, Davey... I shouldn't have come."

"It's alright. I'm glad yuh did. Woulda been pissed as hell if yuh hadn't."

"Yuh sound just like him."

"He'd uh been pissed, too."

"Would he have come for me, is the question."

"What kind of question is that?"

"A legit one, no?"

The plane hit some brief turbulence and shifted Davey's thoughts to the scene at Gina's and how it all came clear as soon as he and Annie walked in. The first clue was the luggage, the soft leather flight and garment bags and matching tote, the St. Laurent knockoffs still sitting there on the floor in the foyer where Mickey or Gina had left them. Another indicator, the box of cigars, Harry's brand, sat on a nearby side table. The dead giveaway was the photos, one of a youngish Esther, another of Mickey and Harry all dressed up at some family affair, smiling for the camera, along with several others, the ones that used to sit on top of the TV. He wondered now as he peered from the plane, why he didn't say anything then and there. His thoughts shifted to the scene at Harry's.

They had agreed to meet at four and to come alone, without the wives, girlfriends or "significant others". The two still-at-large grandsons showed up at Howard's beforehand so the four went over in the Audi with Davey riding shotgun, Josh and Ray Ray sitting in the back. Still in the casual clothes that he had worn to the funeral and still pretending to be straight, Joshie just sat there saying little as he struggled to maintain. Ray-Ray, relatively quiet as well for the rambunctious fourteen year old that he was, fidgeted in the meantime with a worn deck of cards, dealing hands of blackjack to himself as the car moved through the late afternoon cold.

Still adolescent curious and at the same time constantly on the lookout for a new angle like some seasoned downtown hustler, he took the opportunity, as he shuffled, to direct an occasional question about the old man to his uncles.

"Hey, Uncle Dave."

"What is it, Ray-Ray?"

"Yuh really think it was like yuh said?"

"What are you referring to?"

"You know. What yuh said at the funeral, when yuh talked. About Granpa knowin' it was time to go?"

"That he knew his time was up? Yeah, I think it possible, highly probable."

"Now probability's somethin' I know about, and I don't think he coulda known."

Howard chimed in. "What could you possibly know about probability?"

"I read about it in a card book. One of the pros. Scarne. Yuh know. The odds. When to increase the bet... and when not to."

"That's all bullshit," came Joshie's response. "Yuh go when it's time to go and it ain't got nuthin' t'do with cards."

Davey replied. "It does, in the sense that you have to play with the hand you're dealt and make the best of it."

"See! Uncle Dave's smart. He's educated. And he says there somethin' in knowin' how to play the cards."

With that, Joshie quickly reached over with one hand as he powered down his window with the other. Grabbing the deck from Ray-Ray's unsuspecting grasp, he tossed it out.

"I'll show yuh fuckin' cards, yuh little jerk!"

Joshie took an instant to gaze back at the deck now scattered like tossed confetti on the gray-white ice-patched road and turned on his older half brother.

"What'd yuh have to go and do that for! Why yuh gotta go messin' with me all the time?!"

"Show some respect, yuh dumb shit! Yuh know what gran'pa said, about how yuh shouldn't be gamblin' and here yuh are... He ain't even cold yet, and yuhr playin' cards like some asshole!"

His voice raised, Howard interjected. "I already got a fuckin' headache as is and I don't wanna have t' listen t' this. If yuhz can't behave, I just as soon turn the car around and none of yuhz will get anything!"

"But he didn't have to throw my deck out the window!"

"What are yuh? Some kind of crybaby?" came Joshie.

His brother shot back. "Junkie fuckin' asshole!"

Howard veered over onto the shoulder and the car skidded to a halt on the icy gravel. "Okay! That does it! Get out…! The both of yuhz."

The two in the back fell quiet as Howard just stared forward through the windshield, waiting for the rear doors to open. David's voice broke the silence.

"Let's everybody take a deep breath…, just relax. We've all had a long day, already. We got this one last thing to take care of and I was sorta hopin' we could do this like family, in peace, the sons and grandsons, together."

"But Jimmy ain't even here," Joshie retorted.

"Jimmy would be here, if he could. And that isn't the question since he's probably back to Vermont now. What I want to know is can the four of us and your father go up to the apartment and for a short time act like gentlemen, like family, and take care of what has to be done. If the answer is no, then the two of you don't have to get out and walk 'cause Howard'll turn around and we'll all go back to his place."

Howard replied. "I don't want them in the house!"

"Then we'll drop them off wherever."

The nephews remained silent and Davey, after a few moments, signaled for Howard to drive.

They arrived at the agreed upon time, perhaps a family first. Mickey was waiting for them, still huddled in his Corvette, when they pulled into the lot. Like tropical fish conditioned to rise to the top of the tank at feeding time, they converged at the glass entry to the sprawling senior housing complex and took the elevator up in silence, again a rarity. The oldest used his key to open the apartment and they all stepped in. Still playing his game, he suggested that they all take a few minutes and walk through and pick out what they wanted.

Davey couldn't put his finger on it then. Immersed in his own mournful nostalgia and his general indifference toward the material remains of Harry's world, he actually didn't give it much thought at the time but now recalled wondering why the place seemed in such disarray, so unlike his father. It wasn't that Harry was some neatnik, but the place had its own order to it and something immediately struck him as off, not right, as soon as they walked in.

The accordion doors in the hallway stood open and his eye caught the pile of shoes, normally lined in neat rows, heaped in disarray at the bottom of the closet and the stacks of dry-cleaned shirts and sweaters askew on the top shelf. He though it odd, the empty shoulder holster sitting there, but still hadn't put it together. It all seemed strange, how untidy the bedroom seemed with several of the dresser drawers left partly open, again unlike his father, and how the two near-empty jewelry boxes, lids raised, sat there like abandoned nests.

   Stepping into the tiny bathroom, he noticed the emblematic icons of his father's world, sitting there atop the toilet -- the ashtray with a long-abandoned stale stub of a Top Stone, a book of matches alongside, the can of Rapid Shave and razor, the plastic tub of Vaseline, its lid still off, the bottle of Old Spice. Several pairs of hand rinsed boxers and calf length dress socks, polyester grays, dark blues, and olive green, still hung from the curtain rod in the shower stall. As if coming to their rescue, he gathered up the now orphaned socks, one of the few mementoes he would take. Returning to the living room, he noticed the vacant spots at the front of the tea cart, the place where several bottles would have stood. His eye fixed on the empty spaces, the footprints silhouetted in dust atop the television where the family photos normally gazed out into the room. Preoccupied with the memories, he still hadn't figured it out.

   It only dawned on him later, as he spotted Harry's things at the girlfriend's, the realization that two of them had already gone through to plunder the apartment. And now, sitting there at thirty thousand feet, he imagined them, Mickey and Gina, as two comedic cat burglars in matching black, with masks over their eyes, tippy-toeing out of the apartment in the middle of the night, their loot-filled pilfered pillowcases slung over their shoulders. He again wondered why he hadn't said anything.

   Hermina was there at Gina's and he came away thinking about her. This lady with the sad, milky eyes; his father's other woman. How they greeted each other once again and she let him know, not so much with a word, but from the way she took his hand and made eye contact, that everything was cool between them. Connie, Mickey's first and actually Davey's favorite, overcome by her own memories and an already long afternoon's commiseration with a bottle of Smirnoff's, just sat there at the dining room table. When she talked at all, she spoke of Esther as if Harry wasn't even gone. Angela, of course, remained palpably conspicuous in her absence and Gina, hardly one to play the hostess and already observably pissed about something, kept to herself in the kitchen, only appearing on occasion to replenish one of the food trays with cheap cold cuts and to silently pour more coffee when Mickey called to her. None of them really spoke, had anything to say. They didn't have to since the booty from Harry's place, everywhere in plain view, seemed to speak for itself. He and Annie stayed a while, attempted some small talk with a couple of remaining visitors, and left.

   Wanting some time to himself before the rest of the house awoke, Davey had quietly eased himself out of bed without rousing Annie. Pulling on one of the terry robes that Richie had hung in the guest bath and forgetting about the security system on the ground floor, he made his barefoot way downstairs and used the bathroom off the front atrium so as not to disturb the upstairs with his morning sounds.

   It surprised him, almost startled him a bit, to find Howard in the kitchen, fully dressed in one of his charcoal business suits, ready for work, standing there sipping a glass of cranberry by the light of the open refrigerator.

"Yuh goin' in t'day?"

"Yeah, figured I'd better. Got tons t'do, a closing on this big package deal, a mainframe for one of the local banks... Sittin' around here all day would just make me nuts, and I don't think anybody'll come by... Not until tonight, anyways."

"Lookin' to get out of here without sayin' good-bye?"

Howard closed the refrigerator and clicked on the overhead fluorescent.

"Nah. I knew you'd come down before I left. I would've woken yuh if yuh hadn't. What time did yuh say your flight was?"

"Nine-thirty."

Howard glanced at his watch. "It's what? Twenty after six. You got time yet. Richie'll drive yuh."

Davey's eye caught it then sitting there on the island counter, in front of the toaster.

"What's this?"

"I was just about to write yuh a note. Just a little somethin', I thought maybe you should have. To take back with yuh. Nuthin' seemed to interest yuh much at the apartment."

Davey picked up the timepiece and examined it as if it were some old talisman, an ancient amulet.

"Daddy's watch."

"The one Mommy gave him."

"Mickey know you got it?"

"Be serious."

"He's gonna want it, you know."

"He's probably lookin' for it right now. Losin' sleep over it, I hope. It was so obvious he went through the apartment before we got there. Turned the place upside down lookin' for it, I bet. Him and that girlfriend of his."

"So you noticed, too...? How the place was a mess and how stuff was missing?"

"Yeah, but I didn't want to get into it. Not there."

"He's not gonna give up on the watch. He'll figure somebody's gotta have it and he's gonna look straight at you."

"That's why you should take it. Fuck 'im. Mommy prob'ly would've given it to you anyway and I don't need it. Besides, it can't be worth that much. Take it."

"But what am I gonna do with it?"

"It's yours. I don't want it and I'll be goddamned if I let him get his hands on it. I'll put it in the compactor first... You gotta take it. For me..., and for Mommy."

They both just stared at each other as the tears welled up in Howard's eyes. Davey couldn't hold them back either at that point, and the two came face-to-face, arm in arm. Retrieving a Kleenex from the dispenser sitting on the counter, Howard finally sniffled a stilted laugh.

"What time'd you say your flight was?"

"Nine-thirty."

"It snowed last night. It'll take you a good forty minutes, at least. Maybe more with the morning traffic, if it's backed up across the harbor. You should allow some extra time. You probably should get rollin' pretty soon… I'll go up and get Richie's ass out of bed…"

"Hey…."

"What?"

"Thanks."

"For what?"

"For everything. For bein' my brother."

"Yeah, you too."

The snow had started to come down just before dark in wet, feathery clumps, melting immediately as it hit the pavement. Initially covering the grass and the cars and sticking to the branches of the New England hardwoods, the laurel and evergreens, it soon took hold of everything as the temperature dropped. It came down through a good part of the night, stopping well before dawn, and the entire graveyard lay blanketed with a clean white comforter by the time they made their way back.

Davey hadn't mentioned a word about stopping off, but merely asked Richie to turn left at the cemetery when they pulled up at the stoplight, at Fitch and Whalley. As the Audi pulled up by the wrought iron gate, he turned to his wife. "I'll just be a minute. There's something I gotta do."

Annie, understanding immediately, didn't even make a motion to get out as Davey opened the door and stepped into the three inches of wet Connecticut whiteness.

It took him no time to find the grave, its still unsettled earth slightly mounded beneath the snow cover. Pausing there but a few moments to say a silent farewell, he turned and glanced the fifty or sixty yards across the way to the giant poplar by the fenced perimeter, the landmark. As he made his way across, he could feel the winter wetness in the toes of his dress shoes. He thought about how the two of them remained apart, separated, even afterwards.

Squatting down to get closer, he slowly slid the slushy wetness away with his bare hand and uncovered the simple brass plate. The tears welled up and he fought to hold them back as if someone was watching.

"Hi, ma."

Easing his hand into his coat pocket, he came out with the watch and placed it on the marker.

"I thought maybe you should have this."

Pausing then but a moment more, he returned to the car, wiping away the tears as he went, and Richie took them to the airport.

ISBN 142510320-0

9 781425 103200